Greetings from Barker Marsh

Tyson Hanks

For Rachel and Ava. I couldn't have done this without your love and support.

CONTENTS

ACKNOWLEDGMENTS

Unlike the Oscars, there's no orchestra to cue when an author gets long-winded on his acknowledgment page, so I'll do my best to keep this short. I'll inevitably leave someone out here, but just know that a LOT of people helped make this book possible, and I'm forever grateful to each and every one of you. Those that absolutely deserve to be singled out and thanked, though, are as follows:

Alisha Sams and Nicole Vlachos Jordan, for giving me permission to take a chance and submit my first short story for publication. I truly wouldn't be where I'm at if it wasn't for you.

All of my beta readers (you know who you are), for reading my raw material and providing feedback. You're brutally honest when I need it, and I need it a lot.

John Catapano, for the amazing editing work on this book. You're a wizard, my friend, not to mention a mentor and an inspiration.

Richard Livingston, for the amazing artwork . (I mean, seriously, look at the damn cover art on this thing!)

Mitch Hyman and the rest of the Dark Alley Crew, for allowing me to be a part of your merry band of whackos. I'm humbled to call myself a friend and colleague to so many talented professionals.

Mom and Dad, for letting me take my own path in life. You let me read what I wanted, watch what I wanted, and never blinked an eye when it was pretty obvious that my interests were a little on the strange side. It doesn't matter what I do, you're always there to support me. I love you both.

Most importantly, to my wife, Rachel, and my daughter, Ava, for making me the luckiest man alive. For someone who fancies himself a storyteller, I simply don't have the words to describe how much I love each of you, and what your support means to me.

Lastly, I'd like to thank you, the reader, for picking this book up and giving me a chance. I'll do my best to take you on one hell of ride. Now buckle up...

CHAPTER 1

"Riding on an East bound freight train

Speeding through the night

Hobo Bill, a railroad bum

Was fighting for his life

The sadness of his eyes revealed

The torture of his soul

He raised a weak and weary hand

To brush away the cold."

—Rodgers, Jimmie. "Hobo Bill's Last Ride." Victor Talking Machine

Company, 1929

The Drifter stared out the open door of the train as the Midwestern countryside flew by like an old time zoetrope. He loved this part of the country and the effect it had on him. Seeing the Autumn colors in the trees and the gauze-like whiteness that blanketed the scenery could make even bad men feel good.

He was a bad man.

He'd left his job, left his wife, and left any trace of moral decency back in that tiny apartment in Philadelphia. Now the Drifter lived a life of constant movement, riding the rails from one small town to another. Lately he'd steal whatever valuables were available, jump on a train to the next town and sell whatever he'd taken. Sometimes he would break into a home and stare at the families as they slept. Especially the girls.

The Drifter had killed only one person. He'd been sleeping in an empty train car as it rolled Westward, just east of Columbus, Ohio when another vagrant hopped onto the same car. The Drifter was startled awake when the other man started to rifle through his bag. It contained half a dozen watches and a very nice photo album trimmed in silver that he'd taken from an elderly couple a few days earlier. The other man told the Drifter how much he'd liked these items. He'd even offered to perform sexual favors for the Drifter if he'd give them to him. When the Drifter told the other man to "*fuck off*," the man pulled out a filed down screwdriver and grabbed the bag. The Drifter was much larger and wrestled the screwdriver out of his assailant's hand. As the man made one final lunge toward him the Drifter buried the screwdriver in the man's neck, all the way to the duct-taped handle. Bright arterial blood began to jet across the floor of the rail car as the other man fell to his knees and eventually collapsed onto his back. The man made awful gurgling sounds so the Drifter placed his hand over his mouth. Wet, bloody bubbles crept through his fingers until they eventually stopped. After what seemed like an eternity the other man stopped breathing.

When the Drifter looked around at the amount of blood covering the railcar floor, panic washed over him. He snatched up his bag and stood in the doorway of the car. The massive train had started to pick up speed and the Drifter figured he had better jump before the train got much faster. He leaned out and spotted a patch of track ahead that sloped off into what looked like a soft berm of dirt. The Drifter clutched his bag to his chest and when the berm appeared in front of him, he jumped.

When the Drifter landed he'd felt something in his right ankle snap and cried out in pain as he finally tumbled to a stop. The berm wasn't nearly as soft as he'd hoped. He spent the rest of that night limping through the small town he'd landed in. Eventually he broke into a small veterinary clinic, shoved a handful of medications into his bag and got out before the town deputies showed up. He stumbled into a salvage yard and laid up in the cab of a 1949 Ford pickup for three days. He took too much and nearly overdosed on what he assumed were animal tranquilizers. He constructed a makeshift splint and when a vicious rainstorm blew in to help cover his movement, he limped back to the rail yard and jumped another train west.

At first he wasn't sure if he'd broken or sprained his ankle, but six weeks had passed and he still walked with a limp. He moved from town to town, listening to people, hoping to hear details about a murder

investigation, but it would seem that the authorities had not been overly

concerned with a dead bum on a train. Finding dead vagrants on trains was

a fairly common occurrence. Besides, would anybody *really* miss a man that

would suck a cock for some shitty watches and a photo album?

The Drifter didn't think so.

All thoughts of the murdered transient left the Drifter's mind as the

moving picture show outside began to slow down. He fought to keep his

balance as the wooden planks beneath his feet began to buck and jerk. The

long train was coming to a stop. He peered out of the open door and

spotted a town up ahead. There were a few church steeples and an

occasional rooftop above the tree line, but so far there didn't seem to be

anything about this town that made it different than any of the other

countless stops he'd made since he'd adopted his life on the rails. He

limped over to the opposite side of the car so that he could see what the

town had to offer on the south side of the tracks. The Drifter had barely

stuck his head out the door when he recoiled as a sharp temperature drop

hit him. He went back to his bag to pull out a heavy coat as his teeth began

to chatter in sync with the large wheels below the rail car.

Jesus, he thought. *The temperature must have dropped thirty degrees.*

11

Having wrapped himself in the stained jacket, the Drifter made his way back to the left side of the car and once again peered out. What had been a pleasantly mild day in late October was now a cold, dreary afternoon. It was as if he was experiencing the opening act of what was shaping up to be a particularly nasty winter. The Drifter could see a rusted chain link fence up ahead that looked as if it had once been meant to keep something particularly awful from getting out.

A low rumble of thunder erupted and the first patter of rain drops began to sound on the roof of the rail car. The Drifter snugged up the collar of his jacket and rammed his hands into the pockets in an effort to ward off the sharp chill. As the menacing fence grew closer, he noticed a large metal sign hanging askew from several links. By the time he got close enough to read it the light rain had graduated to a hard, cold downpour. Through the heavy rain the Drifter could see that many years of exposure had reduced the sign to rusted metal, but he could still make out the ghostlike trace of some words. "BARKER ZINC COMPANY."

The Drifter looked beyond the sign and fence at a huge structure. The Barker zinc smelting plant appeared to be long out of service. Rusted machinery littered a large lot in front of the building and one of the plant's smoke stacks lay in segments on the courtyard like a giant snake.

The building itself was in no better shape. One entire corner of the building seemed to have been blown off. It reminded him of images of Europe during World War II. There wasn't a single pane of glass in any of the windows on this side of the plant. Graffiti covered the exterior walls like a proud parent's refrigerator. The focal point was a giant penis, complete with veins and hairy balls.

The Drifter shook his head and smiled as the train slowed to a crawl. He peered down the line of cars to make sure there were no Bulls walking the tracks. Bulls—or Cinder Dicks, as some vagrants called them—were plainclothes policemen that worked for the railroad. One of their favorite duties was running off hobos. Most weren't so bad. If you were stupid enough to get caught the Bulls would normally just kick you off the train or evict you from the rail yard. Occasionally though, a Bull with something to prove would come along and beat a vagrant within an inch of his life, or worse, take them straight to jail. The Drifter didn't want to explore any of these scenarios. When he looked down the line it appeared that he had this stretch of track to himself.

He eased himself down from the slow rolling car, still nursing his right ankle. He pulled the hood of his jacket up over his head to block the rain but the damage had already been done. His hair hung down in his eyes in sopping wet ringlets.

"Swell fucking town so far," the Drifter muttered to himself.

13

He began to walk the fence line and eventually came to a gap in the chain link big enough to squeeze through. By now he was cold, wet and his ankle was killing him. The decrepit smelting plant looked like a good place to spend the night. He figured he could find a dry spot to settle in.

Once he was through the fence, the Drifter started limping toward the massive building, cursing the weather every laborious step of the way. He reached an open doorway and stepped inside the plant. To his dismay, the rain continued to pelt him. He squinted up and saw this portion of the plant's roof had a huge, gaping hole.

The Drifter surveyed the roof and spotted a portion that provided some protection from the rain. Directly below this section of roof was a cluster of large boilers or vats of some kind. The brackets supporting these containers were covered in rust and looked as if they could crumble any minute, crushing anyone stupid enough to sleep under them. But the area around these iron death traps appeared to be dry, and at that very moment the Drifter was willing to risk his life to get warm. He made his way through a gauntlet of fallen insulation and jagged, rusted roof girders and finally stopped under a shelter that was blessedly dry.

This portion of the factory floor was shrouded in shadows, and as his eyes adjusted to the dark the Drifter surveyed his surroundings. Almost immediately he startled himself by stumbling into a pile of empty beer cans.

14

The graveyard of Old Milwaukee empties and the stained mattress that he eventually stood over confirmed for the Drifter that he was sheltering in what was most likely a popular party location for the town's youth.

The Drifter slid his sopping bag off his shoulders and dropped it onto the floor next to the mattress. He shook off his heavy coat and dropped it on top of the bag. Having shed his gear, he partially sat and partially collapsed back onto the dirty mattress. It was only then that he realized he'd nearly landed on a pile of used condoms. There appeared to be four or five stuck together like crispy, latex tentacles.

"Holy shit," the Drifter said as he flicked the little cluster off the mattress with one of the empty beer cans. "Who the hell are you kid, Superman?" If the thought of sleeping in someone else's bodily fluids repulsed him, he didn't show it. Instead he slipped his right boot off and began massaging his throbbing ankle. He had slept in worse places and as the rain continued to fall in buckets outside, the rusted and stained surroundings started to look like a palace.

The Drifter's vision had adjusted fully to the darkness, so this time when he looked around he spotted the eyes staring back at him, less than ten feet away.

The other man was squatting low in the shadow of one of the large boilers, his heels flat on the floor. The clothes he wore were every bit as worn and dirty as the Drifter's, so even though his eyes had adjusted, the Drifter could barely tell there was another man there at all.

The stranger continued to stare at the Drifter, not moving. After his run in with the other vagrant and the screwdriver, the Drifter couldn't bring himself to carry a weapon of any kind. As he stared back at the other man, with his filthy clothes and long, disheveled hair and beard, he couldn't help but to succumb to genuine fear at the sight of his almost primal-looking audience. He immediately regretted his decision to not carry a weapon.

The Drifter continually shifted his focus from the squatting man in front of him to the immediate area surrounding the mattress. He was hoping to find a rusted piece of rebar or busted beer bottle—anything that he might be able to use as a weapon to defend himself if the other man decided to attack him. When he couldn't stand it any longer, the Drifter opened his mouth to speak, but the other man spoke first.

"Trampin' huh?" The other man eased some of the Drifter's tension by following up his simple question with a smile. "We don't see many tramps around here much anymore."

A tramp? Jesus, nobody's ever called me that before. Mostly the Bulls just called him "buddy" or "pal" but usually it was something like "fuckface."

16

To the Drifter's knowledge, no one had referred to train jumpers as "tramps" for at least forty years, so the Drifter was fairly confident that the other man wasn't there to arrest him. If he was, the man was dressed as the best undercover detective he had ever seen.

It seemed the other man sensed his apprehension. "Relax fella. I ain't the law." The man didn't move an inch—just sitting there, squatting like a tribal elder in some third world village.

"What do you want?" asked the Drifter.

"Just a little conversation, Lou," said the other man.

"My name isn't Lou."

The man looked at him strangely. "Who said it is?"

"You did. Just now."

The man made a dismissive gesture with his hand. This eased the Drifter's fear, even though he started to get the feeling that this old man wasn't all there in the wits department.

"The hell I did," said the man. "Anyway, *my* name's Harold, but everyone calls me Hasty."

The Drifter gave a single nod. "Okay."

"You don't say much, do you Lou?" Hasty added to the awkwardness by closing one eye when he said this. "Well, that's okay. Hasty Davis can make conversation with anyone, yes-sir-ee. Some folks think it's a lost art ya' know, but I mostly think folks is just lazy and rude these days. Guess maybe they don't got nothing nice to say. 'Course, my momma always told me if you don't got nothing nice to say you shouldn't say nothing a'tall— Guess that's why after that she didn't talk to me much." Hasty followed this up with a bout of laughter that reminded the Drifter of Walter Brennan's toothless character in *Rio Bravo*.

Well, it's official, thought the Drifter. *Ol' Hasty here is a real life "old coot," right down to the long beard and crazy laugh.*

When Hasty was done chuckling he pointed an unusually long finger at the Drifter and closed one eye again. "Say, Lou. Why *are* you here?"

The Drifter had been asked this question many times before, and he gave Hasty his standard answer. "Just looking for work." In reality he was looking for unlocked cars and old folks that still kept their cash under their mattress. The Drifter added, "But right now I'm just trying to get warm."

"Not much work around here, Lou," Hasty said. "Not since this joint shut down." Hasty gestured to their dilapidated surroundings. "Lotsa folks worked up the Hoffner Falls joint, but it burned to the ground years ago."

"Hoffner Falls?" asked the Drifter.

"The looney bin. Baaaad place, Lou. I know cuz I had to stay there some. Courts made me, but them folks don't know the difference between shit and sugar cookies." Hasty let out another burst of shrill laughter. When he was able to pull himself together again he stood up, uncurling himself from his squatting position. The Drifter was a little shocked to see that Hasty easily stood six and a half feet tall. He was even more shocked when the bearded giant held out the remains of a six pack of Old Milwaukee, dangling from the plastic holder. "Anyhoo," Hasty continued, "can't help you much with work, but one of these will help with the gettin' warm part."

The Drifter eyed Hasty like a nervous dog eyeing a stranger with a treat. After a brief round of *what's the worst thing this old fella could do to me?* the Drifter reached out and popped a can free. The can felt surprisingly cool in his hand, as if Hasty had just pulled it out of the fridge. Cold beer was a luxury the Drifter didn't get often, so he cracked open the tab and did his best to enjoy the long pull he took on his first drink. It tasted wonderful, but didn't do much to warm him up. He would have gladly traded the beer for a pint of peppermint schnapps.

"Now you just sit back and enjoy that, Lou," Hasty said. "I'll see if I can't get us a fire going."

"Won't somebody see it?" the Drifter asked, unable to hide the nervousness creeping into his voice.

Now it was Hasty's turn to look at the Drifter suspiciously, his eyes narrowing to thin slits. To the Drifter, he looked like a six and a half foot tall viper with a beard. "The law don't come out here much anymore."

"I just mean…we're technically trespassing. That's all."

Hasty's eyes were still slits. "I s'pose we are, Lou. But like I said, nobody comes out here, 'cept kids when they wanna drink or screw."

The Drifter thought again of the tangled pile of condoms as Hasty walked over to a large boiler and dragged a wooden pallet out from underneath. The Drifter watched as Hasty stood the pallet up on its end and with an almost frightening amount of strength began to stomp on the wooden planks, smashing the pallet to pieces in a shower of splinters and bent nails. Finally satisfied with the pile of tinder he'd created, Hasty constructed a small teepee out of some smaller pieces of wood. Next he pulled out a small plastic bottle from his pocket and soaked the wood with its contents. The Drifter recognized the scent as kerosene. Hasty struck a match with his thumbnail and tossed it on the pile. The tiny structure went up in a surge of light and heat. As the fire established itself Hasty added some larger pieces from the remains of the pallet until there was a good size fire between the Drifter and himself.

The Drifter could feel the heat reflecting off the two large boilers on either side of them, and at that exact moment—with a warm fire at his feet and a cool beer in his hand—he felt pretty damn good.

Still, it wasn't a small fire, and it was bright.

"You sure nobody's gonna see this?" the Drifter asked again.

Hasty gave another of his short, and what the Drifter was assuming could be called "signature" laughs, before he replied. "Ya 'know, Lou, for a guy that's supposed to be here looking for work, you sound an awful lot like someone that's really looking for trouble."

Was that an accusation? the Drifter thought. He started to wonder if this old coot *was* psychic or something. He thought carefully about how to answer Hasty. Finally, he said "No, I'm not looking for trouble, but I don't want any either."

"That's good, Lou. We got plenty of trouble in this town. In fact, seems that's all we've got here anymore."

The Drifter pondered this for a second. There was something bizarre about the way Hasty had said "trouble." It was as if he were a kid and "trouble" was a dirty word, and he didn't want his folks to hear him saying it. The Drifter took another long pull from the beer, draining it. He crushed the can in his hand before looking through the flames at old Hasty Davis. "What do you mean, trouble's all you've got?"

"I mean there's something wrong with this town, son. Like some kind of cancer's taken root here. Brings out the worst in people. That goddamn railroad out there snaked its way through this part of the country like a vine droppin' town seeds, and Barker Marsh is a bad seed, Lou."

The Drifter had seen some rough cities in his travels, and he didn't get the feeling that Barker Marsh was all that bad. "Every little town has its fair share of crime, but it can't be that bad."

"I ain't talking about crime. We got plenty of that. I'm talking about death. And just…bad stuff. Like…like…" Hasty started to get frustrated and began pounding his head with his palm, as if he were trying to knock loose whatever word was escaping him. "Shit, what's the word? Like Elvis only that's not right. Elvis was the King. Shit!"

"You mean evil?" asked the Drifter.

"THAT'S IT! Evil! That's what this place is all right. It's evil, Lou. Boy-oh is it. I could tell you some stories."

The Drifter couldn't help but to feel a little creeped out. There was just something foreboding about the way Hasty talked. He wondered if maybe he had gotten off in the wrong town. Maybe tomorrow he'd move on down the line.

As he was questioning hopping back on the train, nature answered him with a shattering flash of lightning and thunderclap. The Drifter jumped at the sudden atmospheric release but Hasty didn't move a muscle. He just kept staring into the flames between them, as if in a trance. The Drifter decided he'd calm his nerves a little before taking to the rails again. Besides, the fire sure was nice.

"Say Hasty, could I have another one of those beers?" the Drifter asked. Hasty kept on staring into the fire. After an uncomfortable silence the Drifter tried again; louder. "Hasty! You alright, old timer?"

The old man blinked. "What's that, Lou?"

"Could I have another one of those beers?"

"Oh. Sure thing." Hasty plucked another can from its plastic shackle and tossed it to the Drifter.

The Drifter opened the can and took another long drink. Then he stared into the fire, too. The two of them sat in silence for a long time, sharing the warmth. The Drifter could feel the heat and the beer calming his nerves, and when he finally felt relaxed he broke the silence.

"Tell me one," he said.

"What's that?" Hasty replied, confused.

"You said you could tell me some stories about this town. So, tell me one."

Hasty looked at him with those viper-like eyes again, radiating with suspicion and sizing the Drifter up one last time before he made his decision. On the opposite side of the fire the Drifter felt like he'd passed some secret test when Hasty finally grinned at him.

"I suppose it wouldn't hurt nothing," Hasty said.

Then, as the Drifter put it, Hasty told him one.

***

Antipode Theory

"Eat my diamonds

Drinking all my gin

Feast your eyes on

A whole lotta sin"

—Priest, Judas. "Devil's Child." *Screaming for Vengeance*, Columbia, 1982

For many identical twins, the similarities between the siblings extends only as far as their physical appearance. This was the case for Wesley and Wendy Klein.

Wendy was an American sweetheart. She was attractive and smart. She was on every conceivable student club or committee, already had valedictorian in the bag, and had a line of representatives from some of the best colleges in the state ready to offer her a scholarship next Fall. Teachers loved her, her classmates loved her and her mother loved her. She could have easily let all that attention go to her head, but she didn't, and this made people love her even more.

The only person that didn't appear to be smitten with Wendy Klein was her brother. Wes cared about her, for sure, but in the kind of way that only brothers with seemingly perfect sisters can understand. The two weren't very old when Wes became fully aware that he was destined to live in the shadow of his twin sister. From that moment he'd made tremendous efforts to walk a path far from his sister's. That path frequently got Wes into trouble of all kinds, and he spent as much time in detention hall as Wendy spent in student government and cheerleader practice.

His acts of defiance and delinquency started small. He stayed out well after dark, ran with the "bad crowd" that his mother warned him about, and played down by the old trestles, where folks went who were up to no good. Wes's mother raised him and his sister on her own from day one so he had no father figure to offer a paternal influence. He smoked, looked at dirty magazines, and when he was fourteen he stole his mother's old Cutlass and blew the engine out on Joliff Bridge Road. The police brought him home that night in the backseat of a cruiser but they didn't charge him with anything. They figured the experience of being "arrested," combined with the ass kicking he'd probably get from his mother was punishment enough, and that he'd learn his lesson.

He hadn't.

Seeing the speedometer in that Oldsmobile pegged at eighty-five and knowing that he was actually doing well over 100 when the engine blew was worth every lashing he'd gotten from his mother that night. Cars became a frequent cause for the trouble Wes Klein would get into through the years.

Surprisingly, the incident with the wrecked Cutlass wasn't the worst thing that Wes had ever done according to his mother. Wes would lay a bet that Brenda Klein had never been as pissed off as when he'd told her he'd quit the baseball team. Wes had been a pitcher and he was good. He'd known it too. At 6'2", he was tall for a fifteen year old. His height and natural talent armed him with a four seam fastball capable of hitting the high eighties, which was rare among high school pitchers. Quitting was also one of the few decisions *Wes* regretted. He would occasionally sit in the parking lot at the home games, smoking and pretending to raise hell while he actually watched his former teammates and imagined himself standing out there on the mound.

The real tension between Wes and his sister started soon after he'd quit playing baseball. As if the pressure he was getting from his mother wasn't enough, Wendy had taken on the role of a second parent and given him the same line of shit. *"What's wrong with you, Wes? You know you could have gotten a scholarship. Are you trying to throw you future away?"*

After his sister's barrage of questioning Wes had stormed out of the house and into his garage. The Kleins had a normal two car garage attached to the house, but the original garage still stood out back, and Wes had come to think of it as his "safe zone." Behind its old tilt-up door Wes would work on his `79 Monte Carlo. He purchased the car with his own cash, so his mother and perfect sister couldn't hold the car over his head. The night he'd told his family he'd quit playing baseball was also the night he'd added another four barrel carburetor and Hurst shifter to his car. Wes

Klein would spend a lot of time in that garage with his car. It was the only thing in his life that didn't anger him.

When he finally turned sixteen Wes took to the streets in his car and purged a few years' worth of aggression. Two speeding tickets, one year and a decent amount of bragging rights later Wes Klein and his '79 Chevy was the fastest team in Barker Marsh. They were unbeatable, and it would appear that he'd found something else he was really good at—besides baseball.

Other than driving too fast, the Summer before Wes Klein's senior year was relatively trouble-free. He spent most of his time in his car, and he'd slowly drifted away from what his mother referred to as the "bad kids." He'd get in the occasional street race, but mostly he just cruised the backroads of Barker Marsh, listening to old rock and roll. When the first week of school started back up Wes was actually determined to keep to himself and keep his nose clean. He hoped to get a job working on the river after he graduated—anything that would get him away from the Marsh and his sister's shadow. Wes also decided to step up his academics his senior year. To tell the truth, he actually found school easier than his sister, and he was an underachiever by choice.

His classmates bitched when several teachers assigned homework on the first day, but Wes finished it all while he sat in his car during his seventh period study hall. As Friday's first period rolled around that week Wes was feeling pretty good about his senior year.

Then he got suspended.

More specifically, he got suspended because of his sister, and because he had to piss.

Wes had fourth period chemistry and afterwards had to run to the far corner of the school for Senior English. On Friday he decided to cut chemistry ten minutes early to take a piss before fighting the mob of fellow students in the halls. Wes took the time to sneak through the halls so he could take care of business in an isolated restroom across from the music room. Barker Marsh High School didn't have hall monitors, but most of the restrooms were strategically placed next to the Principal's office or teachers that had noses like bloodhounds and could smell smoke through a foot of cement wall.

When Wes arrived outside the restroom door he paused for a moment to listen, making sure Mr. Reynolds wasn't in there trying to squeeze out one of those awkward, segmented squirts that only middle-aged driver's education teachers seemed to be capable of. Convinced that he'd have the place to himself, Wes slipped through the door and entered the farthest stall from the entrance. As he began to piss he thought to himself how fucked up it would be if he got in trouble for cutting class to take a leak. Most would figure he'd gone off to smoke or get into some other trouble. He was thinking that along with working on his grades that year he was going to work on his reputation as a punk too.

That's when he heard the restroom door open.

He stopped urinating mid-stream and held his breath, preparing himself for an ass chewing if it was a teacher. Two voices, much too young to belong to a teacher, echoed in the restroom. Wes breathed a sigh of relief and listened for a moment. He recognized one of the voices as Shane Watkins, a Junior that thought he was hot shit because his Daddy had bought him a Trans-Am earlier that summer.

"Dude, I swear," Shane said, "I made her come like, four times."

In the far stall Wes Klein smiled to himself and leaned against the wall, crossing his arms. Shane Watkins and the other boy, whose voice Wes couldn't quite place, were about to launch into one of those mythical sex stories that only happened in high school boys' restrooms. Wes thought he'd sit back in silence and see just how full of shit these two were.

"You're so full of shit," said the other boy. Wes thought it sounded like Ronnie Tozier, but he couldn't be sure. "You wouldn't have made it five minutes with her. That's *if* you actually fucked her, and you didn't, so that makes you twice as full of shit."

"Oh yeah," Shane retorted, "then where'd I get these, asshole?"

From his sanctuary, Wes squatted low to peek up under the door at the two younger classmen. Ronnie Tozier stared in amazement as Shane held up a pair of yellow panties. From Wes's vantage point there barely seemed enough material in Shane Watkins's hand to make an eye patch, let alone underwear.

Ronnie Tozier shook his head. "No way, dude. You could have bought those yourself."

"Smell 'em if you don't believe me." Ronnie put a hand up to block as Shane tried to shove the underwear in his face.

"Ahhhh! Fuck off man! Keep those away from me!"

Shane Watkins burst into a fit of laughter as he wrestled with Ronnie, teasing him with the panties like it was a poisonous spider.

Wes wasn't entirely sure what happened next, but he remembered Shane finally stopping at some point. And he remembered what the kid said after that. He remembered it distinctly.

"Suit yourself, Ronnie. I'm not sure what kind of fag wouldn't want to smell Wendy Klein's pussy, though."

After that Wes Klein couldn't exactly give a play by play recap as to what happened. He remembered a fury boiling up in him with an intensity he'd never known. He didn't remember exiting the stall he'd been in but Ronnie Tozier did. He'd told Principal Barnes that Wes had torn the stall door clean off its hinges. After that he'd run off to find a teacher, leaving Wes and Shane alone in the isolated restroom.

Wes didn't remember Ronnie running off, but he did remember the pain he'd felt as his knuckles connected with Shane Watkins's front teeth, two of which were permanently removed that afternoon. Wes hadn't thought to even ask Shane if he was telling the truth about his sister, he'd just started hitting him in the face and he didn't stop until he heard—and felt—the kid's nose shatter under his fist.

Wes remembered one other thing about that afternoon quite clearly. As Shane Watkins lay bleeding on the floor, barely conscious, Wes glanced around and found the yellow panties, now spattered with little droplets of Shane's blood. There was no telling for sure if they really *were* his sister's, but Wes prayed they weren't. He picked up the underwear without a second thought and shoved them deep into the garbage bin by the sinks. Moments later the door burst open and Mr. Reynolds rushed in with Ronnie Tozier close behind.

The Driver's Ed teacher looked down at the bleeding student and yelled for Ronnie to get the nurse. He turned back to Wes, and in very un-teacher-like form said, "You really fucked up this time, Klein. *Really* fucked up."

Forty-five minutes later Wes was in Principal Barnes's office with an ice pack on his knuckles while his mother sat next to him, whispering about how lucky they'd be if the Watkins kid's parents didn't press charges. When Mr. Barnes walked back in, Wes didn't look up.

The Principal sat down across from Wes and his mother and cleared his throat. "Well, Shane's on his way to the hospital so they can set his nose. I asked him what you two were fighting about but he wouldn't say." Mr. Barnes removed his steel-rimmed spectacles and began cleaning them with his tie. "So Wesley, would *you* like to tell me what prompted you to break his nose?"

Wes continued to look down, focusing on the ice pack. He said nothing. It was his mother who finally broke the silence.

"You'd better answer him dammit! Or I'll…" Wes had no idea what his mother had threatened to do to him, because he wasn't paying attention. He was trying to think of something to say, because he knew he had to give them something or risk being expelled completely. He certainly couldn't tell them the truth. His mom really pissed him off sometimes but Wes didn't want to put the woman through the embarrassment of hearing that her fuck-up of a son had beat the shit out of a kid for bragging about fucking her little angel of a daughter. Instead Wes came up with the most believable lie he could on short notice.

"It was stupid," he finally said, looking up. "Shane started saying some shit, sorry, some stuff about my car and how his Trans-Am would smoke me. One thing led to another and we started shoving each other. Then shoving turned into hitting."

Principal Barnes put his glasses back on and said, "It looks to me like you were doing most of the hitting, Wes."

Wes shrugged. *What's he want me to say?* he thought, *Watkins is a pussy?*

33

"Funny though," Barnes continued, "that's not the story we got from Ronnie Tozier."

Shit! I forgot about him. Please don't say he told you about my sister's underwear.

"Ronnie said they didn't do a thing to provoke you and you just stormed out of a stall and started swinging."

A flood of relief washed over Wes. *Thank God.* "And you believe him?!? He's Shane's best friend and he's an idiot."

"No, Wes, I don't believe him. But I'm not sure I believe you either. A car is a pretty stupid thing to get in a fist fight over." Principal Barnes stared at him accusingly through his nerdy glasses.

Brenda Klein broke the silence again. "You and that God damn car! Well guess what, buddy—that car is going to stay in the garage for the rest of the year! Let's just see how much you like getting a ride from your sister."

Wes's knuckles began throbbing again as he realized he'd clenched both fists. He was furious. How could his mother do something as drastic as take his car away for five months? He wondered if she would have still grounded him if she'd known the real reason he'd gotten in the fight.

Sensing the first wave of a domestic megastorm, Principal Barnes cleared his throat again. "Look, Wes, I'm not saying you're entirely to blame here, but based on the facts it certainly looks like you were the instigator. We're suspending you for the entire week starting Monday. At least until we can get Shane's version of the story."

So much for starting this year off on the right foot, genius, Wes thought. He felt he should say something mature and reserved.

"Fine," he said. It was the best he had.

"No," his mother said, "it's not fine. Far from it. We'll finish this conversation at home." Then, turning and extending her hand to Principal Barnes, "I'm very sorry. Please convey my apologies to the other boy's parents."

"I will," replied Barnes. "Mrs. Klein, could I have a quick moment with Wes?"

Wes sensed something strange about Barnes's request to speak to him alone, but his mother didn't, and instead responded with a relaxed, "Sure."

When it was just the two of them Principal Barnes got up and walked around to the opposite side of the desk, where Wes was still sitting. Barnes sat casually on the corner of his desk and looked down at Wes. There was something about this sudden informality that made him uncomfortable. Just when Wes thought things couldn't get any weirder a wide grin spread across Barnes's face and he raised one eyebrow mischievously.

"Wes," Barnes hissed as he shook his head disapprovingly. "You're lying, and I get the impression it's because you didn't want your mother to hear the truth."

Wes officially had a genuine case of the creeps, and a nervous tingle started in his stomach and moved into his testicles. He swallowed hard before replying. "I'm not lying."

"Really? So you're saying that you and Shane Watkins were brawling because you got pissed off he was talking trash about you and your car? That he could "smoke" you in a race?"

Wes nodded slowly.

"Why didn't you just race him, then?" Barnes asked.

It was an easy enough question, but it caught Wes completely off guard, and he didn't have a response.

Barnes wasn't expecting one, so he continued. "You could have raced him to settle it, but you're saying you chose to break his nose instead. Well, I don't believe it. You know why?" Again, he wasn't expecting a reply. "Because you're not that stupid. Now you wanna tell me what really happened, just between the two of us?"

This time Barnes *was* looking for an answer, but Wes was too flustered with the fact that Barnes had seen right through him to offer a reply, so he kept staring.

Finally Principal Barnes sighed heavily and threw his hands up. "Have it your way then. You can go. Your suspension starts today."

Wes got up without a word and turned to walk out. He was almost to the door when Barnes spoke again.

"Wes," he said, "not even Shane Watkins is stupid enough to think he could outrun you in that Trans-Am of his. You've got…what…200 horses on him?"

Wes didn't have an answer for that either.

Barnes shook his head, annoyed. "Get out."

Wes left the office and found his mother waiting for him outside. She held out her car keys. "You're driving my car, and I'm taking yours," she told him. "You're following me."

Wes fished his keys out of his pocket, too preoccupied to protest. His mother grabbed the little eight ball swinging from the keychain. "We're gonna have a nice long chat when we get home, buddy-boy."

But Wes didn't hear her. He was busy playing a question over and over in his mind.

Mr. Barnes drives a Volvo. How the hell does he know so much about muscle cars?

***

As promised, Brenda and Wes Klein did have a talk when they got home that afternoon. It was a script that the two had followed many times before. Brenda would say how disappointed she was, and how raising two kids wasn't easy and blah blah blah. The final question varied slightly with each talk, but it was always some version of *"why can't you be more like your sister?"*

After the day he'd had, Wes almost answered that question with *"because I'm not a slut."* In the end he maintained his quiet dignity and sat in silence as his mother dished out her verbal attack. When his mother had nothing more to say Wes went up to his room, shut the door, and collapsed on his bed. Knowing that he had a lot to think over and work out, he began his normal ritual when faced with heavy issues. He put his Quiet Riot cassette in the player and cranked the volume. As the first notes of *"Metal Health"* started, his head hit the pillow and his hand instinctively reached up and behind him to find his autographed Bob Gibson baseball. Wes placed his index and middle fingers across the ball's stitches in a perfect fastball grip. His knuckles were swollen and still hurt like hell, but he began to toss the ball into the air anyway. He'd catch it and toss it up again, flicking his fingers just before release to put a little spin on the ball. Once he'd established this trancelike cadence he began to think.

Did I really have to beat on the kid that badly? he thought. He decided that yes, he did. Shane Watkins was a rich little punk, and even though he hated

38

his sister sometimes for being so perfect, he wasn't about to let that shithead spread a rumor about screwing her.

But what if it's not a rumor? Wes couldn't shake the feeling that Shane Watkins hadn't been lying. Call it a twin's intuition. Maybe Wendy wasn't as sweet and innocent as everyone thought. Wes wasn't one of those naïve brothers that believed his sister was going to wait until she was married to "do it"—he'd lost his own virginity two years earlier—but he didn't think she was the kind of girl that would sleep with a douchebag like Shane Watkins.

Wes was angry with himself for getting suspended, but he didn't regret breaking the kid's nose. What upset him more than anything was his mom taking his keys away (*let's just see how you like getting a ride from your sister*). He shuddered at the thought of climbing out of Wendy's orange Volkswagen as the entire school watched. It was at that moment he decided that the following morning he would pull out his dusty ten speed and air up the tires. He'd have to leave for school thirty minutes earlier, but at least it would be less humiliating than riding with Wendy every day.

He was still flipping the baseball over his head as Quiet Riot demanded he "bang his head." He stopped when he heard the sound of Wendy's Beetle chugging up the driveway.

Shit, he thought. *Here we go.* He wasn't prepared to be lectured by her for his suspension, especially when he considered the real reason behind it.

There was no lock on his door but it would have done him no good anyway. If Wendy wanted to bitch at him she would have stood in the hall pounding on the door until he let her in. Not even Quiet Riot would drown her out. *Maybe she'll just leave me alone for a while.*

She didn't, and minutes later Wendy stood in his doorway, staring at him. Judging him. There was an uncomfortable silence before she finally spoke. "You wanna talk about it?" she asked.

"Nope," Wes replied. He was still flipping the ball in the air, knowing that Wendy's question was just a formality, and that he was about to have a conversation whether he wanted to or not.

"Why would you do something so stupid?!?" Wendy apparently had no intention of getting to the point subtly. Wes continued to toss the ball. He did his best to hide the anger that was building inside him. "And why Shane Watkins?" she continued. "You barely know him and you decide to beat the shit out of him for no reason?"

This time when the ball came down Wes stopped. He didn't toss it again. He was fighting every urge to tell her the real reason he'd gotten in the fight, but the condescending way she scolded him was more than he could handle. When he finally responded his words came out like weapons.

"I hear that *you* know him pretty well," Wes said.

She stared at her brother and swallowed hard. She tried to come up with a reply but she could only sigh heavily. His comment had rendered her speechless, and that's when Wes knew for certain that his sister had indeed slept with Watkins.

"You had sex with him, didn't you?" Wes asked.

Ordinary siblings might have lied about such an accusation, but Wendy and Wes possessed a kind of sixth sense that only twins can understand. There was no point denying it, so instead she tried to sugarcoat it. "It was only once. I was at a party and drank too much, and—"

"FUCK, Wendy!" Wes sat up and swung his legs over the side of his bed, fuming. Wendy quickly looked down the hallway to make sure her mother hadn't heard them, then she stepped into her brother's room and closed the door. When she sat down beside him she had tears rolling down her cheeks.

"How did you know?" she finally managed to ask.

"He came in the bathroom with Ronnie Tozier, bragging about it. They didn't know I was in one of the stalls."

"Oh my God." Wendy buried her face in her hands. As Wes watched her chest heave with sobs, his anger with her started to subside. Wendy finally looked back up at him. "That's why you hit him?"

Wes nodded. "Multiple times."

"Good. I'm glad you did, but I'm sorry you got suspended. How long?" she asked.

"A week."

"Wes. Did you tell mom?"

"No. I told Mom and Barnes that Shane and me got into it over our cars."

"Did they buy it?"

"Mom did." Wes recalled the surprising discussion he'd had with Principal Barnes. "I'm pretty sure Barnes knows I'm full of shit."

"Really? Barnes?" Wendy seemed as surprised as Wes had been.

"It was weird. The guy actually knows his shit when it comes to cars, so he knew Shane would never really challenge me."

Wendy's sniffles finally subsided, and she looked absolutely pathetic when she looked over at Wes. "I'm so sorry, Wes. And I'm embarrassed. It never should have happened."

Wes felt bad for her, and at the same time he was happy to have told someone the real reason he'd gotten in the fight. When Wendy got her second wave of tears he put his arm around her and she cried into his chest. He decided not to tell her the part about the yellow underwear.

Just as Wes was about to give Wendy one last hug and essentially get on with his life, something unsettling struck him.

"Wendy," he said, pushing her off slightly. "How much did you actually drink?"

"Huh?"

"The night you and Shane...you know."

"I don't remember," she said. "That's what's so crazy. I don't remember drinking that much, but I woke up with one hell of a hangover. And I remember random images of us...well, you know."

All of the anger had returned, and Wes's knuckles throbbed again as he clenched his fists.

"Did you really want to do it, Wendy?" Wes asked. "I mean, really?"

"What do you mean?" she asked.

"I mean I'm asking you flat out. Did you voluntarily sleep with him or did he force you to do it?"

Wendy sat in silence again, and once more it was all the answer Wes needed.

"Mother Fucker!" Wes shouted.

Wendy jumped at his outburst. "What, Wes?!? What does it matter now anyway? It's done and over."

Wes got up and began rummaging around the chaos covering his desk. "You were raped. And it matters, Wendy!"

"Wes, what are you doing?" Wendy asked.

"Looking for my spare keys," he replied.

"Why?" But Wendy already knew the answer.

"Because I'm gonna go find that piece of shit and break more than his nose!"

Wendy jumped up just as Wes found his extra key. She grabbed his arms and spun him around. Wes could see the pleading in her face, and when she spoke he did his best to keep an open mind.

"Wes, no! Please don't go after him," she said.

"Wendy," he said, surprisingly calm, "he raped you, and he needs to pay for it."

Wendy's gaze dropped to her feet. "Fine. Then I'll go to the police. But if you go after him again you could get in worse trouble than a suspension. Much worse. And I don't want you getting into any more trouble because I was stupid."

Now it was Wes who grabbed Wendy's shoulders and shook her a little harder than he meant. "You were *not* stupid, Wendy. You were violated and that son of a bitch needs to answer for it."

Wendy shook her head. "Wes, promise me you won't do anything stupid."

Wes looked at the pleading on his sister's face and realized that this had to be incredibly difficult for her to process. Finally, he nodded. "Fine. But we're not done with this."

Wendy smiled and threw her arms around his neck. "I promise we'll talk about it as soon as I get back from practice." With that, Wendy rushed back into the hall, grabbed her pom-poms, and rushed out the door to cheerleading practice.

When the sound of Wendy's V.W. faded, Wes pocketed his spare keys and slipped on his shoes.

***

Two hours later the sun was down and Wes was in his Monte Carlo, heading toward Orchard Drive. He'd spent the last two hours trying to figure out what he was going to do when he arrived at Shane Watkins's house. It was strange; he wasn't running on pure rage like he had been that afternoon when he'd broken Watkins's nose. The thought of beating him to death for raping his sister was definitely tempting, but Wes knew that Shane would probably be home with his parents after spending the afternoon in the emergency room.

So what the hell am I supposed to do when I get there? Wes thought. He couldn't explain it, but there was something pushing him forward, toward the Watkins residence. When Wes Klein turned left on Orchard Drive, he was no closer to having any idea what he was doing there. As the Watkins house became visible Wes realized that it wouldn't have mattered if he'd had a plan.

The first thing that caught his eye was the car parked on the curb in front of the house. It was big, and it was old. Wes recognized it as a fifties model with large, sweeping tail fins. He shut off his own headlights and pulled over to the shoulder of the street. As he crept slowly forward, Wes saw more of the car and he realized he was looking at a very sweet ride indeed. It was a 1959 Cadillac and it was in fantastic shape. The deep red paint job was the thing that really grabbed Wes's attention. Something about that color in the moonlight was almost…threatening.

46

Wes was so enchanted by the Cadillac that he hadn't noticed the Watkins's front door open. When he looked up, what he saw was even stranger than the vintage car parked out front.

Principal Barnes stepped off the porch and adjusted the spectacles on his face. Down the block, Wes sat in his car, unblinking, as Barnes strode across the front lawn, directly to the red Caddy. Wes watched him open the door and slide behind the wheel. For an instant, he panicked at the thought that Barnes might have been there to get the truth from Shane about their fight.

Did Shane tell him? And what the hell is Barnes doing in a car like that? Wes thought. If he restored that car himself it would certainly explain why he'd seen through Wes's lie about the fight. *I'll be damned. Barnes is a gear head.*

A loud growl erupted from the Caddy's exhaust just then, as if Barnes had heard Wes's thoughts. Wes stared as the reverse lights suddenly came on and the sound of the screeching tires pierced the night. Thick, white smoke billowed from the Caddy's wheel wells and the big car shot backwards toward Wes's parked Monte Carlo. Wes slumped down behind the wheel until he could just barely see over his dash. Just as the Caddy passed Wes's Chevrolet, Barnes executed a flawless maneuver known as a "bootlegger's turn." The front end of the Caddy swung around 180 degrees as Barnes threw the car into first gear and sped forward down Orchard Drive, the wheels howling each time he up-shifted.

Wes sat up and turned in his seat. He watched as the Caddy's taillights disappeared around the corner. *So, Barnes can drive too.* As he turned back toward the Watkins house Wes saw the strangest thing yet. There was smoke drifting out of the open front door of the house and Wes could see flickers of orange in the front windows. When his brain finally registered that the Watkins's house was on fire, he was already opening his car door.

He took off in a dead run toward the house. If Shane Watkins was in the house he should have come out by now. Something was wrong, and Wes wasn't about to let his sister's rapist burn to death.

Shane deserved worse than that.

When he reached the front lawn he could see actual flames in the downstairs windows and he could hear the smoke detectors going off inside. Wes's right foot hit the first porch step just as the curtains in the living room started to go up. He was almost inside the door when he finally smelled the gasoline.

When he'd stepped all the way into the living room the thick smoke stole his breath and blurred his vision. Remembering something from grade school, Wes instinctively dropped to his hands and knees and started crawling. The air near the floor was easier to breathe, and through his tears Wes could see that the fire hadn't spread to the hallway at the far end of the room. Between coughing fits, he began to yell.

"Hello! Anybody in here?!?" He didn't hear a reply, but his heart was beating so hard in his ears that he was afraid he wouldn't be able to hear anyone even if they did yell back. When he made it to the hall the air was clear enough that he could stand up again. He turned to look at the living room and saw that the fire had taken over the entire front wall of the house, and it was starting to spread across the ceiling. He didn't have much time, and he realized just how stupid he'd been; rushing into a burning house to save someone that he could have killed seven hours earlier. Wes turned back toward the hall and was about to yell again when he saw the bodies.

Lying at the bottom of the stairs, in a pool of blood and what looked like little grey pieces of brain, were Shane's parents. Wes's first thought was to flee the house and call the police, but the fire had blocked his retreat on the first floor, and he had no choice but to approach the two bodies. The heat of the fire on his back pushed him forward, until he eventually stood over Mr. and Mrs. Watkins.

Shane's mother was lying on her back, her eyes wide open. There was a jagged hole in the center of her forehead. Mr. Watkins was lying next to her on his stomach. His face was turned to the side but Wes could see that the back of his skull was nothing more than a gaping, pulpy mess.

Jesus, Wes thought. *It was Barnes. Barnes fucking shot them and set fire to the house!*

The most gruesome thing about the two bodies at this feet was the smell. Through the thick odor of smoke Wes thought he could smell shit, and the idea of Mr. and Mrs. Watkins losing their bowels as the bullets blew out the backs of their heads is what finally caused him to turn and vomit.

Wes carefully stepped over the bodies and started up the stairs. As he ran up the staircase Wes told himself that he only had time for a quick sweep of the top floor, and then he'd need to find a way out of the house, and fast.

The air on the second floor was clear, but Wes knew it wouldn't stay that way for long. He crept along the hall steadily until he arrived at the first door. He glanced inside and assumed it was Mr. and Mrs. Watkins's room. Content that the room was empty, he proceeded down the hall toward the next door. Just as he was about to enter the room two things happened. The smoke detectors on the second floor went off, startling Wes to the point he screamed, and he sensed a new smell.

It was a coppery kind of smell, like a jar of old pennies. The air was palpable with it.

It smelled like blood.

As Wes entered Shane Watkins's room he saw why. The floor, walls and even the ceiling were covered in blood. On the bed lay what was left of Shane. Wes tasted bile rising in his throat again but he managed to keep it down as he stared at the massacred boy. Shane had been split open from his pubic bone to his sternum. Intestines and several organs had spilled over his sides and they sat glistening on the mattress. His throat had been cut deeply, and Wes could see sharp, white pieces of his windpipe sticking out of the wound. The final act of butchery was still sticking out of Shane's chest. There was a long dagger buried in his heart. The handle was intricately designed in silver patterns and there appeared to be the head of a goat or ram at the end. Wes glanced back up at Shane's face and saw that he had two black eyes and a bloodied bandage covering his nose. A wave of guilt struck him for a moment. But only a moment.

You poor bastard.

Wes knew that he needed to get out of the house, but as he was about to turn around he spotted something on Shane's dresser. There was a very old book and a stack of Polaroid photos. Wes picked up the book and began to flip through the pages. He couldn't read any of the words, but the illustrations gave him enough information. The yellowed pages contained drawings of pentagrams, goat heads and hideous looking creatures and demons.

What kind of satanic shit were you into, Watkins? he thought.

He picked up the stack of photos and began sorting through them as Shane's room began to fill with smoke. There were several pictures of a bunch of figures in black robes standing around some sort of alter. The next photo Wes flipped to showed Shane standing at the foot of the alter. The robe he was wearing was open and Wes could see that he was naked underneath. He quickly flipped to the next photo and froze.

It was Wendy.

She was lying naked on the alter and several of the other hooded figures had stepped up and appeared to be holding her arms and legs. Wes began to cough as smoke poured into Shane's room. He could see bits of burning wallpaper drifting through the hallway.

Wes quickly ran to the doorway, felt the intense heat outside and slammed the door. He turned back to the opposite side of Shane's bedroom and ran to the window. He threw it open and inhaled deeply as the fresh air flooded his lungs. Peering outside, he saw that he could easily jump onto the porch roof and make it to the backyard safely. He could hear sirens approaching in the distance and knew that he needed to move. When the police and fire department showed up he'd have a lot of explaining to do. They'd probably be interested that he'd kicked the shit out of Shane Watkins that afternoon, and now the kid's parents had been shot in the head, not to mention that Shane himself had been gutted like a fucking trout.

As the sirens grew louder, Wes realized he was still holding the stack of photos. He moved the picture of Wendy naked on the alter to the back of the stack and looked at the next one. It was even worse. Shane was kneeling between her legs, Wendy's thighs wrapped around his hips. His head was thrown back in a kind of wild ecstasy. Wes's blood boiled as he kept rifling through the photos. The next photo showed someone Wes didn't recognize in a similar position with his sister. So did the next.

And the next.

She was fucking gang raped! Wes had an intense urge to throw the stack of photos into the fire. Instead, he flipped one more picture.

It was obvious who he was, but there was still something wrong about it. His back was covered in tattoos. The tattoos were illustrations, exactly like those in the book Wes had looked through. Everyone else in the photo had dropped to their knees in a kind of reverence. In this photo it was his sister whose head was thrown back in ecstasy. It was Principal Barnes between her legs.

Wes dropped the stack of photos.

Everything started to make sense. Shane's ritualistic slaying. The ornate dagger. The book of the occult. The photographs made it pretty obvious, but for Wes it was something else that convinced him.

That car. Unnaturally red. Only the Devil, or something damn close to it, would drive a car like that.

Flames were slithering under the bedroom door and traveling up the inside. This, combined with the sirens, helped snap Wes back into action. He climbed out of the open window and dropped onto the roof of the back porch. By the time his feet hit the grass, the lights on the fire trucks were rounding the corner and pulling onto Orchard Drive. Wes ran around the side of the house and slipped into the crowd that was standing out front watching. When he was positive no one had seen him sneak out of the house, Wes made his way back to his car.

He shut the driver's side door just as the first floor windows blew out in the Watkins house. By the time he pulled off of Orchard Drive, the top windows had blown too.

***

He had to get his sister. That much he knew.

Everything was moving at the speed of light. The distance between Orchard Drive and the High School wasn't far, and at the rate Wes was driving it didn't leave him much time to put things together.

We have to go to the cops now, Wes thought. Then he shook his head at his stupidity. *And tell them what? Wendy was gang raped? Where's your proof? You dropped it on Watkins's floor, and it's going up in flames, dumbass.*

It didn't matter. He had to get to Wendy and tell her what he saw, as much as it may hurt her. He needed her wits, because at that exact moment all he could think about was killing Principal Barnes, and from what Wes had seen at the Watkins house, he'd likely end up the one that was dead.

Wendy will know what to do.

Wes put the Monte Carlo into a hard slide as he squealed into the High School parking lot. He breathed a sigh of relief when he saw that Wendy's V.W. bug was still parked outside the gymnasium. He pulled in next to the Volkswagen and killed the engine on his Chevy. Then he was sprinting up the walkway toward the gym doors.

The Barker Marsh Blackhawks varsity cheerleading squad was just wrapping up their practice when Wes Klein burst through the double doors under the South scoreboard. Most of the girls thought Wes was hot in a renegade, James Dean kind of way, so when they saw him approaching they made a point to stick their breasts out a little further than usual.

"Hi Wes," said a raspy voice. Layla Drake was five feet nine inches of blond bombshell that Wes would have ordinarily been more than happy to have exchanged playful flirting with, but now wasn't the time.

"Hey Layla," Wes said, trying to hide the tension in his voice. "Have you seen Wendy?"

"Yeah, she just left with Principal Barnes," Layla replied.

The statement hit Wes in the gut like a blow from a heavyweight boxer. "NO!" he shouted as he put his hands on his knees to steady himself. While he was still looking down at the floor he said, "Where are they going, Layla?"

"No idea."

"Dammit Layla! Doesn't it seem a little weird that my sister would leave at eight o'clock at night with the Princ—" Wes stopped in mid-sentence when he looked back up at Layla's face. Her eyes looked like two black golf balls. He actually took a step backwards.

"What's so weird about it, Wes?" said the strange Layla-like thing in front of him.

Wes looked around at the rest of the girls. They all had the same lifeless, black eyes as Layla, and they were all chewing on their lower lips seductively. The girls were completely in sync. The whole scene reminded Wes of a movie he'd rented once. *The Stepford Wives.* He flinched as Layla stepped forward and grabbed his shoulders. She leaned in to whisper in his ear. "How about it, Wes? You wanna sneak down to the locker room and fuck?" Then she stepped back and turned to the rest of the squad. "You can fuck all of us if you want."

The girls scared Wes, and he was relieved when they didn't chase after him as he turned and ran. They were under some kind of spell, and Wes was sure Barnes had done it. He'd already violated his sister once, and now he'd taken her.

Where? he thought as he sprinted back toward his car. He jumped behind the wheel and cranked the motor. The Monte Carlo roared to life, and it helped Wes regain some of his courage. He closed his eyes and started to think.

He wouldn't take her to his house. That would be too obvious. So assuming he is some kind of fucking devil, where would he go? Hell? Then it hit Wes. Something from his childhood. Not hell, but for Barker Marsh, it was probably close.

The old trestles, where—according to his mother—there were supposedly Devil worshipers aplenty.

That's where Barnes was taking Wendy, and that's probably where the photos were taken. When Wes looked back up, Layla Drake was standing outside his car on the driver's side. She was naked, and she'd grown some impressive fangs to go along with her black eyes. Wes sat frozen as the Layla-thing's hand moved toward the door handle. As its fingertips touched the lever, Wes snapped out of it and slammed down the door lock post, while simultaneously slamming the Monte Carlo into reverse. The stocky Chevy shot backwards through the parking lot, and in a maneuver identical to the one Barnes had performed in his `59 Caddy, Wes suddenly slid the front end around 180 degrees and shot off down the street without slowing. As he pulled out of the fishtail, Wes reached down and snapped on his stereo. The Rolling Stones flooded his speakers and Wes actually laughed at the irony of the song that was playing.

It was *Sympathy for the Devil.*

***

The old Barker Marsh trestles weren't operational, and hadn't been for almost thirty years. The wide trench and a few tons of burned timbers were all that remained of the long since retired train route. Back when there was still coal to be mined below The Marsh, Union Pacific constructed a two mile off-shoot to move six million tons of coal through the town. In 1962 a fire destroyed the better part of this detour. The mine closed not long after, and soon "the Trestles" became an uninhabitable wasteland. Naturally, kids with less than honorable intentions flocked to this space through the years. The younger kids would ride their BMX racers up and down the steep hills and smoke the occasional cigarette swiped from a parent. The older kids frequented the grounds for a steady schedule of drinking, drugs and sex. Wes had certainly spent his fair share of time at the Trestles.

When he was younger his mother would warn him to stay away from the area at night. *"It's where the devil worshipers congregated,"* she'd say. Wes had always thought it was a load of bullshit—just a creative maneuver by parents to keep their kids closer to home. Wes had found the occasional animal carcass among the hills and timber, but nothing that indicated any serious occult rituals.

As he pulled off the main road and onto the charred grounds bordering the Trestles, he was positive that his mother was on to something.

The 1959 Cadillac was parked on the edge of the steep trench that bisected the Trestles and did wonders to confirm this belief.

As he pulled slowly beside the Caddy, Wes thought back to the photos in Shane Watkins's room. At the time he had been focusing on the individual people in the pictures, and not the surroundings. Now, as he shifted into park, he closed his eyes and tried to remember *where* the individuals were. He couldn't be positive, but the photos certainly could have been taken among the Trestles.

Wes glanced over to make sure nobody was in the Caddy, and when he was positive it was empty, he killed the engine. He got out of his Monte Carlo and walked over to the classic coupe parked next to him. Wes peered into the driver's side window and admired the plush tuck-and-roll leather. This, as well as the chrome trim that decorated the interior of the car, was absolutely flawless. He took a step back then and looked at the equally flawless exterior of the vehicle.

Red.

It was a kind of red that Wes had never seen on a car, or anywhere else. It was the color of broken promises. Lies. Lust. Pain.

It was the Devil's red. And Wes Klein was convinced it was the Devil that had his sister.

He could hear voices drifting up from the deep trench. One of the voices he thought belonged to Principal Barnes. The other was much deeper and full of sin and hatred.

Wes crept closer to the trench, following the voices. Even if he wanted to stop he couldn't. That deep, exotic voice kept him moving. He didn't understand the words, but to him they felt like a warm bath, inviting him to slip a little further into the void. A part of Wes sensed that something was wrong, but he couldn't stop walking. He was a puppet, and a part deep inside him had a very bad feeling about who was pulling the strings.

Stop walking, Wes thought. But his legs kept moving.

He could sense that he'd—*stop*—moved out onto—*STOP*—an old trestle, high—STOP—above the deep trench below.

STOP!!!

After what felt like miles Wes finally stopped walking. He looked down at his feet and realized he was standing in the middle of one of the few remaining trestles, 25 feet above the ground.

"Hi Wesley!" said a voice from behind him. Wes snapped around quickly and saw that Principal Barnes was staring at him. He barely had time to notice that Wendy was standing behind Barnes, in some kind of trance. In a split second Principal Barnes's right hand shot up and grabbed Wes's throat. It felt as if his windpipe was being crushed in a vice. Barnes was even taller than Wes, so his feet dangled freely when the older man lifted his face up to his own. Wes was choking. The strength in Barnes's hand was inhuman.

Wes wasn't surprised.

"Listen to me closely, Wes," Barnes said through gritted teeth. "I admire your courage—coming after your sister like this—but there's nothing you can do. I don't want to kill you, boy, but I will. There's no shame in staying down when you know you're beat."

Wes made a last ditch effort to claw at Barnes's eyes, but Barnes simply extended his own arm, putting Wes well out of reach. Barnes shook his head disapprovingly. "Stupid boy. It appears you don't know how to lay down, so I'll have to show you."

With hellish strength, Barnes shoved Wes over the edge of the trestle—and let go. Wes's stomach lurched as he fell, back first, toward the floor of the trench. He had time to look over at Wendy before the ground blasted the wind from his lungs.

Wes was pretty sure he'd blacked out. The good news was that he didn't think he was paralyzed. His back hurt too much. All he wanted to do at that moment was to go to sleep. Instead, he managed to roll over on his stomach, which was plenty agonizing. He suppressed the urge to throw up as a ringing started in his ears and Wes was convinced he was slipping into a coma. The sound suddenly erupted into a familiar growl, and Wes recognized the throaty exhaust of Barnes's big Caddy.

The sound ignited some reserve of energy deep inside Wes, and he managed to push himself up onto his hands and knees. Another burst of exhaust from the top of the trench brought Wes to his feet. When his head finally cleared he was clawing his way up the side of the trench. He reached the top just in time to see the Caddy fishtail out onto the paved road. With a final burst of energy Wes pulled himself over the crest and sprinted lamely to his Monte Carlo. He fired up the motor and seconds later he was gaining on a vintage pair of tail lights.

***

The steering wheel vibrated in Wes's hands as he roared forward toward the Cadillac. His brain was working overtime as he simultaneously tried to focus on the road and figure out why Barnes, or Satan, or whoever the hell he was, wanted his sister so badly. Up ahead, Barnes turned right and Wes mashed the accelerator to the floor in an effort to catch up. When he reached the intersection he slammed on the brakes and jerked the steering wheel to the right, sliding the Monte Carlo sideways past the stop sign. He was closing on the tail lights again.

Barnes must have realized he was being followed, because at that moment Wes could see the Caddy fishtail slightly as its driver accelerated as quickly as the big antique could manage. Wes answered this with his own burst of speed. He didn't care anymore about *why* Barnes had taken his sister. He just knew he had to get her back.

Wes was gaining on them when Wendy's voice began to come through the car's speakers.

"Wes, you have to stop chasing us. You have to let us go."

He shook his head in disbelief, and took his eyes off the road just long enough to look around suspiciously in the car. "Wendy? Is that you?"

As the red coupe made a hard left onto the main highway and Wes quickly followed, his sister's voice spoke through the speakers, again. "Yes, it's me. Now listen Wes, you have to back off."

"But Wendy, I don't understand—"

"Dammit Wes, stop! If you don't he'll kill you. He—"

Wes snapped the radio off. He didn't know how his sister was able to talk to him through his car speakers, but he wasn't about to give up on getting her back.

They were on a straightaway and Wes had pulled close enough to see Barnes behind the Caddy's steering wheel and Wendy sitting in the passenger seat. He looked down at his own instrument panel and saw his speedometer was pegged at 85, but knew both vehicles were doing closer to 120 miles per hour.

Now what? Wes thought. *We just race until one of us runs out of gas?*

As if replying to the question in Wes's head, Barnes suddenly braked hard enough to slingshot down a side road. Wes blew past the road and slammed on his own brakes. He threw the car in reverse and sped backwards toward the side road he'd overshot. Another rubber-screaming maneuver and he was rocketing down the gravel road toward the Cadillac once more.

Both cars slid wildly on the loose gravel but Barnes and Wes both managed to keep the vehicles on the roadway. Wes recognized their location as the entry road to the Barker Zinc-smelting plant. He was right up on Barnes's rear bumper now and could have easily overtaken the Cadillac, but there was no room on either side to pass. Wes swerved slightly so he could see around the Caddy. The gate to the plant was shut, but Barnes showed no sign of slowing down. He was close enough to see Wendy's face in the rearview mirror now. Her eyes seemed to be pleading with him just as much as her voice had been minutes earlier.

He tucked in tight behind Barnes just as the Caddy's front bumper contacted the chain link gate. The large antique tore the gate from the hinges in a shower of sparks. Wes slid into the large, open courtyard and had only a moment to ponder what his next move would be before the Cadillac blazed ahead with an unearthly speed. Wes floored the Chevy but it was no use. The big Caddy had already disappeared around the backside of the smelter before Wes was able to get any traction in the loose rock.

He felt the explosion before he saw or heard it. He rounded the backside of the plant and slid to a stop. Hot tears instantly started cascading down his cheeks when he saw what was left of the Cadillac coupe. Barnes had run head first into a large piece of equipment. It must have been a matter of seconds before the gas tank exploded. Through the tears and the intense flames, Wes could make out the two bodies in the blazing carnage.

Wes hung his head as a primitive wail rose up inside of him.

It's my fault. She's dead because I pushed him.

Him.

Barnes.

The Devil.

Wes's chest stopped heaving then. *If Barnes is some kind of fucking devil then why would a collision and a little fire stop him?*

He looked back up at the wreckage and his heart stopped.

Wendy was staring back at him. She was standing naked in the middle of the flames.

Wendy? Wes questioned. *How is this possible?*

Wendy smiled.

He continued to stare, confused. After an eternity he saw her raise her right hand and put her thumb and forefinger together. Then she slowly turned her hand back and forth, as if dialing a knob.

Wes understood. He reached down and snapped his stereo back on, and Wendy's voice filled the speakers again.

"I tried to warn you, Wes. You should have let me go."

I had to stop him, Wes thought. *He was going to do terrible things to you, Wendy. Worse than he already has.*

His sister threw her head back in the flames and an eerie laughter filled the interior of the Monte Carlo. Behind Wendy, Wes could see what was left of Principal Barnes baking in the wreck.

"And what terrible things do you think he was going to do to me, Wes? Fuck me? Kill me?" she asked.

For an instant Wes thought of how ludicrous the situation was; him having a conversation with his naked sister, who was standing in a blaze of fire, communicating using only his thoughts and his car stereo. However, crazy as it seemed, he couldn't help but respond to her question.

I don't know, Wendy. I assumed Barnes needed you for some kind of ritual or something.

"Because he's the Devil, right?" she continued.

I guess so. Confusion was sweeping over him, but there was a new feeling building in his gut too. It was fear.

"Barnes didn't need *me*, brother." Wendy's eyes flashed a brilliant gold from within the flames. "I needed *him*."

Then Barnes isn't the devil......because—

"I am," said a deep voice that was strangely still his sister's.

Wes watched in horror as Wendy stepped completely out of the flames. Her legs were covered in thick fur, and they tapered down to sharp looking hooves. They kicked at the dust as if she was a bull about to charge. Wendy's breasts heaved with each breath she took.

Wes blinked a couple of times. *But I—*

"Don't understand?" Wendy asked, finishing Wes's thought for him. "Of course you don't. I don't have a lot of time to explain it to you, but if you trace back the Devil's lineage it has consistently hinged on the dichotomy of good and evil."

Wes stared, clueless.

The Wendy-thing rolled her eyes. "Twins, Wes. Through the years Lucifer has always produced twin offspring. A good twin and an evil twin."

Wait. Us? Wes thought.

"Yes, brother. All these years everyone assumed you were the *bad* twin, but surprise surprise—try as you might to be a hardass, you were always good deep down. But me—well," the Wendy-thing laughed deeply. "It doesn't really matter now. I had some other things to do before I took care of you but—"

This time it was Wes that interrupted with his thought. *Are you saying our father was the Devil?*

"You never found it strange that mom doesn't have a single picture of dear old Dad?"

Wes shook his head and moved to a new question. *What do you mean you "have to take care of me?"*

The Wendy-thing threw her hands in the air as if she couldn't believe that Wes could be so dense. "I have to kill you, Wes. Sorry, but that's how it is. The evil twin kills the good twin. It goes all the way back to Cain and Abel."

Cain and Abel weren't twins.

"Really, Wes? You wanna get into this with me right now?"

You won't kill me. You can't. In his heart, as much as it pained him, Wes knew that the hooved thing in front of his car absolutely *could* kill him. That's why he did his best to keep his eyes focused on her while his right hand slipped the car into drive.

"I'm sorry, Wes, but I can and I must."

Wait! What did you need Barnes for?

"Same thing I needed Shane and a dozen others for. Offspring. I have to keep the bloodline going. I'm sorry things got so fucked up for you so fast. Watkins couldn't keep his big mouth shut and you just happened to overhear it. I mean, you were gonna have to die eventually anyway, but I'd hoped we would have a little more time."

Wes's heart pounded at the thought of what he was about to do. He hesitated, then looked down at the beast-like lower half of her body, and the decision became easier. His foot started to let up on the brake. He was going to floor the accelerator and run the Wendy-thing down, but he never got the chance. Wendy's voice came through the speakers once more and it made him hesitate. It was all the pause that the Wendy-thing needed.

"It's too late, Wes. I'm sorry."

Wes lifted his foot to step on the gas, but a piercing shriek made him jerk his head to the left. He was blinded by a brilliant light, and had just enough time to glance down and realize that he'd stopped the car on the railroad tracks that cut through the smelting plant.

A second later 8,000 tons of steel pulverized Wes Klein. The front and rear halves of the Monte Carlo, along with the upper and lower halves of his body would be recovered half a mile apart.

***

By the time the train had passed, the Wendy-thing's lower body had returned to normal. Gone were the beast's hooves—her slender, sixteen year old legs back once again. She looked down the tracks as the sirens rang out in the distance, and then her hands moved up to rub her stomach, caressing both lives that were growing inside.

Chapter 2

"No warm lights flickered around him

No blankets there to fold

Nothing but, the howling wind

And the driving rain so cold

When he heard a whistle blowing

In a dreamy kind of way

The hobo seemed contented for

He smiled there where he lay"

—Rodgers, Jimmie. "Hobo Bill's Last Ride." Victor Talking Machine

Company, 1929

Hasty finished his story and spat a large globule of phlegm onto the

dusty floor. For a moment the Drifter could only watch as his narrator

cracked open a fresh beer and took a long drink. Telling the tale of Wes

and Wendy Klein must have left him parched.

The Drifter glanced around the old factory and all at once realized that

if Hasty's story was true, then Wes Klein would have been struck by the

train not one hundred feet from where he sat. "It happened right outside?"

he asked.

Hasty cut loose with a deep, satisfying, belch. "What's that, Lou?"

"The train. The one that hit the Klein kid. It happened right outside, didn't it?"

"Yes-sir-ee. Although, most of what was left was found half a mile down the tracks. I was there that night, ya' know. Workin' for the town back then so there was a bunch of us got woke up that night to come and clear the wreckage off the tracks. Horrible sight, Lou. Just horrible."

The Drifter tried to imagine what the carnage must have looked like and then immediately shook the image from his mind. Then he asked, "Whatever happened to the sister—Wendy?"

"Oh, she stuck around the Marsh for a while. Had twin babies and then one day she just up and disappeared with those two little ones. Can't say I blame her though, Lou—all those rumors about her being evil and all the sex scandal stuff with that principal fella."

"Do you believe any of it, Hasty?" the Drifter asked. "I mean, all that Devil stuff?"

"All I knows is that this town has a way of making good people go bad—rots 'em sort of. I remember the Klein girl was a sweetheart, and when she turned up pregnant after her brother died and that principal tried to take off with her the rumors started flying. Some thought the babies might have been her brother's, and then there was the question of how she made it out of that car fire alive. Now, is she the Devil? I don't think so, but I wouldn't swear on nothing when it comes to the folks in this town."

"What about the mother?" the Drifter asked.

"Her son dying was hard as hell on her, but when her little girl had them babies and then just took off it was more'n she could take. They had to lock her up at Hoffner Falls. I saw her a few times during my little vacation there."

"Jesus," the Drifter said softly.

Harold "Hasty" Davis let out another of his signature laughs. This one was short lived, and when it tapered off he spoke again. "Whassa matter, Lou? My story shake you up? You're the one that asked to hear it."

The chill had returned and the Drifter began to shiver again, unsure if it was because of the weather or Hasty's tale. For just a moment it sounded as if the rain outside was letting up, but seconds later it started pouring harder than ever, as if the sky just needed a second to catch its breath.

Hasty threw a couple more pieces of wood on the fire and the Drifter welcomed the increased heat and glow from the flames.

"Didn't mean to unsettle you, Lou," said Hasty, "but like I said—you asked for it. And that story ain't nothing, boy-oh."

The Drifter looked through the flames once more at his strange host and felt like he was in Catholic school again, talking with the priest through the screened window during his weekly confession. Finally, he spoke up again. "Don't you have any stories that *don't* involve dead kids or the Devil?"

On the other side of the fire, Hasty's eyebrows went up curiously, but he didn't smile—only considered the Drifter's question. Finally, he said, "Only a few."

Then Hasty Davis cleared his throat.

***

Bruises

"The beast in me is caged by frail and fragile bars

Restless by day and by night rants and rages at the stars

God help the beast in me"

—Cash, Johnny. "The Beast In Me." *American Recordings*, American/Sony,

1994

July was a special month in the village of Barker Marsh. Park league baseball was in full swing. The sweltering heat provided ample opportunities for swimming—day or night. In the evenings the town seemed to glow under the soft light of fireflies and backyard bonfires. Fewer *bad things* seemed to happen in July around the Marsh. It was the cold, winter months that bred the *bad things*, when there was nothing to do but drink and get into trouble.

For Nick Goodman the best thing about July was the annual Barker Marsh Picnic. It was always held on the last weekend in July and Nick had always adored it for as long as he could remember. The event was meant to raise funds for the town's volunteer fire department and was essentially four days packed with carnival rides, games, fair food, and countless other activities that helped hold sleepy little towns like Barker Marsh together.

The experience was a little different for Nick now than it used to be.

Gone were the days of running through the crowds with his friends at break-neck speeds and devouring funnel cakes, only to throw them up again when he rode *"The Stinger."*

He still attended every year, but for the last five he was stuck behind the smoker at "Red's BBQ." Nick had no idea why his employer called it "Red's" BBQ. Merrill Colby ran the business and Nick was pretty sure he didn't have any relatives named "Red." Nick thought maybe Merrill had settled on "Red's" because it sounded like a typical Southern black man that would run a BBQ joint. Ironic, really, considering Merrill Colby was the biggest racist Nick had ever met.

But he gave Nick a job, and that was more than anyone else in town had done when he got released from Menard State Penitentiary. Then again, Colby also paid him less than minimum wage and had told Nick that if he had a fucking problem with it he'd be happy to put a call in to Nick's parole officer for him.

The only person who had *truly* given Nick a chance after his prison stretch was Kara Wheeler, his high school sweetheart. She'd written to him every week while he was incarcerated and had visited him a few times, even though she was married at the time. She was divorced by the time he was released.

Now Nick turned slightly to admire her naked body, sleeping soundly on top of his very numb left arm. Kara looked much younger than her 31 years, despite having been through some hard times. Nick's right hand gently caressed the inner thigh of her right leg. His fingers walked slowly upward to tickle her trimmed pubic hair, causing Kara to stir slightly. Showing a substantial amount of self-control, he continued to run his free hand up across her toned stomach and finally settled on her left breast. He have her nipple the slightest graze before moving his hand to her right breast. His hand stopped there for a long time, tracing the tight, smooth scar tissue that ran a vertical two inches in the center of her breast. The scar was a gift from her ex-husband, who had felt that a small fender bender she'd gotten into was reason enough to bury a kitchen knife in her chest. If he'd stabbed her on the left side instead of the right the blade would have cleaved her heart in two. Kara divorced him on a Monday, and he went to prison on a Wednesday.

Nick got *out* of prison the following Friday.

As he was about to wake her up for what he hoped was an intense round of "wake-up sex," a loud noise made him jump. Kara's trailer sat right on the main highway running North and South through Barker Marsh, so when the big semi-truck hit its Jake brake Nick was convinced that his boss, Merrill Colby, had been right all along, and the "fucking Commie bastards" were invading. He quickly removed his right hand from Kara's chest and pulled apart the blinds to peek outside. He was relieved to see that it wasn't machine gun fire and smiled when he saw that the large truck was hauling the dismantled body of *"The Stinger,"* still going strong after all these years.

There would be a steady convoy of trucks like this coming into town all day long, hauling all sorts of equipment that would eventually become the rides and games at the Barker Marsh Picnic.

Nick glanced up at the alarm clock on his dresser. If the trucks were already rolling into town then it meant Merrill Colby was already at the town park, too. He'd be setting up his own truck in preparation for four days' worth of slow cooking pork and beef. Nick figured if he got dressed and made it to the park in twenty minutes Merrill would only chew his ass for about ten.

He tried to slide his left arm out from under Kara stealthily, but it was no use. Her eyes opened and she smiled up at him.

"Where do you think you're going, mister?" she asked. Her hand slid down and gripped Nick's penis. He stiffened instantly. Kara climbed on top of him and he gave a quick glance at his alarm clock again. As he slid inside her Nick Goodman had just one thought.

Six bucks an hour ain't worth giving this up.

***

Merrill Colby wasn't just mad, he was fuming. Red's BBQ was the top food seller year after year at the Barker Marsh Picnic, and Merrill believed that part of his success was because his food truck was granted the premier location over the entire carnival. This year it was different. He and the "Funnel Cake Faggots," as Merrill called them, were listed to set up at the very back of the park, on top of the tennis courts. Merrill folded the vendor map angrily and shoved it into his back pocket, then he marched off to find out whose bright fucking idea it had been to stick him out in no man's land.

It was Wednesday morning—the day before the big Picnic was to start. The town park was already packed full of vehicles, carnies, and nosey townsfolk. Every year Merrill Colby was the first food vendor to arrive. He liked to set up early and have his smoker going while the rest of the carnies set up their various rides and games. He could make a pretty decent amount before the event ever started just by feeding overpriced pork sandwiches to the hungry workers. His truck was *always* parked in the middle of the action, and this year's decision to move him to the back corner of the park was going to impact him financially. At least that's what he was trying to tell Bud Dillon, the Chief of the volunteer fire department and organizer of the Barker Marsh Picnic.

"What difference does it make?" Bud asked when Merrill finally stopped yelling long enough for him to get a word in. "People gotta eat, don't they? If they're hungry, they'll find you."

"No, Bud, they won't," Merrill retorted. "What they'll do is walk by one of these cotton candy or little fuckin' ice cream dot joints you've got strung out through the main thoroughfare here and stop there. You know why? Cause' they don't wanna walk half a fuckin' mile to get real food, that's why!" Merrill Colby was easily a hundred pounds heavier and a foot shorter than the fire chief, so his protruding belly prevented him from really getting in Bud Dillon's face. It didn't matter, though—the Chief had had enough.

"Merrill," Bud said, "get over it, would you? The layout is set and it ain't changing. Now I suggest you fuck off, or maybe my guys find some fire hazards when they inspect your site later. Let's see how that impacts your finances."

Merrill stared up at the Chief, the veins in his temples throbbing. Finally, he could think of just one thing to say. "Cocksuckers!" Then he turned and stormed off back toward his food truck.

As Merrill waddled off, Bud Dillon put a hand to his mouth and shouted, "Good luck at the Picnic this weekend, Merrill!"

Merrill spun around and gave the Chief the finger. "Cocksuckers! All of you! Cocksuckers!" Then he turned and continued his march. He was almost all the way back to his food truck when he spotted Nick Goodman standing in front of it. Merrill thought Goodman was a decent kid, for an ex-con. He gave the kid a hard time and didn't pay him shit, but the bottom line was that Merrill liked him—as much as Merrill was capable of liking anyone. Still, Merrill also liked punctuality and Nick was late. This, combined with his conversation with Bud Dillon, had primed Merrill to deliver a royal ass chewing.

"Well, glad you decided to show up, shitbird!" Merrill said, trotting up to Nick. "This ain't the kind of fucking job you can just show up whenever you please."

"Sorry, Merrill," Nick said. Then he looked around and realized that the Red's BBQ trailer wasn't in its normal location. "Hey, what gives? Why are we parked way back here?"

Merrill made a sound that was somewhere between a laugh and a cough. "If you'd showed up on time you'd understand the cluster fuck I've been dealing with all morning. That cocksucker Dillon has us shoved back here with the rest of the assholes."

"What's going in our normal spot?" Nick asked.

Merrill didn't know. He'd been so pissed when he saw that his business *wasn't* going to be the center of attention that he hadn't even bothered to check the diagram to see what was in "his" spot. He reached back and pulled the wrinkled page out of his back pocket. There was one name covering the center of the page, marking the carnival's prime real estate.

Kempster.

"Those mother fuckers!" said Merrill through gritted teeth. The Kempsters were a gypsy family that travelled from town to town, carnival to carnival, county fair to county fair. They were old school entertainers. The old man, Abraham, was the patriarch of the family and he was a fortune teller. With him was always a brigade of kids, grandkids, and great grandkids whose talents ranged from knife throwing to fire breathing. One of the granddaughters even did a routine where a Capuchin monkey rode around on the back of some mixed breed mutt of a dog. The people of Barker Marsh loved the Kempsters.

Merrill Colby hated them. He didn't have a particular reason for hating them, until now. He tore up the vendor layout and threw the pieces on the ground, stomping on them for effect.

Nick held his hands out and shook his head in a *"mind filling me in?"* kind of way.

"Fucking gyp bastards," Merrill said. "Those freaks have got center stage while the rest of us *tax paying* folks who are trying to run a legit business are stuck back here. I don't know why Bud Dillon invites them back every year."

Nick knew exactly why the Kempsters were invited each year. People loved their acts, but he wasn't about to tell Merrill that right now. Instead he just let him continue his rant.

"Buncha fuckin' weirdoes, Nicky, I'll tell ya. And thieves, too. You know they're always in and out of Carl's Grocery across the street there— probably shoplifting the whole time. Them gyps are worse than niggers. At least the spooks aren't afraid of earning an honest day's pay. What do *they* do? I'll tell you. Juggle fuckin' knives and belly dance—the girls flashing their hairy snatches if you look close enough. Probably all got the clap, too, from all that—"

Merrill stopped spouting in mid-sentence. Nick could see that he was staring at something and he followed his gaze over to Highway 51, where a caravan of old cars and campers, a dozen long, was rolling up to the entrance of the town park.

"Speak of the fucking Devils," Merrill muttered. He and Nick watched as Bud Dillon jogged up to the first car, where a very old man was getting out of the passenger side. Nick thought that Abraham Kempster was at least 130 years old, but he pumped Bud Dillon's hand with the strength of a much younger man.

Merrill snorted loudly and spat a large wad of phlegm onto the dirt. "Look at em', Nicky. Thick as fuckin' thieves, Bud and the gyp. Bet there ain't gonna be no fuckin' fire hazards in that lot's set up—even with them old jalopies they drive. Probably end up setting the whole park on fire one of these days."

What happened next was very subtle, but it gave Nick the creeps.

Merrill had just finished his sentence when the old gypsy looked up at them from across the distance of the park. Merrill and Nick stared back as Abraham Kempster reached into his pants pocket and came up with a small, silver object in his hand. A second later the flame from the Zippo lighter ignited. Nick couldn't be sure at that distance, but it looked like the old man was smiling at them.

"Jesus, Merrill," Nick said, "I think he heard you."

As Merrill was about to respond they saw the old man fish a cigarette out of his front shirt pocket and light it with the Zippo.

"Right," Merrill said, chuckling, "some fucking psychic."

"Man, that ain't no joke," Nick said. "They say that old Kempster dude is the real deal."

"Yeah, well, *they* are full of shit—and so is he." Merrill jutted his chin toward the old man and the gypsy convoy with him.

Merrill finally stopped his rant about the gypsies and he and Nick proceeded to get the Red's BBQ truck set up. Merrill continued to bitch about their location but Nick didn't really mind too much. He enjoyed the technical process of getting the truck and smoker set up almost as much as he enjoyed the actual cooking process itself. This genuine joy in his work, plus his ability to ignore Merrill whenever he felt like it made for a decent morning. By lunch time they were ready to start cooking.

Shortly thereafter all hell broke loose and Nick almost went back to prison.

***

Of course it was Merrill Colby's fault. Merrill and Nick had started to prep their first fifty pound batch of pork for the smoker. According to Merrill, the most important process of making his famous BBQ was seasoning with dry rub. On this one subject (and one *only*) Nick trusted him completely—Red's BBQ was the best he'd ever had. After mixing the first six spices together they realized they were completely out of brown sugar—a vital component of any good BBQ rub. After overreacting and blaming the potential ruin of his business on Nick, Merrill realized that the issue was easily fixed by simply walking 500 feet over to Carl's Grocery and buying some more brown sugar. So, Merrill went on his shopping trip and Nick was left to finish preparing the meat.

Twenty minutes later Nick heard the commotion and ran up to the center of the park where the Kempsters were setting up their tents and booths.

According to what Merrill Colby would later tell Sherriff Christie, he'd been minding his own business on his walk back from Carl's Grocery (Nick didn't believe this for a second). He'd walked through the Kempsters setup when he was "suddenly" attacked by one of the mixed breed dogs that traveled with the gypsies in packs. Merrill had apparently also bought an economy size jar of chunky applesauce—an ingredient in one of Red's BBQ sauces—and he brought the jar down on top of the dog's head hard enough to shatter the glass and knock the pit-bull cold for a couple of minutes. By the time Nick had arrived at the gypsy's area the dog was lying on the ground covered with blood and chunky applesauce, and Merrill was in a shoving match with what Nick assumed was one of Abraham Kempster's grandsons, or maybe *great* grandsons.

Nick had managed to grab his boss by the shoulders and spin Merrill out of the way in an attempt to come between him and the irate gypsies. The younger Kempster—the one Nick assumed was the old man's grandson—took a swing then and the haymaker glanced off of Nick's right jaw. It would result in one of many bruises that Nick would acquire over the next several days. If the blow had connected squarely it probably would have laid him out, but Nick managed to turn and grab the young gypsy, shoving him backwards and pinning him against the side of the camper, knocking the dirty old fedora he was wearing in the dirt. Nick never intended to hit the young man and only wanted to keep the gypsy from taking another swing at him. However, Sheriff Christie arrived at that exact moment and assumed Nick had instigated the scuffle. It's one of the pitfalls of being an ex-con—*everything* is your fault.

The Sheriff was preparing to put Nick in handcuffs and remind him that assault was a violation of his probation when, to Nick's surprise, Abraham Kempster stepped up and explained that Nick hadn't done anything wrong, and that the whole incident was a misunderstanding. So, unable to hide a sense of disappointment, Sheriff Christie let Nick go.

Nick apologized to the Sheriff and the gypsies and grabbed Merrill by the arm. As they marched off toward the back of the park Nick looked back. The old man was staring at them and it made Nick feel very uneasy. To Nick's relief, he also saw that the dog had woken up.

It was licking at the pile of spilled applesauce on the ground.

***

Merrill Colby was mean during the day, but for all intents and purposes he was sober. At night, on the other hand, Merrill drank. At night he was downright vile. He would get halfway through a pint of Old Crow bourbon and a certain look would slip over his face. His eyes would narrow and it was as if the only emotion he was capable of conveying toward anyone or anything was hatred. In the evening after his altercation with the gypsies, Merrill was absolutely shitfaced and there was only one place he wanted to direct his insatiable hatred.

That goddamn dog.

An hour later Merrill arrived at the park, a full pint of bourbon into the witching hour. His original intention when he'd stumbled to his car had been to simply kill the dog, but the drive to the park had given him some time to come up with something far more sinister.

Now Merrill smiled to himself as he stumbled drunkenly up to his Red's BBQ food truck and began to fumble with the padlock on the door. Once inside he grabbed the two items he needed and then he strolled lazily toward the Kempsters' campers.

There were a few carnival folks milling about the park, but nobody paid any attention to Merrill Colby. It was true that the majority of the workers were sleeping in their campers at that hour, but it seemed there were always a handful of people that couldn't sleep or had over active bladders on their way to or from the plastic porta-johns. It was also common for many of these night owls to be drunk, so Merrill fit right in as he finally arrived at his destination.

The dogs were all sleeping in their pen. There was a half dozen pit-bulls dozing in a pile of fur and teeth, and for a moment Merrill was concerned that he might be too drunk and it was too dark to pick out the mangy sonofabitch that had tried to attack him earlier. Then, as fate would have it, the first dog that stirred and rose up still had matted, congealed blood stuck to the top of its head from the blow Merrill had given it with the applesauce earlier.

"There-roo are," Merrill slurred. "You shlimey little cocksucker."

As if it understood, the injured pit-bull emitted a low, threatening growl and took a step toward Merrill.

"Oh, tough guy, huh? That's O.K. Ol' Merrill's got somethin' for you." Merrill dug around in the large duffel bag he was holding, nearly lost his balance, and eventually came up holding a Tupperware container full of Red's famous BBQ pulled pork. He took the lid off and placed the container on the ground, just on the other side of the pen. The dog must have decided to put his differences with Merrill Colby aside, because as soon as the BBQ hit the ground it instantly ceased its growling and trotted over to the bowl. Merrill chuckled to himself. "Eat up, dickhead. I've won—" Merrill paused to think—"seventeen blue ribbons with that recipe."

Merrill fumbled for a moment with the bailing wire holding the gate to the pen closed, and when he was finally able to free the door he stepped inside the pen. The other five pit-bulls in the pen seemed to sense the intruder in their domain and woke up lazily. When they spotted Merrill standing over one of their pack members they collectively emitted the same threatening growl their mate had produced moments earlier. Merrill's eyes narrowed into hateful slits as he thought of something witty to say to his K-9 audience. After several seconds he decided to simply stagger on drunken legs and give the dogs the finger. Then he reached into his bag and produced three more containers of pork, which he tossed over to the remaining dogs. They instantly ceased their growling and buried their snouts in the piles of meat. When he was content that the other dogs were sufficiently occupied, Merrill reached into his bag for another item.

The stainless steel mallet was cold in his hand and it shined bright in the moonlight. Merrill Colby had probably held the meat tenderizer ten thousand times over the past thirty years, and he'd never given it a second thought. Now he turned it over and over in his hands, studying it. One side of the mallet's head was flat and smooth, the other side was rows of raised points—a medieval tool used to break down tissue into tender sheets of beef and pork. Merrill intended to use it to cave in the dog's skull.

He reached down and scratched the pit-bull behind the ears. The dog apparently had no problem letting bygones be bygones when pulled pork was involved, but Merrill Colby had no intention of letting anything "be gone." Merrill hated the dog, and he hated Abraham Kempster. Merrill hated the old man because of his claims to be a legit fortune teller. Taking good folks' hard earned money in exchange for some line of bullshit was just shady business in Merrill's opinion. Sure, the old man probably got something right every now and again, but Merrill didn't believe for a minute that Abraham Kempster was capable of predicting the future. Merrill didn't believe that Kempster, or any human, could be "all knowing."

"All knowing my ass," Merrill said as he slipped his left hand under the dog's chin and raised its head up to waist level. "We'll just see if he's *all knowing* all right."

The pit-bull raised his eyes just as Merrill raised the meat tenderizer. The dog licked his chops, trying to get pieces of pulled pork off its snout. It looked at Merrill without an ounce of ill intent.

Then Merrill swung the meat tenderizer downward. Hard.

His hand was still under the dog's chin when the heavy hammer connected with the top of its head. There was a loud crack and Merrill wasn't sure if the sound was the dog's jaw snapping shut or its skull splintering. He was prepared to deliver another blow but it wasn't necessary. The dog let out a choked yelp and dropped to the dirt. Its back legs clawed at the dust and then stopped. Soon Merrill smelled shit as the dog's bowels emptied. The rest of the dogs in the pen growled inquisitively but that was it—they went back to their BBQ. Merrill went back to examining the dog at his feet.

I really creamed him, Merrill thought. The dog's left eye had popped completely out of its head, hanging by a tangled optic nerve as thick yellow pus oozed out of the bloody socket. The meat tenderizer had torn a decent sized gash in the top of the dog's skull and thick, grey pieces of brain were slowly leaking out onto the dirt. There wasn't as much blood as Merrill expected, but he still needed to get the dog's body into his duffel bag before somebody came along.

Merrill opened the big bag on the ground next to the body of the dog and rolled the carcass inside. He zipped up the bag and kicked dirt over the blood and brains that had spilled onto the ground. He knew he was too drunk to have gotten every little drop, but he figured he'd done well enough. Having completed the first task of his plan, Merrill slung the heavy duffel over his shoulder, locked the pen up tight, and started back toward the Red's BBQ food truck. He passed a few night owls on the way back but he simply put on the part of a drunken carnival worker out for a stroll and nobody gave him a second thought.

When Merrill finally got back to his food truck he glanced around and when he was confident no one was watching he hauled his cargo inside. He opened the bag and dumped the dog out onto the stainless steel table. Then he flipped a soft lantern on and set his knives out on the table next to the dog. "All knowing my ass," Merrill said as he made his first cut.

An hour later Merrill stepped outside again and walked over to his large meat smoker. He shoved some fresh hickory logs in the smoker and set them ablaze. After that he commenced with the next part of his plan.

***

When Nick Goodman answered the phone and heard Merrill's voice on the other end of the line he assumed he'd overslept again and Merrill was calling to chew his ass. When Nick glanced at the bedside clock and saw that it was only 6:30 he knew that wasn't the case, so he asked Merrill if everything was O.K. Merrill told him that everything was just as *"fine as Fannie's titties,"* and that he was only calling to tell Nick he didn't have to be at the truck until about eleven that morning because he'd had trouble sleeping the night before and got an early jump on the day's first batch of barbecue.

Nick had no idea who "Fannie" was, and wasn't overly interested in how fine her titties were, but he sure was happy—and surprised—when Merrill told him to take the morning off. He thanked Merrill, told him he'd see him at eleven, and hung up the phone. Then he crawled back into bed and put his arm around Kara.

***

At about the same time Nick Goodman was crawling back into bed, Silvanus Kempster was entering the pen to feed the dogs. After dumping a pile of kibble into a trash can lid, the first thing that struck him as strange was that the dogs weren't acting very hungry, and they were normally ravenous at this time of day. Of course, Silvanus had no idea about the dogs' midnight feeding. The second thing that struck him as strange was that there were only five dogs in the pen. Bela—one of the Kempsters' star performers—was missing. He wasn't overly concerned; the dogs did this from time to time. Still, the Picnic started at noon that day and no one in the family had time to go running around town looking for Bela and whatever bitch he'd decided to spend the night with. Silvanus hated to bother his grandfather this early, but the old man would know what to do to keep this minor issue from becoming a major one.

Silvanus locked the pen up tight—they couldn't afford to lose any more dogs—and then marched off toward his grandfather's trailer. When he got there, he stood in front of the door nervously. Abraham Kempster was his grandfather, but nobody wanted to bother the big man—the Rom Baro—this early.

Silvanus had no reason to worry. Abraham Kempster had been awake for hours. Something was troubling him but he wasn't sure exactly what it was; he only knew something wasn't "right." Those with the gift of "true sight," as his people called it, didn't always have a clear picture of what was going on, but they always had a vague notion. That's why he knew *somebody* was about to knock on his door. When he swung it open he startled his grandson, Silvanus, who immediately took a step back and lowered his eyes.

"I didn't mean to disturb you, Bapo," Silvanus said.

Abraham made a dismissive gesture with his hand before speaking.

"What has been stolen?" he asked.

Silvanus gave the old man a look of surprise. "Uh, nothing, Bapo. I mean, I *think* nothing. Bela is missing, that's all. I think he might have run off."

Abraham took two arthritic steps down out of his trailer as Silvanus stepped up to steady him. "Maybe just missing, maybe no," the old man said. His speech was still thick with traces of his native Romani dialect, even though he'd been in America for over seventy years. "But be careful, Silvanus. My think Bela missing is a bibaxt. Don't want it spreading nowhere else."

Silvanus had been born in this country and didn't speak a lot of the old language, but he knew what "bibaxt" meant. Misfortune. Bad luck. For his people that was serious business.

Abraham and Silvanus—Bapo and grandson—walked together back to the dog pen. Abraham was hoping to pick up a clearer impression about what had happened but he was still only able to sense a general feeling of unbalance. It would only be a few hours before he got a clear vision of what had actually happened.

With a worried mind, Abraham exited the pen with Silvanus at his side. Then he invited his grandson back to his trailer and made him breakfast. It was more of a distraction than an act of courtesy.

***

Four hours later Merrill Colby awoke with a start to someone shaking him. He opened his eyes slightly and could make out the shape of Nick Goodman hovering over him.

Jesus, did I dream the whole episode last night? Merrill thought. He opened his eyes all the way and immediately regretted it. The pounding that had started in his head and the lurching feeling in his stomach confirmed for him that at least the drinking part hadn't been a dream.

"For Christ's sake, Merrill," Nick said. "What time did you finally put a cork in it?"

Merrill Colby straightened up in the camp chair he was sitting in and managed to lean forward, catching his clammy forehead in his hands. "I don't know, what time is it?"

"It's almost eleven."

"And you're just now getting here?!? What the fuck's wrong with you, kid?!?"

"Merrill, you called me and *told* me not to come in until now, remember?"

Merrill didn't remember. He asked Nick what time he'd called him and Nick told him it had been around 6:30. He could only assume he'd passed out soon after their conversation.

Merrill stood up then and fought the urge to vomit for a moment. Then the smell hit him just as Nick commented on it.

"Well whatever you did to the latest batch while you were drunk was a good call, Merrill. That smells amazing. Probably didn't think to write down the ingredients did you?"

Merrill didn't need to write down the ingredients. He knew what was in it. He realized then that he hadn't been dreaming. He'd bludgeoned the dog to death, then he'd skinned it, carved it, and was currently smoking it in his cooker. An ordinary person would have thrown up at this realization but Merrill Colby smiled. The smell of the slow roasted pit-bull was actually *settling* his stomach. His head was still pounding, but he'd just have to deal with it, because he still had one last task to complete before his little plot against the gypsies was over.

"We've still got a lot of work to do, Nicky. See, that's just a small batch in there. I feel real bad about our little scuffle with the gyps yesterday so I made them up a special recipe I was gonna take to them for lunch. You know, sorta like a peace offerin'."

Nick looked at him suspiciously. Peace offerings or any other decent gesture toward another human were not a regular staple in Merrill Colby's life, and Nick instantly feared that something was up. He was about to try and pry some more information out of Merrill, but his hung-over boss spoke first.

"Tell you what, Nicky. Why don't you run it over to them? That way I can get a big batch going so we'll be ready for the public when the Picnic opens."

"Sure," Nick said, "I can do that, but level with me, Merrill. What's going on? Yesterday you were ready to burn all of them at the stake."

Merrill smiled, and this made Nick trust him even less. "Well I certainly ain't gonna invite em' over for my weekly poker game but ol' Merrill knows when he's been a prick. Them gyps may be a bunch of fuckin' weirdoes, but they're just trying to make a living, same as us."

Nick realized he was nodding, but he still didn't trust Merrill. Finally he agreed to run Merrill's peace offering over to the Kempsters. After all, what choice did he have?

Nick grabbed a stack of Styrofoam clamshell containers from inside the food truck and then went back out to the smoker.

This really is a good batch, he thought as he opened the lid. He piled the tender meat into a dozen containers and added a piece of Texas toast and container of Red's BBQ sauce to each box. Then he stacked all the containers into two large plastic bags, grabbed a handle in each hand and started off toward the center of the park. As he stepped out of the shade of the food truck he looked back and saw Merrill leaning over the counter. The grin on the fat man's face was downright scary.

When Nick arrived at the area of the town park that served as the Kempsters' "camp" he felt as if he'd stepped back in time. The gypsies were all outside. The youngest of the clan were running in and out of the various campers and booths, chasing after their dogs. Several of the older Kempsters appeared to be setting up their various carnival acts and games. A young woman stepped out of a trailer in full belly dancing attire and Nick did his best not to stare at her ample breasts when she walked by. All of the action centered around the old man, who was seated in a lawn chair beneath the shade of one of the camper's awnings. As Nick approached, a younger man who had been throwing large bowie knives at a heavy disk of oak turned and made no effort to hide that he was pointing the sharp end of one of the knives directly at Nick. Nick recognized him as the young man he'd scuffled with the day before. The young man took a step toward Nick and tipped his dirty fedora back on his head with the knife. The old gypsy in the chair raised a hand and stopped him.

"Stay there Silvanus," Abraham Kempster said, then turning his attention to Nick, "Why you here—wha'choo want, boy?"

Nick held up the two bags of barbecue. "From my boss, Mr. Colby. He wanted me to bring you lunch, along with an apology for yesterday's misunderstanding."

Silvanus Kempster took another step forward, defiantly. He raised his knife slightly when he spoke. "There wasn't any damn misunderstanding. That fat—" Silvanus stopped as his Bapo once again raised his hand.

"Why your boss no come himself?" the old man asked Nick.

Nick had wondered that same thing during his walk across the park.

He had no better answer now than he did during his walk. Nick simply shrugged. "Picnic starts today—we've still got a lot to prep for. I guess he didn't trust me to run the truck by myself. Anyway, I *do* know he was up all night making this batch special for you and your family."

The old man seemed to consider this for a moment, and after a very uncomfortable silence he finally nodded. Without saying a word, the young man called Silvanus and another boy stepped up and took the bags out of Nick's hands without ever breaking eye contact.

"You go now, boy," said the old man with a dismissive flip of the hand.

Nick nodded and gave one last glare to Silvanus before turning around and walking away. He half expected to get a bowie knife shoved through his back but it didn't happen. As he walked back to Red's BBQ truck he thought to himself, *Merrill is right, they are some weird fuckers.* Still, he was glad to have no more dealings with the gypsies.

That feeling wouldn't last long.

***

Thirty years ago Abraham Kempster would have known what happened to his grandson's dog as soon as he stepped foot in the pen, but his old age had taken its toll and his visions simply weren't what they used to be. He certainly wouldn't have *eaten* Bela thirty years ago.

But today that's exactly what he did.

As the Meat Man's young errand boy walked away, the rest of the Kempsters stopped whatever they had been doing and came over to where Silvanus had set the bags full of barbecue. Abraham had given the word and the food was dispersed. It was true that he didn't care for the fat Meat Man, but his people had to eat.

He watched as five generations of his family sat down to lunch, and when they were all thoroughly enjoying their portion of the peace offering, Abraham took his first bite.

And that's when he knew.

The old man only had to swallow one bite and he knew that his people were eating Silvanus's missing dog. He quickly spat the meat out and looked up as the rest of his family stared at him. For an instant Abraham had considered simply blurting out that everyone was eating his grandson's beloved Bela, but then his 90 years of wisdom prevailed. There was no sense in creating a panic among his *vitsa*. Besides, many of them probably would have been sick on the spot, and some of the residents of Barker Marsh had already begun to show up at the park. If they saw half of his vitsa throwing up on themselves it would be bad for business.

In the end he had simply ordered his people to stop eating and throw away the rest of the food. They did so without question.

Abraham suppressed the rage he was feeling inside and none of his family sensed anything was wrong, even the young and observant Silvanus. Abraham was used to being viewed as a minority—that was part of the Romani lifestyle. He was not accustomed to this, though. Abraham felt there was something more than hatred that grew inside the Meat Man. *Something sinister. What kind of man cut up a dog and feed it to his enemy?*

And *why* had the Meat Man done it? Abraham closed his eyes as his family tossed out the slow roasted remains of one of their pets and thought about this. His talents might be dwindling with his old age but he could still get the answers he needed if he thought hard enough.

Then his skin began to prick up, just as it always did when he got a vision, and all at once Abraham Kempster knew why the Meat Man had killed his family's dog and fed it to them.

It was a test, he thought. *That bastard want to see if I knew what he done. Well I do, fat man. I do. You gonna get answer back real soon.*

Then the old man pushed himself up out of his chair and hobbled over to his trailer. He gave strict orders that he wasn't to be disturbed and his people obeyed. Two hours later his door opened and he called for Silvanus.

When his grandson was comfortably seated across from him and the door was closed Abraham Kempster told the young man what his orders were. Then he gave Silvanus a small container and sent him on his way. Silvanus stepped down out of his Bapo's trailer and adjusted his fedora. He squeezed the container in his hand and started walking toward the back of the park—toward the food vendors.

***

It was really no one's fault. Just a simple case of miscommunication and a slight lack of clarity on Abraham Kempster's part. He was an old man, after all.

Silvanus had been told to deliver a package, in a manner of speaking, to the "Meat Man." As he stood back and watched Nick Goodman work the counter of the food truck that's exactly what he thought he was about to do. Nick worked for a barbecue business. Nick had delivered the food earlier that day. Nick *was* the Meat Man. The thought of the fat man who had smashed a jar of applesauce on his dog's head being his Bapo's intended target never entered Silvanus's mind. In Silvanus's mind, the young man behind the food counter had somehow crossed his Bapo and it was his job to deliver the man's *bujo*—his bad luck for upsetting the spiritual balance of his family.

So he watched, and he waited, and when Nick Goodman walked around to the back of the truck to get more paper food trays, Silvanus made his move. He was simply supposed to blow the contents of the container in the man's face, but as he got closer he was presented with an opportunity he simply couldn't pass up. Silvanus had crept to within eight feet and Nick still had his back turned, clueless to Silvanus's presence. *If I had one of my knives I could gut him like a trout*, Silvanus thought.

He pulled his fedora down to cover his eyes. He quickly glanced around to make sure there was no one watching just as Nick started to turn around.

Nick's arms were full of cardboard trays when he turned back toward the food truck. They crashed to the dirt as the fist connected with his left cheek, and he fell on top of them. He tried to look up and see who had sucker punched him but the blood from his sliced cheek was already running into his eye, blinding him temporarily. He could vaguely make out some sudden movement before his assailant's foot caught him in the ribs, driving the air from his lungs.

Nick rolled onto his back, his insides on fire. He silently prayed that the blow hadn't ruptured his spleen or some other organ. He still couldn't see who was attacking him but he sensed the shadow over his face as somebody bent over him. The kick had knocked the wind out of him and he was taking long, labored gasps of air. He inhaled deeply and felt something being blown into his face, which instantly went up his nose, down his throat, and into his burning lungs. Whatever the ashy powder was it was very spicy with a kind of sweetness to it, like basil. He began to cough uncontrollably but he was getting a surprising amount of oxygen, feeling better actually.

And then the real pain hit him. It was suddenly as if hot lead was flowing through his veins. Nick tried to cry out but could only emit a dry wheeze. His eyes opened wide as his entire body started to convulse, and he thought he could make out the shape of a brimmed hat looking down at him. Then everything went black as he passed out.

Silvanus Kempster watched as the man at his feet stopped writhing and appeared to black out. Convinced that his Bapo's curse had taken hold he adjusted his hat and turned to walk away. Then he turned back to the man at his feet, held up the first two fingers on his right hand and spat between them onto the ground.

It would be a solid ten minutes before Merrill Colby would find Nick Goodman lying on the ground, bleeding and still unconscious.

***

Nick awoke at about 6 P.M. to the lingering effects of a dream. He couldn't recall every detail of the dream but he'd been running, and he'd been naked. It wasn't that awkward kind of naked dream, like the stereotypical "naked on the first day of school" scenario. He had felt quite comfortable being naked in his dream. He'd been running, and he was covered in blood. And he was aroused.

He continued to shake off the effects of his dream as he looked around Kara Wheeler's bedroom. He wasn't in the old Barker Zinc Smelting plant, where he had been in his dream, and he wasn't covered in blood, but he *was* naked. And he *was* aroused. He eased out from under the sheets feeling surprisingly, almost unbelievably good for someone who had just had the shit kicked out of him three hours earlier. He had a throbbing erection and he had to piss, which he knew from past experience was a problematic combination.

Nick stood up and strutted to the bathroom. He flipped on the light and winced, not so much from the pain of the bright light as the visual shock of his own reflection in the mirror.

The dark bruise on his left jaw was no surprise. It complimented the one he'd received the day before on his right cheek. Nick continued his visual inspection and turned his body to get a better look at his bruised ribs where his assailant had kicked him. These bruises, although much nastier than those on his jaw, were still not surprising to Nick. The bruises that

111

surprised him were those on his chest, back and legs. They were a sickly looking brown color and they seemed to highlight the bones under his skin. He turned slowly and saw how the bruises on his back outlined the ribs and made a kind of tiger stripe pattern all the way to the top of his buttocks. *What the fuck?* Nick thought. The strangest thing was that none of the other bruises hurt at all, just his jaw and ribs, and even that pain was just a dull throb now. Nick thought that he should barely be able to stand, given the way he looked, but he actually felt good. He turned back around and breathed deeply, inflating his chest. What pain he'd had in his jaw and ribs was only a tingle now, and that tingle had spread across his entire body. He chuckled softly and then raised his hands up next to his head, flexing his biceps. Nick glanced down and saw that his erection hadn't shrunk in the slightest.

Nick was just finishing urinating, awkwardly, when he heard Kara stirring in her bedroom. He turned and stood in the doorway as she opened her eyes. Kara pushed herself up on her elbows and cleared the sleep from her eyes. When she got her first good look at him she stopped breathing. He'd been beaten up when she'd brought him home but he hadn't looked anything like this. He was covered in bruises. Her eyes drifted down to his groin. "Ummm," she said, "other than *that*, are you O.K.? You look awful."

"Yeah, well, I feel great, actually. Especially *this*," Nick said pointing at his engorged penis. Before Kara could react Nick jumped into the air and came down on the bed on his hands and knees. She began to cackle as he covered her in kisses. Eventually his mouth found hers and it stayed there for a long time. Then his mouth started a slow descent down the rest of her body, and eventually landed on her breasts. Nick paused when he reached the shiny scar above her right nipple, a flood of anger washing over him momentarily as he thought of the bastard that had stabbed her. His tongue began to trace the outline of her scar as his knees slid between hers, parting her legs and giving access to the warm folds between them.

Nick eased himself inside her gently and a moan escaped her lips. What followed for the next five minutes was the slow, steady love-making that was typical of their relationship. Then something changed. Nick's excitement seemed to multiply ten-fold and he suddenly increased the speed of his thrusts until he was pounding away at the woman beneath him ferociously. Kara certainly didn't seem to mind. She moaned steadily as her fingernails dug into his back and started clawing their way down to his buttocks.

When the wave of her first orgasm hit her Nick started to feel sick to his stomach. Something strange was happening to him but he had no idea what it was. All he knew for sure was that if he didn't have his own orgasm soon his insides were going to burst. He stopped thinking of Kara as a lover then and thought of her only as a means to a sexual end. He raised up on his knees and sat back on his heels. With a strength he didn't realize he had he slid his hands under Kara and in an instant had lifted her up and on top of him as easily as lifting a sleeping cat off the couch. One hand stayed at the small of her back as the other slid up to one of her shoulders so that he could yank her downward, driving himself deeper inside her. Kara climaxed twice more but Nick didn't care or even notice. He was no longer making love to her as much as he was simply using her body to reach his own climax. He had gone entirely animalistic, and when he finally did orgasm in blessed release there was no romantic, post-coital bliss. Nick simply let her collapse back onto the bed without a word. Kara was sound asleep less than two minutes later.

Nick clutched his stomach. The growing pressure in his genitals had been released but he still felt like he was going to be sick. He glanced at the clock and saw that it was now 6:30—the start of the dinner rush. Nick appreciated the very uncharacteristic gesture Merrill had made by giving him the night off, but Nick felt good enough to work. *Except for this fucking stomach ache*, he thought. He made up his mind then that he was going to head back to the park for a few hours to work the truck. Besides, he hadn't had a chance to talk to Merrill yet and he wanted to try and figure out who had jumped him.

Nick was just about to slide off the bed to get dressed when the most intense wave of nausea he'd felt yet hit him like a truck. He doubled over, fighting the urge to vomit and started making his way to the bathroom. At the last minute Nick decided that he didn't want to wake Kara up with his retching so he continued past the bathroom, down the hall, and eventually out the back door of the trailer.

Nick didn't have time to worry about standing stark naked in his girlfriend's backyard because as soon as his bare feet hit the grass he could feel the bile rising in his throat. He dropped to his hands and knees as a loud, wet belch erupted from his mouth, followed by a surge of the pulled pork he'd had for lunch and what was left of breakfast. He normally would have found the eight foot arc of vomit he'd produced impressive had it not been for the intense burning that was rising from his stomach into his chest. Nick then experienced a series of physical changes and jarring pain in virtually every part of his body. By the time he could focus on one area a new pain somewhere else on his body would distract him.

The burning in his chest was so intense that he instinctively brought his hands up to claw the heat right out of his body. When Nick looked at his hands he forgot about his chest. Long, course hairs were starting to grow painfully out of every follicle on his knuckles and his fingers were actually growing longer before his eyes.

How is this happening? he managed to ask himself before two sharp claws burst through the ends of his ring and middle fingers on his right hand. Nick howled in agony as his skin continued to tear all the way up to his elbow. A fine mist of blood accompanied the jagged rip as it spread up his right side and before Nick could even begin to process what was happening to him a two foot long sleeve of flesh that looked like a deflated balloon version of his arm dropped to the ground. Nick held up a massively muscled arm, covered in thick black fur. He wanted to scream again but as he spread the long, clawed fingers of what used to be his right hand he spotted the bright, yellow moon and it seemed to soothe him.

But only for a moment.

A new agony had erupted in his lower half. He was still on his knees and when he looked back he saw that his feet were growing just as his right, and now left hand had. As the skin on his feet began to separate in a bloody mist he could hear the Achilles tendon in each ankle snap like the fat rubber bands he and his brother used to chase each other around the house with. They were soon replaced with long, sinewy cartilage that ended where his toes used to be. Now instead of toes he had fat paws, each pad with a sharp, brown claw extending from it. Through the pain Nick had a sudden urge to use his new appendages to rip and tear. He thought he'd gotten through the worst of the pain but then all of his ribs snapped inward, breaking and then resetting themselves, expanding the girth of his chest so that his pectoral muscles were almost a solid three feet across. His skin continued to slip off in bloody rags, replaced with thick fur on top of heavy muscle.

Nick prayed that the tearing would stop before it got to his head and face but it didn't. He felt the tops of his ears burst as new, pointed ears grew in place. Then came the worst pain of all. Nick stared up at the bright moon and could not only feel, but actually see his eyeballs tear right down the center. His vision suddenly became crystal clear in the moonlight and he felt like he could also hear every dog, bird and bug within half a mile.

He felt his lips split, and the tip of his nose and he tried to cry out in pain again. But he didn't cry. A low, powerful howl erupted from within him and then the pain was gone. So was any trace of Nick Goodman, the man. Except for the greasy pile of skin at the creature's feet.

It stood up then, nearly eight feet tall. It's newly formed snout turned up into the night air, nostrils flaring as it picked up a powerful scent. There was animal waste in the scent trail but under all of that there was something more intense.

Sweeter.

Redder.

Something that could satiate the painful void in the thing's new belly. Its long tongue licked the air in front of it, wafting the scent further into its nostrils. When it had zeroed in on the source of the smell a low growl escaped its panting jaws.

Then it took off toward the field behind Kara Wheeler's trailer, hopping over the seven foot tall privacy fence without touching it.

***

Warren Filch waved as the rest of his family pulled out of the driveway. He was frustrated as hell and wished he was going with them to the town picnic, but he had work to do. As a farmer trying to support his family in a town full of farmers, he *always* had work to do.

It was four months before the normal birthing season, but somehow a bull managed to impregnate one of his heifers, and she'd been showing signs of calving all afternoon. The heifer had stood off by herself all day, nervous. She'd started lactating at noon and by 4 P.M. her rear end was large and swollen. Warren moved her into the barn. She'd been there for the past three hours—laying down, getting up, and laying down again. That's when Warren knew he'd be trading in an evening of funnel cakes and Ferris wheels for a sweaty birthing session with his cow.

When the tail lights of his wife's minivan disappeared he turned to the barn and pulled the cigarettes out of his shirt pocket. His family had thought he'd quit so he took advantage of any chance he got to poison his lungs openly.

He lit the cigarette, and never saw the large amber eyes staring at him from the hedge row.

***

It sat in the shadows of the thick hedge, staring at the man. Its upper lip curled and exposed the glistening white teeth and red gums. Its tongue once more licked the air and pulled tiny wavelengths of scent into its nostrils. The creature was barely twenty minutes old and already its receptors were powerful enough to pick up hundreds of separate smells, some minute and some so potent that they were already sending its nerves into spasms. It could smell the man's sweat and the bacon he'd had for breakfast that morning. And it could smell the smoke from the man's cigarette. The beast didn't like how the smoke smelled, or the effect it had on the tender tissue inside its nostrils. It wanted to tear the source of that smell from the man's face and it took an angry but stealthy step forward.

Then it sensed new smells and it stopped.

The barn. The beast licked the air and pulled in the spicy aroma of hay, animal waste and dirt. Tractor oil and other chemicals. Underneath all of those smells was something wonderful. It was the same sweet scent that it had picked up moments after awakening behind the trailer—the scent that had brought him here. It inhaled deeply as a soft, low growl vibrated in the back of the beast's throat. It could smell, and almost taste the heifer inside the barn. It could also sense the calf that it was about to expel. The sweet fragrance that had set the nerves on the end of the beast's tongue on fire was the heifer's water sac, which was now starting to ooze from beneath the cow's tail.

It was on its hind legs inhaling the night air and then it dropped back onto all fours in a predatory crouch. It stepped out of the hedgerow just as the man flicked his cigarette to the ground and stepped inside the lighted barn.

***

The heifer was mooing loudly when Warren Filch reached her stall. He got there just in time to see the slimy mucus sack slip from the cows vulva and he could see two tiny hooves protruding from below her tail.

"Easy darlin'," Warren said, rolling up his sleeves, "Don't go gettin' in a rush now." He positioned himself behind the animal and raised its tail with his left hand. He slipped his right hand into the cow's birth canal and soon his arm was gone, all the way past the elbow. *Damn it*, he thought. *I could have been nursing my first stale beer right about now.* He continued to grope around inside the heifer's uterus until he felt what he was looking for and then he hung his head and sighed heavily. "You couldn't make this easy on us could you, you son of a bitch?"

The fact that the cow was a female and as such, couldn't *possibly* be a son of a bitch didn't seem to dawn on Warren.

Warren was frustrated because after inspecting his heifer he discovered that her calf was facing the wrong direction and the hooves protruding from her vulva were attached to the animal's *rear* legs, not the front as he'd hoped. That meant he and the heifer had some work to do. Warren slid his arm out of the cow and she gave an appreciative moo. He wiped the thick slime on his jeans and then eased his heifer forward until her head rested between two swinging gate doors. When she was in the appropriate position Warren pulled a lever and the gate doors swung shut, pinning the heifer's head in place. She moaned angrily and Warren gave her a reassuring pat on the hip. "It's alright darlin'. For your own good."

Warren had helped deliver so many calves in his life that he couldn't begin to guess how many times he'd gone through this routine. Usually he did this in November, when the warmth of the barn was a welcoming treat against the cold winter wind. But it was July, and easily ninety degrees in the barn now. Warren was already drenched in sweat but such is the life of a cattle farmer.

He unbuttoned his shirt and removed it, then he hung it over the stall's railing. Next to his shirt hung a heavy duty chain with two pull handles attached to it. Warren picked this medieval apparatus up and walked back to the rear of the cow. He attached the calf chains to each of the hooves sticking out of the back end of the heifer and then he sat down on the floor of the stall. Warren put one of his boots on each of the heifer's hind quarters and grabbed the pull handles of the chain, one in each of his callused hands. Then he dug in with his feet and pulled.

At first it was like trying to pull a coal train, but then the stubborn calf conceded a little and Warren managed to pull an additional eight inches of leg into the world. After fifteen minutes of an exhausting tug-o-war Warren had most of the calf's rear legs free. He paused and stood up. He stuck his hand back inside the heifer so that he could lay the calf's tail flat— he didn't want to break it on the way out. Satisfied that mother and baby were O.K., he sat back down, tightened up his chains, and pulled.

Like a boot stuck in soggy mud, the calf started slipping out slowly at first and then picked up speed as more and more of its body became exposed. Finally, Warren gave one last pull and the calf fell to the straw covered floor. Warren quickly stood up and knelt beside the slime coated calf. Its tongue was hanging lazily out of its mouth and it didn't appear to be breathing. Warren grabbed a handful of straw and stuck it up the calf's nostrils and almost instantly the newborn made a gagging sound and sneezed violently, spraying Warren's hand with thick snot and leftover birth fluid. The trick seemed to work as the calf's eyes opened wide and it retracted its tongue back inside its mouth. Soon the newborn animal was attempting to stand on his own.

That's when Warren heard the growl. The heifer, head still secured in the gate, heard it too. She began to moan loudly and shuffle around on her back legs nervously.

Warren looked toward the open doors of the barn and saw two yellow eyes staring back at him. He had grown up with animals and worked with them every day, so at first he wasn't frightened. For an instant he thought a coyote had crept up to the barn, drawn in by the sounds and smell. But then the creature lowered its head and crept a little further forward until Warren could see the rest of the head surrounding those yellow eyes.

The head was huge, and Warren was now convinced it was a bear. But that wasn't quite right either. First off, bears didn't live in this part of

Illinois—certainly none *this* big. The snout was more elongated, like a wolf, but there weren't any wolves in this part of the country either. Warren stood up now and the animal in his barn's entrance took a few more steps forward, so that Warren could see its entire body.

Now he began to panic. He could see that the thing was covered in thick, silver fur but it thinned out around the creature's chest and biceps, both of which were massively muscled. The thing in the door curled its lips as another menacing growl echoed in the open barn. The heifer mooed loudly again and jerked her head back against the gates holding her in place, trying to free herself. The newborn calf was still kneeling on the floor, apparently clueless to the predatory beast that was a mere thirty feet away.

Warren's right hand moved instinctively to his pocket where his fingers traced the clip on the folding pocket knife he kept there. He thought of a conversation he'd had with one of the town's deputies once about something called a "twenty-one foot rule." If he remembered correctly, the theory was that a man with a knife could close a distance of twenty-one feet and stab a man with a gun before the second man could clear his holster and fire a shot. Warren Filch wondered if he could get his knife out before the wolf/bear-thing could close the thirty feet between them.

The beast in the doorway didn't give Warren much time to think about it. It lunged forward with a roar and Warren pulled his knife and flicked it open. He pulled it in plenty of time but it didn't matter. He was too shocked to use it. As the creature came within ten feet of Warren it suddenly raised up and took two quick strides toward him on its hind legs. Warren didn't move his knife hand an inch, and barely had time to look up at the eight foot tall monster in front of him before a flash of silver fur streaked across his midsection.

Warren spun around and his back struck the side of the barn. An intense burning erupted in his gut and he suddenly tasted metallic tinges of blood in his mouth. His right hand was still clutching the knife so he instinctively brought his left hand to his stomach. For a moment he could feel four jagged tears in his flesh and then the pain intensified as the tears split into one large, open fissure. Suddenly Warren Filch was holding a handful of his own intestines. They felt hot and greasy in his hand. He began to slide down to the floor as something more important slipped out of the wound in his belly and landed on the floor with a loud splat like an oversized bird dropping.

The pain was intense but there was much less blood spilling out of him than Warren had expected. He looked up through tear-filled eyes as the wolf-like creature that just disemboweled him crept over to the moaning heifer that was still pinned in place. Warren could do nothing but hold his guts in place and watch as the beast reached under the heifer's head with its massive paw and unzipped the thick hide there with a single long claw. The heifer let out a wet moan and Warren could hear the cow's

blood splashing on the floor. Soon the heifer staggered on its legs and

finally collapsed to the floor with its head still stuck in the gate. Warren

watched as a wave of thick cow's blood started to creep across the barn

floor toward his feet. He couldn't believe how much there was, and it was

so thick that pieces of straw floated on top of it like dead mayflies on a still

eddy of river. Warren could imagine a trout rising from the dark red puddle

to slurp down a bug that existed only in his mind. Instead he saw the giant

wolf drop back down on all four legs and start to lap up the pooling blood

from the floor with its oversized tongue. Then Warren Filch glanced down

at the tangle of intestines in his hand and passed out.

He had forgotten about the newborn calf, but when he opened his

eyes again it was laying right in front of him. At least what was left of it.

The wolf was still there too, and apparently it had tried to pull the same

trick with the calf as it had with its mother. Except there hadn't been nearly

as much fat and gristle to slice through so when the thing's claws punched

through the calf's neck they didn't stop. The calf's head had been torn

clean off, and now the beast had its snout buried in the jagged stump of the

calf's neck. It tore a long, sinewy piece of flesh from the newborn and

threw its massive head back as it swallowed the morsel. Then its large

yellow eyes fixed on Warren and it let out another of those hellish growls.

It stalked toward Warren slowly until it was close enough that Warren could smell the musk coming from its pores, mixed with the heavy copper stench of blood.

He was still holding his guts in his left hand and the knife in his right. He was cold all over and Warren could no longer feel his legs. He was dying, and he knew it, but he thought he could muster up just enough strength to give the thing one more surprise. When the thing was close enough that Warren could feel the foul breath on his face he smiled at the beast.

"Fuck you," he said through wet, bloody bubbles. Then Warren swung his right hand up with all of the strength he had left and buried the knife in the wolf's bicep. He was rewarded with a shattering howl as the thing reared back onto its hind legs again and took two surprised steps backward. The beast reached over with a paw that was eerily hand-like and grasped the handle of the knife. It tore the blade free and flung it all the way to the back of the barn, where it landed with a clang. It leaned back down toward Warren with rage in its eyes.

Warren opened his mouth to say "Fuck you" again but he never got the words out. The wolf jammed its thumb inside Warren's mouth as four sharp claws punctured the soft flesh below his chin. He felt no pain, only an intense pressure as the wolf pulled back, ripping his lower jaw off in a thick spray of dark blood.

The last thing Warren Filch saw was the giant beast grab the lower jaw bone—*his* lower jaw bone—in both of its massive claws and snap the bone and flesh in half. Then the beast pounced on him and there was only blackness, and silence.

***

Abraham Kempster stood in the middle of the busy thoroughfare as a sea of carnival patrons swarmed around him. He was staring at a man who, by this time, should not have been a man at all. The "Meat Man" was there, filling the open window of his food truck as he slung his barbecue pork and beef.

Silvanus, he fuck up good, Kempster thought. Merrill Colby should have been running around on all fours, killing and eating his loved ones, but instead he was sweating onto a pile of brisket, grinning like the fat cat that he was. The Meat Man finally spotted Kempster staring at him in the crowd and gave a patronizing wave.

Kempster only squinted in reply.

Finally, the old man turned and started to limp back toward his own trailer with that one thought running through his mind.

Silvanus, he fucked up good. In the distance a wolf howl cut the night, but it seemed that Abraham Kempster was the only one that heard it.

***

The most permanent keepsake that Kara Wheeler's ex-husband had left her was the scar on her chest. The only other item Kara had of her ex-husband's was the rear bench seat from a 1969 Chevy Malibu that he'd torn out and left on her back porch.

Nick Goodman found himself awakening on the sun battered upholstery of this relic. He pulled himself up into a sitting position and raised his hand to shield his eyes from the brutal sunlight. It took Nick a surprisingly long time to realize he was naked.

Fucking A, he thought, *how much did I drink last night?*

He tried to think back to the previous night and it only added to his confusion. It certainly wouldn't have been the first time he'd passed out drunk and naked someplace, but Nick couldn't remember taking a single drink. In fact, the last thing he *could* remember was an insanely hard sex session with Kara and that was it.

Stranger still was that Nick didn't feel the least bit hung over. In fact, other than the sun blinding him he felt great. It seemed that Nick had experienced a good old fashioned black out, plain and simple. He pondered this for a moment and then thought of the beating he'd taken the day before.

Shit, he thought, *what if I have a concussion or something?*

He stood up then, remembered that he was naked, and panicked briefly before he remembered that he was still in the relative privacy of

Kara's fenced in backyard. As he turned Nick caught a glimpse of his face in the reflection from the trailer's window and he froze.

The face looking back—his face—was covered in blood. Panic washed over him again only this time it had nothing to do with his nudity. Something was very wrong with him. The memory loss, the face covered in blood and…something else. But what was it?

Nick stared at his reflection and concentrated, trying to remember what he'd noticed the day before. All at once a single word hit him.

Bruises.

He'd been covered in strange looking, nasty bruises. Nick stood on the tips of his toes and turned, trying to see his sides and back in the reflection but the window was too high to see anything but his face. He ran up the back porch steps and threw open the door. Nick rushed down the hall and into the trailer's only bathroom. Then he turned on the light and looked in the mirror. He had much more dried blood on his face than he'd originally seen in the reflection outside. He looked down at his ribs and saw that the wicked looking bruises were still there, painting his body like tribal tattoos.

He faced the mirror again and leaned in close, trying to find the source of all the dried blood but there was just too much of it. Nick was unable to see any open gashes or scrapes. He turned on the water and splashed it on his face. The sink was soon stained a strawberry pink but Nick still couldn't find any cuts on his face except for the scratch he'd gotten on his cheek from his attacker the day before.

All that blood couldn't be from this little scratch, could it? Nick thought.

Maybe it was a nosebleed or something.

It was then that Nick noticed he had a small scratch on his left bicep as well. It itched, as cuts often do when they're well into the healing process, and the wound was well sealed by a thick scab. There was no way this small cut was responsible for all the blood either. Scarier still, Nick had no memory of cutting himself on his arm either.

What the fuck is wrong with me?

For an instant Nick had an uncontrollable urge to be pissed off at Kara. How could she leave him out there all night, covered in blood? His anger subsided once he stopped and processed it for a moment. If Kara had dozed off after their love-making, which she often did, she might have had no idea he'd gone outside. When she did wake up and he wasn't in the trailer she probably assumed he'd gone into town to work the picnic. Nick shook his head, trying to piece together the last twelve hours as the onset of a wicked headache started taking root behind his eyes.

Kara probably assumed I went to work last night, and assuming I was laying out there all night she would have had no reason to look in the backyard when she left for work this morning. But still, wouldn't she have noticed that I wasn't in bed last night?

None of it made sense, especially the blood that was still running down the sink drain. Nick was suddenly famished, so he went into the trailer's small kitchen and made a quick breakfast of steak and eggs, which he devoured in about four bites. After checking the clock above the stove he concluded that he'd better get dressed and head into the picnic to help Merrill. The old prick was probably livid that Nick had left him hanging on the first day of the picnic.

Nick marched back to Kara's bedroom where he pulled on a pair of jeans. He gave his bruised upper body one more glance in the mirror before covering it up with a faded Asia concert t-shirt.

Five minutes later Nick was walking down the main highway toward the town park. He didn't notice the vintage Plymouth that was following him.

***

Abraham Kempster knew what happened the instant his Grandson had sat down across from him. Silvanus had it out for the young man that worked for the Meat Man ever since their fight on the first afternoon in town. Silvanus didn't like him and that's exactly who he'd gone after with the *lup bujo.*

Damned his old age! If he'd had the strength to overpower the Meat Man himself and infect him with the bujo they wouldn't be in this mess. The Meat Man would either already be dead or at least strongly considering killing himself. But things didn't work out that way. His grandson had laid a curse on someone that didn't deserve it. The young man was no saint— his sight was still good enough to sense that, but a lup curse was serious stuff. Werewolves brought some serious death to an area, and cursing the wrong person was a recipe for disaster.

Abraham looked through the Plymouth's window at the man walking toward town. He could sense the aura surrounding this young man and Kempster knew that in *lup* form he made one powerful beast. He shot an angry look over at Silvanus, who was driving. The anger passed—it was as much his fault as his grandson's.

"Pull over in front of him," Abraham told his grandson. Silvanus accelerated around the young man, who jumped aside slightly as the big coupe passed. Once he'd pulled ahead Silvanus pulled the car over and stopped directly in the man's path.

Nick Goodman had stopped walking about twenty feet short of the Plymouth's rear bumper. It didn't take him long to recognize the silhouette of the brimmed hat sitting behind the steering wheel. Nick knew it was the young gypsy he'd scuffled with a few days before, and he suddenly had an overwhelming feeling that this was the same man that had jumped him the day before outside the food truck. At first Nick was nervous, staring at the thick exhaust pouring form the beat up old jalopy's tail pipe and wondering if the young gypsy was going to throw the car in reverse any second and run him down, finishing the job Nick was now positive he'd started the day before. The nervousness only lasted a moment, and then something strange happened. The nervousness turned to rage, and all at once Nick felt like his senses were on fire. The sound of the Plymouth's big V8 engine was deafening in his ears, and Nick could tell that it was badly in need of a tune up. He could taste the exhaust on his tongue. His sense of smell was the most intense sensation though. He could suddenly smell the gypsy behind the wheel of the car. He could smell his sweat, cigarettes and the tonic he put in his hair.

Then he smelled the other man. The old man.

Nick hadn't even realized there was someone else in the car. The old Gypsy was so short his head didn't stick up over the headrest. Nick was busy analyzing this man's scent when the passenger side window rolled down and a bony, liver-spotted hand emerged. The hand motioned for

Nick to come forward. He should have hesitated but he didn't. He marched confidently toward the big car's passenger side. Under normal circumstances he would have been scared that the Gypsies would try to attack him, but as he neared the door he felt something different. He almost hoped they *would*.

Nick looked in at the little old man in the passenger seat. The man looked straight ahead and never gave Nick so much as a sideways glance when he finally spoke. "Get in the back. I have to talk to you, boy."

"I'm not going anywhere with you, pops," Nick said. Then he watched as the old man took something out of his front shirt pocket. If he'd had time to study the bottle a little closer he would have seen it was silver nitrate, but the old man took the cap off before Nick had a chance to read the label. A pain stabbed Nick deep behind his eyes like an intense migraine. He pressed his palms against his temples and bit down until his jaws started to cramp. The pain was other-worldly and Nick felt as if he was about to vomit. "PLEASE!" he cried through clenched teeth, "MAKE IT STOP!"

Abraham Kempster screwed the cap back on the bottle of silver nitrate and the pain in Nick's head started to dissipate. The old man hooked his thumb toward the backseat. "Get in back."

Nick pulled the heavy door open and slid into the backseat of the car, still massaging his temples. The old man pointed toward the open road ahead without saying a word, and Silvanus pulled back out on the highway.

Then Abraham Kempster laid the whole story out for Nick. Merrill feeding

his people one of their dogs. The *lup bujo* he'd concocted. Silvanus

delivering this *"prikaza"* to Nick my mistake. Nick took all of the old man's

tale in, but the part he found the most interesting was how he was

supposedly a werewolf now.

"You guys are fuckin' nuts, you know that?" Nick said when the old

man finally stopped talking. "There are no such things as werewolves, and

I certainly ain't one."

The old man kept looking out the front window as he spoke. "Oh

yeah," he said, "What you did last night, huh? You can't remember?"

Kempster tapped the side of his head with a bony finger.

Nick started to feel uncomfortable. "That doesn't prove a thing."

"How bout dem bruises, boy?"

That stopped Nick in his tracks for a moment. *How the fuck does this old

guy know about my bruises? Well, the old man is supposedly psychic, right?* "So

what," Nick said, "they're just bruises."

Kempster shook his head. "They not *just* bruises, boy. Underneath all

dem bruises your body changing. Your bones. Your organs. You getting

lup bones; lup organs."

"Lup?" Nick asked.

"It means wolf," Silvanus said from the driver's seat, speaking up for the first time.

Nick smiled in the backseat. He decided to play along. "O.K. So I'm a werewolf. So what do I do now?"

Silvanus laughed and then turned to the old man. "You hear that, Bapo? He wants to know what he does now." His laughter tapered off when he saw the look on his Bapo's face. The old man had daggers in his eyes, and Silvanus instantly knew he'd spoken out of line. When he looked into the rearview mirror he saw Nick staring at him too, hatred in his eyes.

"Keep laughing, pal," Nick said. "If all of this *is* true—and your Gramps here sure seems to think it is—then it was *you* who fucked up and…infected me, or whatever you call it."

Silvanus opened his mouth again to reply, but his grandfather's glare was enough to shut him up for good. In the backseat Nick suppressed his boiling temper and spoke again to Abraham Kempster. "The question stands, old man. What do I do now?"

The old man held up the bottle again and Nick got a sudden pain in his chest as if he could feel some deadly power from the liquid inside. "You drink this," Kempster said. "You drink this and everything will be over."

Nick stared at the bottle like it was a loaded gun. Every instinct he had was trying to tell him how ridiculous the whole scenario was, that there was no such thing as werewolves and that these dirty gypsies were trying to

139

scam him or something. Deep down he knew that it was more than that, though. The gypsies had done *something* to him. He didn't believe he was actually a werewolf, but he also knew that he wanted no part of whatever was in that tiny bottle. All he wanted was to get out of that old Plymouth.

"Man I'm not drinking that," Nick finally said. "Pull over and let me out.

Kempster didn't blink, only stared. He shook the contents of the bottle slightly and Nick winced. Finally the old man spoke up again. "Only one other option for you, boy."

The big car rolled to a stop just outside the gates of the Barker Marsh ball park. Nick could have gotten out right then and been done with this entire encounter but he didn't. He wanted to hear what the old man had to say.

"What's the other option?" Nick asked.

Kempster grinned eerily and lowered the bottle of silver nitrate. He wouldn't need it after all. The intrigue in in Nick's voice was enough for the old man to realize that he had him. "You have to pass the curse to someone else."

"And how exactly would I go about that?" Nick was sure he already knew the answer.

"You wait till you turn lup again, then you bite somebody. That person get the lup curse." Kempster said it as nonchalantly as if he were telling Nick how to change out spark plugs in a car.

Nick laughed, trying to convince the old man, and himself, that the suggestion was ridiculous. "That's it, huh? All I have to do is bite someone else?"

"Bite, not kill," Kempster said, "It's not so easy as you think, boy—to bite one time and stop."

Nick once again thought that the *normal* thing to do at this point was to laugh and get out of the car, washing his hands of this gypsy horse shit. But once again, he didn't.

"Any suggestions on who I should bite?" Nick asked.

The old man didn't answer. He didn't have to.

***

Nick got out of the car and walked through the park entrance. He glanced back at the two gypsies but the ancient coupe was already pulling away.

Must have more gypsy business to attend to, Nick thought. Maybe they have more folks to curse. *Maybe it'll be a vampire this time.* Nick shook his head as he walked, as if that would magically make all the pieces fall into place and make the weirdness of the past two days go away. He walked past all of the kiddie rides as he recapped the last 48 hours in his mind.

Let's see, the Picnic rolls into town, which is normally a good time, but in the past two days I've had to stop my boss from getting into a gypsy war, had the living shit kicked out of me, blacked out for about twelve hours, woke up with the most fucked up bruises I've ever seen, and now I've been told I'm a werewolf. Oh yeah, and the only way to get rid of it is to bite someone else.

Someone else. Nick had asked the old man who he should bite and he'd tried to sound like he was making light of the situation, but deep down Nick was scared that maybe this wasn't all bullshit. The old man didn't say a word when he'd asked but Nick knew that he wanted him to pass this curse on to Merrill Colby. Something else the old gypsy said was replaying in his head as Nick walked into the rear section of the Picnic, among all of the food vendors. *Bite, not kill,* the old man had said. *It's not so easy as you think, boy.*

When Nick finally arrived at the Red's BBQ truck Merrill Colby was leaning against the side. He was talking to Sherriff Christie. Both men stopped talking when they saw Nick approach.

"Bout' time, shitheel," Merrill said in his typical, classless tone. "I give you an inch by giving you the night off and you take a fuckin' mile."

"Sorry, Merrill," Nick replied. "I was in pretty rough shape last night. What's going on, Sherriff?"

Sherriff Christie spat a large stream of tobacco juice on the ground and wiped his mouth with the back of his hand. "You know Warren Filch, Nick?"

Nick nodded. He'd helped Filch deliver hay for a couple of summers before Nick got into the trouble that eventually landed him in prison.

"Yeah, well," Christie continued, "his wife found him torn to pieces last night in his barn."

"No shit?!?" Nick said, "What the —I mean, what the hell happened?"

Sherriff Christie shrugged. "Medical examiner is calling it an animal attack. There was a heifer and a newborn calf in the same stall with him, and they were in the same shape—torn to hell."

Nick could feel a sour concoction brewing in his bowels. "What kind of animal was it?"

"That's what's got us scratching our heads. The tracks in the dirt indicate that it was something big, like a bear."

"There aren't any bears around Barker Marsh," Nick said.

"No shit. You'd make a decent deputy," Christie said sarcastically. This caused Merrill to chuckle from the sidelines, and it caused that new rage to boil up in Nick again. "But that ain't the weirdest part. The bite marks look like a wolf, only M.E. says it'd have to be a wolf the *size* of a fuckin' grizzly."

Nick's skin broke out in gooseflesh and he hoped neither man noticed it.

"The Sherriff was asking me if I've seen anything weird out at my place," Merrill said. "I said I wouldn't know 'cause I ain't been there, on account of covering for your ass."

Nick didn't allow this comment to get under his skin because he was too focused on the thought of Warren Filch being shredded to bits. "It was pretty bad, huh Sherriff?"

Christie spat another stream of tobacco between his boots. "Boy, let me tell you this: aside from that Klein kid that got creamed by that train some years back I've never seen so much blood in all my years on the job."

So much blood, Nick thought to himself. He had a sudden vision of himself staring in the mirror that morning, covered in blood. *So much blood.* Thankfully, Merrill spoke up again and snapped him out of his trance.

"I'll tell you this," Merrill said, inflating his chest, "I hope that big sum'bitch does come by my place. I got something for his ass. I'll knock a hole the size of a fuckin' manhole cover in him. Wonder what a barbecued bear would taste like?"

Merrill laughed at that. The Sherriff only chuckled slightly, and Nick simply glared at his boss. He hadn't wanted to believe the gypsies when they'd told him Merrill had slow cooked one of their dogs, but after Merrill's comment about the bear he was starting to feel that maybe what they'd said wasn't bullshit.

Christ, Nick thought, *maybe none of it was bullshit. And that would mean that it wasn't a bear at all.*

The Sherriff glanced at his watch and then said, "Just don't shoot any of your neighbors or livestock alright, Merrill? You call us if you see any monsters." Merrill and the Sherriff chuckled and then Christie walked away.

When the Sherriff was out of earshot Merrill turned back to Nick. "That cocksucker couldn't find his own asshole if someone drew him a map. He ain't ever gonna catch whatever killed Filch. Anyway, *you're* working the truck for the rest of the day, peckerhead. I was on my own all last night and apparently you needed your fuckin' beauty sleep so I've been up since four getting the smoker ready."

Normally Nick would have apologized, but there was nothing "normal" about this day anymore. "What are you gonna do?" Nick asked.

"I'm gonna have Fannie Pace sit on my face," Merrill replied poetically. "What the fuck you think I'm gonna do? I'm going home and going to bed, then I'm gonna sit up and wait for that bear or wolf or whatever the fuck it is to come past my place, then I'm gonna pop his ass."

"You really think that of all the places around Barker Marsh this thing could roam it's actually gonna wind up on your property?" Nick asked.

"Well what are you, a fuckin' bear-wolf expert now?"

Nick didn't reply. He was afraid that he was much more of an expert than Merrill could possibly know.

***

Red's BBQ was busy that day. It made for a pleasant distraction for Nick. Normally he would have complained that Merrill had left him on his own on the busiest day of the Picnic, but as Nick had established several times that day, normalcy was completely foreign to him now. Besides, Nick couldn't exactly blame Merrill for being pissed at him and heading for the house. He had essentially left Merrill hanging for about 18 hours to run the business by himself.

He was running low on trays, and when Nick stepped behind the truck to get more out of the trailer he had a flashback to the day before and broke out in a sweat. He quickly glanced around, sure that he was about to get jumped again. The anxiety soon turned to that same rage he'd felt in the gypsies' car. A big part of him wished someone *would* attack him. Nick felt like he could tear a man limb from limb and he'd love to start with that gypsy cocksucker with the fedora.

When he was sure that no assault was coming, Nick carried his stack of food trays back into the truck, slightly disappointed. He set the stack of trays down and turned to face his next customer. Kara Wheeler was staring at him from the other side of the counter. She was dressed in her hospital scrubs and she didn't look happy to see him. Nick approached the counter.

"What happened last night?" Kara asked, "You never came over after work."

Nick stared at her, trying to piece together the prior evening's events and once again coming up blank. "Kara, I *didn't* go to work last night."

"What are you talking about, Nick?" Kara replied, agitated, "So where the hell were you then?"

Nick had no intention of explaining the last 24 hours to Kara through a barbecue food truck window, so he did a quick glance to make sure no prospective customers were approaching, then he set a sign on the counter that read, "Back in 5 minutes."

Nick walked with Kara to the grassy field that was serving as the overflow parking lot. He did most of the talking as they walked and recounted as many of the strange events as he could remember. When they finally got to Kara's car Nick was just telling her about his morning ride with the gypsies and the conversation he'd had with Merrill and Sherriff Christie. When he finished, Nick felt sick to his stomach; and for reasons he didn't understand, this sent a fresh wave of panic through him.

"Well that's some story," Kara said. Her tone was distinctly accusatory.

Nick knew that Kara was speaking, and he realized that she hadn't believed a word he'd said. She probably assumed he was off screwing around on her. But the rising nausea and his fight not to throw up took most of his concentration. Her voice faded away as another wave of nausea hit him in the lower gut.

"—full of shit, you know that, Mister? If you want to see other people

148

just say so, don't—" Kara's voice faded again. Nick was sweating now. He wanted to tell Kara she was wrong, that he loved her and didn't want to be with anyone else, but all he could focus on was the pain, and the moon that was growing brighter and brighter in the evening sky.

"—the matter with you?" Kara echoed.

Nick looked up at her as his eyes began to fill with tears. A vision from the night before suddenly flashed in his mind. He could see himself standing in Kara's backyard, his skin splitting and falling to the grass in piles.

"Honey, are you O.K.? Nick? Baby say something." Kara sounded like she was at the far end of a long tunnel, not standing right in front of him. Nick had another vision. This time he saw Warren Filch, with whom he'd helped deliver hay, clutching his belly as his insides poured out through his fingers. Warren Filch suddenly turned into Kara Wheeler. This shocking new vision, combined with the stabbing pains in the backs of his heels dropped Nick to his knees. He could smell Kara—her blood, her sweat, her sex. It wasn't until he could hear her heart pounding in his head that Nick realized what was happening.

The old gypsy was right. He remembered everything now. He'd killed Warren Filch. He could remember ripping and tearing at the father of three, and he could suddenly taste the blood of the heifer he'd eaten the night before, and her calf. The thought of the cow's blood sent sharp, stabbing hunger pains into his abdomen. One of the few remaining parts that was still Nick Goodman cried out as two of his ribs snapped and reset. Through clutched teeth, he shouted, "Kara...run!"

Nick looked up with the last remaining bit of human strength he had. He saw Kara drop to her knees and scream, then his vision went black as the blood vessels in his eyes began to burst.

***

Kara screamed. She had been pissed off at Nick, it was true. But she was only upset because deep down she truly loved him. The man had his faults but Kara would never wish him any harm. What she witnessed happening to the man she loved tore at her. The thing that was her lover fell to its knees in agony, and Kara could hear bones breaking. She could actually see the flesh rippling beneath his clothing as ribs snapped and reset. Thick, coarse hairs were erupting from the flesh Kara could still see. Small beads of blood were turning into tiny rivulets as Nick's flesh began to split. Kara was about to step forward and help him when something that sounded like Nick spoke.

"Kara...run!" it said.

Part of Kara *did* want to run, but another part wanted to reach out and help the Nick-like thing at her feet. She took a step toward him but froze as a low, agonizing growl came from deep within his body. The concert t-shirt Nick had been wearing was now stretched tight across the thing's chest as the muscle and fur beneath continued to grow. The thing reached up with abnormally long fingers and raked its sharp nails across the front of the shirt, tearing it in half. Kara watched as it tried to do the same thing to the blue jeans that were constricting its lower body. Once the thing got a couple of tears started in the jeans the fabric split all the way to the upper thigh. The image reminded Kara of Lou Ferrigno in *The Incredible Hulk*. Just as she was about to take another step forward the last part of the thing's face that remotely resembled Nick Goodman split down the center, spraying her scrub bottoms and white nursing shoes with a fine mist of blood.

Kara screamed, but the sound was lost in a sea of a hundred other screams from the nearby carnival rides. Nick Goodman was gone. In his place squatted a giant beast. Minutes earlier when Nick had told her the gypsies had told him he was a werewolf she had almost laughed at the mental picture—Nick looking like Lon Chaney Jr., with an afro and pronounced under bite, wearing a grey Oxford shirt buttoned up to the collar and tucked into his trousers while he pranced around the Moors on his tip-toes.

She didn't feel like laughing now. The thing crouched before her looked nothing like a Universal movie monster. The creature stood up then on its hind legs, and as Kara looked up at the eight foot tall animal she realized that not even Claude Rains with his silver tipped cane could help her. The werewolf extended its jaws and snout skyward and howled. The sound was so powerful it rattled Kara's insides and made her bladder tingle as she pressed her palms to her ears. When the creature looked back down Kara was already running.

She ran about forty feet and then jogged to her left between two parked cars. For a moment she thought she might actually be able to outrun the beast. Then she heard a terrifying sound. It was a metallic

CLUNK!-POP! CLUNK!-POP! Kara didn't have to look to know that the sound was the werewolf landing on metal roofs as it jumped from car to car. It was getting closer.

The werewolf had her scent, and it leapt from car to car effortlessly. When it was only a car length away the creature pushed off hard with its rear legs and flew nearly twenty-five feet before landing on the hood of a Trans-Am, right in front of its prey.

Kara's feet skidded in the grass as the beast landed in front of her. She tried to back pedal but only succeeded in tripping over her feet. She went down hard and her head struck the rear bumper of a pickup truck. Bright, white explosions erupted in front of her eyes and she could feel warm blood running down the back of her neck. Through her swimming vision she could see the creature crawl down off the car and creep toward her. Her blinks were becoming longer and longer and suddenly she opened her eyes and the thing was in her face. She could feel its breath on her and she prepared herself to feel fangs in her throat any second. Tears stung her eyes.

This is Nick, she thought. *Somewhere, deep down, this thing is Nick.*

"Nick," she said, "I know you're in there." The beast hesitated a moment and growled loudly. "Nick, I love you." She felt intense pressure on her upper chest as the creature laid its paw on her and pressed down. The air was driven out of her lungs so nothing came out when she attempted to scream. The next thing Kara felt was burning as the thing extended its claws and punctured her flesh. The wounds weren't deep, but it was incredibly painful. The werewolf drug its paw downward, tearing open her top. It did this gently, almost as if it was making a conscious effort not to scratch her. Its claws caught the front of her bra and snapped the thin fabric. She made an effort to cover her exposed breast, but the weight of the thing pressing down on her was too great. She could only lay there, waiting for a fatal bite.

It had revealed the bare flesh of her chest with the intention of breaking through her rib cage to get at the organs beneath, but it paused. It looked at the scratches it made and then one of its long claws started tracing the scar on her breast. Something deep inside the creature—something that was still Nick Goodman—forced it to back away from the woman lying beneath it. It could sense many more humans approaching, and the Nick part of it was suddenly thinking of new prey.

Kara's head was spinning but she managed to catch a glimpse of the giant beast as it leapt over several cars and disappeared into the night. A moment later Sherriff Christie was kneeling over her, trying to keep her conscious.

***

Merrill Colby really *did* have every intention to go home and sit on his back porch, waiting for the bear that had killed Warren Filch to come wandering by. A pint of Old Crow bourbon later and Merrill had completely forgotten about his commitment to stake out his back field. Halfway through the bottle of whiskey he had stumbled upon a steamy B-movie on the T.V. about a prostitute that was looking for a way out of the business.

"Hooker with a heart of gold," Merrill chuckled to himself.

He had dozed off and missed a good thirty minutes of the movie, and when he woke up the blond starlet was about to perform fellatio on her pimp at gun point.

Woke up just in time, Merrill thought. *Now let's see some titties.*

The blond on the screen had pulled her top over her head, and just as gravity was about to send her ample breasts plummeting back toward her midsection the television snapped off with a loud pop, along with all of the lights in the house.

"What the flyin' fuck," Merrill said as he cranked the switch on the lamp next to the sofa. The lamp's bulb was still intensely hot, and Merrill grazed it with his knuckles, sending him reeling off the couch in the pitch black. He stumbled over the coffee table and wound up face first on his twenty year old shag carpet.

"Cocksucker!"

Merrill's knuckles and right knee were throbbing as he sat in the darkness. He became aware of how quiet it was. He was listening to the summer sounds of insects outside and before he knew it he was holding his breath, hyper-focused on his sense of hearing.

There was another noise out there.

It was a series of metallic pops coming from the direction of Merrill's barn. The barn was pretty much empty this time of year so the sounds reverberated and echoed loudly across his property. It sounded like someone was walking on the roof out there.

Merrill got to his feet, his eyes having grown accustomed to the darkness. He limped over to his porch window and looked out into the night. He could see a strobe-like light show on the opposite side of the pole barn. It took him a few seconds to realize that it was sparks and electrical bursts from what almost certainly was the electrical box that controlled the power to his home and barn.

"What in the f—," Merrill's voice trailed off as one of the electrical flashes revealed something new. There was someone standing on the roof of the barn, staring back at him. Merrill could only make out the silhouette in the flashes, but whoever it was they were *big*.

"Cocksucker!" Merrill said again. He moved through the darkness toward the gun cabinet in the hallway, dragging a hand supportively along the wall to make sure he kept his bearings. When his hand brushed the glass front of the gun cabinet he reached up and felt for the flashlight that he always kept there. He found it and thumbed the switch. The hallway was bathed in white light. Then he opened the gun cabinet and took out his Remington Wingmaster twelve gauge.

Moments later Merrill Colby was marching across his lawn toward his barn. Whoever had been standing on the roof was gone, but Merrill was sure they were still somewhere on his property. As he reached the open barn door Merrill brought the stock of the shotgun up to his shoulder. At the same time a low, rumbling growl rolled out of the blackness of the barn's interior.

Merrill froze. He suddenly remembered his conversation with Sherriff Christie earlier that day. Something had torn Warren Filch to pieces and the coroner had thought it might be a bear or something.

Fuck me running, Merrill thought. *The sumbitch' is in my barn!* He followed this up with another thought. *How the fuck did the thing get on my roof?*

He continued to stand at the opening of the barn, listening. Merrill broke out in a cold sweat and he wondered if the buckshot in his shotgun would be any use against a bear. He figured if he hit the thing in the face it would do the trick, but he still wished like hell that he'd grabbed his deer rifle out of his cabinet instead of a scatter gun. Another deep growl broke the silence. To Merrill it sounded like the idling motor of a muscle car. He flipped on the flashlight and awkwardly brought it up with the fore grip of the shotgun.

The flashlight's beam cut through the darkness and illuminated a million dust particles all at once. Merrill swept the flashlight and shotgun across the barn, searching for whatever animal had stumbled onto his land. A gust of wind slammed into the barn then, lifting the metal roof slightly and bringing it down on its rafters with a bang.

"Shit!" Merrill screamed. He'd felt his finger flex when he'd jumped at the sound and was relieved that he hadn't accidentally fired the gun. When he was sure that he wasn't having a heart attack he brought the gun and flashlight back up and continued to sweep the barn. The beam was shaking now and it took Merrill a few seconds to realize it was because his hands were trembling. He did his best to steady himself and continued to move the light from left to right across the barn. So far nothing was out of place and there was no sign of the source of those deep growls; only hay and equipment. He kept sweeping, and searching.

The light landed on his old, rusted Massey-Ferguson tractor and Merrill almost didn't see the eyes. In fact, at first he just took them for bolt heads that *hadn't* rusted over yet. Then they blinked, and moved. The tractor was blocking most of the light, but Merrill could see the eyes rise to a height of what had to be seven feet. Merrill knew that grizzlies could stand as tall as twelve feet on their back legs, but there weren't any grizzlies in this part of the country.

This was no bear.

Merrill's heart pounded in his chest. He didn't have a shot and he took a step to his right, trying to get an angle on the beast hiding behind his tractor. The thing at the end of the flashlight beam took a step to its left and for the first time Merrill Colby saw the beast in its entirety.

Before the side effects of being middle aged had sunk their teeth into Merrill and wrapped an extra 150 pounds around his midsection, he was actually capable of getting a date with a woman without having to pay for it. Several of these dates had ended at the Barker Marsh drive-in theater, where he'd end up groping around in some waitress's crotch while some B-horror movie played out on the screen. Oftentimes he'd say something stupid and his date would storm off before the flick even started, leaving Merrill with nothing to do but jerk off and then actually watch the movie. On one of these occasions he'd watched Gene Fowler's *I Was a Teenage Werewolf*. Ever since then Merrill's mental picture of a "werewolf" had always been Michael Landon in blue jeans, engineer's boots, and a wool letterman's jacket.

As Merrill stared at the towering creature in front of him he realized the movie had no idea about what werewolves actually looked like. The beast looked nothing like Michael Landon. It wasn't wearing engineer's boots or a letterman's jacket, although it had the remains of some blue jeans wrapped around its waist.

The thing roared suddenly and Merrill instinctively pulled the trigger of the shotgun that he'd almost forgotten he was holding. The beast reeled backwards, howling in pain.

"Gotcha, you cocksucker!" Merrill shouted.

The thing dropped back down to four legs and turned quickly. It ran toward the back entrance of the barn. Merrill pulled the trigger again and cursed when nothing happened. He racked another shell into the chamber and squeezed the trigger quickly. This time he was rewarded with another thunderous boom as the shotgun slammed into his shoulder. New, tiny shafts of light shone through the far end of the barn where the buckshot had peppered the door, but he had missed the creature.

Merrill turned and ran out the front of the barn on his side. He would cut the thing off on the outside. As he reached the far side of the barn he racked his last shell into the chamber. He stopped and immediately brought his hand up to shield his eyes, dropping the flashlight in the process. The electrical box was still belching a shower of blue sparks, and it had just ruined Merrill's night vision. He spread his fingers and tried to squint through the strobe-like sparks.

Fuck! Is it standing over there? He couldn't tell through the sparks. He considered firing in that direction but he only had one round left. There was definitely a dark shape on the other side of the sparks but he couldn't tell if it was moving.

Another burst of blue sparks. When the shower stopped the big shadow on the other side grew taller as the werewolf stood up again. Another burst of sparks and Merrill started to pull the trigger. A split second later another flash of sparks revealed the beast standing right in front of him. It's massive, clawed hand grabbed the shotgun's barrel and twisted it to the left as Merrill finished squeezing the trigger. The last load of buckshot blew a hole the size of a pumpkin in the side of the barn.

In the next second the gun was torn from Merrill's hands and a rock hard block of fur slammed into his lower jaw, sending him backwards ten feet. He landed on his back and reached up to feel his broken jaw. Before he could feel the swollen flesh the werewolf was standing over him. It brought its foot down hard in the center of Merrill's chest, pinning him to the ground. Merrill felt something, probably a rib, snap in his chest. He tried to scream but his jaw had already swelled so much that he was unable to open his mouth so the scream came out as a muffled grunt.

The werewolf brought its large head downward, stopping when its jaws were a few inches from Merrill's face. Merrill closed his eyes and waited for the thing to tear his throat out. *Well come on then, fucker*, Merrill thought, *get on with it.*

The werewolf opened its jaws wide, but it didn't bite. Something was going through its primitive brain. *Bite, don't kill. It's not so easy as you think, boy.* It didn't understand words any longer but somehow it understood the meaning behind these. If it only bit this man it would pass its curse on to him. There was a part of what used to be Nick Goodman that wanted to do this—bite Merrill Colby and run off, freeing himself from this curse. The problem was that the beast in him enjoyed what he was. *Bite, don't kill. It's not so easy as you think, boy.*

It certainly wasn't. Merrill Colby deserved to die and the human part—the Nick part—soon receded. Only the beast was left, and it had no intention of only biting once.

The creature roared loudly in Merrill's face and then it reached over and grasped his left wrist. Merrill tried to scream again as the sharp claws dug into his flesh. What he felt next was a heavy pressure in his shoulder as the beast starting pulling his arm upward, while still pressing down on his chest with its muscular foot. The pressure grew and finally graduated into pain as his shoulder dislocated with a loud pop. Merrill still wasn't sure what the thing was doing to him until the pain he was feeling increased to pure agony when a muscle in his shoulder started to tear.

It continued to pull upward and Merrill could feel more tearing in his shoulder. A jet of blood splashed across the creature's chest as the skin covering his shoulder finally tore and separated. The creature stood fully above him, holding his left arm. He looked at the jagged meat and bone protruding from the stump and was surprised that the pain was all at once gone. In its place was an icy numbness. Merrill made an attempt to reach with his right arm and feel the pulpy crater left in his opposite shoulder, but the creature had seized his right wrist before he had a chance to feel anything. The creature pulled again and Merrill's back started to come off the ground. The thing pressed down hard with its foot and Merrill's right arm tore free with another pop and splash of blood.

The last thing Merrill Colby ever heard was the sound of his own neck breaking as the creature's massive paw connected with the side of his head.

Merrill's head rolled to a stop ten feet away, and the last thing he saw before the neurons in his brain stopped firing was the creature burying its snout into the jagged stump of his neck.

***

An hour after Merrill Colby had been beheaded, Kara Wheeler was opening her eyes. She'd sustained a concussion when her head had struck the truck bumper. Paramedics had attempted to keep her awake but once they determined that her brain wasn't swelling they had let her sleep. As her hospital room came into focus she had a sudden urge to throw up. Kara closed her eyes quickly in an attempt to ward off the nausea. Everything that had happened to her came flooding back all at once. She had gone to the Picnic to talk to Nick and he had walked with her back to her car. He'd told her a crazy story about a bunch of gypsies putting a werewolf curse on him, and then…

Then he turned into a werewolf. It didn't make any sense but she'd seen it. The man she loved had turned into a werewolf and he'd damn near eaten her. Sherriff Christie had asked her what happened and she had faked unconsciousness, because she had no idea what to say. She still didn't know what to say.

he nausea had passed, and this time when she opened her eyes she sensed someone else in the room with her. At first she feared it was Sherriff Christie, and she didn't think she could fake passing out again. She reached over and thumbed the remote control on her bed to increase the light.

The man in the doorway wasn't the Sherriff. As he stepped toward her bed she saw that this man looked to be three times as old as Sherriff

Christie. Kara nervously considered hitting the call button for the nurse.

She opened her mouth to say something to the old man but he spoke first.

"Your man a lup," he said.

"A what?"

The old man took something out of his pocket, ignoring her question.

"He gonna come for you. When he do, you make him drink this."

Kara tried to speak again, but now she was choking on tears. The old

man placed the bottle in her hand and turned to leave.

"It was you," Kara managed to get out. "You did this to him."

Abraham Kempster paused but he didn't turn around. "You have him

drink that, girl, and it will all be over." Then he walked out of the room.

Fifteen minutes later a nurse came in to check on her stitches and put

something in her I.V. to help her sleep again. When she was on the verge

of dozing her window opened, even though a metal guard had been

screwed in place to prevent it from opening. This didn't strike her as

strange, though. Nor did she find it strange that her room was on the third

floor but someone was still managing to crawl through the open window.

Nick was standing naked at the foot of her bed. There was dried mud

and blood on his face and arms, but in Kara's medicated state she found

nothing odd about this either.

"Hiii Niiiick," Kara said dreamily.

"Hi baby," Nick said. "I'm sorry about tonight. I never meant to hurt you. I just—"

"Why'd you come here?" Kara asked.

"I came to say I love you, and I came to say goodbye."

Kara felt the tears returning and at the same time knew that she was slipping quickly into unconsciousness.

"I can't stay here," Nick continued. "I've killed people and they'll be after me. Mostly I'm scared of hurting you, Kara."

Kara's tears were flowing freely now and beneath her blankets she rubbed the small bottle that the old gypsy had given her. The old man had told her to make Nick drink the contents of the bottle and it would all be over. *Would* Nick drink what was in the bottle if she asked him to? Kara knew in her heart he would, and she knew it would kill him.

She had faked sleep when the Sherriff had asked her about what happened and she was faking now when Nick kissed her cheek. She peeked through half closed eyes as Nick crawled back out the window and onto the third floor ledge that bordered the hospital. Moments later he was gone. Shortly after that a fierce howl cut through the night.

Kara clutched the tiny bottle to her chest and cried until she fell asleep.

***

GREETINGS FROM BARKER MARSH

Four months after several Barker Marsh citizens were tragically killed by a rogue animal and Nick Goodman went missing, an incident report was filed at the Southern State Penitentiary in Franklin, Illinois. Sergeant Jim Brown—no relation to the famous football player turned actor—was the officer that filed the report and it was the strangest he'd written in more than twenty years on the job.

According to Sergeant Brown's report, a team of prisoners was working in the dining hall at 0100 hours, waxing the floor. There were three prisoners and one guard supervising. At approximately 0130 hours the guard heard a disturbance in the kitchen and went to investigate. He found the reinforced door to the kitchen bent off its hinges and his investigation led him to a series of busted doors and bent bars. Fearing an attempted escape had been made, the guard called in a tactical response team and hurried back to the dining hall to secure his three prisoners. When the guard entered the hall he reported finding two of the three prisoners cowering under a dining table, showing symptoms of shock. The third prisoner was lying in seven separate piles throughout the dining hall. He'd been torn to pieces. No blood was found on the other two prisoners and they were ruled out as suspects in the slaying, but they refused to speak about the incident or divulge who had killed the third man. The guard underwent a complete psychological evaluation at the request of the State Board of Prisons because he had also reported finding animal tracks in the victim's blood.

Sergeant Brown's report named the victim as Kyle Wheeler. He was 30 years old and had been serving a 15 year sentence for stabbing his wife in the chest with a kitchen knife.

Chapter 3

"Outside the rain was fallin'

On that lonesome boxcar door

But the little form of Hobo Bill

Lay still upon the floor"

—Rodgers, Jimmie. "Hobo Bill's Last Ride." Victor Talking Machine

Company, 1929

The Drifter threw his head back and laughed.

"*That* was a good fucking story, man!" he said. "Could've come right

out of a Forrest Ackerman magazine."

Hasty wasn't laughing. He simply stared at the Drifter with his cold

eyes. When he spoke there was a hint of a threat in his voice.

"You don't believe that story really happened, Lou?" Hasty asked.

The Drifter stopped laughing and paused for a moment, trying to

figure out whether or not Hasty was being serious.

"Uhh, I mean come on," the Drifter said, "A werewolf? It was

entertaining and all, but that one's a little farfetched."

Hasty spat in the dirt again. "I told you, Lou. This town ain't normal,

no sir'ee. Anything can happen in the Marsh."

"Yeah, but werewolves aren't real." Maybe the beer was getting to him, but for some reason he felt obliged to talk some sense into the old man on the other side of the fire. "There's no such thing—you know that, right?"

"No?" Hasty asked.

Before the Drifter could reply a howl cut through the night. It echoed throughout the empty smelting plant so it was hard to say exactly how far away the source of the spine tingling sound was.

"You gotta be shitting me," the Drifter said. "Let me guess, that was a werewolf, right?"

Once again Hasty only replied with a single word. "Probably."

Another howl echoed through the plant then, this time it caused the Drifter to jump with a start. On the other side of the fire Hasty cut loose with another one of his cackling laughing fits.

"Oh, Lou," Hasty said. "You still don't get it, do you? In this town anything's possible—anything goes. In this town *everything* is bad. Everything is—shit, what'd we call it—evil." Hasty started another of his Walter Brennan laughs. "Including the wildlife."

"What about you, Hasty? You're not evil. Little crazy, maybe, but you seem like an alright guy. Why do you stick around a place like this if it's so bad?" The Drifter didn't bother looking at Hasty while he waited for an answer. He looked around the shadows of the factory, trying to spot movement. He still didn't believe in werewolves, but *something* out there in the darkness was howling, and he didn't want to be bitten by some rabid cur anymore that he wanted to be bitten by a shape shifting monster.

"Well, that's two questions now ain't it, Lou. First off, you don't know me, boy. You say I ain't evil, I say I done things that'll make you vomit. As for why I stay in Barker Marsh, I ain't got no choice—same as a lot of other folks. I have to stay here, Lou."

Now the Drifter looked back through the flames at Hasty Davis and it was his turn to offer up a cold stare. "You don't know me either, old timer. And I've done some pretty bad things, myself." The image of the tramp he'd stabbed flashed in his mind. He could see the man's lifeblood jetting across the wooden floor of the train car.

"Have you now?" Hasty said, mockingly.

The Drifter nodded slowly. "Tell you what—why don't we have us another drink and tell our stories. You go first."

"Well," Hasty said. "The beer's gone, so I guess we'll have to move on to the finer things in life." Hasty removed a full pint of brown liquor from his coat pocket. He tossed the 16 ounces of Wild Turkey through the flames and the Drifter caught the bottle gently. "You're gonna need that, Lou."

"Well, I'm listening," said the Drifter as he unscrewed the cap on the bottle.

"So you wanna know ol' Hasty's story, do ya? Well, Lou, like I said…"

***

Box 247

"Wrong side of the tracks,

Tried to leave, but you came right back

To the wrong side of the tracks

It's in your blood, and that's a fact."

—Clark, Guy. "Wrong Side Of The Tracks." *Somedays the Song Writes You*, Dualtone Records, 2009

A town like Barker Marsh has a way of wearing good people down and turning them rotten. Some folks have a higher tolerance for the town than others and it takes longer for them to go sour. Toby Linkladder lasted thirteen years before the town sunk its hooks in him and turned him "bad." That had been the same year his kid sister had gone missing.

Becky Linkladder had been playing in their front yard the last time Toby had seen her. Their mother had run up town to buy cigarettes and insisted that Toby stay home to keep an eye on Becky. Toby had not been happy about this. He was supposed to be on his way to the town ballpark for a pickup baseball game against Jarrod Ramsey and those pricks from the North side of the tracks. The other guys were going to give him hell when they found out he'd missed part of the grudge match because he had to babysit.

Toby sat on the front porch steps, watching Becky swing on an old rope that was tied to an apricot tree. She had Strawberry Shortcake, her favorite doll, stuffed into a fanny pack around her waist. Toby remembered that doll well, because it had a tattoo of a strawberry on its cheek, which he found weird, and it actually smelled like strawberries when you scratched it, which he found even weirder.

For the first five minutes after their mother had left Becky had bugged him relentlessly to join her on the rope swing, and Toby remembered telling her to "get bent,"—he wasn't going out there because he'd get the rotten apricots on the ground stuck to his baseball cleats. Becky told him she intended to tell their mom he'd told her to "get bent," even though Toby knew she had no idea what the phrase actually meant.

Becky never got the chance.

From his spot on the porch, Toby thought his little sister made a pretty good moving target, and he was strongly considering grabbing a handful of rocks and testing his theory when Bruce Davino came around the side of the house on his BMX racer and slid to a stop in front of the porch. Toby had told Bruce he couldn't leave for the baseball game yet and Bruce reacted exactly how Toby had expected him to—with a barrage of insults, the sum of which basically said that Toby was a pussy that needed to grow a pair, and that their gang was inevitably going to lose the baseball match to that rich fucker Jarrod Ramsey, and that it was all Toby's fault.

Eventually Bruce's insults dried up, and he told Toby he'd wait with him

until his mom got back. Toby would have liked to believe his friend's

decision was a noble gesture of camaraderie, but that was bullshit. Bruce

Davino had offered to stay because Toby had a Nintendo and he didn't.

Toby's suspicions were confirmed when Bruce asked if they could play a

little Mario while they waited.

Toby had been happy for the company and agreed. He figured the

odds were pretty slim that Becky would set the front yard on fire, so he had

told her that he and Bruce were going inside and that she'd better not do

anything stupid or he'd kick her ass. Then he'd gone inside with his friend.

Twenty minutes later the two boys heard Toby's mother pull into the

driveway. They'd abandoned their video game and took off for the front

door. Toby would later remember thinking that if he and Bruce hurried

they might only miss a couple of innings against that rich fucker, Jarrod

Ramsey.

When he'd stepped out the front door his mother was standing at the

bottom of the porch steps, a newly purchased Pall Mall jutting from

between her lips. Toby would remember how the glowing tip of the

cigarette bounced as she asked him a simple and innocent question.

Where's your sister?

He would hear that question over and over in his nightmares for the next six years. He didn't know the answer…then.

At first he'd thought Becky was hiding to get him into trouble, but as an hour of searching turned into two, Toby got scared. By the time he and his mother had started driving through town, frantically hopping from one of Becky's friend's houses to the next; tears of worry and guilt began to stream down his cheeks.

They drove around town until 11 p.m. Then his mother drove to the Sheriff's office and told the deputy on duty that her daughter was missing. The deputy told her that Becky wasn't "officially" a missing person until she'd been gone for 24 hours.

Toby remembered two things very clearly after his mother got back in the car that night. First, after she told him they had to wait 24 hours before they could declare Becky missing he would remember thinking about a boy named C.J. C.J. had gone missing the summer before, and after four days the deputies found his lifeless body washed up on a sandbar in the middle of the Cahokia River. Snapping turtles had eaten several of the boy's fingers. The thought of turtles eating Becky's fingers brought stinging tears to his eyes.

The second thing Toby remembered clearly from that night was his mother breaking into uncontrollable sobs. Then she smacked him hard across the face.

***

The posters had gone up the following week and that was when it hit Toby the hardest. His mother made him ride his bike all over town, hanging missing person fliers with Becky's photo on them. He'd hit every light post and public bulletin board in town. By the time school started again a month later, Becky was still missing and Toby's mother had received no phone calls.

Toby's classmates treated him as if he had a disease. The kids he wasn't particularly close to whispered as he walked by, referring to him as "that guy whose sister disappeared." Worse yet was the way the kids he *was* close to treated him. They avoided him like he was a leper. Even Bruce Davino, who Toby had always been able to count on, gave him the cold shoulder.

To Toby, that first week back at school had felt like a month, and by the time Friday afternoon rolled around he was thrilled to have been given a new task by his mother, because it helped take his mind off of his deteriorating social life. She'd asked him to ride around town again and replace any of Becky's missing posters that might have blown free in the past month. In his heart he knew it was probably useless, but his mom needed to feel like they were still doing *something*. He was happy to help, because deep down he knew that she still blamed him for Becky's disappearance. Even deeper down, he agreed with her.

He spent the rest of that Friday afternoon pedaling through town, stapling fresh fliers onto the telephone poles and getting all kinds of looks from the residents of Barker Marsh. By the time the street lights had come on he'd ridden all the way out on the old highway to the bowling alley, and that's when a simple act of selfishness changed the course of his life forever.

Perhaps "selfishness" isn't the right word. "Desperation" may be more appropriate.

John Morland was a drunk, that much was true, but what was also true was that he was basically a good father, and that couldn't have been an easy task given his situation. Morland's wife had died while giving birth to their only child, a boy with cerebral palsy. Raising a child with special needs financially would not have been easy for most single income families in Barker Marsh, but it was especially hard for John Morland. His particular set of skills and intelligence level left him with only one career option. He performed all sorts of odd jobs around Barker Marsh, ranging from mending cattle fences to clearing out folks' septic systems.

John Morland *did* have enough business sense to understand basic advertising though. That's why, about two weeks after Becky Linkladder went missing, he'd driven down to the stationery store in Chelsea and had a hundred fliers printed up, advertising his services as a handyman. In a moment of genius he printed his phone number over and over in vertical columns along the bottom of each flier so that potential customers could tear off his contact information.

Whether it had been intentional or not, John Morland had stapled one of his fliers over the top of Becky Linkladder's missing person poster. Toby discovered this as he stood in the vestibule of the bowling alley and he became infuriated. He reached up and tore Morland's advertisement free, shredding his thumb on an errant staple in the process. Toby stood shaking, the blood from his mangled thumb soaking the handyman's flier. Toby remembered feeling equal parts of anger and hurt. It had *hurt* him to think that someone could be so insensitive as to put their stupid handyman ad on top of the picture of a missing kid. It *angered* him that the kid in question was his sister.

John Morland.

Toby knew the man, and he knew where he lived. As Toby stormed out of the bowling alley he'd had a thought. *What if someone walked through that lobby that* would *have recognized Becky, but they never saw her because some asshole had stapled their fucking flier on top of Becky's photo?*

John Morland lived on Perry Lane and by the time Toby turned his bike down the road he was convinced that Morland was the sole reason his sister was still missing. Morland's big Dodge van had been in the driveway. There had been several long pieces of PVC pipe and a ladder strapped to the roof the van, supplies for whatever project he'd been working on that week. Toby didn't care about Morland's work; he'd cared about his sister and in Toby's mind John Morland apparently thought his business was more important than Becky.

Toby rode all the way from the bowling alley without giving much thought to what he was actually going to do when he arrived at Morland's house, but as he stood in the driveway staring at the big work van it came to him.

Back then, it was practically a requirement for twelve year old boys to fill their pockets with an assortment of supplies that would make even the most highly decorated Boy Scout proud. In Toby's case, one of those items was a vintage Barlow pen knife his grandfather had given him. He'd opened the knife and crept up behind the van, with the intention of burying the blade in the back right tire. That's all he planned to do, and at first that's all he did. As the hiss of air cut the night and the stale, rubbery scent from the tire's insides filled his nostrils it seemed to fuel his anger even more. Before Toby was able to think twice about it, the entire rear of the van listed and sank as he sliced the rear left radial too. Thirty seconds later Toby had sliced the front tires as well.

His adrenaline peaked and Toby didn't stop with the tires. He'd walked to the edge of the driveway and worked a paving stone loose from the dirt. When he'd turned around and walked back to the van Toby paused to contemplate the odd looking contraption bolted to the side of the vehicle. After a moment he realized what it was.

It was a wheelchair ramp.

There had been a fleeting moment when Toby thought about John Morland loading his crippled kid onto that ramp, and he felt something like sympathy. Then it was gone, shoved out of the way by blind rage again like some high school bully.

Toby shattered the rear glass of the van. Some of his fury had subsided then, but not enough to stop his hands from shaking. That's why it took him half a dozen attempts to light the match once he'd removed the matchbook from the arsenal of supplies in his pocket. Once aflzame, Toby had touched the match to a rag that was in the back of the van. The bottom half of the rag just happened to be stuck inside a can of paint thinner.

Over the next several days plenty of people would ask Toby why he did it and the short answer was that he'd been pissed off, plain and simple. As it turned out that wasn't much of a defense.

A neighbor had seen Toby as he rode off that night after John Morland's van burst into flames. The next morning a Sheriff's deputy—the same one his mother had tried to report Becky's disappearance to a month earlier—knocked on their door.

For a split second Toby thought about denying any knowledge of the vehicle fire the deputy was asking about, but in a moment of maturity—and some would say stupidity—he owned up to it and confessed. As a result of his honesty, Toby spent his last year of junior high attending classes at the Anderson Home for Troubled Youth in Gillespie.

That's where he met Rusty Tomlinson.

***

Rusty Tomlinson was a year older than Toby, but he'd managed to flunk a grade before being shipped off to Anderson Home, so he and Toby were in the same academic sessions throughout the majority of that year. Tomlinson had amassed quite the criminal background by the time he was 15, but it had been a battery charge and a couple of narcotics misdemeanors that had landed him in Anderson. He was a big kid and a bully, and as such he wasn't easily impressed, but Toby managed to capture his attention when word got around that the new kid from Barker Marsh was in for a destruction of property and felony arson. Tomlinson thought that was pretty cool, or as he put it, he thought that was "the tits."

There hadn't been much of an opportunity to get into trouble during their time at Anderson, but Toby and Rusty had managed to land in some hot water after giving each other homemade tattoos using a smuggled razor blade and some India ink. After that the two literally thought of themselves as "blood brothers."

At the end of the following summer both boys were released and they walked out of the Anderson Home for Troubled Youth for the last time. The two vowed to remain friends and they did. They had a bond, like the bonds grown men who had served prison terms or military stints shared.

After days of protesting, Toby had agreed to start his freshman year at Barker Marsh High School like a normal kid. His problem was that he *wasn't* a normal kid. He was still the guy whose kid sister had gone missing a year before but he wasn't unique in that regard any more. During the year Toby had been at Anderson Home two more girls had gone missing. In the eyes of the other kids at Barker Marsh High, this would have only made Toby unlucky, not an outcast. What did make him an outcast was the fact that he was a convicted felon at 15, and while the Anderson Home for Troubled Youth was a far cry from the federal penitentiary in Marion, he might as well have been on death row as far as the other kids were concerned. Even the troublemakers steered clear of him and more often than not Toby would find himself sitting alone during lunch. The only time he wasn't ignored was when he acted out in his classes and he began to do that so frequently that it became the expectation. He had a permanent seat in detention and Toby had thought on more than one occasion of bringing in some photos or other personal effects to spruce up what he'd come to call "his" office in the corner of the library.

Rusty Tomlinson had not gone back to school after leaving Anderson Home, and while Toby Linkladder wasted away in freshman English and Home Economics, he slept in, read shoplifted copies of Swank magazine and smoked a lot of dope. Then every weekday at four o'clock—about the same time his friend Toby was getting out of detention—Rusty would grab his skateboard and head up to the parking lot of Huck's filling station. Toby would show up shortly after on his trusty BMX racer, and then the two would head out on the town, Toby pedaling hard while Rusty held on to the bicycle seat and got towed along on his board. A year later Toby traded his BMX for a beat up Pontiac Fiero. Rusty thought the car was a real piece of shit, but it beat getting dragged around town on a skateboard, and it wasn't as if he had a car of his own.

If the mission at Anderson Home had been to reform its tenants, Toby Linkladder and Rusty Tomlinson were complete failures. The two had fully embraced an adolescence full of petty crime. Shoplifting, vandalism, underage drinking, and the possession and use of marijuana were among their favorite pastimes. Life pretty much continued on that way for the next four years. Toby had grown an impressive set of mutton chop sideburns and also somehow managed to graduate high school. Also, six more girls had gone missing. Toby Linkladder's 19th summer also served as the critical point he would add robbery and accessory to murder to his list of criminal behavior.

***

"The plan", as they'd come to call it, had started as a joking conversation over a 12 pack of Keystone Light and two joints. The initial discussion was no more than three minutes long.

Several weeks later, one of their crew, Josh, had brought up the conversation again and said, "You know, I've been thinking; that bank robbery idea could really work."

One month later, Toby Linkladder sat in the backseat of a non-descript Oldsmobile Cutlass Sierra, sweating his ass off. The air conditioner was broken and August was a hot month in Barker Marsh. Rusty Tomlinson had wanted a much cooler getaway car, like an old Dodge Challenger or something, but the other three members of the gang proved to have cooler heads and convinced Rusty that a beefed up muscle car *would* be badass, but it would also draw a lot of attention before and after they initiated "the plan." Besides, their entire plan hinged around the idea of them not needing to run from the police anyway. So, in the end, Toby Linkladder, Rusty Tomlinson, Josh Ray, and Brian Wells had pooled their beer money together and bought a used Oldsmobile with a broken A.C. for $1,100.

Josh Ray was sitting behind the wheel and when a Rollins Band tune came on the radio he thumbed the volume knob, blasting the inside of the Olds and its occupants with punk-infused hardcore rock.

"Will you turn that shit down?" Rusty said from the passenger seat. "I can't fuckin' hear myself think."

"Sorry," Josh said as he backed the volume back down. "I'm just nervous I guess."

"Well, quit being a pussy," Rusty replied. He tried to sound like a textbook ringleader—cool, calm and collected—but he was unable to quell the nervousness in his own voice.

In the backseat, Toby and Brian Wells looked at each other and made a face as if to say "ooooh, I'm so scared." The two young men did no better hiding their own fear than their friends had in the front seat.

Rusty glanced at his watch. "Ten minutes."

Toby fingered a Zippo lighter, flipping the lid open and shut with a satisfying "*schlock*." Finally, Brian dug a pack of Kamel Reds out of his shirt pocket and shook four cigarettes out onto his palm.

"For fucks sake, Toby," Brian said, "if you're going to keep doing that at least put the damn thing to good use." He passed the cigarettes out and Toby fired up the Zippo. He lit all of the smokes, and no one mentioned that Toby's hand was trembling as he passed the flame around. None of them said a word for the next five minutes, each lost in a cloud of thought and cigarette smoke. The silence finally got to Rusty, and he reached over and turned the radio up again. They all banged their heads lightly to the gravelly voice of Henry Rollins for the next five minutes.

Rusty checked his watch again and then flicked his cigarette outside the car. "If we're gonna do this, we gotta do it right now."

Silent agreement passed between them, and then Josh dropped the gear shift lever into drive.

The plan was actually a pretty good one, but it required three critical steps that had to be timed perfectly. As the Oldsmobile cruised through Barker Marsh on its way to that first step, Toby continued to flip open the Zippo and close it. The irony hadn't really hit him until that moment, and it made him shake his head a little. Although his life had really changed on the day his sister had gone missing, it was a fire that had truly started him down his current path in life. And so it would be another fire that would change his life again.

He'd burned John Morland's van to the ground on an impulse. What he was about to do now was something different—it was a deliberate, premeditated act of arson. But given the list of felonies that the men would rack up by the end of that day, it really wasn't anything special.

The Oldsmobile rounded an "S" curving road at the end of Dwyer Avenue. Barker Marsh was surrounded by farmland, and Dwyer Avenue marked the border of the town's Southernmost fields. It was here that the homes grew further and further apart, offering up some geographical isolation for those willing to work the fields. The old Marsters place was one such location. In its day, the home had been a beautiful two story dwelling on top of 40 acres of rolling farmland, but a warped floor and a variety of other examples of poor luck had resulted in the house sitting vacant for the last 16 years. Sixteen stifling summers and freezing winters had taken their toll on the house. The wood was rotten, the foundation crumbling. The place should have been condemned. None of the four men knew who actually owned the property now, but they justified their actions by telling themselves that whoever owned it was going to make out just fine with the insurance company.

Josh Ray brought the Oldsmobile to a stop in front of the Marsters place, then he put the car in reverse and backed down the gravel driveway. The overgrown weeds were three feet high and they scraped and flicked the underside of the car as it reversed. Eventually Josh brought the car to a stop at the backside of the house. Anyone driving by would be able to spot the white Oldsmobile parked behind the abandoned house, if they were looking for something out of place. It wouldn't be wise to dawdle with this part of "the plan."

"Okay," Rusty said as he turned around and looked at Toby. "Do your thing."

Toby glanced around at his three friends, making sure to lock eyes for a moment with each of them. "You guys sure you wanna go through with this?"

Josh and Brian replied by dropping their gazes to their laps. Rusty simply looked at his watch and then held his wrist up to Toby.

"Tick tock," Rusty said.

Toby took a deep breath, inhaling confidence, then opened his door and got out. From the driver's seat Josh popped the trunk and Toby grabbed the supplies he needed and started toward the back door of the house. The gasoline cans were heavy and his hands were sweating, but the adrenaline kept him from dropping his supplies as he took the porch steps two at a time.

He wasn't surprised when he found himself unable to turn the doorknob on the back door. He put down the cans and prepared to force the door open. What did surprise him was the fact he didn't need the crowbar he'd brought after all—the door jamb had rotted behind the strike plate and with a little pressure the door slid open without needing to turn the knob.

Toby picked up the gas cans and stepped over the threshold. His blood froze and his heart leapt as something hit him in the chest. He dropped the gas cans again and started to swat at the creature attacking him. At first his mind was convinced he was battling a giant vampire bat, but when the thing flew back to the splintered mantle over the fireplace Toby was able to gather his wits enough to see that the creature was nothing more than a large, black crow. He watched as the bird ruffled its feathers and cawed loudly, announcing its intention to make a second attack run. It left the mantle and flew toward Toby again. Toby raised his hands to protect his face, but at the last minute the bird diverted its flight path and maneuvered around Toby and disappeared through the door.

He took a moment to catch his breath and make sure the crow didn't' have reinforcements in the house. When he was sure the crow had been a rogue pilot, Toby retrieved his gas cans and continued inside the house.

The floor was piled with plaster and an assortment of other junk. The shelves had been torn from the walls and splintered. What wall paper was left on the walls flapped lightly as a phantom breeze flowed through the house. There was an antiquated player piano in one corner and Toby half expected the instrument to begin playing by itself at any second. The first floor was riddled with empty beer bottles and graffiti. The focal point of the living room was a stained and shredded mattress. Toby had heard the rumors about a large number of high school girls who had spent time on that mattress, so he grinned a bit when he upended the first gas can and soaked it with fuel.

Toby continued walking through the first floor, splashing gasoline in all directions. Eventually he made his way to the enclosed staircase that led up to the second floor. He opened the second gas can and poured a wide stream along the stairs as he made his way up. When Toby reached the landing he set the can down and kicked it on its side. The gasoline poured out of the spout in surges and puddled on the floor as Toby turned and descended the stairs. As he stepped back into what was left of the living room he pulled the Zippo out of his pocket and flipped it open. He thumbed the flint wheel and for the second time in his life Toby Linkladder intentionally set a piece of property that wasn't his ablaze.

When the flame touched the fuel soaked fabric of the old mattress the fire spread faster than Toby had imagined. The layer of debris covering the floor provided plenty of kindling. Toby knew right away that the old house was going to burn with no trouble at all. The gasoline he'd poured simply accelerated the process and the flames quickly trailed off down the hall toward the staircase.

Toby turned and ran out of the house. He leapt from the rear porch, and sprinted to the car. He could hear his own heart pounding in his ears and the sudden rush of adrenaline caused him to fumble with the door handle before he was finally able to open it.

Toby's three accomplices stared at him as he slid into the back seat. Brian Wells was actually rocking back and forth with nervous anticipation.

"Did you do it?!?" Brian asked. "Did you fucking do it?!?"

"Yes, I fucking did it!" Toby shouted. "Get us out of here!"

Josh Ray dropped the car into gear and floored the accelerator. The Olds slid sideways in the overgrown grass as Josh pulled around to the side of the house. He was on the verge of losing control of the car and driving straight into the burning home when the tires found the gravel again and the car righted itself. At the same time, the trail of fire inside the house had found its way upstairs and reached the gas can Toby had left on the landing.

Even inside the car the men could feel the concussion as a wave of fire

burst from the second story windows.

"Holy fuck!" Rusty yelled.

Josh slid the car back out onto Dwyer avenue and sped back toward

town. When they reached the "S" curve the Oldsmobile almost lost control

again.

"SLOW DOWN!" Rusty hollered. "If we wreck or get pulled over

this entire plan is fucked!"

Josh didn't speak, just nodded in reply and let off the accelerator. As

the car slowed so did the heart rates of its passengers. They had started it.

"The plan" had begun.

"O.K." Rusty said, much calmer now. He checked his watch again.

"Now we make the call."

Josh drove the speed limit through town. All four boys glanced back

to the Southwest and could see the black smoke from the Marsters house

curling into the sky. They all shared an unspoken concern. It had already

been established that for their plan to work the timing had to be perfect,

and the gang hadn't counted on the house going up so fast. They needed to

hurry, but not so much that they drew unwanted attention.

The Oldsmobile leapt over the suspension-jarring train tracks, and

when they reached the end of the street, Josh turned east on Main street and headed up to Huck's filling station, where Toby and Rusty had met after school on so many afternoons. Thankfully, the parking lot was relatively empty, and they'd done a good job in selecting the Olds. No one was paying attention to them.

Josh pulled up next to the payphone on the West side of the building and parked. Rusty got out and walked over to the phone, popped in a quarter, and dialed. After two rings there was a voice on the other end of the line.

"Perry County emergency services," the voice said.

"Uh, yeah," Rusty said, clearing his throat. "I'm not sure if anyone has called it in yet or not, but I was just driving down Dwyer Avenue over in Barker Marsh and there's a big old house on fire."

"O.K. sir, do you have the address of the property on fire?"

"Oh geez, no, I don't. I'm not from around here. I know it's Dwyer Avenue, after some curves heading south of town." Rusty hoped the dispatcher on the other end of the line wasn't trained to pick up on lies in the voices of callers.

"O.K. sir, that should get us close enough. What is your name?"

Rusty didn't answer. Instead, he hung up the phone and ran back around to the passenger side of the car. When he was seated, Josh started driving back toward the center of town. As soon as he turned on Main Street they could hear the sudden shriek of fire engines.

"Holy shit, it's working!" Rusty said. "Pull over here for a second."

Josh pulled over to the curb and the four men watched as two fire engines pulled out onto Main, less than a block away. One of the signature characteristics of small towns like Barker Marsh is that *everything* is on Main Street. One could park and watch the lifeblood of the town flow freely. Within a two block radius from where they were parked sat the town's volunteer fire department, two bars, a café, a barbershop, a hardware store that was no longer in business and a tiny post office.

There were two other buildings on Main Street, and both played vital roles in "the plan." The first building was half a block from where they were parked. It was the First National Bank of Barker Marsh, and they were going to rob it.

The second building was a little further south down Main Street, next to the fire station. It was the Barker Marsh Sheriff's station, and the four men in the white Oldsmobile Sierra needed that building to be empty or the only thing they would have accomplished by the end of that day would be burning down an abandoned house.

Rusty looked at his watch for what had to have been the 300th time that day and muttered something under his breath. He stared at the front of the Sheriff's office for what seemed like an eternity. His heart started to sink and he could almost sense the despair radiating from the other passengers as well. He was about to say something when the front door of the Sheriff's station flew open and Sheriff Christie came running out, followed by two deputies. They all jumped into three different squad cars and seconds later they were screaming south after the fire engines. As the last of the squad cars' tail lights disappeared over the train tracks Rusty spoke up.

"FUCK YES!" he yelled, pumping his fist. The other three men only smiled. Rusty closed his eyes and exhaled deeply. When he opened his eyes he checked his watch for the three hundred and *first* time.

Now came the part of "the plan" that was completely out of their control. Fortune had shined on them so far and all four silently hoped that their luck would hold out. Two very long minutes later, fate provided the answer.

The men smiled because in the distance they could faintly hear the sound of a train whistle. Their good fortune was holding out.

***

As it turned out, geography played as big a part as luck in "the plan." Barker Marsh was a coal town, and as such, it was also a train town. The town was really only about two miles square, and its Northern and Southern halves were separated perfectly down the middle by a set of railroad tracks which ran East and West. That meant that if a slow moving coal train was travelling through Barker Marsh, the town's North and South sides were completely cut off from each other.

That's what made their plan so simple. All of the town's emergency personnel, including the entire Barker Marsh Sheriff's department, was on the south side of the tracks dealing with the fire at the old Marsters place. Their timing had been perfect. The four men had studied the Illinois Southern route schedule, and all of Rusty's watch checking was paying off. Every public servant that could possibly respond to a crime—like a bank robbery—was about to be completely isolated from the North side of town.

The men figured that they could pull off the actual robbery in the time it would take for the train to pass through town, but they'd added a little additional insurance to "the plan" anyway. An hour before the train was scheduled to pull through town and thirty minutes before Toby set the Marsters house on fire they'd carried an old car hood out onto a remote section of tracks and laid the scrap metal across the rails. The big coal trains were equipped with plow-like devices on the front of the engines, and they were capable of knocking stalled pickup trucks off the tracks if necessary, but Brian Wells' uncle worked for the railroad and he knew they would stop the trains, walk ahead along the tracks, and clear the debris by hand rather than risk a derailment.

The tell-tale squealing, banging, and rattling of the train cars indicated that that was exactly what was happening now. The long train eased to a stop, blocking every railroad crossing in the Barker Marsh town limits. Their barricade was in place. They figured it would be at least fifteen minutes before the train would get rolling again, and twenty minutes before the first crossing would be open to allow the police to respond to any calls on the North side of town. They gave themselves ten minutes to get in and out of the First National Bank of Barker Marsh.

In the backseat of the Oldsmobile, Toby's stomach rolled, and a nervous tickle crept into his testicles.

Rusty turned around to look at Toby and Brian in the backseat. "Alright Brian, open the bag. Let's go."

If Brian Wells was feeling any hesitation, the nineteen year old with fire red hair didn't show it. He unzipped the gym bag in his lap and removed eight items. Four of the items were black wool ski masks. There had been some debate among the gang as to what they were going to wear over their faces to disguise themselves. Josh and Brian had been hell bent on wearing latex Star Wars masks, but Rusty and Toby had convinced them that ski masks were the more practical way to go. They offered a wider range of vision and they were generic. A report of a bank being robbed by Yoda, Chewbacca, and two storm troopers was sure to gain more attention than "four masked men."

They pulled the ski masks over their heads and then Brian passed out the other four items—three pistols and a sawed off pump action shotgun. If "the plan" continued to go as expected, they wouldn't need to use the guns.

Josh dropped the car back into gear and drove the short distance to the front of the bank. He had enough presence of mind to back into the parking spot—no sense in trying to perform a fancy bootlegger's turn should they need to make a quick getaway.

The nervous sensation Toby had been feeling in his gut and genitals grew in intensity then as he came to a frightening realization.

He didn't want to go through with this.

He looked around at his co-conspirators, hoping to see some sign that at least one of them felt the same way. If any of them *did* feel the same hesitation their ski masks didn't betray their emotions. Sweat had already started to run into his eyes. He could see that on that front, at least, he was not alone. All four of them were absent mindedly wiping sweat from the skin they could actually get to around the wool masks. As usual, it was Rusty that broke through the tension in the air.

"O.K. Brian, Josh—you guys have got the cash drawers. Toby and me are going for the safety deposit boxes. I'll be watching the clock, and when I say it's time to go, we fucking go. Got it?"

Toby wanted to vomit. He nodded instead.

"Alright," Rusty said, "let's go then. Josh, don't forget to pop the trunk."

Rusty was the first one out of the car. Toby and Brian filed out next and Josh, after pushing the yellow trunk release button in the glove box, was the last one to exit the vehicle.

They rushed through the front doors of the First National Bank of Barker Marsh, and from that point forward "the plan" barreled forward at full steam. The first thing they all collectively noticed was that the bank wasn't as crowded as they had expected it to be. Then again, it was only 11:15 on a weekday, and most of the folks that did their banking during their lunch hour wouldn't be out quite yet.

The second thing they all noticed as they stood in the bank lobby was that nobody was saying anything. There was only one teller working at the counter and he looked up and spotted the four masked gunmen. He didn't speak or seem to panic in any way, he only stared at them. Soon, the four patrons standing in line turned and looked too. They all wore the same blank look on their faces. Under the wool ski masks, Toby and the others sported similar expressions. It was as if all parties involved recognized that a robbery was taking place, but nobody knew what to do next.

Shit! Toby thought. *Somebody needs to say SOMETHING.* It wouldn't be him though. His tongue felt like a dried out piece of carpet in his mouth. He just assumed it would be Rusty that would step up and take charge, as he usually did, but Rusty was just as frozen as the others.

As it turned out, it was Brian who finally broke the awkward silence, albeit in a voice that shook with nervousness. "Alright," he said as he raised his pistol and pointed it at the five people on the other side of the room. "You all look like pretty smart folks, so you've probably figured out that this is a robbery."

Whatever spell the four patrons and bank teller had been under was broken then as a woman they all recognized, but couldn't address by name, began to scream. The scream elicited a response in Toby that surprised everyone in the lobby, including himself. He began to laugh. They all stared at him until finally Brian stepped up again and began waiving his pistol at the five people standing opposite them.

"Everybody get your faces on the floor, right now!" Brian yelled. The four patrons—two women and two men—dropped to their knees and prepared to flatten themselves out on the tiled floor. The young teller behind the counter started to drop to his knees as well.

"Not you, slim," Brian said as he stepped forward and aimed the pistol directly at the young man's head. "You've got work to do." He threw an empty nylon gym bag at the teller and then instructed him to start filling it with cash from each of the drawers on his side of the counter.

Rusty, Josh and Toby were driven into action. Josh stepped up and trained his weapon on the patrons on the floor while Brian moved from cash drawer to cash drawer with the young teller, filling the gym bag with money. Rusty and Toby moved further into the bank and collected the rest of the employees, which turned out to be two tellers working the drive-through window, two loan officers, and the bank's vice president. Together, they walked the troupe back through the bank at gunpoint. When they passed by the four patrons lying on the floor, they stopped.

"Pardon me folks," Rusty said as he squatted down. The four patrons lifted their frightened gazes upward toward the masked man with the shotgun in his hands. "We're gonna need you all to pitch in and give us a hand. Now get on your feet." When the four people on the floor simply stared up at him, Rusty tried to use more persuasive language. "Let me rephrase that: Get your dicks up off the ground or I will shoot each of you in the fucking head! NOW MOVE!"

This scared the quartet into action and they all rose to their feet. Rusty, Josh and Toby started walking their nine hostages toward the rear of the bank. Brian and the teller approached from the other direction, the teller in the lead with the gym bag full of cash, Brian behind him with his pistol pressed into the small of the teller's back.

"Five minutes left," Rusty said as he passed Brian.

Brian nodded and continued escorting the teller out of the front doors and over to the open trunk of the Oldsmobile. The teller threw the gym bag into the trunk and then Brian quickly walked him back inside the bank where they joined the others in front of the wall of safety deposit boxes.

This was the part of "the plan" that was a bit of a gamble. The truth was a small bank like First National, in a small town like Barker Marsh, did not have a large amount of cash on hand. Brian had kept a casual tally as the teller had filled up the gym bag from the cash drawers, and he estimated that they might have $10,000 in the bag—certainly not the robbery of the century by any stretch. They could have gone for money in the bank's vault, but Josh had read that many bank vaults had silent alarms that could be tripped if they weren't opened just right. The coal train had isolated them from the police, but the group decided not to push their luck by tripping an alarm before they were able to load a single bag of cash.

Instead, the four men decided to take a chance with as many safety deposit boxes as they could fit in the car. They were counting on the idea that at least some of the boxes would contain some expensive jewelry or other valuables that they could cash in at their leisure. As it turned out, each of their ten hostages was able to carry two deposit boxes each, and there were only 40 boxes in total. They were going to get them all.

On the first trip the group stacked twenty boxes in the trunk on top of the bag of cash. On the second and final trip out to the car they were shoving deposit boxes into all available floor space in both the front and rear seats of the car. When all of the boxes were loaded, the Oldsmobile was squatting precariously on its springs.

Rusty checked his watch again, and then said, "Time."

The other three gunmen quickly escorted the 10 hostages back inside the bank. They ordered everyone on to the ground again and the hostages obeyed. Then Rusty told them to count to two hundred and at that point they were free to do whatever they wished. Then Rusty, Toby, Josh, and Brian turned and exited the bank one final time.

That's when the wheels came completely off "the plan."

They never figured that the hostages inside would actually wait almost four minutes before sounding an alarm, but apparently some brave soul inside had barely waited for the gunmen to step outside the front door before rushing to whatever switch tripped the bank's burglar alarm. It certainly wasn't a silent alarm.

As the four men were attempting to crawl into the car on top of the safety deposit boxes, a loud wail burst from the top of the bank's roof. The alarm was surprisingly piercing, and it caused all four of them to pause briefly.

"Fuck it," Rusty said, "we knew this was gonna happen—doesn't change anything. Cops are still on the other side of the train." They all nodded and went back to the task of piling into the Oldsmobile when a new voice caught their attention from further up the street.

"What's going on over there?" the voice asked.

All four of them turned to look at the source of the voice. Toby was caught up in the excitement of the moment, and while he recognized the man's face, he couldn't immediately associate it with the man's name. His brain began to process details about the man's appearance—A tightly cropped crew cut, wire rimmed spectacles, white smock, black pants; Toby's eyes went back to the man's right hand. It was holding something bright and shiny. Finally he recognized the man was holding barber's shears and that's when the man's name came to him.

Phil Whitman.

Phil was the proprietor of the cleverly named Phil's Barbershop, which happened to be two store fronts north of the First National Bank of Barker Marsh. Phil opened his mouth and said something else, but Toby never heard it. The next four seconds or so seemed to drag on for ages, and for this reason Toby was able to save several crystal clear images to his memory. He glanced back at the scissors in Phil's hand and then movement to his left caused him to turn in time to see Rusty raising the shotgun to his cheek. He turned back to Phil Whitman, who had started to step backwards. Rusty yelled something, but Toby didn't hear him, either. In fact, all he *could* hear was his own heartbeat pounding in his ears. Toby's vision began to narrow as his brain continued to process what was happening. Forty feet away, the town barber continued to backpedal toward his shop.

Toby felt the gunshot more than he heard it, the concussion blast rattled his bowels and sent a tingle through most of the nerve endings in his body. When he focused on Phil Whitman again he noticed something strange. The barber had raised the hand not holding the scissors up in front of him, as if to tell Toby and his friends to "halt." Suddenly two of the fingers on that hand—the index and the middle—disintegrated in a red mist of blood and bone fragments as the buck shot tore through him. The cluster of small steel ball bearings passed through Phil Whitman's hand and slammed into his chest. The man's white smock suddenly erupted in red as what looked like a gallon of gore and viscera belched forth from the man that had given Toby his first haircut when he'd been two years old. The impact lifted the barber off his feet and a split second later he lay sprawled on his back, his life spilling out onto the dirty sidewalk.

Oh Jesus! Toby thought. *We just fucking killed someone!* He knew Phil Whitman, and worse yet, he *liked* him. Burning down an empty house was one thing, armed bank robbery was another, but now they'd murdered someone. He turned back to Rusty, who was still holding the smoking shotgun to his shoulder.

"What the FUCK did you do, Rusty?!?" Toby yelled.

Rusty continued to stare at Phil Whitman's lifeless body, and answered calmly, "He had a gun—I had to shoot him."

Toby looked back at the body now, and once again focused on the item that was till clutched in the barber's right hand. "Jesus Christ! That's not a fucking gun, it's scissors! He's a fucking BAR-BER!"

Rusty finally blinked, then the reality of the situation hit him. He didn't say anything for several seconds, then finally looked away from the man he'd just killed and turned, looking directly at Toby but addressing the entire group. "Fuck it. It's done. We knew this could happen, but we gotta get the fuck out of here."

Brian and Josh didn't need to hear anything else; they immediately went about climbing into the vehicle again. Toby wasn't moving, though. He stood staring at Rusty, his blood boiling. They could have gotten away without harming a single soul, but instead Rusty just blew an innocent man in half and his justification for the act was *fuck it, we knew this could happen.*

Toby's temper erupted. He threw a vicious right cross that connected squarely with Rusty's jaw. Pain shot through his hand, despite the wool ski mask cushioning some of the blow. Rusty stumbled backwards and fell against the side of the car, but managed to say on his feet. Toby prepared himself to fend off a counter attack from Rusty, but no punch or physical attack came. Instead, Rusty leveled the barrel of the shotgun at Toby's head and racked another shell into the chamber.

Toby was terrified, but he had no intention of showing it and giving

Rusty the satisfaction. He managed to suppress the terror and simply stared over the barrel at his friend. Finally, it was Josh that interrupted the stand-off.

"Come on guys!" Josh shouted. "We're almost out of this. Both of you need to keep your cool until we're out of town. You guys really wanna fuck this up for all of us?"

Toby and Rusty both shifted their gazes to Josh, and then back to one another. Behind them, the shrill alarm from the bank droned on. There was another sound now, coming from the opposite side of the train tracks a block away. It was a police siren. The train had begun to creep forward again and was serving its purpose by keeping all of the police on the south side of town, but it wasn't going to stay that way forever.

"O.K., we move," Rusty said.

Rusty kept the shotgun aimed at Toby until he was seated in the back of the Oldsmobile on top of some safety deposit boxes, and then he climbed into the front passenger seat.

When all four doors were closed, Josh shifted the car into gear and started Northbound on Main Street. In the rearview mirror they could all see the flashing lights of the police cruisers through the gaps in the slow moving train cars. Josh accelerated and blew through the stop sign at the end of the street, sliding the Olds out onto the main highway.

As the car rocketed Westbound, the bank's burglar alarm and the wailing cry of the police sirens melted away into silence. It was silent inside the Oldsmobile too.

They'd pulled it off, but none of them felt like celebrating.

***

Baker Creek was one of those fishing holes that every small Midwestern town seemed to have. It was in the middle of nowhere and sported a seldom used and dilapidated boat ramp that served far more water moccasins looking for a place to sun themselves than it did actual fisherman. It was a shame, too, because Baker Creek was an excellent catfish hole. The water was dark and very deep, and a swift current brought a steady flow of bait from the waterways to the North.

All of these factors—the isolation, the water's depth and murkiness, and the fast moving current—made it an ideal spot to dump a vehicle. The men had driven out to Baker Creek, where they'd parked Brian's old International Harvester pickup truck that morning. They weren't concerned if anyone had driven by and seen the truck parked there—it would only support their alibi. On the off chance that they were ever questioned about their whereabouts on the morning the First National Bank of Barker Marsh had been robbed, they'd simply say they had all driven out to Baker Creek in Brian's truck and then walked the banks for hours hunting for bluegill and channel cats.

They transferred the bag of cash and the safety deposit boxes to the back of the truck, then they drove the Oldsmobile to the edge of the steep and crumbling boat ramp. They rolled down all the windows, put the car in neutral, and shoved the vehicle down the ramp. It had landed in the water with a splash, and for a terrifying moment the car actually bobbed up and down, as if it was going to float all the way to the Gulf of Mexico. Then the weight of the engine pulled the front of the car down, and when the water level reached the open windows the car was quickly sucked under the brown, swirling eddy in a spray of water as the last of the air was forced out of the passenger compartment. When the deed was done there was no sign that the Oldsmobile had ever been there.

Having rid themselves of their getaway vehicle, the four climbed into the International Harvester and drove further north until the paved road gave way to gravel and dusty farm trails. They found an old derelict barn and backed the truck inside. Here they started to tally up the payoff from the robbery.

"Nine thousand, seven hundred and sixty two," Josh said as he sat the final dollar bill down on top of the stack of cash in front of him. Subtracting the cost of the Oldsmobile, the cash alone had resulted in a little over two grand for each of them. It wasn't a huge sum, but it was a decent start. None of them, except maybe Rusty, felt good about it though, especially Toby. Toby would have given all of the money back in an instant if it meant bringing Phil Whitman the barber back.

"O.K.," Rusty said, "let's get to work on these boxes."

They set to work on the safety deposit boxes with an assortment of tools; crowbars, screwdrivers, and hammers. Josh was the first one to gain access to one of the boxes. It turned out to be worthless, full of nothing but photographs and savings bonds in someone else's name—nothing they could cash in. They'd expected to have a few of these in the bunch, but when six more boxes revealed more of the same worthless junk, their respective hearts sank.

Finally, Brian managed to crack the latch on a box that showed at least some promise.

"Hey guys," Brian said. "I've got some more cash here." He removed several stacks of bills and began counting.

"Does it make sense to you to keep cash in a safety deposit box?" Josh asked. "I mean, why not just put it in an account—it's already *at* the bank."

Rusty spoke up. "Sure it makes sense. It could be someone's 'Get outta Dodge' money, or some old boy's whore fund. You put it in an account and there's a record of it, so *somebody* knows about it. Throw it in one of these boxes and nobody's the wiser. Anyway, who gives a shit? It's ours now. How much we get?"

Brian laid the last bill on the pile. "Exactly two grand. Not bad."

"Yeah, well, it ain't exactly making my dick hard either," Rusty replied. "Keep working at them." He went back to work on his own box then and moments later looked over at Toby. "You're awful quiet."

Toby offered no reply. He didn't even look up from the box he was prying on.

"Look," Rusty said. "For what it's worth I wish like hell it didn't go down that way. It looked like he had a gun. Either way, the guy was rushing us."

Toby's head remained down, but his eyes shot up to Rusty. "Is that what he was doing? Rushing us? He was an old man, Rusty. He heard the fucking alarm and came outside. He spots four guys wearing ski masks and holding guns. So what goes through his head? 'Gee, I think I'll disarm these four dudes with my fucking scissors!'" Toby shook his head then. "You murdered an innocent man, and you made all of us accessories to it."

Now it was Rusty who shook his head. "An innocent man? Right. Phil Whitman illegitimately fathered how many kids in this town again? How many D.U.I.s has he had?"

Toby surprised himself by laughing. "And that's a good reason to blow a man in half? The guy was a drunk and had a problem keeping his pecker in his pants, and that justifies killing him?"

"Come on brother," Rusty said, "did you really think we were gonna come outta this spotless?"

Toby stopped jimmying the box with the screwdriver he was holding and buried the tool in the dirt with an angry flick of his wrist. "Yes! That's exactly what I thought! Because that was the fucking plan! We're in, we're out, and nobody can do shit about it because they're all trapped on the other side of town." Toby reached down and yanked the screwdriver from the dirt. He took a step toward Rusty and pointed the screwdriver at him.

"You killed an unarmed man."

"He wasn't entirely unarmed," Rusty said as he raised his shotgun and pointed it at Toby. "The man was holding scissors. You could kill someone with scissors, ya' know—same as you could kill someone with that screwdriver."

Toby stared down the barrel of the shotgun for the second time that day. Rusty's threat was loud and clear, and he dropped the hand holding the screwdriver back to his side. Behind him, Brian and Josh sat in silent anticipation.

"Fine," Toby said, "we divvy this shit up and then we go our separate ways."

Now it was Josh that stood up and entered the conversation. "You don't think that'll look just a little suspicious?"

"He's right," Rusty said. "Us four lovers have been palling around every day for the last two years. Small town like this, cops will notice if you go breaking up the band, Toby."

Shit! Toby thought. *He's right.* He stood there, battling with his own emotions for some time. Finally, he accepted that what was done was done and there was no changing it. Phil Whitman was dead, the house was burning, and the bank was robbed. He turned back to the safety deposit box at his feet and went to work at it again with the screwdriver.

Rusty lowered the shotgun. "That's better."

Brian and Josh both breathed an audible sigh of relief now that there no longer seemed to be the prospect of their friends killing each other. Then they went back to work on their respective boxes.

Josh was the next one to get a box open, and upon looking at the contents he erupted in laughter.

"Holy shit!" he said. "You guys aren't gonna believe this!"

The others stopped messing with their own boxes and watched as Josh reached into the open box at his feet and pulled out a handful of women's underwear, and they certainly weren't of the conservative variety.

"No shit?!?" Rusty exclaimed. Even Toby cracked a smile.

"Oh wait," Josh said, "it gets better." He reached back into the box and pulled out a stack of Polaroid photographs. He started to flip through the photos, going faster as he neared the end of the stack. The grin on his face was so big Toby feared it might actually do some kind of medical damage.

"Come on, Goddammit!" Brian shouted, buckling under the anticipation. "What are they?"

Josh didn't answer, he simply passed the stack of photos to Brian as the tears of laughter streamed down his face. Brian looked at the first three photos in the stack and then burst into his own laughing fit.

Rusty, getting visibly irritated that he wasn't in on the joke said, "Alright you cock knockers, what the hell is it?!?"

Brian pulled himself together long enough to say, "Well boys, it appears to be...pussy." With that, Josh and Brian went to pieces again. Now Toby and Rusty both got up and walked over to Brian with their hands stuck out. They each took a stack of photos and started to sort through them. Each picture contained the image of a random woman. All of the women were naked and in a variety of positions, and they were all showing the camera what Toby's mother would have called their "lady business."

"Jesus," Toby remarked. "You think we know any of them?"

Rusty shook his head. "It's hard to say. Doesn't look like you can see any of the faces in any of these, but come on—if these broads are local you gotta figure we know at least some of them, right?" Rusty flipped to the last photograph in the stack, and then he started laughing too. "Holy fuck! Look at this one!"

He turned the Polaroid around for the other three to see. They stared with wide eyed fascination at the woman in the picture. As with the other photos, the woman's face wasn't visible, but almost every other part of her anatomy was. She was kneeling on a bed, bent over in front of the camera and she had a very impressive red dildo sticking out of her ass.

"Now *that* is a talented woman!" Brain said as he slipped into another laughing fit.

Josh picked the safety deposit box up off the ground and turned it over in his hands, hoping it contained more lude treasures. It did indeed. The same large, red sex toy that was in the photo Rusty was holding slid down to the opening in the box where it became lodged grotesquely.

Toby looked at the slick rubber object in the box and then back to the obscene photo in Rusty's hand. "No way. You think that's the same one?"

The question set them all squealing with laughter again. Finally Rusty answered him. "Man, does it really matter? My question is why would some guy keep all this shit in the bank?"

"Wait," Brian chimed in, "how do we know it's a guy?"

Rusty looked back down at Josh. "Is there anything else in that box that tells you who it belonged to?"

"Well, it's kinda hard to see around the giant rubber cock, but there doesn't seem to be any other identifiable items," Josh said with a sarcastic laugh.

"I guess it's safer than a shoebox in the closet," Toby added. "I mean, if you were into some seriously kinky shit and didn't want your wife—or husband—to find out about it, why not keep it all in a safety deposit box? It'd definitely stay safe, and if you trust the bankers you can pretty much rest assured that you'd be the only one that could get access to the contents."

The other three stared at him for several seconds and then they all chuckled again. Rusty threw the photos back down in the dirt at Josh's feet.

"This shit may be funny," Rusty said, "but unless that dildo is made of gold or we can use these photos to blackmail some rich housewife, none of it does us much good."

Josh's discovery had certainly offered some much needed light-heartedness, but they all knew Rusty was right. They'd all had a hand in burning down a house, robbing a bank, and killing a man. They needed those boxes to contain more than just dirty photos for them to justify their actions in their own minds. Josh put the photos back into the box and then they all went back to busting open new boxes.

Another half an hour went by and they'd managed to raise their spirits a little more when Toby cracked open a box of jewelry. They all inspected the items closely, discarding any pieces that had personal inscriptions on it (no sense in risking getting caught if they tried to pawn the stuff) and threw the jewelry in the bag with the cash. They guessed, conservatively that the jewelry added another $5,000 to their total haul.

As they neared the end of the process of inventorying their loot, they all seemed to be comfortable with what they had so far. Several more valuable items and two more stashes of cash brought their total to somewhere around $40,000. None of the guys were able to suppress their grins as they worked open the last of the deposit boxes.

Rusty was loading the loot into the bed of the International Harvester while the other three worked on the last of the boxes. Josh and Bryan both struck out with their boxes, dumping nothing but worthless junk into the dirt. When Toby got his box open his first impression was that he'd struck out as well, and that the contents were nothing but worthless keepsakes. There was an assortment of keys, a dozen or so bottle caps, and there was also jewelry, which should have elicited some kind of excitement.

But this jewelry was strange.

None of it seemed to be of any value. There was no gold or silver; no pearls. It was all cheap plastic and cosmetic. Most of it looked like it could be bought for a buck in the toy aisle at Carl's Grocery. It was that observation that was the most disturbing to Toby. He was holding children's play jewelry.

He tilted the box and more of its contents slid down into the opening. Toby swallowed hard as he looked at what had fallen to the ground. The situation was no longer disturbing—it was frightening.

At Toby's feet were several bunches of hair, each one bound tight with a rubber band. They were all different colors. More items had fallen out of the box and landed at his feet. At first Toby's brain couldn't process what the tiny white objects were. He picked them up, one by one, and held them in his open palm. Once he had half a dozen resting there in his hand the realization of what he was holding hit him. His blood turned to ice.

They were teeth.

More specifically, they were small teeth. They were children's teeth.

"Jesus Christ!" Toby yelled as he dropped the teeth back on the ground. The others stopped what they were doing and looked at Toby.

"What's the problem!?!" Rusty asked.

"This one's got fucking baby teeth in it, man!" Toby replied.

Rusty shrugged. "Lots of people hang on to their kids' teeth when they fall out. Don't be such a pussy."

Rusty made a good point, and Toby could even use that same rationale to explain the locks of hair, but something wasn't sitting right with him. He picked up the safety deposit box again and shook it to see if it contained any more items. No more objects fell out, so Toby slid his hand into the box to feel for any papers that might identify the owner.

There was something else in the box, wedged at the very back. Toby got a hold of it and pulled it out. This time he kept holding the item and dropped the security box instead. The metal box clanging on the ground startled the other three and someone—probably Rusty—had asked Toby what his fucking problem was. Toby didn't answer, and if he'd even heard the question he gave no indication. He simply stared in horror at the item in his hands.

He'd seen it many times before. Once he'd even soaked it in water and stuck it in the freezer just to make Becky cry when she'd discovered it frozen stiff.

It was his sister's doll—Strawberry Shortcake. Toby ran his thumbnail over the image of a strawberry on the doll's cheek and could smell the faint

chemical scent of strawberry. The last time he had seen the doll was on the

day his sister had gone missing six years earlier.

It had been sticking out of a fanny pack she'd been wearing around

her waist.

***

The rest of that afternoon was a blur for Toby Linkladder. He didn't tell the other boys why he'd reacted so strangely to the bizarre items in the box, and he hoped they just contributed his behavior to a case of the jitters based on everything that had happened that day.

He could vaguely remember them stashing the cash and moveable jewelry in bags and hanging them high in the rafters of the barn; their intention was to leave the loot for some time before they went back for it, which they hoped would prevent any of them from blowing their cut on something extravagant and drawing unnecessary attention from the law.

The traceable items and useless junk went back into the security boxes, and in turn were driven back to Baker Creek and thrown into the rushing water at various points along the bank.

Not all of the "junk" made it back into the boxes, though. Toby had managed to hide the contents of his last box in his pockets without the others seeing. Strawberry Shortcake had been forced to make the trip back to town in the far more uncomfortable location in the small of Toby's back, tucked into the waist band of his trousers and covered by his shirt.

They'd managed to avoid roadblocks on the way back into town, and by the time Toby jumped out of the back of the pickup truck and walked up his porch steps the sun was going down and Barker Marsh was bathed in the sienna glow of dusk.

Toby's mother worked nights over at the Westbrook resort in Draper, washing linens, so he had the house to himself. He walked to his bedroom

at the back of the house and turned on his stereo before collapsing onto his

bed. The radio was tuned to WBKR, "The Rock of the Marsh." Toby

found it strange that a town that only had one traffic light was apparently

big enough to have its own radio station. Bill Stearn had been The Rock's

disc jockey for as long as Toby could remember, and aside from the

occasional political rant—Stearn was a devout democrat and liberal—he

played a pretty good stream of classic rock. Tonight, however, Stearn broke

the evening "rock block" with what he called a "platter full of breaking

news."

It was a platter-full alright, and Toby had a hand in every bit of it. Ol'

Wild Bill laid everything out right there on the air. The old Marsters place

had burned to the ground, the First National Bank of Barker Marsh had

been robbed, and old man Phil Whitman had been gunned down in the

street in the process. That was certainly some heavy shit to process, but

Toby was focused on something else.

He pulled the strange items out of his pockets and placed them on the

nightstand next to his bed. He didn't set Strawberry Shortcake down,

though. He held the doll lovingly and then wiped tears from his cheeks.

Toby thought of his sister, and he also thought of a number.

247

That was the number on the safety deposit box that held the doll and the other strange items. He memorized it before throwing the empty box into Baker Creek. That three digit number could change his life forever, and Toby knew it. Something deep down told Toby that whoever owned box 247 was responsible for his sister's disappearance. His misspent youth, his mother's depression and grief—it could all be answered for, *if* he told the authorities what he'd found in that box.

But if he did that he'd also be implicating himself in almost half a dozen capital crimes, up to and including murder. A sickening feeling crept into Toby's stomach as he considered this. He knew that a decent person, and a good brother, wouldn't have thought twice about going to the authorities. Toby was torn by the question of whether or not he had any decency left in him. Could he go the Sheriff and turn himself in, finally bringing justice and peace to his sister? Or had the Marsh sunk its evil fangs in him too far to salvage anything good?

When Toby closed his eyes and drifted off to sleep these questions were still fresh on his mind.

***

Toby had terrible nightmares that evening, most of which he couldn't remember when he woke the following morning. One dream stuck with him, though, its details so clear and vivid he might as well have been watching his favorite movie.

In it, Toby, Rusty, Josh, and Brian were all coming out of First National again, having just robbed the bank and ready to make their getaway. The dream continued to follow the actual events of the day as Phil Whitman stepped out of his barber shop and yelled "What's going on over there?"

At this point in the dream Toby knew what was coming next, and he looked over at Rusty just in time to see the boy raise the shotgun and shoot Phil Whitman in the chest.

Now the dream started to deviate from what had actually happened. Instead of jumping in the car and speeding away, Toby ran toward the dying man on the sidewalk. He prepared himself to see the bloodied remains of the town barber, but what he actually saw as he stood over the body was more terrifying than anything he could have imagined.

It wasn't Phil Whitman lying at his feet, but his sister, Becky. Her chest had been perforated by the shotgun blast and he could hear a wet, wheezing sound coming from somewhere deep in the wound. In one hand she held Strawberry Shortcake. The doll was covered in freckles of bright, red blood. Becky's other hand reached up for Toby. She attempted to speak but was only able to produce a bloody bubble that grew from her lips before popping and leaving a streak of dark crimson on her cheek. Toby wanted to wipe the blood away but when he brought his hands forward he saw that *he* was holding the smoking shotgun. Becky expelled another bloody bubble, and this time she was able to produce a sound.

"W-w-why?" she whispered.

Toby wanted to tell her that he didn't know, that he didn't mean to shoot her and that he was sorry he left her in the front yard by herself, but now it was Toby that was unable to make a sound.

There was a clicking sound behind him and Toby turned to see another shotgun barrel pointed directly at his face. The opening of the barrel looked big enough to swallow him up. The figure holding the weapon was shrouded in shadow and Toby couldn't see his face. Then the figure spoke in a voice too deep to be natural.

"Let it go," the voice said.

Toby never had a chance to reply. The figure pulled the trigger and there was a blinding light.

Toby Linkladder awoke from the dream screaming and drenched in sweat. He brought his hands up to make sure his face was still there. When he was confident that his head had not been blown off he thought back to what the figure in his dream had said to him.

Let it go.

He understood what the figure meant, and who it was supposed to represent, but Toby had no intention of letting anything go. He'd made up his mind.

He was going to the Sheriff's station.

***

The receptionist at the Barker Marsh Sheriff's station must have been in a bad mood. The condescension was thick when she referred to him as *Mr. Linkladder*, and informed him that the Sheriff was extremely busy. She asked him if he was aware of the tragic events that had happened the day before.

Toby told her he'd heard something about it on the radio.

She asked him if he had any idea what kind of workload that put on the Sheriff.

He said he did.

When she realized that he wasn't going to leave voluntarily, the woman told Toby he could wait in the lobby, but it might be a very long time before the Sheriff came back.

Toby told her that was fine, he'd wait.

And so he waited.

Ordinarily he'd have been a nervous wreck waiting on the Sheriff, but Toby was surprisingly calm. He thought about what a strange relationship he had with Ted Christie for half of his life. Christie was the Sheriff now, but once upon a time he'd been the deputy who his mother had spoken with when his sister had gone missing, and he'd been the deputy who had taken Toby into custody for burning John Morland's van. Toby had an odd kind of respect for the Sheriff. He almost looked at the man as a kind of uncle that he saw every few years or so, and somehow this put Toby at ease when he thought about what it was that he needed to say.

Toby only had to wait until lunch to actually say it.

***

"We're a little busy around here," Sheriff Christie said as he and Toby each took a seat on opposite sides of the Sheriff's desk. "What's on your mind, son?"

"Do you remember when my sister disappeared, Sheriff?" Toby regretted asking the question as soon as it came out. That was a stupid way to start the conversation.

Sheriff Christie could have replied many different ways, several of which would have made Toby feel like an idiot. Instead, he simply said, "Yes, I do."

Toby wasn't sure where to go from here. He froze. He'd hoped to work up to the point in the conversation where he would tell the Sheriff about his involvement in the prior day's events. However, his stupid opening question had left him with no choice but to lay everything out on the table.

"Sheriff," Toby said. "I think I have some information that might help find out what happened to her."

The Sheriff frowned, and Toby's palms began to sweat. Christie sighed heavily and removed his round brimmed hat, which he dropped on his desk before replying. "Toby, I understand that you and your momma have been through a lot—with your sister going missing and your little trouble soon after, and son, I'd love to hear what you've got to say, but I'm in the middle of trying to solve an arson, robbery, and murder all at the same time. Now how 'bout you come back in a couple of weeks and tell me all about your idea."

Toby shook his head. For a moment he thought of following Sheriff Christie's advice and waiting a couple of weeks. Maybe by then he'd change his mind all together and let the whole awful business go. But then he thought about Becky again, and he pressed on.

"I know something about all of that stuff too, Sheriff," Toby said. There was no turning back now. The cards were on the table and Toby tried to stay focused on his ultimate goal of solving his sister's disappearance.

"How's that, now?" Christie said, leaning forward in his chair.

"I know about everything that happened yesterday," Toby said.

"And why is that?"

Toby cleared his throat. It was time to go all in. "I started the fire at the Marsters place." Toby waited for the Sheriff to say something, but the big man on the other side of the desk only looked at him with cold eyes, so Toby continued. "And I was involved in the robbery. I didn't shoot old Mr. Whitman, but I know who did."

"O.K., who?" Christie said.

Toby was surprised at himself that he never hesitated for a moment. "Rusty Tomlinson shot him. And Brian Wells was there and Josh Ray, too. And me."

Sheriff Christie laid his hands out flat on the desk and Toby could see the muscles in his forearms flex. For an instant he thought the Sheriff was about to beat him to death. Instead he exhaled through his clenched teeth. When he spoke again his voice was controlled and full of authority.

"Listen to me very carefully," the Sheriff said. "What you're saying is goddamn serious, Toby. It's probably the most serious thing you've ever said, or are ever gonna say, you understand me?"

Toby nodded. He understood, but the Sheriff was wrong. In Toby's mind confessing to the prior day's crimes wasn't the most serious thing he was ever going to say, but telling him what he'd found in box 247 *was*.

"Now I need you to tell me," Christie continued. "Are you telling the truth?"

Toby nodded again.

"O.K., then. I have to arrest you, Toby. Do you understand?"

Toby nodded.

"You have the right to remain silent. Anything you say can be used against you in court, do you understand that?"

Toby nodded.

"You have the right to an attorney. If you can't afford one the court will provide one for you. Do you understand?"

Toby nodded.

"I need you to answer me, son. Do you understands your rights?"

"Yes," Toby said. "I understand."

Christie removed a form from his desk drawer and picked up an ink pen out of the coffee mug in front of him. He took a minute to fill in some information on the form, then he looked back up at Toby. "O.K., start from the beginning."

Toby did start from the beginning. He told the Sheriff about how the four of them had come up with the plan, about burning the Marsters place, robbing the bank, and Rusty shooting Phil Whitman. He told him about Baker Creek and the barn where everything was stashed. When Christie asked what all of this had to do with his sister, Toby told him about box 247 and what was inside it. When he was done Sheriff Christie pinched the bridge of his nose and closed his eyes.

"So what happens now?" Toby asked.

"Well, now I've got to check out your story. I'm gonna drive out to that barn. If the stuff is there then I'm gonna bring in your friends."

"What about my sister?" Toby asked. "And box 247?"

"I'll send an officer to your house to check it out. You said everything, uhh—" Christie looked down at his notes. "—the hair, the teeth, and the doll are in your room?"

Toby nodded. "That's right."

"We'll find out who used that box and go from there, but look Toby, this whole thing is complicated, and you're still in a hell of a lot of trouble."

The Sheriff stood up then. "For now, I gotta lock you up here until we can get you over to County, you understand?"

"Yes, sir," Toby said.

Christie had Toby empty his pockets then and remove his belt before he frisked him to make sure he had no weapons. After that the two walked out of the Sheriff's office and down the hall to the single holding cell at the far end of the building. Toby stepped inside and Christie locked the sliding door behind him. The Sheriff started to walk away without a word, but after a few steps he stopped and turned back around.

"Toby, let me ask you something," he said as he stood in front of the cell once more. "If you hadn't found that stuff in the box, if you didn't believe this was gonna help with your sister's case, would you still have come to me? Would you have confessed?"

Toby thought about the question before answering, and then finally he did. "Yes."

Christie nodded. "For what it's worth, son, I believe you would have."

With that, the Sheriff turned and walked away.

***

It was four days before Toby spoke to the Sheriff again. Barker Marsh had more than its share of strange and tragic events, but never before had so much happened in such a short time span.

The Sheriff had driven out to the abandoned barn to search for the money and jewelry from the robbery. The bags had not been in the rafters, as Toby had said. From there he decided to bring in Rusty Tomlinson, Brian Wells, and Josh Ray for questioning anyway.

Upon arriving at Rusty Tomlinson's home, Sheriff Christie found Rusty's stepmother standing in the driveway, screaming frantically at him. She told the Sheriff that Rusty and his friend, Brian Wells, had loaded her van with bags and guns and driven off. She seemed less concerned with the fate of her son than she did with getting her mini-van back.

The Sheriff assumed that Rusty and Brian had double-crossed Toby, and possibly Josh Ray, and made a run with the money from the robbery. Having gotten the information he needed from Rusty's mother, his next port of call was Josh Ray's home.

Josh had been home when Christie knocked on his door, and if there was any question as to the boy's knowledge or involvement with Rusty's and Brian's double-cross, it was cleared up when Josh collapsed into a sniveling wreck after hearing the accusations made against him. He immediately confessed to the robbery and was taken to the county jail, so as to keep him separated from Toby Linkladder. In the meantime, Sheriff

Christie launched a manhunt for Rusty Tomlinson and Brian Wells.

It took less than 18 hours to find them.

They had driven thirty miles to a town called Ripley, where they rented a cheap motel room. What they were doing in Ripley no one would ever know. The only reason the motel owner even took notice is that neither of his guests had a credit card to put on file for room damages, but they offered the proprietor $500 in cash as collateral instead. Nine out of ten small business owners would have kept their mouths shut, happy to just have the business. This particular businessman, however, immediately gave the two men a room and then dialed the Ripley police department, telling the dispatcher "that something wasn't right about the two guys." The owner gave the police the license number off the minivan the two men were driving and within ten minutes, and thirty miles away, the phone on Sheriff Ted Christie's desk started to ring. An hour after that Christie, along with twenty more officers made up of both the Barker Marsh Sheriff's department and Ripley Police surrounded the Wayward Inn.

Christie had addressed Rusty and Brian through a bullhorn, running the typical police jargon: *We've got you surrounded. Give yourself up. Don't make this harder than it has to be.*

The two suspects answered by busting out a window and opening fire on the officers outside.

The uniformed officers, many of whom had never drawn their

weapons on the job before, returned the gunfire. The exchange only lasted twenty seconds, and when Sheriff Christie's command to cease fire was finally heard over the barrage, the property around the Wayward Inn was eerily quiet, for a moment.

Just as Ted Christie picked up the bullhorn in an attempt to draw out some sort of productive civil exchange with Brian and Rusty, the silence was shattered by a deep, bellowing gunshot. A few officers returned fire, but Christie quickly wrangled the task force in. After ten minutes of trying to talk the boys down through the bull horn, Christie and a dozen officers rushed the door of the motel room. There wasn't much left of the door itself, so it didn't take much force to break it down. The task force rushed into the room, prepared to engage in a close quarters shootout with the two suspects.

They need not have worried.

Brian Wells lay in a crumpled heap just inside the door. Four of the bullets had apparently found their mark, and he'd been struck in the leg, twice in the chest, and once in the throat. He'd bled to death before the officers could get to him.

Rusty Tomlinson lay further in the room. He'd apparently seen that there was no hope for escape or winning a gunfight against twenty armed officers. The final gunshot the officers had heard was Rusty placing the barrel of a shotgun—the same one that had killed Phil Whitman back in

Barker Marsh—in his mouth and pulling the trigger. The upper portion of Rusty Tomlinson's head was splashed on the ceiling above the bed. A good sized portion of flesh and hair dropped to the floor with a wet splat and two of the Ripley officers quickly retreated out of the room before the contents of their stomachs were retched up onto the ground. It seemed that the officers from Barker Marsh were a little more accustomed to seeing the kind of horrible carnage that was drying on the ceiling in that motel room.

Sheriff Christie and his men recovered several duffle bags from the room and all but $400 was accounted for from the robbery.

It was the following day when the Sheriff finally got around to checking on box 247. Toby Linkladder had told him about the strange contents of the box, but it wasn't until he was standing in the young man's room, dropping the teeth and hair into an evidence bag that Ted Christie realized just how creepy the situation actually was. He left Toby's home and drove up town to the First National Bank of Barker Marsh.

He entered the bank and Mickie Green, the bank's president, came out to greet him. She invited Sheriff Christie into her office, and once inside the Sheriff asked her to see a ledger showing the stolen safety deposit boxes, and their respective owners. When Mickie Green returned moments later with a thick, leather bound journal he grinned when he opened the cover. Christie had been expecting a somewhat modern computer printout, but this book and its records were all hand written. Each page was divided into several columns within which you could jot down a member's name, the date they opened an account, and in this case, their account number or safety deposit box number, if they had one.

The Sheriff traced his finger down the page, searching for the number 247. When he got to the third page he found it, and then drug his finger over to the Name column. Written there was a name he recognized.

Harold Davis.

Not many folks knew the man as "Harold" Davis. Most folks in town only knew him as "Hasty" Davis. Christie himself couldn't remember exactly where the nickname came from, but Hasty had been Hasty for as far back as he could recall.

One could guess as to how old Hasty Davis actually was, but there was really no telling. He was one of those guys that had lived a tough life, and liquor and cigarettes had a way of aging someone prematurely. He'd lived in Barker Marsh for a long time, but he hadn't been born in the area, and he had no other family to verify his age, or where he came from. It was as if one day he just drifted into town and stuck around, but nobody could pinpoint exactly when that had been.

Once upon a time Hasty had been a city employee, and that's how Ted Christie had briefly interacted with the man. He'd been a rookie deputy at the time, and Hasty was essentially the groundskeeper and maintenance man for the village of Barker Marsh. If the outfield needed mowing at the town ballpark or a dead animal needed to be scraped up off of Dwyer Avenue then Hasty was the man for the job. Occasionally it was drag racing teenagers that needed scraping up and Hasty would help with that too. It was on those nights that Ted Christie had gotten to know him.

Christie racked his brain on his trip out to Hasty Davis's house, trying to remember when the man had retired from city employment. The Sheriff found that Hasty's departure from public service was as covert as his arrival in the town many years before. There was just no pinpointing the exact date. Christie didn't even feel comfortable spit balling a year. Hasty was still doing odd jobs around town—cutting grass, mending fences, stuff like that—but he was doing all that on his own now, not as a city employee.

There was no denying that Hasty Davis was a strange guy, but keeping children's teeth, hair, and toys in a safety deposit box went beyond weird. If Toby Linkladder's suspicions were correct, Hasty was potentially responsible for the disappearance of seven or more young girls. It was with this thought that Sheriff Christie pulled into the rocky driveway in front of Hasty Davis's home. He put the cruiser in park and then pulled his revolver out of his holster, swung the cylinder open to check that he had a full six shots, and then re-holstered.

Christie's deputy, Keith Hudgins, watched his boss from the passenger seat and then removed his own pistol and checked it in the same way.

Hudgins asked the Sheriff if he was expecting trouble with Hasty Davis, and Christie told him that if the last 48 hours were any indication of the condition of people's mental states he was not going to take any chances.

Both officers walked up the drive and then mounted a few steps to a wooden front porch that had seen far better days.

Any police officer in the world will tell you that one of the most nerve wracking things about the job is knocking on a suspect's door. There's always a part of a cop's mind that expects a shotgun blast to tear through the door at that exact moment. Much to Christie's relief, his chest wasn't shredded, and the interior door swung open slowly instead.

Harold "Hasty" Davis stood there, staring at Ted Christie. He had a strange little grin on his face and it widened into an actual smile as a sense of recognition came over him.

"Lou!" Hasty said. The man stuck his hand out, and out of instinct Sheriff Christie took it and pumped it up and down. Ted Christie had never in his life been known as "Lou," but he remembered that old Hasty Davis called everyone Lou from time to time. Why? Nobody knew, but it didn't take long for someone to realize that old Hasty's elevator didn't go all the way to the top floor.

Christie asked if he and deputy Hudgins could come in and chat with him a moment. The Sheriff was a little surprised when Hasty ushered them both inside without a moment's hesitation. He didn't even bother to ask what it was the Sheriff and Hudgins wanted to ask him about. He simply opened his home up to them, as if he was thrilled just to have the company.

The two officers sat on a couch while Hasty simply sat across from them on the floor, Indian-style. The Sheriff started the conversation by telling Hasty they were there as part of their investigation of the bank robbery earlier that week. They explained that Hasty's safety deposit box had been stolen and that he and deputy Hudgins were meeting with all of the owners of those boxes to put together a list of the contents so that they could start canvassing local pawn shops and other, less reputable establishments.

The Sheriff had paused then, looking at Hasty and waiting for some kind of nervous reaction, but the man simply nodded and told the officers he was happy to help. Hasty verified that box 247 was indeed his, and he told them that there wasn't anything of much value in the box—just some old family photos and baseball cards that had belonged to his father.

Ted Christie sat quietly for a moment and simply looked at Hasty Davis. The man was either a very good liar or Toby Linkladder had gotten his wires crossed about which box the teeth, hair, and doll had come out of. Either way, it dawned on Christie how thin all of the evidence was, anyway. No judge in the state would sign off on a search warrant to bring Hasty in, even if the man did seem to be hiding something, and he certainly did not. It would seem that the only thing Hasty Davis was clearly guilty of was being strange, and arresting a man for being strange in Barker Marsh was like arresting a fish for being wet.

The Sheriff stood then, a little frustrated at his own quickness to put so much faith into what Toby Linkladder had told him. So as not to convey his frustration to Hasty, or more importantly his deputy, Christie chalked it all up to exhaustion as a result of the events of the previous three days. He ordered Hudgins to take a detailed report from Hasty as to the complete contents of his box, and then he asked Hasty if he could use his bathroom. Hasty pointed him in the right direction and then the Sheriff walked down the hall, cursing to himself as he went.

Christie entered the small bathroom and closed the door behind him. As he unzipped his trousers and took care of business, he surveyed the cramped bathroom and marveled at the realization that—although he might be a little nuts—Hasty Davis was impeccably clean. The bathroom was spotless. The white toilet bowl had not a stain on it, the trash can was completely empty, and there wasn't so much as a speck on any of the fixtures or the mirror. Christie was a bachelor himself, and quite familiar with the usual, lazy attributes of a bachelor's bathroom, but the water closet he currently found himself in was so spotless it might as well have been in a high end hotel in St. Louis.

The Sheriff performed the mandatory three shakes, zipped up, and then moved over to the basin to wash his hands. At the same time, the air conditioner in the old house kicked on. The home had a central air system, so Christie looked down at the vent in the floor as a sudden wave of cool air crept up his pant leg. He shut off the faucet and that's when the smell hit him.

It was a putrid smell with a faint, underlying sweetness to it. Only one thing smelled like that and Ted Christie had been around enough decaying dead bodies to recognize the scent at once.

He stayed in the bathroom a few more minutes, gathering his wits. Earlier he'd thought to himself that no judge would issue a warrant based on the evidence they had up to that point. But now Christie would swear that somewhere in that house something was dead. He felt like that would be enough to get a search warrant.

He was right.

***

Christie had a search warrant in hand by that evening, and the following morning a State Police forensic team arrived from Springfield. Two of the investigators entered the crawlspace under Harold "Hasty" Davis's house with methane probes. It took them less than ten minutes to find the first body. By that evening the team dug up a total of 12 victims, in varying stages of decomposition. Initial observation suggested that none of the victims had been much older than early teens at the most, and several were far younger.

Hasty Davis was arrested.

Four days after Toby Linkladder had turned himself in, Sheriff Christie visited him in the County lockup and told him everything that had happened in the previous 72 hours. He told him about Josh Ray's arrest, which Toby took pretty well, and about the shootout with Rusty Tomlinson and Brian Wells, which he took a little harder. Then the Sheriff told him that Harold "Hasty" Davis had been arrested and charged with twelve counts of murder. Toby asked if it was Hasty who had kept the bizarre trophies in box 247, and Christie told him it looked that way. He told Toby that his turning himself in and providing the information he did should earn him some points with the judge regarding his own case. At that exact moment Toby didn't seem to care. He asked the Sheriff if they'd found his sister. Christie told him that nothing was confirmed yet and that the state police were running tests on the remains to determine the identities of the victims.

Toby asked the Sheriff if he would come back and tell him as soon as they identified the remains. Christie told him that he wouldn't be able to do that, as any findings would be part of a major investigation.

Toby said he understood.

A week later the Sheriff stood outside of Toby's cell. The big man didn't say a word, he just looked at Toby, nodded once and then Toby knew. He thanked the Sheriff as tears began to flow down his cheeks. As Ted Christie turned and walked away, he heard Toby Linkladder say one more thing, to no one in particular.

"Rest easy, sis."

***

Toby Linkladder was sentenced to 20 years in prison for his participation in the arson, robbery of First National Bank of Barker Marsh, and the murder of Phil Whitman.

Josh Ray was sentenced to 25.

Both were assigned to the federal penitentiary in Marion, and ultimately that's what saved their lives.

They're still incarcerated today.

Toby is eligible for parole in two years.

***

Harold "Hasty" Davis was charged with 12 counts of kidnapping and murder. An unknown reserve of funds had bought Hasty a very good lawyer, and instead of receiving the death penalty, Hasty was declared mentally unfit, and was sentenced to a life term in the Hoffner Falls institute for the criminally insane, conveniently located just outside of Barker Marsh.

Seven years later Hasty died in a fire that consumed Hoffner Falls, along with the rest of the village of Barker Marsh.

Chapter 4

"As the train sped through the darkness

And the raging storm outside

No one knew that Hobo Bill

Was taking his last ride"

—Rodgers, Jimmie. "Hobo Bill's Last Ride." Victor Talking Machine

Company, 1929

"That's bullshit," said the Drifter.

"Which part?" Hasty asked. "The part about me killing a dozen little girls or the fact that I'm dead?" He waited a moment for the Drifter to respond, but it soon became clear that Hasty's last tale had rendered the man a bit speechless. That or the Drifter was subscribing to Hasty's mother's rule and couldn't think of anything nice to say at the moment. "Oh, that's O.K., Lou. I guess both ideas throw you for a fucking loop, huh?" He broke out in another laughing fit.

"Just stop!" yelled the Drifter. "Fuck the being dead thing right now. If you made the thing up about murdering kids you're fucking nuts! And if you're telling the truth…well…you're still fucking nuts. So let's assume for a minute that you really did those things. Tell me why."

"Why does an artist paint? Why does a writer write? See I told you that this town made a lot of people real bad, but I was born that way. I can't help the fact that I was a murderer, Lou. I was born with the devil looking over my shoulder, and I suppose he's been with me ever since. Or maybe he's a she, if you still believe that story about the Klein girl."

The Drifter shook his head, trying to process everything Hasty was telling him. "And you're dead, is that what you're saying?"

"You betcha," Hasty answered. "Dead as Disco."

"So then what, you're a ghost or something?"

"Hell if I know, Lou. All I knows is I fried like a chicken gizzard the night this town went up in flames. Them assholes at Hoffner Falls kept us locked in our rooms at night, and the fire that took us spread so quick that the orderlies didn't bother trying to get us out. I can remember seeing the piss green paint bubble up on the walls of my cell from the heat, and I can remember a really bad smell—like burned bacon—that turned out to be me. Then I remember pain. The worst pain I ever felt, Lou. Then it was gone and I was standing on the railroad tracks, not more'n three hundred feet from where we sit right now."

"Do you know what started the fire?" the Drifter asked.

"Sure as hell do! But it ain't so much 'what' started it as 'who.' But that's a looong story. It's a good one, though. Hell, it's the best one! It explains why this place is the way it is." Hasty eyed the Drifter carefully.

"You sure you got the time to hear it, Lou?"

"Storm doesn't seem to be letting up at all, so I got nowhere to be, and according to you, you have all the time in the world, Hasty."

"And then some," Hasty said. With that he removed two items from his inside coat pocket. They appeared to be books; one relatively new and one that looked very, very old.

"What are those?" asked the Drifter.

"Journals," Hasty answered. "I told you this was a long one, Lou. You want the whole picture you're gonna have to stick around for a spell."

The Drifter took another swig from the bottle of whiskey Hasty had given him, and then said, "Are you kidding? I'm not gonna pass up the chance to hear a ghost story from an actual ghost."

Hasty smiled, and began.

***

The Burning

"You know that it would be untrue

You know that I would be a liar

If I was to say to you

Girl, we couldn't get much higher

Come on baby light my fire

Come on baby light my fire

Try to set the night on, fire"

—Doors, The. "Light My Fire." *The Doors*, Elektra, 1967

Secrets are hard to live with. But like anything else, the more you practice something the easier it gets. Eddie Willis was practically a professional secret keeper. Some of his secrets were small, some were big, and two were so great that he'd spent most of his adult life trying to forget them.

But when Eddie was asleep—when he dreamed—the details of his two biggest secrets would slam into his subconscious mind like a coal train; the images so vivid that Eddie would wake up screaming and thrashing in his bed. Thankfully the nightmares were coming much less frequently than they used to, but they hadn't gone away for good. Once every few months he'd drink a little too much and collapse on the bed with his alcohol steeped mind still firing, and that's when he'd dream about them. It was always one or the other—he never dreamt about both of them in the same night.

Tonight it was Sister Agnes.

The powerful scent of Fiddes & Sons furniture polish filled his nostrils and he knew then that he was dreaming. Normally this realization would snap him out of other dreams. He'd had plenty of sexual fantasies cut tragically short by this phenomenon. But that trick never worked when he dreamt about Sister Agnes. He couldn't make himself wake up, even though he knew he was dreaming.

He was twelve years old again, and he was in trouble. He should have been outside, enjoying recess with the rest of his classmates at Saint Benedict, but he was stuck inside the church with Sister Agnes because he'd placed a dead cockroach on top of Brenda Cartwright's head. The girls in class had screamed, but the boys—even his stick in the mud brother, Donald—had laughed their asses off. Sister Agnes did not laugh. She'd thrown an eraser at him, which connected perfectly with his forehead, and happily informed him that he'd be spending his recess with her.

So there he was, freezing his ass off in the high loft that overlooked the rest of the church. He had the can of Fiddes & Sons open and he was vigorously polishing the great organ that was the centerpiece of the balcony. Behind him, Sister Agnes was draping ivy garland over the low railing that protected the choir from plummeting forty feet to the pews below. He'd had this dream many times, so Eddie knew what Sister Agnes was about to say.

"Are you asking God for forgiveness, Edward?"

"Yes, Sister."

"You do *want* to be forgiven, don't you, Edward?"

Eddie nodded without turning around. "Yes, Sister."

"That's good, because you know what would happen if you didn't ask for forgiveness don't you? You know what would happen if you were run over by a car on your way home today without asking for the forgiveness of your sins? You'd burn in hell, Edward. You don't want to burn in hell, do you?"

Eddie stopped polishing and turned to her, shaking his head. "No, Sister."

He meant it. He didn't want to burn in hell.

Sister Agnes picked up a large wreath made of poinsettias. "Good. Then I'd also suggest that you confess to Father Stanley on Sunday and tell him what you did to poor Brenda."

Eddie turned and looked at Sister Agnes. "Yes, Sister." She was leaning over the railing, trying to hang the large wreath on a nail somewhere far below the top of the railing. For a split second Eddie thought of pushing Sister Agnes over the railing and instantly regretted the thought. At that time in his life, Catholic guilt still had a powerful hold on him, and Eddie feared that the mere thought of pushing the nun to her death was as good as making a reservation in hell.

Eddie immediately repented, closed his eyes, and started to pray to himself. *Forgive me my sins, O Lord; forgive me the sins of my youth and the sins of mine age, the sins of my soul and the sins*—Sister Agnes's scream cut his prayer short.

Eddie's eyes snapped open just in time to see the nun's feet flipping over the railing. A second later Eddie could only see Sister Agnes's ten fingers gripping the balcony railing. Then she began to call to him.

"Edward! Please, help me!"

Eddie's heart pounded in his chest as his feet began to slide slowly along the carpet toward the railing.

"EDWARD! You *must* help me!"

Finally Eddie reached the railing and leaned out over the edge. Sister Agnes stared up at him desperately. She looked like a wild woman. Her habit had fallen to the pews below and her long hair had come unpinned. Her eyes bugged wildly in their sockets and Eddie could see the muscles in her jaw quivering from the strain of her clenching teeth. Her eyes narrowed then to small slits, and when she spoke again her voice had lost the traces of panic that he'd heard previously. Now she sounded like the old Sister Agnes—condescending and contemptuous.

"Give me your hand, boy."

Eddie didn't move an inch. He couldn't. One of the fingernails on Sister Agnes's left hand snapped then and Eddie's own left hand shot up to his mouth to stifle his scream. The nun didn't make a sound. The bloody nail started slipping on the railing, along with the rest of the Sister's fingers.

"Look at me, Edward," she said. Eddie looked down at her. Chills ran up his spine as she smiled at him. "You'll burn in hell for this, boy." Then she let go of the railing and fell.

Eddie stepped back from the railing and listened as Sister Agnes's body crashed onto the pews below. He waited a moment, expecting to hear her cry out in agony. The church remained silent. Eddie crept back to the edge and looked down.

She was there, staring up at him. Her head was canted awkwardly to the left as a result of her broken neck. Blood trickled from the corner of her grinning mouth. One leg stuck obscenely up in the air, revealing a thick brown stocking that had slipped down below her knee. Eddie knew he should run and tell someone what had happened, but his feet wouldn't budge. He simply stared at the lifeless body below.

Eddie was glad she was dead. She deserved to be dead, for all of the awful things she had done to him and his classmates. For the guilt, for the pain, and for the masks. He hated her for the masks most of all.

Eddie turned then and walked down the steep staircase to the ground level. He turned to face the pews where Sister Agnes had fallen and he froze. She was gone. Eddie took a single step forward and then heard the floor creak behind him. He could hear her breathing. It was a strange, rattling sound as a result of her fractured windpipe. He turned slowly and looked into Sister Agnes's crooked face, just as her hands came up and wrapped around his throat.

Eddie Willis began to scream.

***

Eddie's cheeks were still wet with tears when he woke up. His phone was ringing, and it was doing nothing to help his hangover. After what felt like an eternity the ringing stopped. He closed his eyes again and was about to count his blessings when the phone started ringing again. Whoever was trying to reach him was being awfully persistent.

Eddie swung his legs over the edge of the bed and put his face in his hands. His head was pounding and at that moment the telephone was just about the most annoying thing Eddie could think of. He stood up and the room started to spin. He put a hand on his night stand to steady himself. The phone continued to ring, drilling into his head. Eddie finally staggered to the other side of the room and picked up the receiver.

"What?!?" he said with a grimace.

"Mr. Edward Willis?" The voice on the other end of the line had an underlying air of sophistication in it. Nobody Eddie associated with these days was sophisticated.

"And who is this?" Eddie asked.

"My name is Bishop Alvin Lancaster," the voice said.

Eddie sighed loudly. "I'm sorry you wasted your time, Bishop. I'm not exactly in a position to make a charitable donation." Eddie had turned his back on the Catholic religion long ago, but he still knew enough to recognize how odd it was that a Bishop was cold calling for donations.

"I'm not calling about donations, Mr. Willis. Not at all. I'm calling about your brother."

"Donald? What about him?" Eddie hadn't spoken to his brother in years. He was utterly confused.

"I'm very sorry, son, but Father Willis passed away late last night. It seems you're the last family member he had left."

"Shit," Eddie whispered. If he felt any remorse cussing at a Roman Catholic Bishop he didn't show it. The receiver suddenly felt ice cold in his hand. "How did it happen?"

"Father Willis died of a fever. It happened very fast. I'm sorry we were unable to reach you prior to his death, there was just no time, son."

Would it have mattered if they did reach me? Eddie thought. Would he have bothered to visit his brother on his deathbed? In the end Eddie knew he wouldn't have gone. "What caused the fever, Bishop?"

There was a moment of hesitation on the other end of the line and then the Bishop answered. "We're not sure son, but with your permission we'd like to authorize an autopsy and then hold Father Willis's funeral on Thursday evening."

"An Autopsy?" Eddie asked. "Is that allowed?" Eddie couldn't remember if Catholics thought of autopsies as a desecration.

"It certainly isn't normal," said Bishop Lancaster, "but your brother's soul is now with the heavenly Father, and in the spirit of helping others in the future we would approve it. But you're the last of his family, Edward, and the decision should be yours."

"Of course," Eddie said.

"God bless you," said the Bishop, and then, "Mr. Willis, will you be attending your brother's funeral?"

The question caught Eddie entirely off guard. He hadn't seen his brother in over ten years. He found himself answering the Bishop before he'd had time to think it over. "I'll be there."

"Bless you my son. Bless you."

"One question, your Excellence. Where is "there", anyway?"

"St. Louis," the Bishop answered.

Eddie's heart sank. The drive time between Florida and Missouri wasn't a huge issue, but the decrepit state of his Chevy pickup was. Eddie doubted he'd be able to make it past Atlanta without the truck breaking down. Before Eddie could speak, Bishop Lancaster broke the silence.

"There's a plane ticket waiting for you at Orlando International, Edward. Your flight leaves at 6:20 PM and I'll have a car waiting for you when you land in St. Louis."

Eddie guessed that the Bishop was grinning. He could almost hear it in his voice. Eddie was surprised to find that he was grinning too. "That was awful presumptuous of you, your Excellency."

"It's not presumption, son. It's faith."

They said their goodbyes, and Eddie hung up the phone. He glanced at the clock and saw that he had just over eight hours before his flight. With a heavy heart, Eddie Willis began to pack. He started with the dark blue suit that hung in the back of the closet.

He hadn't worn it since his mother's funeral, ten years earlier.

***

He'd fallen asleep almost as soon as the plane had taken off, and he immediately dreamt of his mother. She was on her deathbed again and she was talking out of her head.

"I need to feed Goldie, Eddie," she'd said.

"Don't worry, Ma," Eddie would say. "I'll take care of her for you." Goldie had been a horse that his mother had when she was ten years old, and the old Paint had been dead for over 40 years. But Eddie would pat his mother's frail hand and reassure her that he'd take care of the horse, and she would cringe from the pain.

At the very end the cancer had reduced her down to a skeletal eighty pounds. Very little of what she said made sense. The worst part of her sickness was the smell. His mother's room was saturated in it. It was a mix of urine, vomit, and a strange chemical smell that was almost sweet. Eddie was convinced it was a result of the chemotherapy.

Eddie was alone with her on the day she died. His brother, Don, had been by that morning to deliver her last rights. Don had gone out with his Aunt Evelyn to pick up some deli sandwiches for lunch and Eddie was left to keep his mother company. She had spent most of the day sleeping, but around noon she began to moan and writhe in her bed. Eddie had gotten up and walked to the dresser to wet a wash cloth. When he turned around his mother was standing there, her face a mere inches from his. Eddie gasped and instinctively tried to step backwards. His mother's hands shot up and grasped the sides of his face and she let out a high pitched wail. It only lasted a few seconds, and when she collapsed back onto her bed she was dead. For ten years he'd been haunted by the image of his mother standing in front of him in her nightgown, the patches of hair that hadn't fallen out standing in all directions. Her eyes were dark and sunken. When her dried, cracked lips parted to allow that horrible scream to escape, Eddie focused on her teeth, once a brilliant white, now stained a coffee brown— another side effect from the chemotherapy.

This particular version of the dream was different. The body that had fallen back on the bed was no longer his mother. It was his brother, Don, dressed in his cassock. He had the same cancer induced eyes and teeth. His brother parted his cracked lips, and it wasn't a scream that escaped his throat. It was hundreds of large, green blowflies.

That was when Eddie woke with a start, kicking the seat in front of him. A man, easily a hundred pounds heavier than Eddie turned around and frowned at him.

"Sorry," Eddie said to the man.

Before the man could reply the pilot's voice came through the cabin's loudspeakers and announced that they were only twenty minutes from

landing in St. Louis, where the air temperature was a comfortable 65

degrees but the weather was rainy. Eddie, having offered up his apology to

the behemoth in front of him, turned to look out his window at the

landscape below. It was raining and dark. He couldn't see much at first,

but eventually he could make out the dark, serpent-like footprint of the

Mississippi river. Eddie could see the lights of the city and tried in vain to

spot the gateway arch.

Twenty minutes later the plane taxied to the gate, and twenty minutes

after that Eddie entered the main terminal at Lambert International Airport.

He took the escalator down to the baggage claim and when he stepped off

he spotted a very young looking priest standing among a half-dozen limo

drivers. The priest was holding up a sign with Eddie's name on it.

"I'm Edward Willis, Father," Eddie said as he approached the young

clergyman.

The man looked Eddie up and down. "Ah," he said, "I might have

guessed. You look like Father Willis. You have the same eyes."

Our Mother's eyes, Eddie thought.

"I'm sorry for your loss," the priest said.

"My brother's probably more your loss than mine, Father," Eddie said, and then instantly regretted it. "That came out wrong. I just mean that Don and I kinda lost touch over the years. Anyway, I'm pleased to meet you, Father…"

"I'm so sorry. It's Carillo, but everyone calls me Father Felix. It's nice to meet you." Father Felix extended his hand and Eddie shook it.

They turned and walked to the baggage carousel to retrieve Eddie's luggage. A short time later Father Felix was coasting the black Lincoln town car onto the interstate. Eddie had been trying to replay the last twelve hours in his head when a question came to him.

"Hey Father," Eddie said, "how far a drive have we got, anyway?"

"Oh, about an hour I guess."

"An hour?!?" The surprise in Eddie's voice was enough to make Felix take his eyes off the road and give him a sideways glance.

"Did you not know, Eddie?" Father Felix asked. "Your brother took over the Saint Benedict parish in Barker Marsh. You both grew up there, right?"

Eddie stared at the rosary beads hanging from the car's rearview mirror for a long time before answering. "Yeah, we did."

Barker Marsh.

Jesus, Don, Eddie thought, *what the hell were you thinking?*

***

Eddie hadn't been to Barker Marsh, Illinois in better than twenty years. He had absolutely no reason to have visited after his sixteenth birthday. At a young age Eddie realized that Barker Marsh wasn't a normal town. On the surface, like a decorative landscaping stone, Barker Marsh was normal—even beautiful, with a scenic river bisecting the town on an East and West axis, a railroad track bisecting it North and South. However, upon closer inspection, much like turning over a beautiful landscaping stone, the town throbbed with dark, creeping things that did their best to avoid the light of day. Eddie's second grade teacher, Sister Agnes, was one of those creatures.

Eddie wasn't sure how old Sister Agnes was when she died. He thought that she acted, and purposely tried to look older than she actually was. Eddie would have guessed she was in her early forties when she fell to her death from the choir balcony. Every now and again Eddie remembered thinking that he could see just a hint of rouge on her cheeks, as if she'd had it on the night before and couldn't get it all off before Mass the following morning.

Eddie remembered Sister Agnes well. He also remembered the first time she made him wear the mask.

Sister Agnes was fond of launching erasers at Eddie and his classmates when they misbehaved. The erasers in her classroom stayed pretty clean because of this, albeit at the price of a healthy coat of chalk on everything else in the room as a result of her aerial bombardments. One particular day the erasers themselves were a little more thickly coated than usual so Sister Agnes had Eddie, Billy Deets, Lucy Pinehurst, and Wendy Sawyer each grab a handful of erasers and follow her.

Eddie never questioned the bag Sister Agnes carried, or its contents. He barely gave it a thought when she led the four of them through an isolated door and down a dark stairwell to the boiler room under the school. The smell hit Eddie first—a damp, musty smell that stayed in his clothes and hair for days after.

Sister Agnes pulled a flashlight out of the bag she carried and lit the narrow tunnel in front of them. Eddie's heart jumped in his chest as his surroundings came into focus. The scene reminded Eddie of the Dalton junkyard that he sometimes visited with his dad when they were looking for parts for the Charger. This was a different kind of junkyard, though. Down in that dark, damp boiler room there were no Fords, Dodges, or Chevys rusting away.

There were statues.

Joseph, Mary, and the Saints. There were even a few of Christ himself. There must have been thirty or forty total, and all of them were flawed.

Most were chipped or broken, some just slight imperfections and some missing entire limbs. One particular rendition of Saint Christopher was completely charred on one half, the victim of some mysterious fire. Eddie tried to remember if he'd ever heard anything about a fire in the church and he couldn't recall anything.

They pressed on through the tunnels, the statues staring at them like sentries until they reached a small office. Sister Agnes directed them inside. The Sister turned on a single overhead bulb. There was a metal desk and swivel chair. On the desk sat an ancient looking contraption that looked like a sewing machine. Sister Agnes flipped a switch on the machine and a belt began to rotate within its workings, which in turn spun a heavy duty brush attached to a wheel on the outer portion of the machine. Sister Agnes showed them how to run the erasers across the brush and warned them that if they weren't paying attention they'd lose a finger. Looking back after all those years Eddie realized that what happened next was *worse* than losing a finger. When all the erasers had been thoroughly brushed clean Eddie and Billy Deets started piling them up in their arms when Sister Agnes told them they "weren't quite finished yet."

Sister Agnes reached into the shopping bag she had carried down with her and removed four items, setting them on the metal table.

They were Halloween masks. There was nothing special about

them—they were of the cheap plastic variety and could have been found in any drugstore in the state. There was a high cheek-boned Princess mask, complete with tiara, a Casper the friendly ghost, Droopy Dog, and a Dr. Zaius mask from Planet of the Apes.

"Now, each of you grab a mask," Sister Agnes said as she swung the old swivel chair around and sat in it.

Eddie and Billy practically climbed on top of each other to get to the Dr. Zaius mask. Billy's extra reach prevailed in the end and Eddie found himself unwillingly holding the Droopy Dog mask. When they each had their masks Sister Agnes told them to put them on. Eddie and his classmates did as they were instructed and moments later stood giggling at each other in their disguises. Sister Agnes spoke again and they all stopped laughing and stared at her through the eye holes in their plastic faces, positive they'd misheard her.

"I said take off your clothes." Sister Agnes didn't blink when she said this. Neither did Eddie or his classmates. Eddie had clearly heard what she said but his seven year old mind couldn't process it. He wouldn't have thought twice about taking his clothes off if it had been his mother who had asked him, or his doctor, but Sister Agnes was his *teacher*, and she was a nun. Under no circumstances should she have been asking him to take his clothes off. The other three children must have been thinking the same thing because they all stood completely still until Sister Agnes spoke again, this time with more menace in her voice.

"Children," she said, "You will do as I say and remove your clothes or you will spend eternity frying your little asses off in hell. Now strip!"

The nun's threat set them in motion and the children began to take off their clothes. Eddie couldn't remember much else about that first trip down to the boiler room. He remembered Wendy Sawyer pushing her Princess mask up on top of her head as she tried to unbutton her blouse and he remembered Sister Agnes slapping her hard across the face and telling her under no circumstances was she, or any of them, to remove their masks until she said so. He also remembered thinking it was strange that Billy Deets was wearing boxer shorts. Eddie's mother had only ever bought him briefs—tighty whiteys as he would later call them. He remembered looking at the girls in their stupid plastic masks—a Princess and Casper the Friendly Ghost cowering in floral underpants.

Eddie Willis could remember what happened next, too. The touching. He was forced to touch his friends and they touched him. He remembered watching in horror from behind his own mask as Sister Agnes touched herself.

What Eddie remembered most was the guilt he felt. It wasn't the guilt of what he was doing, or what he was watching Sister Agnes do to herself;

it was who he was doing it in front of—the statues. The last memory he

had of that first day was hanging his face in shame, hidden behind a cartoon

dog mask as that congregation of busted saints and apostles stood witness

to what Sister Agnes had made him do.

✳✳✳

Many years later the Catholic Church had come under fire as accusations of sexual molestation seemed to be a weekly occurrence. Eddie remembered hearing the names of priests and wondering how many of them were actually guilty. What he couldn't remember was a single occurrence in which a nun had been accused. He assumed that was more scandalous than the public could possibly imagine.

But Eddie could imagine it. He'd lived it, for five years until Sister Agnes fell to her death. Though he'd never mentioned a word of it, Eddie's brother Don had lived it, too. Every other month or so Don would be selected to clean erasers, only to join the rest of the class on the playground forty-five minutes later, his head hanging in that ashamed way Eddie's would when it was his turn.

Sister Agnes had changed both of their lives forever, but Eddie and his brother certainly took two different paths. Eddie had watched her die— he'd been *happy* she died. He spent the next several years acting out and getting into all sorts of trouble until he was finally expelled from Saint Benedict for smoking grass behind the rectory. He'd spent the next two years attending public school during the day and awkwardly pursuing girls in the backseats of cars by night. Those sexual pursuits only enhanced his anger and depression. He had Sister Agnes to thank for that as well. On the rare occasions when he managed to actually go all the way with some girl he had to close his eyes and picture Sister Agnes lying beneath him before he could get off. Thankfully he'd learned to suppress that. Soon after he became old enough to drive Eddie packed his belongings into the back of a pickup truck and started driving. He hadn't been back to Barker Marsh until today.

His brother, Don, processed the abuse from Sister Agnes in an entirely different way. He devoted himself entirely to the Catholic religion (which Eddie always found to be a disgusting example of irony) and about the same time Eddie was leaving Barker Marsh to become a rock musician Don was leaving to attend the Seminary. Five years later Eddie had traded his dreams of becoming a professional guitar player for dreams of becoming a commercial fisherman. Don's dreams hadn't changed. He entered the Priesthood on a Monday and by that Friday he was on a plane to Rome, where he spent the next two years studying at the Vatican. By his 25th birthday Don would have said his biggest achievement was working on a project regarding sainthood directly with the Pope. Eddie's greatest achievement was winning a darts tournament at Blackie's Pub in Point Clear, Alabama.

Eddie Willis smiled at the thought as he stared out the window at the rolling Illinois landscape.

Father Felix noticed him grinning and broke the silence. "What is it,

Eddie?"

"It's nothing," Eddie replied, "I was just thinking about my brother and how differently we turned out."

Father Felix nodded without taking his eyes off the road. "Father Donald was a good man."

Is he implying I'm not? Eddie thought. Well, he was probably right. "It's just kinda surprising that Don would go back to Barker Marsh. My memories of that place are...not the greatest. I can't imagine Don's were any better."

"We priests go where the Lord needs us, Eddie," Father Felix said.

Eddie looked ahead at the familiar T-intersection at highways 50 and 75 and knew that they only had about another twenty minutes of driving before they arrived in Barker Marsh. He thought of saying something else to Father Felix but elected to keep it to himself instead. *I'm sure the Lord doesn't need me back in Barker Marsh.*

Eddie was surprised at the butterflies in his stomach as they approached the outskirts of town. A sign that read "The village of Barker Marsh welcomes you" loomed on the side of the road. There was a sense of false comfort about the sign. It reminded Eddie of a Venus fly trap. Eddie knew just how accurate the analogy was. On the surface Barker

Marsh appeared to be a cozy little town, but spend enough time there and it would eventually close in around you and gobble you up.

Below the hand painted sign was a smaller piece of driftwood. Burnt into the wood was the word "Population," followed by "1300."

And falling, Eddie thought as the reality of his brother's death sank in again. Just beyond the sign was the Barker Marsh high school, where he had managed to get through three years of academic underachievement before leaving town for what he'd hoped was the rest of his life. Oh how wrong he'd been.

They'd barely driven past the school when the steeple of Saint Benedict Catholic Church came into view. At the sight of the church the butterflies in Eddie's stomach suddenly turned into what felt like a flock of crows. It wasn't until Father Felix started speaking that Eddie realized he'd been holding his breath.

"Sorry, what?" Eddie said.

"I asked if you preferred to see your brother now or if you wanted to settle in first," replied Father Felix.

"Now," Eddie said. "Let's get it over with."

Almost immediately Father Felix started braking and put on his turn signal. The Ramsey funeral home was conveniently located directly across the street from Saint Benedict. In Barker Marsh, *everything* was located across the street from each other. The town was only about two miles square, and there were only two major roads that intersected each other, dividing the community into four separate quadrants.

Father Felix pulled around to the side of the funeral home and parked. Eddie took a deep breath and got out of the car. Moments later the side door of the funeral home opened and Peter Ramsey's massive frame filled the opening.

"Good evening, Father," Ramsey said. "I've gone ahead and—." Ramsey stopped and stared at Eddie. Eventually a look of recognition washed over his face. "Well, Eddie Willis. As I live and breathe."

With that Peter Ramsey stepped outside and lumbered up to Eddie, extending his gorilla-sized hand in the process. Eddie half expected his own hand to be crushed in the funeral director's massive paw, but Ramsey's grip was remarkably gentle. In a town like Barker Marsh he'd had plenty of practice delivering consoling handshakes to the survivors of the dead.

"I'm sorry for your loss, Eddie," Ramsey said, as if on cue. "Folks here in town really loved Father Don."

"Thanks," Eddie said.

Ramsey led them inside. Eddie had never been in this part of the funeral home. The visitation parlor was pleasantly decorated; comforting. But here in the back of the building, where the dirty work took place, it was a different story. Here it was cold and sterile. The lighting was harsh and bright, not soft and soothing like out in the parlor. The walls were an institutional grey, and it smelled like chemicals, and death. The smell reminded Eddie of his mother's cancer.

The smell grew worse as they approached a pair of stainless steel swinging doors. Eddie stopped walking when he reached those doors. The reality of the situation seemed to hit him all at once. His big brother was lying in there, and he was dead.

"You going to be alright, son?" Ramsey asked.

Eddie nodded. "I'm fine, let's just get it over with."

Ramsey and Father Felix glanced at each other, then the big funeral director pushed his glasses up on his nose and opened the doors. Eddie was prepared to see his brother laid out on the embalming table like Frankenstein's monster, but the big stainless steel table was empty and spotless. Ramsey continued over to a wall of about a dozen small doors with handles like a walk-in cooler. Eleven of the doors were open, the storage chambers inside empty. Ramsey grasped the handle of the only closed chamber and opened the door. He slid the rolling table out of the chamber and carefully pulled the white sheet back from the body that was lying on it.

Eddie looked down in shock. He wasn't shocked at seeing his brother dead—he was prepared for that. What shocked him—what he *wasn't* prepared for—was how his brother looked. Don Willis had only been born a mere 19 months before his younger brother, but the body lying on the mortuary table appeared to be at least twenty years older than Eddie. He hardly recognized his own brother. Don's cheeks were sunken in a way that reminded Eddie eerily of how their mother had looked on her own death bed. The crows' feet and frown lines indicated a life that appeared far harder than that of a normal 43 year old man, especially a man of the cloth. The wrinkled, turkey-like neck ended in an intersection of two ghastly scars where Peter Ramsey had recently put the final touches on his autopsy. The big funeral director followed Eddie's gaze and adjusted the sheet slightly to cover up the scars.

The wrinkled and weathered skin was strange enough, but to Eddie the most disturbing thing about his brother's appearance was his hair. The men in Eddie's family had been blessed with a genetic disposition for coal black, wavy hair, his brother included. The body in front of him had snow white hair. Eddie was again reminded of the agonizing death of his mother.

For an instant Eddie was moved to reach out and touch his brother's cheek but he quickly repressed the urge.

Eddie turned to Ramsey. "What happed to him?"

The funeral director exhaled heavily and then said, "Best we can tell, Eddie, his heart just gave out. He'd been sick for about a month ya' know?"

Eddie hadn't known, and he turned to Father Felix, his eyes pleading for some kind explanation.

"We asked Father Don if he wanted us to contact you," Father Felix said, "and he...vehemently protested. Doctor Mason did his best to slow the pace at which your brother was deteriorating, but as Mr. Ramsey said, in the end he was just too weak and his heart gave out."

Eddie could feel himself growing angry. "No, they told me over the phone he died of a fever," he said, shaking his head.

"The fever was just another side effect," Father Felix said.

Eddie turned to the two other men. "So what you're saying, is that my brother died of old age, at forty three?"

"All we're saying," said Ramsey as he placed a giant hand on Eddie's shoulder, "is that the cause of your brother's death seems to be natural."

For some reason the anger Eddie was feeling didn't subside much, he didn't want to accept the funeral director's answer, but that's just what he did. He gave one more glance down at the brother he hadn't talked to in years, and then Peter Ramsey pulled the sheet back up over his head.

When they'd taken care of additional arrangements and were back outside, Father Felix asked Eddie where he was staying while he was in Barker Marsh.

"I figure I'd just get a room up at the Paramount for a few days," Eddie said.

Father Felix chuckled lightly. "You *have* been gone a while, haven't you Eddie? The Paramount Motel was torn down 15 years ago, at least."

"No shit?" Eddie replied, quickly regretting his swearing in front of a Priest. Father Felix either didn't notice or didn't care, so Eddie asked the next logical question. "Are there any motels in town?"

Father Felix shook his head. "Not many folks want to stay in Barker Marsh much anymore, as I'm sure you can relate. Chances are you're going to want to go through Father Don's belongings anyway, so why don't you just stay in the rectory?"

Eddie was caught completely off guard by the chill that shot up his spine and he was unable to hide the shiver that passed through his body.

Nothing bad had ever happened to him in the rectory, so why was he so uneasy at the thought of sleeping there? Eddie glanced back across the street at the large Victorian house that served as the Priests' living quarters. Aside from looking haunted there was no reason Eddie should have been uncomfortable.

For fucks sake, Eddie thought, *just call a spade a spade. You're scared.* He *was* scared, and it wasn't because of the mansion across the street. It was the church behind it, and the schoolhouse behind that. Most of the really awful things that had happened in his life had happened in that church, or the school with its eight rooms, and the boiler room of course.

"Are you alright, Eddie?" Father Felix asked.

Eddie shook off the uneasiness. "Sure thing. I just have a lot of memories about this place and not all of them are good." Eddie expected Felix to say something comforting and Priest-like, but he didn't. He simply nodded and waited for Eddie to get back in the car.

Father Felix drove across the street and pulled around to the back of the old Victorian house. Eddie got his first view of the schoolhouse in almost 25 years and this time he *was* prepared for the chill that swept over his body.

Father Felix followed his gaze and spoke up. "The school isn't open any more either. It's a shame really, but there just aren't enough parishioners that have their hearts set on sending their children to Catholic school, so most of our youth attend the public school. The few that do go to Catholic school attend Saint Mary's over in Waverly."

"So what's the school used for then?" Eddie asked.

"Right now, storage. The Diocese considered converting the classrooms into office space, but then we realized that there's not a big demand for office space in Barker Marsh, either."

For some reason the thought of the school sitting there abandoned made it twice as creepy for Eddie. He'd grown up in Barker Marsh and was no stranger to ghost stories but he didn't put much stock into things like haunted houses. However, if ever there was a building that he felt could actually watch him, it was that old school.

Eddie and Father Felix both got out of the sedan and made their way to the back door of the rectory. Eddie didn't like turning his back on the school. It made him feel cold.

Father Felix eased the door open and Eddie stopped breathing suddenly and listened. He felt as if he was actually hearing a ghost. A series of sharp little clicks were progressing toward him from the darkness of the house. Childish as it was, Eddie also thought he could hear rattling chains.

His feet were bolted to the wooden planks of the rear porch, and he was preparing himself to be attacked by whatever entity was dwelling inside his brother's house. As the source of the clicking and rattling came into view Eddie was still terrified, but then the big Australian Shepard crossed over the threshold and leapt up, planting its front paws squarely on Eddie's chest.

"Uhh, what's this?" Eddie asked awkwardly.

"Ahh. That'd be Mesha," Father Felix said, chuckling. "I guess in a way he'd be your nephew."

"Don had a dog?" Eddie didn't notice the strange look Father Felix gave him, or the fact that he didn't answer.

After an aggressive session of scratching Mesha behind the ears and on his belly, Eddie finally stood up and stepped into the house, his mood much brighter. Father Felix led the way deeper into the house, turning on lights as he went. The further they got into the house the further Eddie slipped into a blanket of déjà vu. He'd walked this path through the rectory many times before, on his way to see the priest after doing something disruptive in class.

It was the smell of sickness that finally snapped Eddie out of his daydream. He was standing outside of what could only be his brother's bedroom. The sharp, sweet chemical smell drifting out of the room reminded Eddie of his mother's death bed. Eddie had always associated that smell with the slow, internal rot of cancer, but Don hadn't died of cancer. It was still unclear as to what *had* killed him, but it hadn't been cancer. It was then that Eddie realize the sweet smell was death itself, and the cause of death didn't change the fragrance. Mesha could smell it too, and the dog stopped short of the open bedroom door, whining gently. It was strange and sad, but Eddie realized that the dog was suffering a greater loss than he was. With that, Eddie reached into the room and closed the door. There seemed to be a hint of gratitude in Mesha's eyes.

"Some of the parishioners have volunteered to clean Father Don's belongings out," said Father Felix in an attempt to break the awkward silence that Eddie and the Australian Shepard seemed to be sharing. Eddie's reply caught him off guard.

"No, I'll do it. I owe him that." Having said his piece, Eddie took over the lead and continued down the hall, ending the conversation about his dead brother's belongings for the time being.

Eddie remembered there being an additional bedroom on the opposite side of the Priest's office. Assuming that his brother had kept the same office, Eddie marched forward. He opened the door of the office, took two steps into the room, and froze.

His brother's office did not look like the typical office of a priest. It looked like something you'd see in a horror movie about vampire hunters or something. One bookshelf was overflowing with ceremonial looking daggers and hideous looking statues and trinkets, none of which appeared to be Catholic in origin. High on one shelf sat a heavy looking steel mask with rows of sharp spikes protruding from the inside. Eddie recalled that the mask was called an Iron Maiden—one of the few facts he found interesting from History class. He couldn't remember the name of the movie, but he could remember seeing Barbara Steele placed in such a device after being condemned as a medieval witch. He was positive that Don had *not* seen the movie, so Eddie had no explanation as to why his brother had one of these torture devices in his office.

Eddie continued his inspection. In one corner stood a bizarre, humanoid bundle of cornstalks that resembled a scarecrow. It was easily six inches taller than Eddie.

"What the hell is all this stuff, Father, and why does Don have it in his office?" Eddie asked as he stepped over to the large mahogany desk and began examining the paraphernalia littering the surface.

"This was your brother's work," Father Felix replied. There was a detectable trace of surprise in his voice, as if he didn't expect Eddie to be asking about the strange items in the room. "I mean, his primary job was to serve the parishioners of Saint Benedict of course, but for the last five years or so that was pretty much a job that only occurred on Sundays. So, he spent the rest of his time working on this."

"I'm not following you, Father," Eddie said.

Father Felix smiled slightly. "You really *weren't* in contact much with Father Don were you? Eddie, your brother spent two years at the Vatican studying the Occult, Satanism; pretty much anything or anyone that opposed the Catholic religion."

Eddie stood behind the desk, trying to process what Father Felix was telling him. His brother, who had been afraid to jump off the high diving board at the town pool when they were kids, was some kind of soldier of God, like Dracula's Van Helsing. Eddie's confusion multiplied tenfold when he picked up his brother's bible and opened it. He ran his fingers over the raised bumps on the pages, his forehead a wrinkled map of confusion. Suddenly, Eddie realized what he was touching.

"This is braille," he said.

"Of course it is," Father Felix said. "Your brother was blind."

***

Eddie and his brother hadn't been even remotely close. There was nothing unusual about that—siblings often grow apart as they got older. Eddie couldn't believe that Don had gone blind and he'd never told him. When Father Felix had told him, Eddie found himself growing angry at his dead brother and the fact that he'd kept his condition to himself. Then Eddie realized it would have been pointless. It's not as if Eddie would have come running back to Barker Marsh to be at his brother's side if he'd known. No, apparently only death could make him do that.

Father Felix had explained that the blindness had struck Don while he was working on his last case, over a year before. Apart from being trained by the Vatican in all sorts of satanic practices, Eddie's big brother was apparently also the only priest in the Midwest certified by the Church to perform the rights of exorcism. It was while attempting the exorcism of a possessed sixteen year old girl that it had happened. Father Felix explained that Don had gone into the girl's home to perform the exorcism, which he attempted for 36 straight hours. In the end the girl had died and Don was carried out of the house, having been struck blind and his hair turned snow white.

That's what Eddie had been thinking about when he finally laid down in the spare bedroom to sleep that night. He knew he would have nightmares, and was prepared for a lousy night's sleep, so Eddie wasn't surprised when he woke up screaming at three o'clock in the morning.

What he wasn't prepared for was seeing Sister Agnes standing at the foot of his bed.

Eddie blinked long and hard, hoping the nun who he'd seen die almost 25 years earlier would disappear. When he opened his eyes she was still there, looking down at him with empty eye sockets that were centered in the middle of a molding skull. Her head was the only part of her that actually looked dead. The rest of her body seemed to be flesh and blood. This was confirmed as Eddie watched her lift the front of her tunic with a hand that was very much alive. The flesh there between her legs was living too. He watched, horrified, as her other hand slid down the front of the black lace underwear she wore. Her fingers began to roll and writhe beneath the thin material as a sound came out of the skeletal mouth. It was an awful, raspy sound; something like a wet, poisonous laugh. Eddie tore his gaze from the dead woman and scrambled to reach the lamp at his bedside. When he was finally able to turn the light on, the bedroom was blanketed in a soft glow and when Eddie turned back to the foot of his bed Sister Agnes was gone. He *knew* he had seen her, and he wasn't the only one.

Mesha was standing at his bedside, staring at the spot where Sister Agnes had stood. Eddie had forgotten that the Australian Shepard had followed him to the spare bedroom and curled up at his feet when he'd gone to bed. Now the dog growled at something Eddie could no longer see.

"What's the matter, boy? She's gone now," Eddie said. And then, "Shit, she *is* gone, right?" The fur on the back of Mesha's back was standing straight up as he began to creep slowly toward the open bedroom door. That was all the answer Eddie needed.

He swung his legs over the side of the bed and stood. There was someone, or something, in his brother's house. Eddie looked around the room for something he could use as a weapon. He finally picked up the heavy crucifix that was on his nightstand. Eddie's intention was to use the cross to bludgeon an intruder, but, if he really *had* seen a ghost, he was hoping it would provide a different kind of protection as well.

Mesha crept slowly forward toward the doorway and the black hallway beyond. Eddie followed, happy to let the dog take the lead. When they reached the door Eddie did his best to peer into the dark hallway but the soft light in the bedroom didn't penetrate the darkness very far. Eddie groped clumsily for the hallway light switch. When he finally found it and flipped the switch he wasn't entirely surprised when the light didn't turn on. Eddie started to panic but was distracted when Mesha started to press further into the dark hall, her growling growing more intense.

The light from the lamp ended at a point midway down the hall and that's where Eddie stopped. Beyond that point he could see only faint variations of shadow. The dog crept on, his nails making clicks on the wooden floorboards. They sounded like hammer blows in the suffocating silence. Mesha's outline started to fade as he got further into the house, then he disappeared entirely as he entered what Eddie remembered was Don's office. Eddie held his breath and listened intensely for any sound coming from the office.

Eddie stifled a small scream as the lights in the office suddenly turned on.

Did the damn dog just turn on the lights?!? Eddie thought. Then, just as suddenly as they'd turned on, the lights went out again.

Something brushed Eddie's leg and this time there was no suppressing the scream that escaped him. He looked down, expecting to see the contorted corpse of Sister Agnes crawling along the floor. Somehow what he saw frightened him even more.

Mesha stared up at him with terrified eyes. He was whimpering and shaking and looked nothing like the dog that Eddie had seen—just moments before—walking into the office at the other end of the hall. In a state of momentary insanity Eddie asked the dog what the hell was going on, fully expecting it to answer him, but before it could the light in the office turned back on.

This time it was Eddie who took the lead. He held the crucifix in front of him, relying solely, it would seem, on its protective powers now. When he was close enough to the open office door to see inside he was relieved to find that there didn't appear to be any intruders—living or otherwise—waiting for him inside. Keeping his guard up, Eddie stepped all the way into the office. He did a quick scan of the room to make sure nothing was lurking in the corners of the room. It was empty.

Old house, old wiring, Eddie thought in an attempt to explain the strange happenings with the lights. He was about to leave the office and head back to bed when he spotted an open book lying on the desk. It was handwritten. Eddie slid behind the desk and sat down in his brother's chair. He picked up the book. It didn't take him long to realize that what he was holding was his brother's journal, highlighting the details of his last exorcism case, which had rendered him blind. Eddie started to read.

In the doorway Mesha laid down, put his chin on his paws, and whimpered. He would come no further into the room.

Eddie gave the dog a quick glance and then resumed his reading.

***

FATHER DON WILLIS'S JOURNAL ENTRY

NOVEMBER 3RD

I'm recording notes today regarding the Pearcy family, new members of the Saint Benedict parish in Barker Marsh, Illinois. Jeremy and Suzette Pearcy have two children, a sixteen year old daughter named Dakota and a five year old son named Ben.

Last Sunday Mrs. Pearcy approached me and expressed some concerns about some strange happenings in her home. When I asked her to elaborate she became visibly upset and started reciting a list of bizarre occurrences. I jotted a few down. (NOTE: May need to put these on a formal document on the chance that a motion to the Arch Diocese needs to be made.)

• The family took a trip out of town and when they returned to the house 4 days later a single candle was burning on the kitchen table. Suzette assured me that no friends or relatives would have gone into the house while they were gone and the candle wasn't lit when they left

- The doorbell has rung several times and upon opening the front door no one is there. (this could be a simple child's prank)

- On two separate occasions Jeremy and Suzette awoke in the middle of the night to find all of the taps in the house turned all the way on. (I asked the Pearcys if they've had a plumber check out their faucets. They haven't)

- Unexplained noises (this usually isn't enough for me to even consider researching a home)

The more compelling stories revolve around the two Pearcy children, Dakota and Ben. On one occasion Jeremy and Suzette went out for the evening and left Dakota to watch Ben for the night. The following morning Suzette had difficulty waking Ben for school and he was very groggy throughout the morning. Ben told Suzette that he was tired because Dakota wouldn't stop coming in his room the previous night and she kept him up. When Suzette asked Dakota about this the girl stated that she had put Ben to bed at 9 p.m., per her instructions, then she'd gone

back downstairs to do homework for an hour or so before going to

bed herself.

Several weeks later Ben was found trying to tie off an

electrical cord to the second floor bannister that overlooked the

staircase. When Jeremy and Suzette asked Ben what he was doing

the boy said he wanted to swing from the rope like he had seen

Dakota doing.

By the time Mrs. Pearcy had finished expressing her concerns

she was visibly distraught. She invited me to supper tomorrow

night and asked that I might walk through the house and bless the

property. I'll conclude these notes after my visit to the Pearcy

house.

FATHER DON WILLIS'S JOURNAL ENTRY

NOVEMBER 5TH

In my last entry I said I would conclude the notes on the
Pearcy family, but after my visit to their home last night I feel like
their experiences merit further investigation. I'll recap my
observations from last night.

I arrived at the Pearcy home a little early, as I wanted to walk
through the house prior to supper. Suzette and Jeremy met me at
the door and welcomed me inside. I felt no negative energy as the
Pearcys started their tour of the house. They walked me room to
room, pointing out the locations of strange occurrences as we
went. At that point, I felt most of their claims could be explained
by old floor boards and plumbing. Then we went up to the
second floor. My immediate impression was that there must have
been several windows open on the second story. The temperature
was easily twenty degrees colder. I asked the Pearcys about this
and they had no explanation for it. Jeremy had called a

serviceman to inspect the air conditioning and heating unit, which was found to be fully functional. There were occasions, according to Jeremy and Suzette, where the heat had been turned on to max but the second floor of the home maintained an uncomfortable chill. The phenomenon occurs approximately 2-3 times each week.

The temperature drop is certainly worth noting, but the first truly substantial piece of evidence occurred when we entered Ben's bedroom. When I stepped into the boy's room I was completely shocked at what I saw.

The boy was in the process of constructing the most impressive house of cards I've ever seen. In fact, "House" isn't the right word to use here. It was more of a metropolis, complete with what appeared to be streets, courtyards, and even fencing by way of vertically balanced playing cards. The structures took up nearly every available bit of free space and must have been comprised of no less than two dozen decks of Bicycle playing cards. When I turned back to Jeremy and Suzette they must have seen the shock on my face, because Suzette commented that she

"must have forgotten to mention Ben's new obsession with

cards."

I told Ben his creation was very impressive and more as an

afterthought I asked him if he'd built all of it himself. Ben shook

his head and said something like "It was mostly me but I had help

on the really hard parts."

With that I turned back to Jeremy and Suzette and they both

shook their heads, indicating that it wasn't them who had helped.

I asked Ben who had helped him with the hard parts, expecting

him to tell me it was Dakota. He told me the "skinny man" had

helped him.

The honest truth is that the boy's reply caught me off guard

and chilled me even more than the drastic temperature drop had.

I remember asking him who the "skinny man" was, and Ben

simply shrugged his shoulders without looking up at me or

pausing while he attempted to stack a playing card on a towering structure as high as the boy himself. When I asked the boy if the "skinny man" lived in the house he simply answered "sometimes."

We left the boy to continue working on his empire of cards and the Pearcys continued to escort me through the upper part of the house. As we walked I asked them if Ben had ever mentioned having an imaginary friend before. To their knowledge, he hadn't.

Up to that point, the temperature fluctuation combined with Ben's massive house of cards and comments about a "skinny man" was enough for me to justify a room to room blessing of the house, but then we entered Dakota's room.

The girl was sitting on her bed reading when Suzette knocked and we entered. I expected the girl to react a little awkwardly, as most sixteen year old girls would if her parents came into her room with a Catholic priest in tow, but Dakota smiled and very cheerfully said "Hi Father Don!"

Visually the girl's room appeared to be pretty normal by sixteen year old standards. The posters on the wall and stuffed animals throughout were typical of the decorations found in that limbo land where girls were transitioning from childhood to womanhood. Everything in the room is pink. Again, visually there was nothing abnormal about Dakota's bedroom. There was certainly no re-creation of Rome with playing cards in there.

What was disturbing about walking into that room was the smell. The room reeked of rotting meat and decay, with undertones of vomit and feces. I have smelled this stench before on previous cases.

Each of those cases involved an inhuman, demonic entity.

After smelling the foul odor last night I fought the urge to cover my mouth and nose, and instead turned back to Jeremy and Suzette so that I could gauge their reaction. I was surprised to see that it was very apparent the two could *not* smell anything. What happened next is stranger still, and more disconcerting. Dakota got up off her bed and said she was going out for a bit before dinner. As the girl walked closer toward me the stench became worse and I actually gagged a little, which I had to disguise as a cough. Also, I can't be 100% sure, but I think Dakota winked subtly as she walked past me. Once the girl was halfway down the hall the smell cleared up without a trace.

I'm recording it here and now that if further investigation reveals some type of malicious presence in the house I fear it may have attached itself to the girl, not Ben as I initially thought.

After my tour of the house was compete I decided to walk through the house once more and bless each room. I returned to the first floor, donned my cassock and started burning a generous amount of myrrh in the thurible I had brought along with me. I walked through each room on the first floor and prayed, swinging the thurible on its chain and alternating between the Lord's Prayer and reading Luke 10: 5-9.

When it was time to head up to the second floor I started up the stairs and only made it about four steps before the ember in the thurible went out. I relit the incense and started back up, only to have it go out again at the top of the stairs. I kept this up for about 5 minutes before I gave up and accepted that no matter what I did the coal simply would not stay lit. At that point I went back downstairs and returned with a flask of holy water. After that I was finally able to compete my blessing of the home. By that time it was near 7 p.m. and Suzette had finished preparing dinner.

Jeremy, Suzette, Ben, and I all sat down just as Dakota came back in through the front door. She sat down at the table across from me, and with her came the offensive stench again. I was asked to bless the meal and could barely get through the prayer without gagging. I looked up and Dakota was grinning at me, almost as if she knew what was troubling me.

If it had just been the smell I wouldn't be so troubled. What troubles me is that I was the only one that could smell it.

I'm sure the roast Suzette made was delicious, but I was only able to pick at enough so as not to come across as rude. The smell destroyed any semblance of an appetite that I might have had.

After dinner Dakota and Ben went upstairs, and blessedly took the foul reek with them. Jeremy, Suzette and I retired to the living room for coffee. I told them that I think the blessings I laid on the house should help, but to keep me posted on further developments, specifically with the children. The Pearcys thanked me and I walked out of the house.

I placed my bag in the trunk of the car and as I opened my door to get in I glanced up at one of the second floor windows. Dakota stood there, staring at me. She was wearing only a towel wrapped around her so I quickly looked away and got in the car for fear of what she might have done next.

I'm afraid that I will have more notes on the Pearcy family, for I can't shake the feeling that it wasn't the house that needed the blessing.

FATHER DON WILLIS'S JOURNAL ENTRY

DECEMBER 7TH

This is a continuation of my notes on the Pearcy family. After my visit to the Pearcy home over a month ago I thought that I may have been wrong, and that perhaps a simple blessing of the home was all that was needed. I talked with Jeremy and Suzette on two consecutive Sundays following my visit and they said that the strange happenings in the house had decreased considerably.

Then I didn't see or hear from them in over two weeks. At first I thought maybe they had gone out of town for the Thanksgiving holiday, but when they weren't in Mass again last Sunday I feared something was wrong. Suzette finally telephoned me yesterday and confirmed my fears.

She was crying at first, and all I could make out was that something was wrong with Dakota. When Suzette was finally able to pull herself together she went on to tell me that over the past several weeks Dakota had displayed frightening behaviors.

It started, she said, late one night when Suzette and Jeremy awoke to an incessant creaking noise. They searched the house, looking for the source of the noise, and they discovered that Dakota wasn't in her bed. They continued to frantically search the house until they finally looked outside on the front porch, where they found the source of the creaking.

Dakota was there, sitting in the wooden porch swing, rocking gently back and forth. Suzette said the girl was wearing only a thin nightgown and temperatures were near freezing, but when they got to Dakota's side she didn't have so much as a single goose pimple. When they asked her what she was doing outside at that hour she simply said "thinking." With that they walked her back inside and put her to bed without another word. Suzette was very hesitant to tell me the next part, and she preempted telling the tale by saying how embarrassing it was, and asking me to please not judge her daughter. It was only after I reminded her that I was a priest and was used to hearing all kinds of sins during confession that Suzette continued.

About a week after they found Dakota sitting outside Suzette came home from the grocery store and upon opening the garage saw, as Suzette put it to me, "something horrific." Dakota was having sexual intercourse with a boy from school, and Suzette went on to say that it wasn't the kind of natural love making that occurred between a man and woman but something "far filthier." Suzette sent the boy running home and swore she would contact his parents. (Suzette never mentioned if she actually did)

At this point in the phone call Suzette got choked up again and finally told me that when she attempted to have a stern conversation with her daughter Dakota simply threw her head back and laughed heartily. Suzette said at that point she could only cry until Jeremy got home from work and she told him what had happened.

Jeremy, apparently, reacted differently. It was hard for Suzette to tell me, and had I not reminded her again that I am used to hearing confessions she probably wouldn't have. Jeremy reacted as many fathers would, he stormed upstairs and burst into

Dakota's room to confront her and she began to laugh in what

Suzette called "that patronizing way." At that, Jeremy slapped

her hard across the face. Suzette said this stopped Dakota's

laughter for a brief moment, but then she started up again.

Suzette said what happened next didn't make sense.

When she started laughing again, Jeremy brought his hand

up to smack her again, but this time Dakota caught his hand in

her own. According to Suzette, the next thing she knew Jeremy

was on his knees, howling in pain as Dakota squeezed his hand.

The girl grabbed Jeremy by the throat and picked him back up.

Dakota said something to him in a voice that wasn't her own

before dropping Jeremy back to the floor, unconscious. When he

woke up his hand was swollen and tender so Suzette drove him to

the emergency room in Waverly. His hand had been broken.

Hearing that the girl exhibited abnormal strength and spoke

in a strange voice was enough for me to decide to visit the Pearcy

home again, but I asked Suzette if anything else had happened.

Her response backs up my earlier finding.

Suzette told me that Dakota smells. She described it as a foul, rotting odor, but she's too frightened of her daughter to say anything to her about it. I don't understand why the Pearcys couldn't smell it weeks ago when I first did. Either way, I'm going back to the Pearcy home tomorrow to continue my interviews. I feel that this may be a case of possible possession and I'm sending a transcription of these notes to the archdiocese should I need approval to perform the rites of exorcism.

***

Eddie set the journal down on the desk and rubbed his eyes. As disturbing as the book's contents were, Eddie was still happy to be reading it. In some strange way it made him feel closer to his brother. Thinking of Don made Eddie think of Don's funeral, and this in turn made him glance at the clock on the wall.

Shit! Eddie thought. *It's 6 a.m. I've been in here a lot longer than I realized.* Eddie would have to continue his reading later. Right now he had to prepare to bury his brother. As he stepped around to the other side of the desk Eddie remembered what had brought him into the office in the first place and he stopped. The faint light of dawn had started to slither into the house through the windows on the east side of the rectory, so Eddie was able to see all the way down the hallway leading back to his bedroom. There was no sign of Sister Agnes or any other ghosts, and Mesha didn't seem to sense anything either. The dog got up from his resting spot in the doorway and walked over to stand by Eddie's side, his tail wagging eagerly. Together, the two started down the hallway.

An hour later Eddie was showered and shaved and he was laying his suit—the dark blue one; the one that he hadn't worn at his mother's funeral—on the bed. In his head, he practiced what he was going to say to the total strangers when they offered him their condolences.

What the hell do I say? Thanks? Hey, you knew him better than I did?

One thing Eddie knew for sure was that he was *not* looking forward to the next eight hours or so. He wanted the funeral to be over and done with because, crazy as it was, he wanted to return to reading Don's journal.

Eddie started to dress and had managed to get his pants and dress shirt on when there was a knock at the back door. Eddie trudged through the house to answer the knock, and when he opened the door Father Felix was standing there, dressed in a fine looking cassock, holding a cardboard tray with two steaming cups of coffee in one hand and a box of donuts in the other.

"Thought you might be able to use some breakfast," Father Felix said.

"Don't take this the wrong way, Father, but you're a God send," Eddie replied, smiling.

"So I'm told," replied Felix with a smile.

Eddie stepped aside as Father Felix entered. A minute later the two were sitting at the small kitchen table. Eddie picked at one of the donuts absent-mindedly, his appetite apparently having been left in Florida. He was savoring the coffee, however. It was hot and strong and the caffeine was doing wonders for his system.

"Thanks for breakfast," Eddie said, raising his styrofoam cup in a toast.

"Any time," Father Felix replied. "So, how'd you sleep?"

"Not real great. Nightmares. Then I stayed up half the night reading in the office."

"Anything good?" the priest asked.

Eddie debated for a moment whether he should be honest and tell Felix what he'd been reading, and ultimately came to the conclusion that lying to a priest at 8 a.m. was not the way to start your day. "Actually, I was glancing at Don's notebook, reading about his last…case or whatever you'd call it."

Father Felix's face folded into a look of deep concern. "That really isn't something you should be reading, Eddie. Those manuscripts should technically be sent to the archdiocese to be filed with the official case notes."

"I understand," Eddie said, "it's just that I haven't said two words to my brother in over ten years. I know it sounds crazy but reading his notes somehow makes me feel like I'm making up for lost time."

Father Felix's scowl eased a little and something new started to shine through. Pity maybe? "Look, I can stall for a while, but eventually those books *do* need to be packed up and sent to St. Louis. But Eddie, I really wish you *would* leave them alone. Those notebooks contain details of some truly horrific occurrences. I'm talking evil. Don went through years of training and conditioning to be able to deal with them. I doubt very much that reading those books will help you with those nightmares you mentioned."

This made Eddie think of seeing Sister Agnes standing at the foot of his bed the night before. "I appreciate the concern, Father, but it's almost a quest for me now. I need to at least finish reading his notes on the Pearcy girl." Eddie paused a moment and then added, "How is the family, Father?"

Father Felix shrugged. "Hard to say. After the girl died the family moved out of the house and left town. They went somewhere out West is all I know."

The two men finished their coffee and then Father Felix told Eddie he had to step next door to prepare the church for the funeral Mass and that he'd meet Eddie at the funeral home after that for the visitation.

By the time Eddie finished getting ready it was almost 10 a.m., and the visitation was to begin at 11. Eddie decided that he would go across the street to Ramsey's funeral home early. He pulled on his suit jacket and walked into the office, where he gave Don's journal a quick glance, and then stepped through to the back door and out of the house.

A cold, light drizzle had begun to fall, and Eddie pulled his collar up tight around his neck as he walked across the street to the funeral home. When he stepped under the shelter of the awning the front door of the funeral home opened and the doorway was all at once filled with Pete Ramsey's giant frame, dressed smartly in a black suit.

"Good morning, Eddie," Ramsey said, extending that hand of his that was the size of a first basemen's mitt. "Shame the weather isn't cooperating with us today."

Eddie shook his hand. "Yeah. Shame."

Ramsey looked for a moment like he was going to say something else, but after a respectful silence he simply stepped aside and allowed Eddie to enter the foyer. The big funeral director walked over to the panel door that led to the main parlor and slid it back.

"I'll give you some privacy," Ramsey said. "I'll be in my office if you need me and I'll let you know when the other visitors arrive."

"Thanks Mr. Ramsey," Eddie said. He took a deep breath and stepped into the parlor. Ramsey slid the door closed behind him, and Eddie found this a bit strange. He assumed that a funeral director would stay at the family's side throughout the whole ordeal, armed with tissues and comforting words for grieving widows and children. Ultimately, Eddie shrugged the idea off—he was neither a widow nor a child; just the fuck-up estranged brother.

The viewing parlor was cool and dark, and there was already gentle organ music playing through the overhead speakers.

I need to make sure I have a playlist noted in my will, Eddie thought. *I think the Ramones and maybe some Sex Pistols would make a good soundtrack for my funeral.*

There was maybe a dozen or so rows of folding chairs set up for the visitors and this gave Eddie a moment's pause. He never did understand that concept. Why would somebody want to hang out with a dead body to the extent that they needed to sit down and rest? Eddie knew the answer though, or at least had his own opinion, and it repulsed him. He believed that in small towns like Barker Marsh, funerals were a social event, and social events needed places where folks could sit and socialize. Thinking of it turned his stomach a little.

Eddie looked beyond the rows of chairs to the front of the parlor and there it was—Don's coffin. And lying in it, presumably was Don. Eddie couldn't see his brother from the back of the parlor but he knew he was lying there. *On display,* Eddie thought. *Might as well get this over with.*

Eddie made his way up the center aisle until he was standing in front of the coffin. He looked down and a fresh wave of sadness washed over him. There was Don—his brother—looking peaceful in his cassock. In his folded hands was a beautiful black rosary that looked hand carved. Eddie wondered where Don had gotten it and when he realized that his brother would never be able to tell him, another pang of regret stabbed him in the chest.

He reached down and put his hand on top of Don's, expecting it to be as cold as ice, but it wasn't. He wondered to himself how Pete Ramsey had managed to pull that one off.

"I'm sorry, big brother," Eddie said. "I'm sorry we didn't have more time to get close again. Truth is, I didn't want to. I guess I was jealous. I mean, you did something pretty noble with your life, and everybody respected that. What did I do? Ran out on you and Mom so I could be a rock star. I might as well have joined the circus."

Eddie chuckled a little, not so much because what he said was funny, but because it helped to fight off the tears that were stinging his eyes. He stepped back to admire the silver casket. "I gotta tell ya, Don, you got a pretty sweet ride here, man. I mean it, this sucker's nice!"

When he had no more to say, Eddie looked down at his brother's corpse on final time and said, "Let's both try to get through today best we can, alright? Then we can have a drink."

After that Eddie turned and sat down in one of the chairs in the first row. Outside, the light drizzle had progressed to a solid downpour and a flash of lightning worked its way through the parlor's blinds, followed by a rumble of thunder.

The graveside service is going to be a blast, Eddie thought, and then, looking at Don's casket again, he said, "At least *you'll* be dry."

He spent the remainder of the 10 o'clock hour sitting in silence, trying to conjure up as many happy memories about his brother as he could. At one point he had walked over to the left side of the parlor, where there was a sea of floral arrangements. There was also an easel, containing a collage of photographs of his brother. Most of the pictures were of Don with what Eddie assumed were various members of the Parish. There was one lonely photo of Don and their mother, taken right after Don had entered the Priesthood. There wasn't a single photo anywhere on the board of Don and Eddie.

Eddie was sitting, wondering if he and Don had ever even *had* a photo taken together when the parlor door slid open and Pete Ramsey stepped in. "Eddie, folks have started to arrive. You want a few more minutes?"

Eddie shook his head. "Nah, I've said what I needed to say. I'm ready; send em' in."

Ramsey nodded and went back outside. Meanwhile, Eddie took his place standing at the foot of Don's casket. Moments later the parlor doors slid open again and people started filing in.

For the next two hours Eddie stood like a sentry over his brother's body while a constant barrage of mourners and well- wishers filed into the funeral parlor. Most of the people that came through were surprised to see that Don had a brother. Eddie recognized a handful of visitors from his childhood and spent a little extra time making small talk with them, but for the most part Eddie spent the visitation shaking hands with strangers, many of whom knew his brother better than him, and this caused a low, burning dislike for most of the people he spoke with. When it was finally time to head back across the street to the church for Mass Eddie was irritable and on edge. The driving rain he had to walk through did nothing to help matters.

Eddie stepped through the vestibule and into the church and quickly forgot about his soaking shoes. The reality of where he was standing seemed to hit him all at once, and he was suddenly overwhelmed by a strange mix of nostalgia and utter fear. He stood staring at the spot where Sister Agnes had fallen and broken her neck when he was a boy and suddenly he was unable to breathe.

Oh fuck, I'm having a panic attack, Eddie thought. He closed his eyes and tried to clear his head but it only made it worse. With his eyes closed all he could picture was Sister Agnes lying there, ten feet from where he now stood, her head twisted grotesquely and a strange smile on her face.

(You'll burn in hell for this, boy!)

"Eddie, you O.K.?"

Eddie tried to scream when Father Felix touched his elbow, but thankfully no sound came out. He quickly glanced over at the spot Sister Agnes had been lying in his vision, and was relieved to see half a dozen funeral patrons sitting there now. That, combined with Father Felix's sudden presence seemed to comfort Eddie and stave off the panic attack he'd nearly had.

"You gonna be O.K., Eddie?" Father Felix asked.

Eddie nodded. He really *did* believe he would be O.K., but all the same, he couldn't wait to get out of the church. Father Felix walked him to the front pew and then left him to return to the rear of the church to begin Mass. Eddie hadn't attended Mass in over twenty years, and he surprised even himself when he managed to remember a handful of the prayers. What he'd forgotten was how many times he had to transition from sitting to standing to kneeling throughout the service. Each time he had to glance sideways secretly so he could take his cue from the other parishioners.

Outside it continued to thunder and lightning, resulting in a kaleidoscope effect when the sudden flashes shone through the stained glass windows. During one of these light shows Eddie glanced back over his shoulder at the rest of the congregation. The church was packed. He shifted his focus upward to the choir balcony, high above the rear pews. The balcony was empty and dark, but when another crash of lightning lit up the church Eddie saw her standing up there. Sister Agnes was watching him, and once again, Eddie couldn't wait to get out of that church.

Finally Father Felix announced that Mass had concluded, encouraged everyone to go in peace and to love and serve the Lord, and informed everyone that the funeral services would conclude at Antioch Cemetery, on the edge of town. Eddie made a half-assed sign of the cross, and rushed down the center aisle and out the front of the church without so much as a glance toward the choir balcony.

The rain was falling in buckets, and Eddie soon remembered that he didn't have an umbrella, or a car to seek shelter in, so he squeezed back under the church's awning. A few patrons tried to talk to him on their way out, but thankfully most of them were too focused on dashing to their cars to make a lot of small talk. In the street, a long black hearse sat idling, exhaust puffing lightly from the tailpipe. Soon other vehicles started lining up behind the hearse and turning on their hazard flashers. By the time

Father Felix came outside, the funeral procession was nearly forty vehicles long.

"Hey Father," Eddie said. "I sorta forgot I don't have a car. Can I get a lift?"

"Of course," Father Felix replied as he popped open a large umbrella. "Get under here. I've got an extra one in the car you can use when we get to the cemetery."

"Sounds good to me," Eddie said.

The two men splashed their way to the rear of the church again and climbed into Father Felix's big sedan. Moments later, Felix eased the car through the procession so he could pull in behind the hearse. Once in position, the entire convoy started heading east toward Antioch Cemetery. Father Felix switched his wipers on full speed, and then turned to Eddie. "How you holding up?"

Eddie shrugged. "Hanging in, I guess. I mean, honestly Father, I've accepted losing Don. I feel some guilt that we drifted so far apart and now I won't have a chance to make up for it, but that's not what's weighing on me. It's being back in this town, and that church."

"Could your experiences in a church really be that bad, Eddie?"

Sister Agnes lying dead in the pew flashed in front of Eddie's eyes. "Trust me, Father, they're that bad."

Eddie waited for Father Felix to make another comment—perhaps try to coax a confession out of him, but the priest simply focused on the road through the blinding rain, and eventually followed the hearse as it turned down the appropriately named "Cemetery Road." By the time the procession stopped at the gates of Antioch Cemetery the thunder and lightning had thankfully passed by the area, but the steady rain remained. Father Felix reached into the backseat and came up with another umbrella, which he handed to Eddie, then the two men got out of the car.

Eddie opened the umbrella as the back of the hearse was opened and six men he didn't recognize slid his brother's coffin out. The pallbearers carried the casket through the cemetery, as the visitors brave enough to face the weather followed.

The grave diggers had had enough forethought to place a large canopy over the grave location, so at least there was some shelter for Eddie and a handful of other visitors. He looked at the contraption that his brother's casket was set upon and marveled at how far technology had come since the days when coffins—wooden coffins—were still lowered into the ground using rope and brute strength. Behind the chrome bars of the lowering mechanism stood Don's gravestone, brilliant and shiny and new.

Eddie focused on the epitaph above his brother's name, from Matthew something or other:

He that endureth to the end shall be saved.

Eddie didn't know who had chosen the epitaph (it certainly wasn't him), but he found it to be appropriate. It did strike up the question of just what *had* Don endured to the end, though. Eddie thought of Don's journal, resting on the desk at the rectory. He suddenly had a longing to get back to it, positive that it would provide much needed answers.

Father Felix began the graveside service but Eddie wasn't paying much attention. He was trying to remember his mother's funeral and he couldn't recall much, other than the weather was infinitely better. Part of his memory loss was probably a result of the fifth of Popov vodka he'd consumed following the funeral.

Father Felix must have sensed that Eddie, and the other graveside mourners, were getting tired of standing out in the rain, because when Eddie had finally stopped daydreaming about his mother's funeral the young priest was offering up his final prayer.

"Heavenly Father, we ask that you remember Donald, whom you have called from this life. In baptism and holy orders he died with Christ; may he also share his resurrection."

There was a collective "Amen" from the congregation and then Felix concluded the services. A few folks shook Eddie's hand and told him they'd see him at the lunch back at the parish hall, which Eddie had completely forgotten about. Finally it was just Eddie and Father Felix left. Eddie placed a hand on the silver casket and said quietly, "Good bye, Don. Rest easy, brother."

The two once again walked aback to the car and started toward Saint Benedict. This time they rode in complete silence, and Eddie was grateful for it. He was exhausted and tired of talking to people. He wanted to get back to his brother's home, change out of his wet clothes, and get back to reading the journal. By the time they pulled back down the alley at the church the last thing Eddie felt like doing was eating lunch with strangers he'd just spent his entire morning with, but that's just what he was going to have to do.

Father Felix and Eddie got out of the car and they entered the parish dining hall together. Only about half of the visitors had made it back to the hall for lunch, but Eddie still felt like that was a pretty good turnout given the weather. Felix said a quick prayer over lunch and then everyone sat down to eat. That's when the afternoon truly took a turn for the awful.

He hadn't intended on being rude; he just wasn't that hungry. That's why Eddie only grabbed a glass of iced tea when he went through the serving line. The large cookers full of barbecue looked appetizing enough, but the day's events had driven any semblance of an appetite far away. When he reached the end of the line with nothing but a glass of tea, a large, aproned woman stared him down.

"That's not all you're plannin' on havin' is it?" she asked.

"Well," Eddie said, "actually...yeah. I'm not that hungry."

She put her giant hands on her equally large hips and cracked a smile that contained just a hint of a threat. "Now come on, son. This here's the best barbecue in the county. Try some."

Eddie stared at the mound of sopping meat the woman had shoved in front of him and did his best to maintain his own smile. "Really, I'm good. Thanks though."

The smile faded from the portly woman's face completely as she lowered the plate of food. "No reason to be rude. Eatin' some of this *free* food, even if you ain't hungry is only the polite thing to do."

The comment caught Eddie completely off guard and his temper instantly boiled to the surface. Part of him was trying to remind his subconscious self that he was the brother and only family member of the deceased and that he should simply take the food from this woman and sit down. Another part of him—the part that generally got him into deep shit—took the woman's defiant stare as a direct challenge and her rude comment as a provocation. Before Eddie could stop himself his own smile faded and he said, "Lady, I don't *WANT* your fucking food."

A few people at the closest table heard him and stopped what they were doing, but he'd said his comment soft enough that most of the folks in the dining hall still had no clue what was going on.

Eddie stood his ground, staring at the plump woman and she stared right back, equally unrelenting. Finally, the woman moved. Eddie watched as she slid the plate of barbecue closer toward him, and as she did this the woman's thumb dipped into the moist meat. It may have been the act of defiance itself, or it might have been the mere thought of eating the barbecue after the woman's grubby thumb had been in it, but what Eddie did next shocked even him after the fact. In one swift movement he brought the hand that wasn't holding the iced tea up and knocked the plate of food clear out of the woman's hand. The barbecue splattered a nearby wall and the plate crashed to the floor.

Eddie could feel all the eyes in the room on him, but he kept staring at the woman standing in front of him. He expected the woman to be appalled and step back but she didn't budge. That threatening smile had crept back into the corners of her mouth. "Well, then," she said softly.

For some reason the comment got under his skin more than anything the woman had said or done previously. Eddie feared that he would strike the woman, so instead he hurried past her without a word and ran out of the hall. He was halfway across the old playground that stood between the hall and the rectory when he heard Father Felix hollering after him. He was all the way to the back porch of the rectory by the time the young priest caught up with him.

"EDDIE! What in the world happened?!?" Father Felix asked.

Eddie didn't bother turning around. "I'm sorry, Father. I think I've just reached my capacity for social interaction for the day."

Eddie opened the door and stepped inside. Father Felix climbed the steps onto the porch and opened his mouth to say something else but Eddie shut the door in his face before he could say another word.

Behind Eddie came a series of clicks and he turned around quickly to see Mesha standing there, looking up at him. He kneeled down and gave the dog a monstrous hug. It wasn't so much that he was happy to see the animal, it was because Mesha was unable to talk to him.

***

Eddie spent the next hour simultaneously feeling horrible for what he'd done and trying to figure out why the woman had pushed him so far in the first place. He'd gotten out of his wet funeral clothes and showered, and as he slid on a pair of sweatpants and an Elvis Costello concert shirt he was no closer to feeling better about his actions at the dining hall or understanding why the fat woman had been so insistent upon him eating. To complicate matters even more, the appetite that eluded him earlier and played such an intricate part in the scene he'd caused had returned to him with a vengeance. The last thing he wanted to do was go back to the dining hall, so Eddie rummaged around for a phone book. When he found one he began dialing pizza joints. After four attempts he finally found a pizzeria that would deliver, and by the time his large pepperoni, sausage, and pepperoncini pie arrived, another hour had passed and Eddie's hunger had escalated to the ravenous level. Eddie brought the box to his brother's office and quickly devoured two slices before he even bothered picking up Don's journal again.

When he finally killed his hunger pangs Eddie wiped his hands off and picked up the journal. He'd waited all day to get back to reading Don's account of the exorcism that had taken his sight. He opened the book to where he'd left off, grabbed another slice of pizza, and began reading again.

***

FATHER DON WILLIS'S JOURNAL ENTRY

DECEMBER 9TH

I've just sent an official request to the archdiocese for approval to perform the rights of exorcism on Dakota Pearcy. After my interview with her last night I have no doubt that the child has been possessed by an inhuman entity. I believe I have enough documented evidence that St. Louis will support my recommendation and I hope to have official confirmation from them in the next three days. In the meantime, here are my notes from my last interview with Dakota Pearcy:

I arrived at the Pearcy home a little after 6 p.m. yesterday. Suzette greeted me at the door. Jeremy was home but he's clearly upset by this entire ordeal. He was seated in the living room and didn't get up and greet me. When I peeked my head in he was scratching the exposed skin around the cast on his hand, and there was an open bottle of Scotch on the coffee table.

Something I must note is that when I first entered the house I was instantly hit with that foul, assaulting odor. Previously this only happened when I was directly in Dakota's presence, but Suzette told me that the girl was upstairs in the bedroom. I did a quick walkthrough of the first floor, and other than the smell, everything seemed to be in order. After that, Suzette led the way to the second floor.

Once again, I felt that same extreme temperature drop I'd experienced during my initial visit a month ago, and the smell was certainly stronger on the second floor. As we walked down the hall I could make out Dakota's voice, and then another muffled voice. I stopped and asked Suzette where Ben was and she informed me that he had gone to play at a friend's house. I asked who was in Dakota's room with her, at which point Suzette gave me a disturbing little grin and said something like, "That's what I was hoping you could tell *me*, Father." Her statement made me uncomfortable, to say the least.

Standing just outside her door it became obvious that the second voice in the room was male. I don't remember how long I stood outside the door—it couldn't have been more than a few seconds—but I distinctly remember the male voice on the other side stopping in mid-sentence, at which point I opened the door.

Dakota was sitting on her bed, Indian-style and staring at me in the doorway, almost as if she was expecting me. She was grinning, but it wasn't the kind of grin common among sixteen year old girls. It was the kind of grin members of rival street gangs gave each other before breaking out in a knife fight. I stood in the doorway for a moment, pondering what I should say to start the interview, when Dakota started the conversation for me.

"Come on in, Father. Don't be nervous."

I stepped in the room and told her I wasn't nervous. Suzette and I looked at each other and with a silent understanding she closed the door. For the next twenty minutes or so we had a conversation, and Dakota kept trying to take the conversation in a sexual direction. It was obvious she was trying to make me uncomfortable, and I made a mental note to mention it on my official report. Eventually she said something that stopped me in my tracks.

When I wrote up the official report for the archdiocese I described a piece of the evidence as "Retro-cognition" without going into detail. I'm hoping they will simply take my word for it that Dakota was able to recall events from the past that she had no way of possibly knowing. However, I feel obligated to get the specific details down in writing. Well, most of them.

As I already mentioned, Dakota was attempting to take every question I asked in a sexual direction. This goes hand in hand with Suzette's claims that the girl has taken a very nonchalant approach to sex in general. I can't remember exactly the question I had asked her, but at some point in our conversation the girl began to touch herself inappropriately. After several attempts to stop her, Dakota said something like "You didn't seem this offended when you were watching Sister Agnes."

She rendered me speechless. I'm choosing to not go into

details in this journal, but Sister Agnes was someone from my past, and there's no way Dakota Pearcy could have known that. I asked her how she knew about Sister Agnes. Who had told her? She calmly replied with, "She did."

Dakota claims that a dead woman from my past is giving her information, but I keep going back to something Ben said during my first interview with the family. He mentioned talking to a "skinny man." I believe that this same entity is what has taken possession of Dakota.

At any rate, I told Dakota that I didn't believe her. Her face became twisted and strained, the corners of her mouth creeping into an almost maniacal grin. I watched as her pupils dilated to the size of dimes and then she replied with, "I don't give a fuck what you believe."

The voice was hers, but it was almost as if there was another voice coming out of her mouth at the same time—a deeper, more sinister voice. Just as the girl said this a candle on her dresser lit up with a flame, seemingly on its own. I turned in time to see the flame rise to a height of almost two feet before the wax melted down to a puddle in a matter of seconds. At that point I rose and walked over to the dresser. I turned and removed a small vile of holy water and held it up to Dakota. I asked her how she would feel if I splashed some on her and she replied, in that same dual voice, that "it would not end well." I placed the vile back in my pocket, as at that point I felt I had enough evidence with which to have the exorcism approved.

I turned to leave and promised Dakota I would be back to see her soon, and in her normal sixteen year old girl's voice she said, "I look forward to it, Father."

I went back downstairs and asked if I could speak with Suzette and Jeremy outside in the driveway. I wasn't comfortable having a conversation anywhere in the house. Once outside, I explained to the Pearcys that I believe something sinister had latched onto Dakota and that I would be reaching out to the Archdiocese for approval for an exorcism. Neither of them took it well. Jeremy got upset and stormed back inside the house; Suzette broke down in sobs. I've seen both reactions several times before, but I still needed confirmation from one of them that an exorcism was the path they wanted to take with Dakota. Suzette asked me if Dakota's problems could be medical. Again, it's a question that most parents ask. I told her that I wasn't a medical doctor, and that she certainly had the right to consult a physician before making a decision, but I also told her that I truly believed that what's ailing Dakota is not medical, but spiritual. I asked Suzette what she believed in her heart, and two minutes later I had her approval to proceed with the requisition for the rites of exorcism.

As I mentioned at the beginning of this entry, I just placed my official requisition paperwork in the mail, and I'm scheduled to have a phone conversation with Cardinal Robert Rollins tomorrow morning. I'm confident that the evidence in this case is more than enough to get approval. Dakota has displayed almost superhuman strength, a (possible) aversion to holy water, excessive sexual acts, retro-cognition, and I've seen objects

spontaneously combust in her presence. Add to that the strange

voice that came out of her mouth and the other strange

happenings in the home and I'd say that the Pearcys have a

serious problem.

I pray that I'm able to help.

FATHER DON WILLIS'S JOURNAL ENTRY

DECEMBER 19TH

I received a signed confirmation this morning from the

archdiocese approving the rites of exorcism for Dakota Pearcy. I

immediately called the Pearcy house and spoke to Suzette. We

agreed that I am to proceed with the exorcism tomorrow

afternoon. I've asked that both Suzette and Jeremy be present, but

I asked that Ben not be in the house tomorrow. The Pearcys are

driving the boy to his grandmother's today.

I'll cut this entry short as I must spend the rest of today preparing myself for the work I must do tomorrow. My next journal entry and accompanying audio recording should mark the end of this case.

***

The remaining pages in the journal were blank.

Eddie flipped through the last third of the notebook frantically.

This can't be it, he thought. *Don* had *to have finished the notes.*

But how? He'd been struck blind during the exorcism according to what Father Felix had told him. Then Eddie remembered the bible, written in braille. He picked it up from the corner of his brother's desk and opened it. He ran his fingers over the rows of dimples and he was struck with a new idea.

He typed it.

Eddie began to look throughout the office for typewritten notes. There was nothing in the desk so he moved to the large bookcase. None of the loose papers were what he was looking for. Eddie removed all the books and rifled through the pages, hoping that his brother had stuck notes randomly inside one of them. He hadn't. Eddie removed all of the artifacts from the shelf and checked every nook and cranny for some sign of the notes. For half an hour he searched the office before he finally gave up.

Feeling utterly defeated, Eddie fell back into the office chair and rested his forehead in his hand. In the doorway, Mesha whined as if he could sense Eddie's frustration. Moments later the dog went tiptoeing through the kitchen. Feeling as if even Mesha had given up, Eddie put his head back in his hands. Suddenly, Mesha began to bark from the front hallway. At first, Eddie didn't pay much attention, but the dog wasn't letting up, so he got up from the desk and went out in the hall.

"What's your problem, huh?" Eddie asked when he arrived at the dog's side.

Eddie realized where he was standing. He was overcome by a sense of hope, and at the same time, fear. He had closed Don's bedroom door the night before and had forgotten that the room was even there. Now here he was, standing in front of it, and somehow he *knew* the missing journal pages were inside. Mesha must have known too. Eddie reached down and scratched the shepherd behind the ears.

"You're something else, you know that?" Eddie said.

Mesha must have sensed that his work was done, because he stopped barking. He backed up to the other side of the hallway, laid back down, and put his chin on his paws before he started up with that nervous whine again.

"O.K., that doesn't help much, buddy," Eddie said as he reached out and turned the doorknob. He swung the door open and prepared himself, as he half expected to see Sister Agnes, or maybe even Don himself sitting there on the bed. To his relief, the room was empty. Eddie flipped on the light switch and stepped inside the room, doing his best to ignore the smell of sickness that sill lingered about, and the images of his dying mother that came with it.

It didn't take him long to find the notes. They were hidden between the matrasses of the bed. Eddie also found ten audio cassette tapes between the fabrics. He took the notes and the tapes back to the office, locking Don's bedroom again before he went.

Eddie sat down at the desk again and placed the folded pages and tapes on the desktop. It was several minutes before he could bring himself to pick up the pages and unfold them.

Then he finished reading his brother's story.

***

TYSON HANKS

FATHER DON WILLIS'S JOURNAL ENTRY

FEBRUARY 25TH

I debated whether I should finish my notes on the Dakota Pearcy case, and ultimately I've decided that I have to, more for my own recovery than anything else.

It's been more than two months since I attempted, and failed to perform the rites of exorcism for the girl. My failure resulted in the child's death. I was lucky enough to have just been struck blind and I'm told I'm left with a head full of snow white hair. I feel unworthy to have even been given that much.

I recovered from my own injuries in two weeks, but it's taken me this long to learn how to read and write in braille. I suppose there's a silver lining in that. Reading the Word of God in braille truly gives one the opportunity to ponder and study the intended lessons. The problem is that without sight there's nothing that can provide a visual distraction when outside thoughts start to creep in. For me those thoughts bring with them horrible visions—the last visions I ever saw—and not even scripture can make those visions go away.

And maybe that is God's penance for me.

I arrived bright and early at the Pearcy home on the morning of December 20th and found Jeremy and Suzette both waiting for me at the front door. Once inside, I went over what was to happen and when I was convinced that the Pearcys were as prepared as they could possibly be, we prayed together and went upstairs.

Dakota was in her room, sitting on her bed just as she had been during my previous visit. She grinned at us when we walked into her room and I got the eerie sensation that the girl had somehow been preparing for us, as well.

I laid out the tools I would be using and when I was ready to begin administering the rites

I asked Dakota if she knew why I was there and what we'd be doing. She very calmly informed me that she did, indeed, know why I was there.

I commenced by reciting the Lord's Prayer, and almost as soon as I started to speak, a low, clicking kind of growl came out of Dakota. It wasn't angry or frightening; it was clearly just meant to annoy me. I prayed out loud for almost an hour and a half and never once did Dakota stop that low, growling sound. In an hour and a half she never paused to take so much as a single breath. She simply made that reverberating "Ahhhhhh" noise. When I felt like my praying was getting nowhere I closed my bible. At the same time Dakota stopped making the noise.

"Well," she said, smiling at me, "that was fun. What's next?"

I ignored her and went back to my bag. This time I turned back around with my bible in one hand and an open vile of holy water in the other. The mischievous grin that had been on Dakota's face disappeared at once. What happened next was the first of many intense moments that would occur that day. I'll try to get down the basics of what happened.

I made a mistake by not restraining Dakota before we got started. When the girl saw the bottle in my hand she immediately became agitated and backed up until she was pressing herself flat against the bed's head board. I began my prayer and at the same time flicked a few drops of the holy water at Dakota, and when the liquid touched her, her skin immediately began to blister and she screamed. The scream seemed to be comprised of two voices, similar to what I'd heard in my last interview. I commanded that Jeremy and Suzette help me restrain the girl. Jeremy grabbed her right arm and I grabbed the girl's feet. We both turned to look at Suzette, who we'd expected to take Dakota's left arm, but Suzette was sitting fast in a chair. I had an audiotape recording at the same time, so it will reveal exactly what was said, but either Jeremy or I asked Suzette why she wasn't helping us and she told us that she was unable to get out of her chair. Jeremy got upset and yelled but I could tell by the look on Suzette's face that she was terrified. After insisting that she still couldn't get up Jeremy and I both instinctively let go of Dakota to help her mother. We each grabbed Suzette under her arms and lifted. The woman didn't move an inch.

Suzette Pearcy couldn't have weighed more than 130 pounds, but Jeremy and I couldn't budge the woman. It's as if she was held fast by invisible restraints. What's stranger still is that we couldn't budge the chair she sat upon either. Despite our combined efforts the chair wouldn't move.

The tapes will show how long we actually struggled to get Suzette free (it probably wasn't more than thirty seconds) but the next thing I knew Dakota was on top of me, frantically clawing at my face. Her finger nails sliced open the skin on my forehead and cheeks, and I'm told I still bear the scars today.

Suddenly, Dakota stopped and let out the most horrific scream I've ever heard. When I opened my eyes to see what had happened I saw that Jeremy had picked up my bottle of holy water and dumped the entire contents on top of Dakota's head. The skin on her scalp and face started to blister and split as if the bottle had contained acid instead of blessed water. At the same time whatever force had pinned Suzette to her chair seemed to be lifted and she got up and rushed to Dakota's side. The three of us managed to lift Dakota back onto her bed and we secured her arms and legs with restraints that I'd brought with me for that purpose.

At that point Dakota started to writhe back and forth on the bed and emit a low groan. She kept this up for the next six hours.

I have to stop typing now. Reliving all of

this has made me ill. I'll finish later if I'm able.

***

Don hadn't been able to finish, after all.

Eddie dropped the stack of pages onto the desk and pressed the heels of his palms against his eyes in an attempt to press his frustration out of his skull. He sat that way for a solid minute before he dropped his hands and opened his eyes again.

He immediately focused on the stack of cassette tapes sitting on the desk. The rest of the story *had* to be on those tapes. There was a heavy tape deck on one of the bookshelves in the office and after swapping out batteries from a flashlight in the kitchen, Eddie had the cassette player working.

For the next several hours Eddie listened to the tapes. The first five provided an audio version of what he'd already read. Halfway through the sixth tape the low groaning sound Don had referred to in his writings stopped and Dakota began to speak.

Eddie turned up the volume on the tape player.

"*Speak, priest.*" The voice on the tape sent chills up Eddie's back. It was as if two people were speaking at the same time, just as Don had written.

"*Who are you?*" Don asked. "*What is your name?*"

"I am no one." There was a brief pause and then the voice continued. *"Keep that shit away from me!"*

"Why do you fear blessed water?"

"Because."

"Because why?" Don asked.

"Fuck yourself, priest!"

"WHY DO YOU FEAR IT?!?" Don yelled.

The voice inside Dakota spoke lower this time, almost in a shameful tone. *"Because it hurts us."*

"You mean demons?"

"We have many names, priest."

"What is yours, specifically?" asked Don.

"We are many."

"You are one. What is your name?"

"We ARE MANY!"

"In the name of Jesus Christ I command you to tell me your name!" Don yelled.

There was a sharp hiss on the recording then, followed by a cry of agony. Eddie figured that Don must have splashed the girl with the holy water. The moans soon turned into a diabolical laughter, and then Eddie heard the sharp sound of someone in the room breaking wind. The evil laughter increased.

"You find that funny, do you?" Don asked.

"I do indeed."

"And would you continue to laugh if I place this rosary around your neck?"

The laughing on the tape ceased, and Eddie assumed that his brother had indeed placed the rosary around the girl's neck, because what followed on the recording was another sudden howl of agony. When Don spoke again on the recording he had to yell in order to be heard over the girl's screaming.

"WHAT IS YOUR NAME, DEMON?!?"

The next voice on the recording was a new one, and Eddie presumed that it was Suzette Pearcy.

"Oh God, Father!" she shouted, *"look at her side!"*

"Is that writing?" asked a new voice. It had to be Jeremy Pearcy.

"Step aside," Don said. *"Let me look. It is a letter—it's an 'A'. This might be the entity identifying itself. IN THE NAME OF CHRIST, WHO ARE YOU?!?"*

"There's another one!" cried Suzette.

" 'N' " Don said. He then proceeded to read off the letters one by one as they formed in the girls flesh.

"G"

"U"

"S"

"Your name is Angus?" Don asked. The entity didn't reply. *"So you're not the Devil. What is your last name?"*

Once again, Don read out loud the letters that were being etched into Dakota's skin.

"D"

"R"

"U"

"I"

"M"

"E"

"I"

"N"

"Druimein?" Suzette said.

"It's Scottish," Don said, *"equivalent of the modern day 'Drummond'. So your name is Angus Druimein?"*

The moaning ceased, and the evil laughter started again until the dual voice inside Dakota spoke up again in an almost mocking tone. *"Angus Druimein. A.D. Anno Domini."*

"Or 'A Demon'," Don said. *"Well Angus Druimein, you and I have a lot to discuss."*

Eddie was startled suddenly as the tape deck shut off with a loud 'click'. He fumbled with a new tape and pressed play. After a few seconds his brother's voice filled the office again. Don could be heard asking several questions of the entity now known as "Angus Druimein." For twenty minutes or so there was no response from the entity, then Don seemed to strike a nerve.

"I know something about you, Angus Druimein," Don said. *"I know you're frightened and you're weak, otherwise you wouldn't have latched on to a sixteen year old girl."*

The moaning stopped, and Angus Druimein spoke through Dakota Pearcy. *"And I know something about you, Father Donald Willis. I know your mother was a filthy whore, and I know your brother killed her."*

The words coming out of the tape deck's speakers hit Eddie like a right hook from a street brawler. He attempted to press the stop button on the cassette player but his hands were shaking so badly that he missed the button on the first try. Eddie stared at the tape deck for a long time. There was suddenly something alien and menacing about it.

I heard that wrong, he thought. *That thing didn't say anything about mom.*

Eddie hit the rewind button on the tape deck. He hesitated a few seconds before finally pressing the play button again.

"—filthy whore, and I know your brother killed her."

Eddie didn't realize he was holding his breath until his lungs began to burn, and only when Don's voice came from the speakers did he take a breath again. His brother's voice was much softer than it had been before.

"My mother died of cancer," Don said. *"In her own home."* Eddie thought

352

he heard a trace of uncertainty in his brother's voice.

"Yes, but who was with her when she died?" the other voice asked. When Don didn't respond the voice inside Dakota Pearcy continued. *"Your brother held a pillow over her face until the bitch swallowed her own tongue."*

"NOOOO!" Eddie screamed as he slammed his fist down on the tape deck, stopping the recording and breaking off the fast forward button in the process. His heart was pounding in his chest and he had tears streaming down his face.

She was suffering, Eddie thought. She *was withering away to nothing— rotting in her own piss and shit. And for what? Where was the quality of life in that?*

Eddie thought back to the day his mother died. He'd told the rest of the family she'd gone peacefully and that was basically the truth. She did grab his wrists when he'd pressed the pillow onto her face but she only struggled for a moment. Then she almost seemed to caress his wrists gently with her gnarled hands.

She was thanking me.

He'd never told a soul what he'd done and why should he? His mother was at peace. Eddie had just given that peace to her a few weeks, maybe even *days* earlier than it would have happened naturally. Hearing someone recite out loud what he'd done somehow made it official. He'd murdered his mother, and some demonic entity had told his brother about it.

Eddie sat in silence while outside the house the rain started again, a large flash of lightning announcing its return. After 15 minutes Eddie pressed the play button again.

"You don't know anything about my mother, or my brother," Don said. *"You lie, Angus Druimein."*

The thing inside Dakota Pearcy began to laugh softly. *"Then why do you weep, priest?"*

"I think it's time for a break," Don Said. *"Jeremy, Suzette, let's go downstairs."*

The cassette stopped.

Had Don believed what that thing said? Eddie wondered. Given all the other evidence up to that point Eddie didn't see any reason Don *shouldn't* have believed it. *How come he never said anything to me about it?* Eddie concluded that Don had been handed enough to worry about without having to question whether or not his own brother had committed matricide.

It didn't matter now, anyway. Don was dead; whatever his feelings were toward his brother had gone to the grave with him.

His brother was dead. Eddie was convinced now that he'd died because of something that had happened in that girl's room. Eddie needed closure, and that closure was somewhere on the remaining cassette tapes. He stuck a new tape in the player and pressed play.

For the next hour Eddie listened as his brother prayed and the girl resumed her uninterrupted moaning. There didn't appear to be any sign of the entity called "Angus Druimein." Another hour and another tape revealed more of the same. Halfway through the last tape Angus Druimein returned.

"I grow tired of you, priest."

"Then you must leave this child's body in the name of God!" Don yelled.

"I am older than your God. His name means nothing to me."

"Then what are you, Angus Druimein, if you're older than God?"

There was a response to Don's question but Eddie had to rewind the tape three times and turn the volume up all the way before he could hear it clearly. Even then, the reply made no sense to him.

"Wen-di-go" whispered Angus Druimein.

What followed was more words in a tongue Eddie didn't recognize.

"Oshikiniigikwewe boogidi. Nibaa hachi miskwi."

"Your gibberish means nothing to me," Don said. *"What do you want?"*

"Zagaswe wakti anaamisagamig mazinagigan."

"Enough," Don said, frustration creeping into his voice. Or was it pain?

"Diba'igiiziswaan."

"STOP IT!" Don was yelling now.

"Father, are you o.k.?" Suzette said from what sounded like the other side of the room.

"Maanadikoshens."

Don's screams on the recording grew more agonizing. *"My eyes are burning!"*

"Oskenzhig!"

The scream on the recording then was so intense that the tape deck's speakers started to crackle. Eddie's hand instinctively shot up to turn down the volume. His brother's wail carried on for a solid ten seconds before stopping.

"*Oh my God!*" Suzette Pearcy said. "*Jeremy, help me!*"

"*Father, what's wrong?!?*" Jeremy asked.

"*I—I can't see.*" Don started to cough. At first it was subtle, but then the coughing fits increased in intensity until Don was gagging and hacking so badly that he was no longer able to speak. Shortly after, Suzette could be heard screaming.

"*JEREMY! DAKOTA'S NOT BREATHING!*" she cried.

"*What?!? OH MY GOD, SUZETTE, CALL 911!*"

The tape continued for another five minutes. All that was left on the recording were the sounds of Don and Suzette screaming and Jeremy trying to revive his daughter. With a final, definitive "click" the tape turned off.

Eddie Willis sat at the desk in silence for a long time. He'd heard everything now, and somehow he still felt empty. Eddie thought of Angus Druimein and how he still didn't fully understand who or what he was. He'd said something in that strange language. *Wen-di-go.*

The word made Eddie think of a man—a man named Henry Blackwater.

Henry Blackwater used to be an anthropology professor at Cahokia College. When Eddie was younger, Blackwater had spoken at a county fair of some sort about the Native American tribes that had been indigenous to their part of the state. He'd brought an impressive collection of artifacts with him, including arrow heads and many other primitive weapons and tools.

Eddie had been fascinated. The bizarre dialect on Don's recording sounded to Eddie to be somewhat Native American, and he figured if there was anyone in the area that could make sense of it, it was Henry Blackwater.

Cahokia College was only a short fifteen minute drive away. For a brief moment Eddie had panicked because it dawned on him that he didn't have a car, and he really didn't feel like trying to track down Father Felix after what had happened earlier at the lunch. After a quick search in the kitchen he managed to find the keys to his brother's sedan. Thirty minutes later Eddie stood at the welcome desk in the Cahokia College's administration building, only to be told that Henry Blackwater had retired five years earlier. However, after a little flirting with the receptionist Eddie acquired Blackwater's home address. Luckily he still lived in the area.

Eddie pulled into a hidden driveway that snaked a quarter mile through overhanging trees before the house became visible. A porch wrapped around all visible sides of the house and in the very front sat Henry Blackwater. Eddie put the car in park and stepped out into cold rain. He trotted up to the porch steps and stopped when he saw the tomahawk sitting in Henry Blackwater's lap.

"If you're here to rob me I'm afraid you'll come up short-handed," Blackwater said as he theatrically ran his thumb over the tomahawk's glistening edge.

Eddie pulled his jacket up over his head to block the rain. "Sir, I assure you I'm not here to rob you, and I'd like to keep both my hands."

Henry Blackwater studied him for a moment before setting the tomahawk down in his lap. "Come on up here out of the rain then, before you drown."

Eddie stepped up onto the porch, grateful to be under the shelter of the awning. "Sir," he said, extending his hand, "my name is Eddie Willis. I met you once when I was a boy. You were giving a talk at the county fair on some of the local Indian tribes that lived in this area."

Blackwater shook Eddie's hand. "I'm guessing you didn't drive all the way out here for an autograph."

"No, Mr. Blackwater, I did not. I was hoping you could help me with something else. My brother, Don, was the priest at Saint Benedict Parish in Barker Marsh."

Blackwater nodded. "I believe I read about his recent passing. I'm sorry for your loss."

"Thank you. Did you happen to hear anything about the details of his death, Mr. Blackwater?"

"Nothing more than rumors, really. Developed some health problems after some unfortunate business with another local family, didn't he?"

"Chances are the rumors you heard were true," Eddie said. "My brother was attempting to perform an exorcism on a girl. She died in the process and my brother was rendered blind."

If the story made Henry Blackwater nervous or uncomfortable in any way the old man didn't show it. "So what is it that you want from me, Mr. Willis?"

Eddie reached into his jacket and came out with the cassette tape he'd brought with him. "This is a recording of part of the exorcism my brother performed. The…thing—whatever it was—that was inside that girl spoke a strange language. It sounds like Native American but I'm certainly no expert. Could you listen to it and tell me what you think?"

"Why?" Blackwater asked. "What difference does it make to you?"

The man's reply caught Eddie a little off guard. He hadn't planned on justifying his position and he had to fight the urge to become angry. "Honestly sir, I'm not really sure. The truth is, my brother and I grew apart over the last 15 years or so. I guess I'm just trying to get some closure. Figure out why he died, I suppose."

"He died because that's what was in the stars for him. We're all going to die, Mr. Willis, nothing we can do to change that. When it's our time, it's our time."

Now Eddie *did* get angry. This man was his last chance at figuring out what happened to Don. "Yeah, well what about the time we spend living? I'm telling you I *have* to find some answers, otherwise my brother's death is gonna eat away at me for the rest of my days. You were a professor, Mr. Blackwater, isn't there something to be said for the pursuit of knowledge?" Eddie realized that his eyes were filling with tears, and he turned around to look out at the rain-drenched woodlands. "I'm just looking for answers, Mr. Blackwater."

The old man continued to stare at Eddie as if making a final decision as to how he should proceed. Finally he cleared his throat. "Fair enough, Mr. Willis. Fair enough."

Eddie spun back around. "You'll help me?"

"I'll try," Blackwater said, extending his hand, "but first you have to help me up."

Ten minutes later Eddie was sitting in Henry Blackwater's study, sipping a very good bourbon. The old man placed a tape deck on the coffee table between them and then slowly sank into a chair, taking care not to spill his own whiskey. When he was settled he leaned forward, elbows on knees, and rested his chin on top of his interlaced fingers.

"O.K., Mr. Willis," Blackwater said, "let's hear what you've got."

Eddie put the cassette in the player and pressed play. He'd rewound the tape to the point just before the demon known as Angus Druimein started speaking in its strange tongue. When the voice came through the speakers Eddie sat back in his own chair. A contemplative look crept across the old man's face, but that was the only emotion he showed as he listened to the tape. Only when the cassette player clicked off did Blackwater take his chin off his hands.

"Well," Blackwater said with a long exhale, "It *is* Native American, but it's not indigenous to these parts—not Chickasaw or Illini or Shawnee."

"O.K.," Eddie said, "so what is it."

362

"I believe it's Ojibwe, but it's an extremely old dialect."

"What did she say?" Eddie was on the edge of his seat.

"I only caught bits and pieces—I'm not really an expert on Ojibwe. I need to hear it again, but first you're gonna need another drink."

Eddie looked down. He hadn't realized it but he'd completely drained his glass. "Why do I need another one?" The apprehension in his voice was palpable.

"If I heard what I think I heard, we're *both* gonna need it."

Blackwater topped off their glasses again and Eddie rewound the tape to roughly the same spot, then pressed play.

"I grow tired of these games, priest."

"Then you must leave this child's body in the name of God!"

"I am older than your God. His name means nothing to me."

"Then what are you, Angus Druimein, if you're older than God?"

"Wen-di-go."

"Stop it there," Blackwater said.

Eddie reached down and hit the stop button. "What does that mean, *wen-doh-to?"*

Blackwater sat back in his chair, a look of deep concentration on his face. "Wendigo," he corrected. "It's a legend among Algonquin tribes. It's sort of a demonic half-human, half-beast creature. Hold on a minute, I think I have a picture of one around here someplace."

Eddie watched as the old man got up out of the chair and went over to an overflowing bookcase. After searching for a moment he brought down a dusty volume. The Professor flipped through the pages for a moment and then found what he'd been searching for.

"Here we go," Blackwater said as he handed the book over to Eddie.

The creature in the photo was hideous. It was very tall, with an almost wolf-like head, though the eyes were sunken deep in the skull. The beast appeared emaciated and gaunt with dark, sickly flesh pulled tight over its bones. This particular rendering showed the beast with tattered, blood covered lips on top of sharp looking fangs, as well as long fingers like daggers.

"It looks like an anorexic werewolf," Eddie said as he sat the book down on the coffee table.

"The wendigo is one possible origin of the modern werewolf mythos." Blackwater replied.

"So how did this thing possess a little girl?"

Blackwater shook his head. "Don't think of it as a *thing*. What you see in that photo is simply its physical form. It is first and foremost a demon; malevolent and with great spiritual power. It could easily take over a human in its spiritual form."

"But why Dakota Pearcy?" Eddie asked.

"I don't know. It's strange. The wendigo is part of the belief system of many tribes. Ojibwe, Cree, Innu. Details vary but all the legends agree on one thing. The wendigo is conjured when humans indulge in the practice of cannibalism."

"You think Dakota Pearcy *ate* someone?" Eddie asked, surprised.

Blackwater shrugged. "I'm just telling you the legend. I don't know how it happened, but if the spirit of a wendigo took possession of that girl's body then your brother was up against some serious evil. Wendigo is one of the most feared legends in Native American culture. Let's keep going—press play."

Eddie turned the cassette player on again and the two men listened together. Eddie cringed at the strange gibberish and his brother's agonizing cries while Henry Blackwater only furrowed his brow as he mentally deciphered what was being said by the evil thing inside Dakota Pearcy.

Finally, the tape ran out again.

Blackwater sat back in his chair again and slugged down the remaining whisky in his glass with one gulp. He didn't speak.

"Well?" Eddie said. "What about the rest of it."

"At first it just says some very unflattering things about the girl." Blackwater said.

"Why was my brother screaming?" Eddie asked.

"It cursed him," said the old man. "His eyes. His vision. What we just heard was the equivalent of your brother's eyes being burned out of his head."

Eddie didn't speak, only sat there with a faraway look.

The old man could see that Eddie was torturing himself with his thoughts, so he broke the painful silence. "What does the name 'Angus Druimein' mean to you?"

Eddie blinked and looked back up at Blackwater. "Uhh, nothing. It sounds Scottish. Why would an Ojibwe spirit refer to itself as a Scotsman?"

"Why indeed," said Blackwater. "But cursing your brother wasn't all it did. Your brother's praying must have been hurting it—it only cursed his vision as retaliation. Before that it started to answer his questions.

"How so?" Eddie asked.

"Your brother was asking what it was, and what it wanted. At one point the thing says something about his answers being in a book. It goes on to say that this book is hidden somewhere beneath the church."

Eddie pondered this for a moment and then shook his head. "No, that doesn't make any sense. There's nothing below that church—no basement." As soon as he'd said it the realization came to him and his skin broke out in gooseflesh. "The basement is under the school. The school was a church, originally. The current church was built in the early 1900s; my great granddad helped build it."

"Well, according to the thing on this tape there's a book down there—maybe that's where your closure is, Mr. Willis."

"God help me," Eddie whispered.

***

Eddie hadn't set foot in the basement under the school since he was twelve years old but he could remember it vividly. He knew how many steps it was from the base of the stairs to that awful office room where Sister Agnes had led him so many times. (*Ninety six.*) He remembered the dim lightbulbs along the tunnel, shrouded in their metal cages. He remembered how even during the driest part of summer there were always puddles of water here and there along the floor. What Eddie could picture most vividly were the statues at the end of the tunnel.

Eddie was still thinking of the statues, and of what Sister Agnes made him do in front of them, when he pulled back into the driveway at the rectory. It was after 10 p.m. and the rain was still coming down in sheets. Eddie shut off the car and ran up the back steps to the house in a hurry, though he wasn't sure why—it wasn't as if he could get much wetter. He inserted the house key into the lock and as he turned it he noticed a note stuck to the glass. It was from Father Felix. He'd apparently stopped by to check on Eddie once more after the meal that afternoon. Felix went on to say that he'd done his best to smooth things over with the ladies who had prepared the food, especially "Violet", who was apparently the plump little woman whom he'd had his altercation with. Felix ended his note by telling Eddie he'd check on him tomorrow.

If I haven't been killed by a cannibalistic ghost, Eddie thought as he opened the door and stepped inside the house. He grabbed a flashlight from the kitchen, stopped long enough to give Mesha a scratch behind the ears, then stepped back out into the pouring rain.

He walked across the grassy lot toward the school like a condemned man heading for the gallows. When he was finally standing under the protective awning of the school's side entrance Eddie pulled his brother's keys out of his pocket and went to work on the padlock holding the double doors closed. After a few attempts he found the right key and the lock clicked open.

For the first time in almost thirty years Eddie Willis stepped inside the school. The hallway was very dark and for a moment he thought about trying the light switch on the wall, but then thought it best if no one driving by outside knew he was there. He pulled the flashlight out of his back pocket and thumbed the switch, half expecting the light to flicker a few times and go out, just like in the movies, but the beam lit up, steady and strong.

He made his way slowly down the hall until he was standing in front of a decrepit wooden door. Here he paused for a long time. Beyond that door was Eddie Willis's personal hell. He'd experienced the most traumatizing events of his life down there and now he had to go back. Eddie thought about what Henry Blackwater had said. *Maybe that's where your closure is, Mr. Willis.*

Blackwater had given Eddie a small leather pouch on a string before he'd left the old man's house. He'd told Eddie it was a medicine bag of sorts and that it would provide some protection against insidious spirits.

Eddie had the bag hanging around his neck and he reached up and touched it. He'd have preferred to have had an army of religious crusaders armed with crucifixes and wooden stakes, but for now the small leather pouch would have to do. With as much courage as he was able to muster, Eddie pulled the door open and started down the stairs.

The smell was worse than he remembered. It was a musty, wet smell that had been there since he was a kid, but there was also something else. There was a smell of rot and decay. Eddie recalled his brother's journal entries about the smell in the Pearcy house and he once again touched the medicine bag around his neck.

Eddie reached the bottom of the stairs and shined the light down the long hallway. The hallway was crowded with stacks of student desks and chairs from upstairs. Eddie took a step and then froze.

He heard something.

Eddie shined the light far down the tunnel. He heard the noise again. It was a heaving clicking sound and it was coming from someplace beyond the reach of the flashlight's beam. Eddie held his breath and listened and he heard the sound again, closer this time but still beyond the reach of his flashlight. It sounded like…hooves.

The noise echoed badly off the concrete walls in the basement but Eddie was positive that's what he was hearing. Suddenly the clicking noise broke into the unmistakable triplet beat of galloping, coming toward him.

CHHIT! CHHIT! CHHIT!, CHHIT! CHHIT! CHHIT!

The light began to shake as Eddie's hand trembled uncontrollably. The sound grew louder as if some beast were running right at him. Before he'd realized he'd done it, Eddie's hand instinctively shot to his side and found a set of light switches on the wall. The hall was suddenly bathed in a dim light when he flipped the switches. It wasn't well lit by any means, but Eddie could see the tunnel in its entirety. It was empty. The sound had stopped.

He took a deep breath as a wave of adrenaline coursed through his body and turned off the flashlight. He placed it once again in his back pocket and started down the tunnel, grateful to have the protection of the overhead lights now. He'd barely made it ten feet before the first light bulb blew. It was the one at the far end of the tunnel, and Eddie had barely processed what had happened when the next bulb in the line blew out.

This time the sound of falling glass accompanied the event.

A wave of blackness began to roll down the tunnel toward Eddie as each light bulb blew out, one by one. Eddie could hear the echoing sound of hooves again, as if something was coming toward him, protected by the advancing blackness. Eddie was frozen with fear, and when the light above his head finally exploded he found himself in complete, paralyzing darkness.

He stood there, silent. The sound of the approaching hooves was gone but a new, foreboding feeling crept up on him. Eddie felt that there was something, or *someone*, standing right in front of him. He waited for something soft and cold to brush his cheek. Finally, when the anticipation became too much he reached into his back pocket and fumbled for the flashlight. He was shaking and the light slipped from his hand and clattered to the floor. Eddie crouched down and began feeling for the light, praying that his hand would find it before he touched whatever was making the hoof sounds. He continued to grope around on the floor as another sound started from the far end of the tunnel. It was a low, groaning "ahhhhhh" sound.

Oh Christ, Eddie thought, *it's the same sound that was on Don's recording of the girl!*

At that moment Eddie decided that he was going to turn and feel his way along the wall back to the stairway. He was giving up on finding his "closure." However, at the same time he was about to stand up his left hand touched the comforting grip of the flashlight. Eddie pulled it to his chest as if it was the most valuable item in the world and flipped on the switch. The flashlight's bulb flickered for a second and then went out again.

Must have jarred the batteries a bit when I dropped it, he thought.

He gave the light a couple of good whacks with the palm of his hand and the bulb flickered on and off again before finally emitting a dim, but steady light. Eddie shined it down the length of the hallway.

There, at the farthest reach of the light's beam, stood Sister Agnus, dressed in her black dress and habit. She was standing in the center of the hallway, looking at Eddie and grinning crookedly as a result of her twisted, shattered neck.

The flashlight flickered out again.

Eddie slapped the light against his palm again and the flashlight flickered back on. Sister Agnes was fifteen feet closer. Her dress and habit were gone and she stood there in the center of the tunnel naked. Her neck was no longer twisted at a grotesque angle and her long black hair fell perfectly around her bare shoulders. Her breasts cast perfect shadows on the wall next to her. Eddie continued to stare. The flashlight illuminated the voluptuous curve of her hips and the dark triangle of hair between her long, slender legs.

Eddie was enchanted. He lusted after her and suddenly he wanted to put his hands on her body. He took a step toward her and then he heard his brother's voice in his head.

(*"Stop, Eddie! She isn't real! And even if she was, think about what she did to us down here!"*)

Don's subconscious intervention was enough to grant Eddie a moment of clarity, and he quickly turned the flashlight off, leaving him once more in total darkness. The clicking noise once again began to echo through the tunnel.

CHHIT! CHHIT! CHHIT, CHHIT! CHHIT! CHHIT!

Eddie turned the light back on and screamed. Something was standing in the tunnel, fifteen feet away from him now. It was taller than the height of the tunnel and it was bent sharply at the waist. The thing's face vaguely resembled Sister Agnes and was covered in sickly grey skin. Instead of a nun's habit the thing bore large, antler-like appendages. It had arms that tapered into long, clawed fingers that nearly touched the floor. The things broad chest quickly collapsed into an emaciated and hollow looking stomach. Sister Agnes's legs had been replaced by stocky, hair covered hind quarters that ended in large hooves.

Here it is, Eddie thought. *Wendigo.*

The flashlight started to flicker again. On. Off. Light. Dark. Each time the tunnel became illuminated the Wendigo was closer. Sometimes it was the beast, sometimes it was Sister Agnes in her habit, others it was the nude version of Sister Agnes. Eddie was still frozen in place with fear but when the thing was finally standing directly in front of him he tried to step backwards, tripped over his own feet, and went down hard on his back. There, in the flickering glow of the flashlight, stood his dead mother.

She looked just as she had on the day she died. *The day I killed her,* Eddie thought suddenly. She was wearing her light yellow nightgown, stained with piss and vomit, and what hair she had left stood up in disheveled little tufts. Eddie had forgotten how bad she'd looked at the very end. She was even more emaciated than the Wendigo-thing, and now Eddie could smell her, too. He could smell her waste and the faint chemical smell from the Methotrexate the doctors had pumped into her in an effort to destroy the cancer that was eating away at her.

Eddie's throat tightened and he could feel hot tears on his cheeks. A low moan escaped him and eventually formed words. "Ohhhhhh, Mom."

"You killed me, Eddie," his mother said.

Eddie tilted his head slightly at the sound of his mother's voice, only it wasn't *entirely* her voice. There seemed to be two different voices coming out of the thing standing there. One voice was distinctly his mother's, and one was something else entirely.

"You killed me," the strange voice repeated. "You suffocated me just when I was getting better."

Eddie shook his head, "No, mom. I helped you. You were dying. Suffering. I-I gave you peace."

"Then so shall I giveth you."

The thing that looked like Eddie's mother bent awkwardly at her waist and placed both hands on the concrete. She started to crawl toward him, placing one leg over each elbow alternately like some kind of circus contortionist.

You're not my mother, Eddie thought as the thing reached out and wrapped its hands around his throat. It squeezed with an inhuman amount of strength. As Eddie brought his hands up to grab the thing's wrists he had another thought, this time of something else that Henry Blackwater had said.

"It is first and foremost a demon; malevolent and with great spiritual power."

The thing choking him was not his mother, it was a Wendigo, and this realization made Eddie remember the leather bag that was around his neck.

He reached up and grasped it, and then he tugged on it, hard. The leather band that was around his neck snapped and Eddie did the first thing that came to mind—he slammed the bag into the thing's face.

An inhuman howl erupted from his mother's mouth and she let go of Eddie's throat as she leapt off of him. He was still holding the medicine bag in front of him as if it was a crucifix warding off a vampire. The bag suddenly burst into flames and Eddie quickly dropped it. The thing that looked like his mother looked at the flaming bag with eyes that had suddenly gone jet black, and she howled at Eddie once more. Then she twisted her body into that crab-like position again and scuttled backwards down the tunnel, knocking over several of the stacks of student desks along the wall. When she was no longer in the range of the flashlight's beam Eddie stood up. The thing was gone.

When he'd first entered the school he hadn't had a clue as to where he should start looking for the mysterious book, but now that he was down here in the basement and had seen how badly the Wendigo wanted to stop him from proceeding he had a pretty good idea where to look for it.

He entered the large room at the end of the tunnel and could tell by the feeling in his stomach that he was getting close. The statues were still there, right where he'd left them thirty years before. Several of them opened non-existent eyes and turned their heads to follow him as he walked by. Eddie remembered what Blackwater had told him and moved calmly past the moving statues.

"You're not real," Eddie said as a chipped and fractured Saint Francis reached out with his marble hand and tried to grab him. It took every ounce of self-control he had, but eventually Eddie had navigated the gauntlet of stirring relics and entered the office where so many awful things had happened to him as a child.

Eddie pulled the chain that was connected to the single bulb hanging from the ceiling and was a little surprised when the light came on. He turned off the flashlight and stuck it back in his back pocket. Being back in that office was making him nauseous, but he'd come too far to stop now. Somehow he knew he was in the right place to find the book, but he had no way of knowing its *exact* location.

Eddie started feeling along the floor for loose stones and when that turned up nothing he checked the ceiling, finding only concrete. His eyes fell upon the wall of filing cabinets that made up one side of the office. The cabinets barely had an inch of clearance from the ceiling but there was enough of a gap between two of them to shine his flashlight so the wall behind them was visible. From the floor to about chest level the wall appeared to be the same cinder block construction as the rest of the basement, but then the construction changed and Eddie could see through the gap that the upper portion of the wall was made of individual stones and masonry. He realized he was looking at the foundation of the original church, and he was positive the book he was searching for was somewhere behind those stones.

It took Eddie a good bit of time and a lot of sweat to move the large filing cabinets, but eventually he was able to access the stone wall. He started checking the wall, brick by brick until he finally found one that was loose and managed to work it out. Eddie shined his light into the void left by the missing brick and it revealed a cavernous crawl space.

"This is a lot of fucking work for some closure," Eddie said to himself as he swung the brick he was holding hard at the wall. Forty minutes later he'd managed to create a hole big enough to crawl through. He pushed himself up on his forearms and shimmied into the crawlspace.

As Eddie crawled further into the void beyond the wall it became increasingly more difficult to control his paranoia. He was afraid that with each subsequent sweep of his flashlight he would find himself staring face to face with the Wendigo, or Sister Agnes, or worst of all—his mother. Finally his flashlight did land upon something but it was neither beast, nor nun, nor mother.

To Eddie, it was more frightening.

The flashlight's beam cast a bright reflection from the plastic mask. Eddie stared into the blank eyes of Droopy Dog as a wave of dread washed over him. He had a dozen thoughts hit him at once—memories of the things Sister Agnes would do to him while he wore that mask. For a moment it appeared as if someone, or some *thing* was wearing the mask, but it was only a trick of the shadows cast by the mask itself.

There's no way that could be in here, Eddie thought. He took a moment to compose himself. *There's no way a bunch of statues could move on their own, either, or that you could have a conversation with your dead mother. Remember, asshole, the Wendigo is first and foremost a demon; malevolent and with great spiritual power.*

With some of his courage replenished, Eddie crawled forward and knocked the evil token from his childhood aside, revealing the prize that was lying beneath it.

The book was there, just as the voice on the recording had said it would be. Just as Eddie had *known* it would be. It looked ancient, and Eddie was cautious as he picked it up. He soon realized he had nothing to worry about—the book was heavily bound in thick leather and protected by a layer of dust inches thick. There was no title on the cover or the spine of the book, but when Eddie opened it and saw the first page it became clear why this was important to his understanding Don's death.

The Journal

Of

Father Angus Druimein

Eddie shimmied his way backwards out of the crawl space. He was relieved to be back in the relatively open office. It was time to get the answers he'd been looking for. Eddie thought for a moment about sitting at the desk but when he recalled everything that had happened to him on that desk he opted to sit on the cold, hard floor instead.

Eddie Willis shifted on the floor until the light from the single overhead bulb was just right, then he opened the journal and began to read.

***

Father Angus Druimein's Journal Entry

17, July 1672

I am truly blessed to be in the midst of such exciting events.

Three days ago our party broke away from the main river to float

a tributary in the hopes of finding a substantial amount of

unclaimed territory ripe with agricultural promise. I daresay I am

both giddy and as boisterous as the other men for I believe we

have found our destination!

We've landed on the shores of a flat and fertile looking plains.

The scouting party reports plenty of vast, open range perfect for

planting and hunting, as evidenced by the deer the group brought

back to the boat. The animal was most impressive, much larger

than the deer in Scotland!

Most importantly, there are no signs that this territory is

inhabited by the indigenous savages we've encountered so many

other times along the Main River. Also, by all accounts it would

appear as if we've beaten the French here!

The men are currently butchering the deer and I must confess that I can't wait to bless the fruits of their labor and indulge. I have a positive feeling that we may have found a new home here.

23, August 1672

Life on the river bank is flourishing! Ample lumber has provided our party the means to build permanent dwellings. I'm happy to say that I very nearly have my own church—well, four walls and a floor anyway. We were able to find plenty of stones manageable enough in size to construct a solid foundation and our final wall was raised yesterday. I imagine we'll have the roof complete in another fortnight. What a joy it will be to conduct a service in a solid church again. A shaded hollow is a fine place to gather and worship, to be sure, but I must confess that I long for my own structure, of stone and wood, to keep up and provide for the congregation.

Enough about my selfish desires!

We've made contact with another tribe of natives lately. At first they only made their presence known at night when they would encircle our camp. Many a member of our group got little

rest that first week, for fear of the same sort of savagery we'd

experienced from other native war parties along the big river. It

became clear, however, that this tribe was different. Finally, after

a period of about ten days, two scouts from the natives

approached our camp in the daylight. After a period of primitive

communication it was obvious that these people meant our group

no harm. We learned that this group was not indigenous to these

lands, and were looking to establish roots among these fertile

plains, much like our own people. There may have been some

initial concerns regarding territoriality but these were quickly

dispatched when our group and theirs agreed that there was

plenty of suitable land in this valley to support both our

communities. That first meeting ended with a trade—some of our

weapons for a few of their horses, and I'm elated to say that a

friendship has sprouted.

10, September 1672

I have a church! We've completed the roof, and earlier than

expected, thanks to the help of our new friends, who we've

learned are called "Ojibwe." We've managed to construct a few

rows of pews, and I've already started holding services. Those

that have no seats are perfectly content to sit on the floor.

The weather in the valley here has grown quite pleasant.

Gone are the stifling hot days we encountered when we arrived

almost two months ago. The days are now perfectly comfortable

and the nights are growing quite mild (I daresay, even cold.) This

pleasant climate has caused a frenzy among the men in our group.

They've managed to harvest a good amount of the fast growing

summer crops that were planted upon our arrival, and those lads

not farming were busy in the woods or on the river bank, filling

our drying huts with fish and game. We're still not sure what

type of winter to expect, but we're attempting to preserve as much

food as possible should the coming months prove to be especially

harsh.

The Ojibwe are proving to be excellent neighbors. They're quick to donate men when our group needs assistance with a particularly large project and they've shown us new methods of smoking meats for preservation. A few Ojibwe have even attended a few of my sermons, probably more out of curiosity than anything else, though I am optimistic that I might convert a few!

29, September 1672

This entry will be far more disheartening than most of my previous writings. Under different circumstances I'd not even place these thoughts on page, but as the only clergyman in this part of the territory, I've no one to whom I may confess my sins so this book will have to serve as the vessel by which I can cleanse my soul.

My first love is for the Lord, and I've spent my life thus far loving only him. Save and bless me Father, for I have sinned. My sin is that I have love for another. Perhaps love is not the appropriate word here, as I am speaking not of the kind of love a priest has for his congregation, or any child of God for that matter. I refer to the kind of love—nay, lust—that men of the cloth have taken a vow against.

A young Ojibwe girl, called Istas, has attended my last three sermons and I confess, while I carried out the appropriate stages of the service, the girl commanded my thoughts completely. She is beautiful beyond words and the damnable reality of my situation is that by simply writing of her beauty I am a sinner.

I have done more than write, though.

The girl was there again at my service this morning, and after hastily shaking the hands of my congregation as they exited the church I rushed to catch up with the group of Ojibwe as they walked through camp. I asked if I might have a moment to walk alone with the girl, surprising even myself at my brazen act. Under ordinary circumstances I'm sure the Ojibwe would have been very much against a girl strolling alone with a foreign white man such as me, but they recognized me as a holy man and acquiesced my request with little hesitation.

I wish they had not.

Istas and I walked down to the river's edge. The girl was silent the entire time and I prattled on like a juvenile. I can recall little of what I actually spoke, but what seemed like a short stroll was soon discovered to have been much lengthier than I'd realized, for the sun was low in the West and there was a noticeable drop in the temperature. At that point I removed the cloak from around my shoulders and wrapped the garment around Istas's shoulders. My hands brushed her bare skin as I did this and from that point my memory of what happened is a maelstrom of images and emotions. I remember the girl shying away from my touch at first, but then, as if swimming in a cool spring, she seemed to melt into the moment and she pressed herself against me. I can remember looking at her when the hide she had wrapped around her body fell to the ground. The next thing I can recall is laying on top of her, sweat slicked and exhausted from my efforts. Istas was smiling after it was over, and Lord help me, so was I.

1, November 1672

I thought that this valley would bring happiness and prosperity when we arrived four months ago, but now I fear that our landing here could have been the Devil's work, as evidenced by the catastrophic events of my own life.

My affair with Istas has continued over this past month, despite my many requests for the Lord to intervene and grant me the strength to suppress the evil urges that have taken over my conscious mind. My sins culminated two days ago when Istas told me that she is with child. She went on, in her primitive way of communicating, to say that she wished to be with me, presumably as my wife. I did my best to explain to her that this was impossible but the girl has no sense of my God, or the vow I've taken to serve him. She persisted in her efforts, even as we re-entered the outskirts of the camp, to the point that she was causing such a commotion that I was forced to strike her several times. She responded with tears and what I can only assume was a salvo of berating in that strange language of hers. As painful as the whole episode has been, I thought that it was behind me, along with the temptations.

I was wrong.

This afternoon a group of Ojibwe rode into camp, their faces painted in the black and red streaks indicating their war colors. They were not their usual, cordial selves. Istas rode with them, and when she spotted me she went off on a tirade, pointing and gesturing at me. Soon the men in the party joined in. Their accusations were clear to me, but thankfully they were still lost on the other members of our camp. One thing was clear: our friendly relations with the Ojibwe were over.

The pinnacle of the encounter occurred when an ancient looking Ojibwe rode out of the party and stopped just short of the church entrance, where I stood. There was no anger on the old man's face, only a stoic grimace. He pointed a gnarled finger at me and spat a series of phrases before finally throwing the carcass of a headless rabbit at my feet. With that, the Ojibwe rode off toward their camp.

2, November 1672

Strange events to report. I sat up late last night discussing the encounter with the Ojibwe with several of the men in our camp. The men picked up on the fact that the Ojibwe's change in temperament seemed to be directed at me, and I did a good job of feigning bewilderment. It was decided that a scouting party from our own camp would ride east to see what the Ojibwe tribe was up to.

We woke this morning to freezing temperatures, and as the scouting party began their trip the valley began to swirl with snow flurries. Those of us that remained in camp went to work processing firewood for what was starting to look like the inauguration of the winter season. When our party returned in the afternoon the flurries had progressed to fat, wet snowflakes which we found strange, given the information we'd learned about the area's seasonality. Stranger still was the news that the scouting party brought back with them.

The Ojibwe tribe has gone. Vanished. They've apparently torn down their camp overnight and moved out of the area, taking all signs that they were ever here with them. Our little village seems to be taking the news with equal parts confusion and sadness at the disappearance of what most considered "friends." I pretend to share their sentiments, but let me write and confess to it here on these pages that I am relieved to see the Ojibwe gone. The news of Istas carrying my child presented a world of evils, and I feel her and her people simply disappearing is the best resolution.

19, November 1672

Peculiarity continues to abound in our valley, and the situation is becoming more and more dire. When winter made its brutal arrival two weeks ago our camp's main concern was with firewood to heat the village. We've managed to keep up with the

season's demands by organizing daily wood processing tasks and
rotating members of the village. Our main threat now is a lack of
food, which makes no sense to us.

Prior to the beginning of November we had ample meat and
vegetables stored to get us through winter. The cold arrived,
which should have made preservation even easier but somehow
over half of our cache has spoiled. It is bitter cold, and even when
packed in ice the meat we stored in the summer is turning rancid.
Many villagers have turned to me for answers, hoping that prayer
will bring an end to this bizarre, and threatening situation. The
surrounding forest, once full of game, is now barren and devoid
of life. The village elders have met and we've elected to ration our
remaining food supply and post guards on the storage sheds.
This will buy us a small reprieve, but if we're not able to secure a
reliable source of fresh food I fear the worst.

10, December 1672

Our situation has reached the precipice of desperation. Our

remaining food cache lasted far less than we'd expected. We haven't had fresh meat in camp in over a week. I believe some of the villagers stocked away their own personal reserves, but most of us in camp are suffering from the onset of starvation. The pain in my stomach is rivaled only by the pain in my head, so I must cut this entry short.

15, December 1672

One of the men shot a crow today and we were able to feed some of the children, but this is only a minute ray of hope in an otherwise bleak situation. For most of the camp, myself included, it's been a week since we've eaten anything. The pain in my gut feels as if a hot iron is being stuck right through my middle. We thought that our salvation may come by way of fish but the bitter cold has frozen the river near our village. The ice is so thick that none in the camp has the energy to chop through it. I've turned to the Lord for answers, and while he has yet to provide a solution to our plight, I do believe he has provided an answer as to the cause.

Last night I dreamt of the Ojibwe, and specifically of the old man that had hurled the rabbit's carcass at my feet. I believe now that the old heathen laid a curse on our village that day, and it is this curse that has spoiled our meat, frozen the river, and caused the game in the valley to vanish. I wish now that I had never laid eyes on the girl Istas, or at least drowned her in the river when she told me she was with child.

29, December 1672

The first of our villagers, a boy of eleven, has succumbed to starvation. The boy died early this morning. His father set out to bury him at first light but the frozen ground, combined with his own weakened state prevented him from removing a fraction of earth sufficient enough for a grave. We've elected to keep the boy's body in one of our drying sheds as they certainly aren't being used for food storage right now. We'll give the lad a proper burial in the spring when the earth thaws. That's, of course, assuming there are any of us left.

3, January 1672

Another of our villagers has died. A woman this time. We placed her in the drying shed with the boy. I know her name but for some reason can't think of it right now. I've barely the energy to write. The cold has kept most of us inside for a month now, but this morning I left the church to collect some snow to melt for tea—the only nutrition available right now. As I looked across the village I spotted someone kneeling in the snow. I walked closer and found John Barclay clawing frantically at the frozen ground. His fingers were bloodied and the snow immediately around him was pink from his efforts. I asked what he was doing and he told me he was trying to get to his garden, where he was sure he'd missed a handful of potatoes earlier in the fall harvest. I managed to get him back to his wife and then returned to my church, where I collapsed from the whole ordeal before waking and writing in this journal.

I don't think we'll make it much longer.

5, January 1673

My hands shake even now as I attempt to record the events of the past two days and nights. My heart and soul ache over what I've done but deep down I know that the decision made by myself and a few other villagers have sustained the lives of those in our community for at least another fortnight.

Perhaps I should start at the beginning. Heaven help me should anyone find this book.

Two nights ago three men from village came late and knocked on the rear entrance of the church. At this time I'm leaving the men's names out of this record. The three were in the same famished state as most of the other villagers, and when they first told me the purpose of their visit I dismissed it as the ravings of desperate men. But then they began to explain their plan in detail, and God help me if I didn't rationalize it.

Their plan was simple enough. They would sneak the bodies of our two deceased villagers into the forest, and they would butcher them into portions that would be unrecognizable as human remains. Then they would roast the meat and disperse it among the village.

As I said, my first reaction was one of pity and silent disgust, but soon the aching in my own guts drove me to ask some questions of these men. I asked what would happen when the bodies were discovered missing from the drying shed. The men had planned for this. One of them would claim to have seen an animal—a wolf or one of the large cats we'd seen in the summer— drag the bodies out of the shed and into the forest. Then they'd say the three of them pursued the animal and killed it, and that's what they'd be serving to the village.

I asked what was to be told to the families regarding the recovery of their kin's corpses. The men said they would tell the village that the corpses were so badly mutilated that they elected to bury them in the forest, in the earth made soft by the fire used to cook the very beast they'd swear allegedly took the bodies in the first place.

I also asked the men what they planned to say when no

animal tracks were found around the village. They were confident that after more than a month with no substantial food no villager would question too severely the means by which such a hearty bounty was acquired.

My final question was why they had come to me at all. Why hadn't they just carried out their plan? They said they wanted my blessing, and they wanted confirmation that a person's soul had no attachment to their earthly body once they'd died, and that no matter what happened to the remains on earth, a person's eternal life would not be diminished. I told the men I couldn't be sure, but at that point I'd already made up my mind to support the plan. My life and the lives of many villagers depended upon it. I told the men that to be safe I would accompany them and say a blessing over the bodies before they carried out their deed.

And that's how it came to be that late last night four of us snuck the two corpses deep into the East woods. I blessed the remains, as I said I would, and the men went to work with their knives. I tried to focus on the fire we'd built, and its warmth, as the men went about their butchering. By the time dawn started to preside over our actions, however, I was a participating member in the grotesque process. As the meat finished cooking I would wrap it in the animal skins we'd brought for that purpose. Lord forgive me, but the smell! It was the most glorious fragrance I've ever experienced.

By the time the sun was at its highest point today we had a cache of roasted meat that weighed near 120 marks. As we descended back down to the valley there was no trace of regret over what we'd done. We went to each family in the village and distributed a hearty ration of the meat. The villagers were elated. Some laughed at our sudden good fortune while others cried.

Ian McConnell cried when he accepted his portion. He sobbed and asked me why God would have taken his son only a week before providing our village with such a bounty. I had no answer for him, and he became downright inconsolable when we told him the beast we had slaughtered had actually stolen his son's corpse from the drying shed.

When the sun went down I retired to the church with my own

portion, which by that time had completely cooled. It didn't

matter. After my first bite of the tough, but flavorful meat I

became ravenous and devoured the entire portion without hardly

taking a breath.

It was the most fantastic meal I've ever had in my life.

15 March, 1673

Easter is upon us and yet winter continues to embrace our

valley in its brutal clutches. It seems that our quartet of butchers

is destined to repeat the events of that first night in January every

four weeks or so. That first distribution of the meat managed to

sustain most of the villagers through the beginning of February,

but then another of our group starved to death. We followed the

same process as before, only this time the deceased's family

actually managed to bury her, so we had to dig her up before

butchering the meat. That was a month and a half ago, and

there's been no food since. I was told this morning that a family of three had just been found in their cabin. It appears that the

child starved to death, and the mother took her own life in her

grief. Her husband, having returned to find his wife and child

dead, turned the same knife his wife used to open her throat on

himself. As there are no remaining family members to bury the

bodies I've told the villagers that I, along with the three other

men, will take the bodies into the forest to bury them and that we

may do a little hunting while we're there.

I'm confident that we'll be successful.

1, May 1673

Winter has gone. I wish that this news brought joy to our

village, but it does not. It is true enough that the temperatures are

perfect, the foliage in bloom and the river thawed, but somehow

our food situation remains as dismal as it was in the heart of

winter. Not a deer, nor fowl nor fish of any kind is to be had in

our valley. I am fully convinced that now that the old Ojibwe

cursed our camp last Autumn, his intention to starve us out of the valley. The old fool failed to account for a Scot's resourcefulness and the extremes we'll endure to survive!

I suppose the sanest way to describe my latest actions is to say that I simply had to elevate our level of resourcefulness in recent days. The improved climate has made it much easier for all of our villagers to sustain life without food. No one has succumbed to starvation in nearly two months. While most of the village sees this as good news, my conspirators and I see it differently. Simply put, with no villagers dying we've no way to provide food for the community as a whole. That's why I'm confident that God will forgive us for our actions this day.

A man called Seamus has been bedridden for a month after succumbing to an infection following an accident in the forest with an axe. His leg had to be amputated and his health has been failing ever since. This morning we four men—men who have single handedly kept this village alive—visited Seamus and conducted what I must vehemently stress was a mercy killing. Three of us held him down while the fourth squeezed his throat until what miserable life the man had left fled his body. Again, I must stress that this man was already at the precipice of death.

At any rate, our foursome is off to our clearing in the forest this evening to do what must be done.

We shall survive yet!

8, June 1673

I don't know why I continue to write in this book, for I realize now that it has become a record of the heinous actions of a madman. Something drives me, or at least my quill, to continue though.

Two major events have affected our village in the last month.

The Ojibwe have returned.

One evening last week a boy came running into the church, shouting that a band of demons had entered the village. The boy had been lighting torches and lanterns along our village's main thoroughfare, and when he reached the end he told me they were there, at the edge of town and they surrounded him while mounted on steeds that could only have been raised in the bowels

of Hell. Upon hearing this news I took to the street myself and

summoned as many of the men in town as I could muster. When

our posse arrived at the edge of town I realized that it wasn't an

army of demons on hell steeds that the boy had seen, but an

Ojibwe scouting party. I recognized at once that the old medicine

man was among their ranks. I stepped forward and prepared to

confront the old man; to demand that he remove the curse he'd

laid upon us, but before I could utter a word the old man made a

gesture toward me and said something in his savage tongue. I

was hit with a horrible pain in my gut, far worse than anything I'd

felt as a result of the many months of starvation. I fell to the

ground in agony and began to writhe about. At the same time the

medicine man had dismounted his horse and was soon standing

above me. None of the villagers had the nerve to approach me or

the old man. He leaned over me and pressed his thumb onto my

forehead. I could feel him smearing some kind of oily substance

onto my flesh, and then he repeated a single word in Ojibwe three times. It's the only term in Ojibwe I've ever been able to recall.

Wendigo.

I fainted at that point and when I awoke I was back in my bed, having slept for an entire day and half another. I spent that day in fear that the old man had made our curse even worse when at some point that afternoon a commotion arose in the center of our village. I went to find the cause of the whooping and hollering and when I reached the congregation I saw that the Ojibwe were not the only thing that had returned to our valley.

At the feet of two young men lay three of the largest deer I've ever seen. I joined the crowd in cheering and then the game was quickly hauled off to be processed, as a bountiful feast was planned for later that evening. Hours later, when the roasted meat was placed in front of me I did my duty and blessed the meal, as well as our good fortune. I joined in with everyone else as we all did our best to remain dignified in our dining habits, even though this was the first real food they'd had in months. I managed to consume three bites before I suddenly fell victim to the same agonizing, stabbing pains in my stomach that I'd felt in the presence of the Ojibwe several nights earlier.

So, for four days the villagers have gorged themselves on fresh meat and I've not been able to take a single bite without being overcome with that crippling pain in my midsection.

I still starve, and long for sustenance. But, Lord save me, it's not wild game, fish, or herb that I long for.

It's the flesh of man.

20, June 1673

I cannot understand why I'm compelled to continue this journal, this record of evil and darkness. Perhaps it's so I'll have some written record to prove that I'm not utterly insane. Let it be written here: I have done terrible, heinous things but not by my own volition.

I have now murdered 3 villagers since the day the old Ojibwe touched me. I murdered them, and then I ate them. All of them. Muscle, fat, hair—even their bones. And yet my hunger is still not sated. The ecstasy I feel when I swallow their flesh lasts but a fraction of a second, and then I ache for more. The more I eat the more ravenous I become.

The rest of the village has remained clueless to my deeds, as I've consumed all of the evidence. That no longer matters. My physical appearance has altered so much that I dare not walk the village during the day. I have consumed the weight of three men and yet still my stomach is hollow and emaciated. This I could hide with clothing. What I cannot hide is my growth in height. I must be near half again as tall as I was this past winter. My clothing no longer fits and I find my own appearance so grotesque that I've destroyed all of the mirrors in the church. I've kept the other villagers at bay by telling them through closed doors that I'm showing symptoms of cholera.

Will this nightmare never end?

1, August 1673

I'm barely able to write any longer. My hands have

transformed into hideous claws and holding a quill is quite awkward. No matter; this shall be my final entry.

I am all that remains of our quaint little village. After I ate nearly a dozen people the majority of the townsfolk fled downriver. They feared the Ojibwe were somehow responsible for the disappearances.

I ate the villagers that remained.

Now I have nothing left. No parishioners. No neighbors. No food. The hunger pains I feel are beyond excruciating, and that's why I'll be taking my own life this afternoon. I'm fully aware that suicide is a damnable sin, but I wager it is a minor one given everything else I've done over the last year. I'm burying this journal beneath the floorboards of the church and then I'm going down to the river to drown myself.

Should anyone ever find this book I can only say that I'm sorry.

***

Eddie closed the journal with mixed emotions. On one hand the mystery of Angus Druimein was somewhat clearer. Henry Blackwater had been right about the Wendigo legend. Druimein was a cannibal all right, but that didn't explain how he was able to possess a teenage girl over 300 years later. And what about the rest of those villagers? Weren't they technically all cannibals too, even if they didn't realize it? Were they wendigos? Eddie finally conceded that he was never going to fully understand what had happened in this dreadful town or why his brother had died for it. All he cared about now was getting on a plane and going back to sunny Florida. Goodbye wendigos, goodbye Sister Agnes, goodbye Barker Marsh.

For a brief moment Eddie thought about keeping Angus Druimein's journal, but somehow he knew by doing so he'd never truly be able to put his brother's death, or Barker Marsh behind him. He threw the book back into the crawl space and stepped out of the office. He glanced back into the room at the cold, metal desk. He thought of Sister Agnes.

"Burn in hell, you bitch," Eddie said.

As he walked slowly down the hallway toward the stairwell Eddie could see out of the corners of his eyes that the statues were once again turning their marble and alabaster heads to follow him down the tunnel. He didn't speed up, or panic. He waited to hear that dreadful sound of hooves behind him but it never came. Somehow he felt like reading the journal had given him some kind of immunity over the Wendigo's power.

He climbed the stairs and was back in the main hallway of the school. He felt like a weight had been lifted from his shoulders as he started toward the door. Eddie had made up his mind to leave that night. He would go back to the rectory, pack his bags, leave Father Felix a note, and then drive back to St. Louis where he hoped to catch a red eye flight back to Orlando. He'd leave the keys to the sedan behind the fuel cap door so Father Felix could retrieve it, and then he'd be done with the whole mess.

Eddie was reciting the letter he was going to write in his mind when he stepped out of the school and back into the damp night. When he glanced up and saw the woman standing in front of him he would have sworn that it was Sister Agnes, but as the woman stepped forward he saw that she was much shorter and far more plump. Eddie Willis barely recognized her as the woman he'd argued with over lunch that day when someone came from behind him and brought a heavy steel pipe down on his head.

**

Eddie couldn't see or hear, but he could taste, and it tasted like he had about two dozen pennies in his mouth. Then there was a new taste—this one taking root far back in his nasal passage. It took Eddie a few seconds to register the smell and taste of smoke from a fire. Slowly his other senses began to return. He could hear the crackling fire, and muffled voices. Finally he'd regained enough awareness to attempt to open his eyes. The heat and glare from the fire, combined with the throbbing pain in the back of his head almost caused him to pass out again. A sudden, sharp slap across his face brought him crashing back to reality. Eddie's eyes snapped open fully just as the plump little woman reared back and slapped him again.

"ALRIGHT GODDAMIT!" Eddie shouted. "Fuck, lady! I'm awake!" Eddie instinctively tried to bring his hands up to guard against another blow, and that's when he realized he was unable to move. A quick glance around him revealed that Eddie was lashed tightly to a thick tree. He struggled for a moment until the ropes began to cut into the flesh of his wrists. He looked up at the fat woman. "What the hell do you want?"

"My my," said the woman, "aren't you a foul little creature. That's three curse words in a matter of seconds. Your brother was a priest, for heaven's sake."

"Hell doesn't count as a curse word. It's in the bible." Eddie had a sudden feeling as if he were twelve again, trying to argue with Sister Agnes after he'd been caught cursing.

The woman shook her head in condescension. "No matter, it's still blasphemous. Anyway, do you know who I am, Eddie?"

"Yes, you're the bitch that tried to get me to eat your shitty barbecue earlier today."

The woman's eyes narrowed to snake-like slits and she inhaled sharply through her clenched teeth, clearly angered by Eddie's insistence on using curse words. "My name, you little potty mouth, is Violet Drummond."

"Congratulations," Eddie said, "Now why am I tied up?"

Violet just stared up at him for a moment. "My name doesn't' mean anything to you?"

"Should it?" Eddie asked.

"Oh for the love," Violet said as she rolled her eyes. "Violet Drummond? DRUMMOND."

Finally it hit him. *Drummond. The modern day version of—*

"Druimein," Violet said, finishing Eddie's thought for him. "Took you long enough, smart guy."

"But how? I mean…" Eddie couldn't get his brain to form the question, but somehow Violet Drummond managed to come up with the answer.

"It was the Indians," she said. "The Ojibwe. See, apparently old Angus had a problem keeping his filthy, Scottish pecker in his pants, and he impregnated some poor Ojibwe girl. I suppose that would be my...."

Violet looked upwards and crinkled her nose, as if trying to figure out a math problem. "Great, great, great to the fourth power grandmother or something like that. Anyway, the Ojibwe slap this wendigo curse on Angus, but what they don't realize is that a wendigo curse is some seriously bad juju, and it not only cursed old Angus, but his entire family, which happened to consist of one unborn and illegitimate child. So when my great great whatever it is grandma was born they found out the hard way that the child would only eat flesh. Boy, makes you feel sorry for the Mom and wet nurses don't it? Anyway, the rest of the tribe banished mother and child and forced them to take on the name of Druimein. Well, The Druimeins actually managed to flourish over the years, and eventually became 'Drummonds' and viola, here we are!"

"We?" Eddie asked.

"Oh, Barker Marsh has bred quite the population over the years of us folks with...ummm...*particular* culinary tastes."

"You mean cannibals?"

Violet sighed heavily. "Boy, you have a real talent for getting under folks' skin, you know that?"

"But how?" Eddie asked. "I mean, the rest of the town would have caught on if you were eating people left and right."

"That's where my people come in," said a gruff, booming voice. Peter

Ramsey stepped out of the shadows and into the firelight. "You see, Eddie, my family's been in the funeral business a long time in this valley, and you grew up here—you know how many unfortunate things can happen to folks in Barker Marsh. Sorry about your head, by the way. I guess I cracked you a little too hard."

Eddie stared in disbelief. "So, you mean…the graveyard…the bodies…"

Pete Ramsey nodded. "Let's just say there's a lot more old phonebooks and sandbags buried in Antioch Cemetery than actual bodies. Oh come on, Ed, we don't eat *all* of them; it really only works for closed casket funerals. They tend to not taste very good after they've marinated in formaldehyde you know. I gotta get them processed when they're fresh."

"Fucking monsters," Eddie said as he lowered his head.

"Hey!" Violet shouted. "You think this is easy on us? I mean, we have like, the worst food allergy on the planet. Put yourself in our shoes."

"O.K., so what happens to me now?" Eddie asked.

"Isn't it obvious?" Ramsey asked in return.

The condescending grin drained from Violet Drummond's face, leaving a sinister glare in its place. "We cook you, and then we eat you."

Eddie watched in horror as Violet Drummond and Peter Ramsey began to change. It wasn't until Violet's floral print dress split, revealing the same emaciated torso he'd seen down in the school's basement that

Eddie began to struggle to free himself. It was no use; he couldn't budge.

Peter Ramsey, who ordinarily stood over six and a half feet tall, was now

towering almost 14 feet tall. When he was completely transformed the

Ramsey-thing squatted, bringing its height down to a mere six feet, and

then it threw its head back and laughed. The sound that rose from the

creature was a deep, crackling rasp.

Eddie actually grinned a little then. After everything he'd been

through since his brother's death he didn't believe anything could surprise

him, and yet here he was, about to be devoured by two malevolent demons.

"Well come on then," Eddie said. "I hope you fuckers choke!"

Both of the wendigos took a step toward him. Eddie made one last

futile attempt to free himself from the ropes. He knew it was useless—

there was nothing left for him to do now but die. As the wendigo that had

once been Violet Drummond stepped closer Eddie spat at her—the last act

of a condemned man.

She stopped in her tracks.

For a moment Eddie thought he might have suddenly developed some

kind of superhuman spit capable of warding off evil spirits, and then he saw

the crude looking arrowhead protruding from the creature's chest. As he

stared a second arrow erupted from the thing's torso, sending a jet of tar-

like black fluid toward Eddie's bound feet. The second creature—Pete

Ramsey—turned and looked at its partner with the arrows sticking out of it.

As the Ramsey-thing turned its giant head to see where this attack was coming from, another arrow suddenly erupted from the back of its skull. It let out a piercing shriek and dropped back to its knees. The Violet creature turned toward her mate just as another arrow burst through the side of her skull, too. She also dropped and joined in that horrific shrieking.

Eddie looked up to see where the barrage of arrows was coming from. At first he thought the fire and smoke were playing with his vision. As the Indian limped toward the fire there was no mistaking the stocky frame of Henry Blackwater. Before Eddie could say a word Henry took his tomahawk out of his belt and sliced through the rope that was holding Eddie fast to the tree.

"What the hell are you doing here?" Eddie asked.

"I kept reading after you left," Blackwater replied, "I realized that if these things were real you were getting in way over your head. Here, hold this."

Blackwater handed Eddie the tomahawk and then reached into the buffalo hide satchel he had slung over his shoulders. Eddie expected him to pull out some Indian artifact, and was more than a little surprised when he came up holding a quart size bottle of Gatorade. As soon as Henry unscrewed the cap it became obvious that what was inside the bottle was *not* a sports drink. The smell of gasoline was overpowering and did nothing to quell the headache that was still throbbing in Eddie's skull thanks to Pete

Ramsey.

"What's that for?" Eddie asked.

Henry Blackwater turned toward the two creatures writhing on the ground. "Everything I read tonight says there's only one way to destroy a Wendigo." Blackwater didn't need to say anything else for Eddie to figure out what was about to happen. The Indian dumped the contents of the bottle over both creatures, then he grabbed the safe end of a burning branch and removed it from the nearby fire.

There was a sudden WHOOSH! sound when Blackwater touched the brand to the Ramsey-thing's back. The wendigo was immediately engulfed in an intensely hot flame; the kind you can feel more than you can see. It began to shriek horribly again and writhe violently on the ground. In its agony, the thing rolled into the side of its partner, and soon what had only minutes before been Violet Drummond began to flail about in that same hot blaze.

Blackwater stepped back and dropped the stick. "Let's see how that works."

Eddie opened his mouth to ask Blackwater how he could be so sure the fire *would* work when there was a sudden inhaling noise as if the atmosphere immediately around the two wendigos was struggling for air. Then the two creatures exploded in an intense ball of heat and when Eddie was able to open his eyes again all that remained of Peter Ramsey and

Violet Drummond was a swirling blizzard of black ashes and a few glowing embers.

"Jee-zus!" Eddie exclaimed. "I'd say the fire thing works."

"Did you find the book?" Blackwater asked.

Eddie nodded. "You wouldn't believe it. Angus Druimein was a priest! He was one of the founders of this village. He and a handful of others resorted to cannibalism to survive a bad winter, and according to his journal an Ojibwe medicine man placed a wendigo curse on them. The book ended with Druimein saying he was going to drown himself in the river."

"And he may very well have," Blackwater said, "but that would have only destroyed his physical body. His soul, and the wendigo, would have gone on living, free to possess who or whatever it wanted. I'd say that's what's been happening ever since."

Eddie gestured to one of the black spots on the grass, scorched from the intense heat. "Violet Drummond said she was a descendant of Angus."

"How is that possible?" Blackwater asked.

"The book spelled it out. Angus apparently got some poor Indian girl pregnant." Eddie paused for a moment, thinking. When he spoke again the color had drained from his face. "The old medicine man could have cursed more than just Angus. He could have cursed the whole town, or at least anyone that ate human flesh, right?"

Henry Blackwater nodded. "That follows, sure."

"So anybody that's still around these parts who happens to be the descendant of an original founder could be one of those things, too. And Violet said something about Barker Marsh having quite the population of folks with her *particular tastes*."

"That means you could have a whole town full of those things, bucko. You got a plan?" Blackwater asked.

Eddie nodded. "Yeah, I think I do." He fully intended on telling Blackwater what his plan was, but when he looked up at the Indian he froze, unable to speak. Blackwater picked up on his look of terror.

"Eddie, what's wrong?" he asked.

Sister Agnes stepped up behind Blackwater; Eddie raised his hand and pointed at her. He wanted to do more; wanted to tell Blackwater to watch out, or run...something. Blackwater started to turn to see what Eddie was pointing at, but he stopped suddenly as the wind was knocked out of him. The Professor looked down and was surprised to see a hand protruding from his chest. There was something bulky, wet, and shining in the hand and it was pulsing rhythmically. Before he could process what it was, his vision faded to black. He thought he heard Eddie screaming from someplace far, far away. Then there was only silence.

Sister Agnes retracted her arm from the gaping hole in Henry Blackwater's chest and the man dropped to the ground like an empty suit of clothes. Eddie stared in horror at her naked body, now slick and dark with Blackwater's blood. She dropped what was left of the man's heart to the ground and turned her gaze to Eddie. As she took a step toward him Eddie's right hand tightened around the grip of the tomahawk. He'd forgotten that he was still holding it. He couldn't even be sure if she was real or not, or if the tomahawk would have any effect on her. She was real enough to tear out Blackwater's heart, and Eddie didn't exactly have time to siphon another Gatorade bottle full of fuel to throw on her.

When Sister Agnes took another step Eddie brought his arm up and back, and with all his might he hurled the tomahawk at the woman who'd haunted his dreams for so many years. Eddie realized that it didn't take near as much skill to wield the weapon as he would have thought. The weight of the axe head took care of most of the work and it connected perfectly with the center of Sister Agnes's forehead. She rocked back in a scream and then collapsed to her knees. When she brought her head forward, Sister Agnes was gone, only the wendigo remained. It was clearly hurt, and more importantly, it was *distracted.*

Eddie turned and ran, praying that Blackwater had left his keys in his truck. When he'd closed the distance to the pickup truck by half he had a sudden thought and veered off toward the back of the rectory. When he reached the back door he flung it open and called for Mesha, who was at his side in an instant. The man and dog turned and both sprinted to the light blue truck parked in the road. When they reached it Eddie yanked the door open, grateful it was unlocked. Mesha jumped up in the cab ahead of Eddie, the key was still in the ignition. Eddie turned it and contrary to his fears, the engine roared to life. When he turned on the headlamps he saw that the wendigo was on its feet again. It took a step toward him. Eddie slammed the gear shift lever into reverse and stood on the gas. The truck lurched backwards in a spray of gravel, and when he found the hard top he cut the wheel hard and spun the truck so it was facing East. Then he dropped the truck in first gear and punched the accelerator again.

***

Henry Blackwater asked Eddie if he had a plan. He did, and it was a simple one. It was obvious that fire worked on the wendigos, so if you come across a wendigo, you burn it. If you come across a *town* full of wendigos, you burn the town.

Eddie had made two stops in the last hour and a half. His first was at the old zinc smelting plant, where he scavenged until he'd found as many 55 gallon drums as he could fit in the back of the truck, which turned out to be five. The he'd gone to Huck's filling station—the only one in Barker Marsh—and purchased 130 gallons of fuel. In a town like Barker Marsh there as nothing strange about a man filling a truck bed full of gasoline.

After that Eddie had driven out to the old Barker Marsh trestles. He used to play there as a kid, against his mother's wishes (she thought the place was full of Devil worshipers). The trestles were built to haul tons of coal from the mines below, but in 1962 they burned after a mine explosion. Eddie was thinking about that disaster as he eased the truck to a stop, a quarter mile into the remaining mine entrance. His Grandfather had told him about the mine disaster of `62 and there was one thing that Eddie distinctly remembered about the story. His grandpa had said that the bad part about a coal fire was that it burned for a long, long time. Sometimes even years, smoldering away. Eddie was counting on this part of the story being true.

When he could go no further he got out, and opened the tail gate of the truck. With considerable effort he managed to roll the drums—each half full of gasoline—out the back. It took hours but he rolled each of these into what he hoped was a strategic place in the mine and poured the contents of the drums on the ground. When he'd rolled the second to last drum into a fairly tight cavern the smell of sulfur almost dropped him to his knees. Eventually Eddie got his bearings and figured the smell was a good sign—it should help this portion of the mine go up like a Roman candle. He made damn sure not to create any sparks in this particular area.

When he was down to the last drum Eddie was struck with the realization that he had given zero thought to how he was going to ignite all of that gasoline. In the end it was Saturday morning cartoons that provided the answer. He'd seen Wiley Coyote attempt to blow up the Road Runner by placing a handful of bird seed on top of a barrel of black powder, then pouring a trail of powder back to his place of safety behind a rock where he would light the powder trail and hopefully be feasting on roast fowl that night. Of course the Road Runner had moved the barrel behind the rock while the Coyote was pouring the trail of powder so in the end he succeeded only in blowing himself up. Still, at this stage in his own game, Eddie thought the theory was sound.

He took the last drum of gasoline and removed the cap. He kicked the drum on its side and rolled it into each cavern he'd placed another drum until he'd created a trail of gasoline from the mine entrance to each of the locations within the mine. Eddie had a quarter of a barrel of fuel left when he'd completed his task. He managed to roll the drum back outside the mine and into the bed of the pickup truck.

When he'd done everything he could, Eddie sat in the driver's seat as the truck idled eagerly. He looked over at Mesha and said, "You think there's a chance in hell this is gonna work?"

The Australian Shepard gave an enthusiastic bark and that was all the reassurance Eddie needed. He put the truck in reverse and rolled down the window. With the truck's cigarette lighter he ignited a page from and Atlas he'd found in the glove compartment and when the sheet was fully ablaze he dropped it onto the puddle of fuel outside the truck. A blue streak immediately started racing toward the mine entrance as Eddie popped the clutch and started racing backwards toward the hard road. As he turned the truck around and dropped it back into first gear he glanced in the rearview mirror.

Come on, he thought. *This has to work.*

Eddie's ears popped suddenly as the atmosphere around the truck seemed to have the air sucked out from all sides. Deep in the abandoned mine the flames had reached the first cavern and when the explosion from the fuel mixed with the residual sulfur in the air it created a hyper-intense wave of heat and flame that desperately craved oxygen. The wave of fire rocketed upwards toward the mine entrance where it belched outward into the night sky like a geyser from some hellish middle-earth. Eddie saw this and floored the accelerator. He'd barely made it a quarter mile when a second blast, much larger than the first, erupted from the center of the old trestles. Somewhere off to his right, several blocks over, another fireball lit up the sky. Eddie said a silent prayer that no innocent people would be harmed, but he knew that there would be some collateral damage in his actions. His chest thumped as another explosion shook the air somewhere ahead of him. He kept driving.

When Eddie Willis reached the western town limit of Barker Marsh he pulled down a farm road and stopped the truck short of the railroad tracks where he had the best vantage point of the Marsh. He got out of the cab and climbed into the bed of the truck where he took a seat on top of the drum of gasoline. Mesha jumped into the bed with him. The two looked out across the freshly harvested corn field at the town.

Bright orange blazes had popped up all over the town where the explosions from within the mine had found vulnerable pieces of earth and burst forth to the open air, fueling the flames.

Eddie sat there for almost an hour, and by the time the impending dawn started to brighten the sky on the opposite side of town tall flames had begun to lick the horizon in half a dozen places where the coal fires had found more than just air to fuel themselves. He smiled as he watched the tall steeple of Saint Benedict topple in a web of flame and black smoke.

He listened to the sirens of the fire trucks throughout the town and wondered how many of the volunteer firemen were wendigos.

They're wasting their time, Eddie thought. *The bad thing about a coal fire is that it burns for a long, long time. Sometimes even years, smoldering away.*

As Eddie thought of his grandfather's words he spotted the figures on the opposite side of the field. It was still dark enough that he could only make out the outlines. There were probably two dozen in all—some were clearly human and others were much taller, and skinnier. There seemed to be one at the front of the pack that was leading the group on their march across the field. Eddie recognized the curves of the body and the sway of the hips, both of which were extremely unbecoming of a Catholic nun.

Run, you bitch! Eddie thought.

But he knew it wasn't *really* Sister Agnes. She was dead—Eddie had witnessed it. No, the thing leading the horde of wendigos across the field was the spirit of a man named Angus Druimein.

For a split second Eddie thought of running—just hopping in the truck and driving all the way back to Florida. But that thing out there had killed his brother, and countless other people. Eddie had killed, too. He'd killed his mother, and while at the time he thought it was out of love Eddie realized that he needed to answer for that horrible sin. In the end Eddie elected to stay right where he was. He had a little payback to dish out.

He turned to Mesha. "You better take off, boy. You don't want to be around for this."

Mesha gave him a pleading whine and licked his hand.

"Come on, now," Eddie said. "Don't make me cry. Thanks for everything. Now get out of here."

The dog gave him a final, pleading look and then jumped out of the back of the truck. Mesha ran along the tracks, leaving Barker Marsh, and Eddie, behind him.

Eddie turned back around and when the horde of wendigos were halfway across the field he knocked the barrel of gasoline over, soaking the bed of the truck and himself in cold fuel. He hopped out of the truck and leaned against the side as the wendigos grew closer. He took a Zippo lighter out of his pocket.

When they were twenty feet away the group stopped. The thing that looked like Sister Agnes stared him down, her breasts heaving with anticipation.

"I wish you really *were* her," Eddie said. "That'd make this far sweeter."

With that, Angus Druimein abandoned his Sister Agnes disguise and took on his pure, wendigo form. With a howl, he and the rest of the creatures rushed Eddie.

At the same time, Eddie flicked the flint wheel on the Zippo and when the orange flame danced from the top of the lighter he dropped it at his feet.

Eddie never felt the heat. The last thing he saw before his own eyes melted was the look of shock and terror on Angus Druimein's grey face, moments before he exploded in a swirl of ash and sparks.

For a split second Eddie Willis felt a tremendous sense of revenge, and then penance, and then peace.

And then Eddie Willis felt nothing at all.

Chapter 5

"It was early in the mornin'

When they raised the hobo's head

The smile still lingered on his face

But Hobo Bill was dead

There was no mother's longin'

To soothe his weary soul

For he was just a railroad bum

Who died out in the cold"

—Rodgers, Jimmie. "Hobo Bill's Last Ride." Victor Talking Machine

Company, 1929

By the time Hasty finished his story about Eddie Willis and the
destruction of Barker Marsh, the rain outside the Barker zinc smelting plant
had all but stopped.

It had been a long story indeed.

The first faint glow of daylight started to creep into the dilapidated
surroundings of the plant. The Drifter had a pretty good drunk weighing
him down at that point, and he was still trying to wrap his swimming head

around the story.

"But that just doesn't make sense," the Drifter said. "I mean, an entire town can't burn to the ground just like that, man."

"Weren't you listening, boy," Hasty replied. "Coal fires burn a long time. They still burnin' now."

The Drifter shook his head. "Nah, I saw the town last night when I rolled in. I saw the buildings and none of them were on fire."

Now it was Hasty who shook his head. "You saw what the town *wanted* you to see, Lou. You don't believe, you go see for yourself, now that you know a few of the Marsh's dirty little secrets.

The Drifter stood up, and between the booze and his injured ankle it took a moment for him to steady himself. He *did* want to see for himself, and he started limping toward the opening he'd come through the night before. The approaching dawn had made it easier for the Drifter to see his surroundings, so he was comfortable leaving the relative protection of the fire. When he was halfway to the opening, he turned around, half expecting Harold "Hasty" Davis to be gone—he was, according to his story, a ghost after-all.

Hasty was still there. He looked up and met the Drifter's eyes, then he went back to poking at the fire with a stick. The Drifter continued toward the opening and when he reached it his first reaction was that the old man might have been quite the raconteur, but he was ultimately full of shit. The large, empty lot in front of the plant looked the same as it had the previous day. There was still a fleet of rusted equipment, and the giant, crippled smoke stack still lay on the ground, although now it appeared to be floating in a lake thanks to the torrential rains.

As the Drifter stepped further out into the courtyard the sun started to peak out over the horizon to the East, but the sky directly overhead and over the majority of the town was still blanketed in an overcast fog. It was as if the sun's rays hit an invisible barrier just outside of the smelting plant, and there was no breaking through.

The Drifter turned back to the West and froze where he stood, oblivious to the fact that the puddle he was standing in was soaking through this worn work boots.

The town was essentially gone.

When he'd hopped off the train the day before, the Drifter had seen the tops of several buildings and a few church steeples stretching above the tree line. There was still technically a tree line, but the trees were charred and dead, like hundreds of giant black skeleton hands bursting through the smoldering earth. No church steeples were visible now. In their place were towering tendrils of black smoke.

Hasty was right. The town had burned. It was still burning. The Drifter could smell the fire and it reminded him of his childhood days as a boy scout, when it would take days to wash the smell of campfire out of his hair after a weekend trip with his troop.

Smell wasn't the only of his senses that was assaulted as he stood there in the water. He could also feel the heat coming from the heart of the town like an infectious fever.

His head began to swim as his body dealt with the smell and the sight of something that he would have sworn was impossible. He bent over at the waist then and vomited into the puddle of muddy water at his feet. When he finally stopped retching and opened his eyes he saw that his feet were splashed in dark, thick blood. A coagulating mass of blood floated on top of the soupy water where the drifter had been sick.

Fear gripped him as he straightened back up, and that's when the Drifter noticed that his chest and stomach were soaked in sticky blood that hadn't been caused by him throwing up. He patted his wet t-shirt in several places and when he brought his hands away again they were covered in blood.

What in God's name is happening to me? he thought.

The Drifter attempted to wipe blood from his mouth with the back of his hand and succeeded only in smearing it across his nose and cheeks. Then he turned and walked back toward the opening of the plant and stepped back inside.

Hasty was standing now. The stick he'd been using to poke at the fire was planted between his feet; the other end cupped by his hands and his chin was resting on top of them.

"Whatcha' think now, Lou?" Hasty asked when the Drifter finished limping back over to the fire.

"What the fuck is going on?" the Drifter asked. "I mean, what's happening to me?"

Hasty laughed like a loon again before answering. "And people says *I'm* simple. Chrissakes, Lou, ain't you figured things out yet? Everything is dead. This town. Me. And here comes the shock ending, Lou—you're dead too."

"The hell are you talking about?" said the Drifter, before spitting another bloody mass at his feet.

"Look at yourself. All that blood's from bullet holes."

The Drifter looked down at his blood soaked shirt while his mind continued to reel. He ran his hand across his chest; when he felt something jagged under the fabric of his shirt he touched the area with his finger. It disappeared up to the second knuckle. He lifted the shirt up and he probed a total of 7 bullet holes in his chest and abdomen. The Drifter lowered his shirt and looked back up at Hasty. He opened his mouth to ask more questions, but the old man held a large hand up before he could speak.

"Give it a second, Lou," Hasty said. "It'll come to you."

The Drifter stared down into the flames of the fire until, as Hasty put it, "it came to him." At first, he had a flash of his struggle with the other hobo, and he could plainly see himself burying the screwdriver in the other man's throat. The vision shifted back to what he assumed was the present and Hasty Davis was there on the other side of the fire, leaning on his stick. Before the Drifter could say anything there was another flash and he was back on the train, but only briefly, because he was jumping off again. He could feel the pain in his ankle as if it had just that moment been sprained. Another flash and there was Hasty and the fire again.

Flash!

He was breaking into the veterinary clinic, searching for medications to dull the pain in his ankle.

Flash!

Hasty and the fire.

Flash!

Now he was seeing something completely new—it wasn't a memory from the night he'd killed the other man.

Only, it was.

The Drifter saw himself coming out of the back door of the veterinary clinic with his hands full of medication. Suddenly he was blinded by a bright light and a voice told him *"not to move an inch!"*

What the hell is going on? the Drifter thought. He wasn't sure if he was actually back at the vet clinic or standing in the smelting plant. If he was having a flashback he didn't remember this part of the night he'd murdered someone. He'd gotten out of the clinic and hid out in a salvage yard, doped up on animal tranquilizers.

Hadn't he?

The blinding light lowered a bit and the Drifter could see a very young police officer pointing his pistol at him.

"Drop the weapon!" the officer shouted. The Drifter could tell that the officer was panicked, and after guessing the man's age he thought this might very well be the first time the officer had ever drawn his weapon on someone.

The Drifter started to tell the officer that he didn't have a weapon, but before he could the blinding beam of the flashlight socked him in the face again. He instinctively brought his hands up to shield his eyes and when he did a glass vile of horse anesthetic slipped from his hands. He watched as it fell, heard it shatter on the concrete at his feet. As the Drifter looked down at the busted glass something else caught his attention. A dark red spot appeared on his tattered t-shirt and started to blossom. Then the Drifter heard the gunshot. He found it funny that he'd seen the bullet hole in his chest before he'd heard the shot. He looked back up at the young officer to see if he thought it was funny, too, and he was just in time to see six more flashes from the barrel of the officer's service weapon. The impact of the bullets shredding his torso drove the Drifter backwards until his bad ankle gave out and he fell on his back. As his head struck the pavement there was another flash of light, and suddenly he was on his feet again, back in the smelting plant and looking at Hasty and the fire.

He felt very cold and his skin prickled as realization washed over him. "Jesus, I'm dead."

"I know that's thick to swallow, Lou," Hasty said, "but like they always said: 'Life's a bitch and then you die.' Well, you have, son."

"Then this place—Barker Marsh—it's hell?" the Drifter asked.

Hasty shrugged. "For some, I s'pose. Not sure if it's *your* hell or not, Lou. You see, if you're here it means you did some bad shit while you was alive, you follow?"

The Drifter nodded. He followed.

"So like I told you when you first came in here," Hasty continued, "Barker Marsh is just a train town. There's hundreds—hell, probably *millions*—of towns like this spread all throughout Limbo, or whatever the hell we're in now, and they're just waiting to gobble up sinners like you. Like me. Where you decide to get off and do your time is up to you, Lou. Barker Marsh is just one option. You decide to stick around, I'll show you the place; introduce you to some of the lads."

In the distance, the Drifter heard a train whistle approaching. "And if I decide I don't want to stick around?" he asked Hasty.

"It ain't my job to try and keep you here, if that's what you're getting at," Hasty said. "If you feel like our quaint town ain't for you then hop back on that train and move on down the line. But you're gonna have to get off somewhere, Lou. Can't ride the rails forever."

The Drifter thought back over the past 12 hours or so. *Shit, what did time even mean anymore? It might as well have been 12 years.* He thought of the four tales the old man had told him. He thought of the death, and the evil that apparently ran deep through that town. He was scared, and confused, and had no idea what to expect in the afterlife, but there was one thing he knew for sure: He didn't want to spend any of it in a shithole like Barker Marsh.

The train whistle blew again. It was much closer now and the Drifter could hear the wheels clanging along the track, as familiar to him as his favorite rock and roll song.

"You can't ride the rails forever," Hasty repeated.

"Yeah, well I can try," the Drifter replied, "and if I do get off, it's not gonna be a place like this."

"You sure about that, Lou?" Hasty asked.

"There's not much I am sure about any more, old timer, but I *am* sure about this. Goodbye, Hasty."

"Goodbye, Lou. And thanks for listening—I like telling them stories."

The Drifter turned then and headed back outside. He laughed out loud because the pain in his ankle was gone. He was still riddled with bullet holes, but those didn't hurt either.

The train slowed as it reached the outskirts of Barker Marsh and as the Drifter got his first look at it he realized that this was no ordinary train. It was not a coal or freight train like he was used to stowing away on. This was a passenger train, and an ancient one at that. An old steam locomotive pulled a dozen or so passenger cars, and while the Barker zinc smelting plant certainly didn't sport a passenger platform, the train stopped in front of the plant anyway.

As the Drifter approached he could see the passenger compartments were full of apparitions of all kinds, in varying degrees of death and decay. Hasty had told him that he couldn't ride the rails forever, but he planned to make a go of it. Judging from the appearance of some of the train's passengers, he wasn't the only one who planned to ride the rails for a long time.

An ancient looking conductor stepped out onto the ladder leading into the first passenger car and bellowed, "All aboard!"

As the Drifter got closer to the conductor he could see that the man was sporting an impressive handlebar mustache, and his uniform was perfect. Aside from the fact that most of the left side of his skull was visible through torn flesh, the man was the perfect stereotype of an old West conductor. Hell, he probably *was* an old West conductor.

"I don't have a ticket," the Drifter said when he reached the ladder.

"Course you don't," replied the conductor, as he looked the Drifter up and down with his one good eye. "No ticket needed to ride this train, son. Come on up."

The Drifter stepped up on the ladder and shook the ghost conductor's hand. The train started moving almost immediately; the Drifter turned back to the Barker zinc smelting plant.

Hasty Davis stood in the opening in the side of the building.

The Drifter waved and Hasty waved back. Then he found an empty seat and prepared for his trip.

As the train continued West, Harold "Hasty" Davis watched it roll through Barker Marsh.

"You gonna stand there all day, old timer?" said a voice from behind him.

Hasty turned as Wes Klein walked up, sporting a Barker Marsh Blackhawks baseball t-shirt and jeans. Before Hasty could reply there was a howl from within the shadows of the plant, and soon after a naked Nick Goodman walked into the light and joined them. A nice trail of paw prints followed him.

"Well if ain't Hot Rod and the Old Coot," Nick said.

Wes shot a foul look at Nick. "Jesus, put some pants on would you, Fido?"

The tell-tale click of a Zippo lighter—the same one that had burned Barker Marsh to the ground—caused all three to turn then as Eddie Willis lit a cigarette and joined the trio. Eddie gestured toward the departing train with the cigarette. "He didn't want to stick around, huh Hasty?"

"They never do," Hasty replied. "They never do."

"Shit," Eddie said. "Who can blame them?"

THE END

Looking for something else to read?

Iraq, 2003. Army Sergeant John Armstrong leads his team into the middle of the desert in search of Weapons of Mass Destruction. What they find is something far more terrifying...and alive.

A short story by Tyson Hanks, available now on Amazon Kindle.

Dr Sarcophagus returns to the off-season compound in Winter Haven, FL with three new acts for the Carnival. A short time later a grisly murder in the woods nearby leads him to believe there is a shape-shifter in their midst. Can he figure out who the killer is before the next full moon? If he does how can he stop it?

John Catapano presents the sequel to his popular "Clarence." The enigmatic Doctor is embroiled again in an arcane mystery.

A Dark Alley Crew story.

Sixteen-year-old Jason McCreary is living a nightmare within a nightmare. Not only is he trying to survive in a post-apocalyptic world overrun by demons from Hell, he also shoulders the burden for humanity's fate as it was his mother who opened the gates in a scientific experiment gone wrong.

In a last ditch effort to redeem his family name and erase his guilt, Jason joins a squad whose mission is to travel to Paris and close the Hell Gate. Once there, they discover an environment more frightening than anything they could imagine and demons more terrifying than they had ever encountered before.

Time is now against them.

Can Jason gain his redemption along with the respect of his peers, or will a new web of lies threaten to rip apart his world and jeopardize his team's only chance for success?

Scott M. Baker, a member of the *Dark Alley Crew*, presents his first young adult post-apocalypse novel, available Fall 2016.

ABOUT THE AUTHOR

Tyson Hanks is a fan of horror—both literature and film. He has yet to receive a literary award, but he did get a gold star on a middle school English paper once. He is also an Army veteran and served in Iraq during Operation Iraqi Freedom. His work has been published in Sanitarium Magazine, as well as the World War I horror anthology "Kneeling in the Silver Light." He lives in Florida with his beautiful wife and daughter.

Follow Tyson at www.tysonhanks.com
and
https://www.facebook.com/authortysonhanks

Photo Credit: Pine Castle Films

www.ingramcontent.com/pod-product-compliance
Lightning Source LLC
Chambersburg PA
CBHW051434260626
47162CB00001B/85